Cap'n Dan's Daughter

Joseph C. Lincoln

Contents

CAP'N DAN'S DAUGHTER

BY

Joseph C. Lincoln

CHAPTER I

The Metropolitan Dry Goods and Variety Store at Trumet Centre was open for business. Sam Bartlett, the boy whose duty it was to take down the shutters, sweep out, dust, and wait upon early-bird customers, had performed the first three of these tasks and gone home for breakfast. The reason he had not performed the fourth--the waiting upon customers--was simple enough; there had been no customers to wait upon. The Metropolitan Dry Goods and Variety Store was open and ready for business--but, unfortunately, there was no business.

There should have been. This was August, the season of the year when, if ever, Trumet shopkeepers should be beaming across their counters at the city visitor, male or female, and telling him or her, that "white duck hats are all the go this summer," or "there's nothin' better than an oilskin coat for sailin' cruises or picnics." Outing shirts and yachting caps, fancy stationery, post cards, and chocolates should be changing hands at a great rate and the showcase, containing the nicked blue plates and cracked teapots, the battered candlesticks and tarnished pewters, "genuine antiques," should be opened at frequent intervals for the inspection of bargain-seeking mothers and their daughters. July and August are the Cape Cod harvest months; if the single-entry ledgers of Trumet's business men do not show good-sized profits during that season they are not likely to do so the rest of the year.

Captain Daniel Dott, proprietor of the Metropolitan Store, bending over his own ledger spread on the little desk by the window at the rear of his establishment, was realizing this fact, realizing it with a sinking heart and a sense of hopeless discouragement. The summer was almost over; September was only three days off; in another fortnight the hotels would be closed, the boarding houses would be closing, and Trumet, deserted by its money spending visitors, would be falling asleep, relapsing into its autumn and winter hibernation. And the Dott ledger, instead of showing a profit of a thousand or fifteen hundred dollars, as it had the first summer after Daniel bought the business, showed but a meager three hundred and fifty, over and above expenses.

Through the window the sun was shining brightly. From the road in front of the store--Trumet's "Main Street"--came the rattle of wheels and the sound of laughter and conversation in youthful voices. The sounds drew nearer. Someone shouted "Whoa!" Daniel Dott, a ray of hope illuminating his soul at the prospect of a customer, rose hurriedly from his seat by the desk and hastened out into the shop.

A big two-horsed vehicle, the "barge" from the Manonquit House, had stopped before the door. It was filled with a gay crowd, youths and maidens from the hotel, dressed in spotless flannels and "blazers," all talking at once, and evidently carefree and happy. Two of the masculine members of the party descended from the "barge" and entered the store. Daniel, smiling his sweetest, stepped forward to meet them.

"Good mornin', good mornin'," he said. "A fine mornin', ain't it?"

The greeting was acknowledged by both of the young fellows, and one of them added that it was a fine morning, indeed.

"Don't know as I ever saw a finer," observed Daniel. "Off on a cruise somewhere, I presume likely; hey?"

"Picnic down at the Point."

"Well, you've got picnic weather, all right. Yes sir, you have!"

Comment concerning the weather is the inevitable preliminary to all commercial transactions in Trumet. Now, preliminaries being over, Daniel waited hopefully for what was to follow. His hopes were dashed.

"Is--is Miss Dott about?" inquired one of the callers.

"Miss Dott? Oh, Gertie! No, she ain't. She's gone down street somewheres. Be back pretty soon, I shouldn't wonder."

"Humph! Well, I'm afraid we can't wait. We hoped she might go with us on the picnic. We--er--we wanted her very much."

"That so? I'm sorry, but I'm afraid she couldn't go, even if she was here. You see, it's her last day at home, and--we--her mother and I--that is, I don't believe she'd want to leave us to-day."

"No; no, of course not. Well, tell her we wish she might have come, but we understand. Yes, yes," in answer to the calls from the "barge," "we're coming. Well, good by, Captain Dott."

"Er--good by. Er--er--don't want anything to take along, do you? A nice box of candy, or--or anything?"

"No, I think not. We stopped at the Emporium just now, and loaded up with candy enough to last a week. Good morning."

"How are you fixed for sun hats and things? I've got a nice line of hats and-- well, good by."

"Good by."

The "barge" moved off. Daniel, standing dejectedly in the door, remembered his manners.

"Hope you have a nice time," he shouted. Then he turned and moved disconsolately back to the desk. He might have expected it. It was thus in nine cases out of ten. The Emporium, Mr. J. Cohen, proprietor, was his undoing in this instance as in so many others. The Emporium got the trade and he got the good bys. Mr. Cohen was not an old resident, as he was; Mr. Cohen's daughter was not invited to picnics by the summer people; Mrs. Cohen was not head of the sewing circle and the Chapter of the Ladies of Honor, and prominent socially, as was Mrs. Dott; but Mr. Cohen bought cheap and sold cheap, and the Emporium flourished like a green bay tree, while the Metropolitan Store was rapidly going to seed. Daniel, looking out through the front window at the blue sea in the distance, thought of the past, of the days when, as commander and part owner of the three masted schooner Bluebird, he had been free and prosperous and happy. Then he considered the future, which was bluer than the sea, and sighed again. Why had he not been content to stick to the profession he understood, to remain on the salt water he loved; instead of retiring from the sea to live on dry land and squander his small fortune in a business for which he was entirely unfitted?

And yet the answer was simple enough. Mrs. Dott--Mrs. Serena Dott, his wife- -was the answer, she and her social aspirations. It was Serena who had coaxed him into giving up seafaring; who had said that it was a shame for him to waste his life ordering foremast hands about when he might be one of the leading citizens in his native town. It was Serena who had persuaded him to invest the larger part of his savings in the Metropolitan Store. Serena, who had insisted that Gertrude, their daughter and only child, should leave home to attend the fashionable and expensive seminary near Boston. Serena who--but there! it was all Serena; and had been ever since they were married. Captain Daniel, on board his schooner, was a man whose word was law. On shore, he was law abiding, and his words were few.

The side door of the store--that leading to the yard separating it from the Dott homestead--opened, and Azuba Ginn appeared. Azuba had been the Dott maid of all work for eighteen years, ever since Gertrude was a baby. She was married, but her husband, Laban Ginn, was mate on a steam freighter running between New York and almost anywhere, and his shore leaves were short and infrequent. Theirs was a curious sort of married life. "We is kind of independent, Labe and me," said Azuba. "He often says to me--that is, as often as we're together, which ain't often--he says to me, he says, 'Live where you want to, Zuby,' he says, 'and if you want to move, move! When I get ashore I can hunt you up.' We don't write many letters because time each get t'other's, the news is so plaguey old 'tain't news at all. You Dotts seem more like home folks to me than anybody else, so I stick to you. I presume likely I shall till I die."

Azuba entered the store in the way in which she did most things, with a flurry and a slam. Her sleeves were rolled up, she wore an apron, and one hand dripped suds, demonstrating that it had just been taken from the dishpan. In the other, wiped more or less dry on the apron, she held a crumpled envelope.

"Well!" she exclaimed, excitedly. "If some human bein's don't beat the Dutch then I don't know, that's all. If the way some folks go slip-slop, hit or miss, through this world ain't a caution then--Tut! tut! tut! don't talk to ME!"

Captain Dan looked up from the ledger.

"What?" he asked absently.

"I say, don't talk to ME!"

"We--ll," with deliberation, "I guess I shan't, unless you stop talkin' yourself, and give me a chance. What's the matter now, Zuba?"

"Matter! Don't talk to ME! Carelessness is the matter! Slip-sloppiness is the matter! Here's a man that calls himself a man and goes mopin' around pretendin' to BE a man, and what does he do?"

"I don't know. I'd tell you better, maybe, if I knew who he was."

"Who he was! I'll tell you who he was--is, I mean. He's Balaam Hambleton, that's who he is."

"Humph! Bale Hamilton, hey? Then it's easy enough to say what he does--nothin', most of the time. Is that letter for me?"

"Course it's for you! And it's a week old, what's more. One week ago that letter come in the mail and the postmaster let that--that Hambleton thing take it, 'cause he said he was goin' right by here and could leave it just as well as not. And this very mornin' that freckle-faced boy of his--that George Washin'ton one--what folks give such names to their young ones for I can't see!--he rung the front door bell and yanked me right out of the dish water, and he says his ma found the letter in Balaam's other pants when she was mendin' 'em, and would I please excuse his forgettin' it 'cause he had so much on his mind lately. Mind! Land of love! if he had a thistle top on his mind 'twould smash it flat. Don't talk to me!"

"I won't," drily; "I WON'T, Zuba, I swear it. Let's see the letter."

He bent forward and took the letter from her hand. Then, adjusting his spectacles, he examined the envelope. It was of the ordinary business size and was stamped with the Boston postmark, and a date a week old. Captain Dan looked at the postmark, studied the address, which was in an unfamiliar handwriting, and then turned the envelope over. On the flap was printed "Shepley and Farwell, Attorneys, ----- Devonshire Street." The captain drew a long breath; he leaned back in his chair and sat staring at the envelope.

Azuba wiped the suds from her wet hand and arm upon her apron. Then she wrapped it and the other arm in said apron and coughed. The cough was intended to arouse her employer from the trance into which he had, apparently, fallen. But it was without effect. Captain Daniel did stop staring at the envelope, but he merely transferred his gaze to the ink-spattered blotter and the ledger upon it, and stared at them.

"Well?" observed Azuba.

The captain started. "Hey?" he exclaimed, looking up. "Did you speak?"

"I said 'Well?'. I suppose that's speakin'?"

"'Well?' Well what?"

"Oh, nothin'! I was just wonderin'--"

"Wonderin' what?"

"I was wonderin' if that letter was anything important. Ain't you goin' to open it and see?"

"Hey? Open it? Oh, yes, yes. Well, I shouldn't wonder if I opened it some time or other, Zuba. I gen'rally open my letters. It's a funny habit I have."

"Humph! Well, all right, then. I didn't know. Course, 'tain't none of my business what's in other folks's letters. I ain't nosey, land knows. Nobody can accuse me of--"

"Nobody can accuse you of anything, Zuba. Not even dish washin' just now."

Azuba drew herself up. Outraged dignity and injured pride were expressed in every line of her figure. "Well!" she exclaimed; "WELL! if that ain't--if that don't beat all that ever I heard! Here I leave my work to do folks favors, to fetch and carry for 'em, and this is what I get. Cap'n Dott, I want you to understand that I ain't dependent on nobody for a job. I don't HAVE to slave myself to death for nobody. If you ain't satisfied--"

"There, there, Zuba! I was only jokin'. Don't get mad!"

"Mad! Who's mad, I'd like to know? It takes more'n that to make me mad, I'd have you understand."

"That's good; I'm glad of it. Well, I'm much obliged to you for bringin' the letter."

"You're welcome. Land sakes! I don't mind doin' errands, only I like to have 'em appreciated. And I like jokes well as anybody, but when you tell me--"

"Hold on! don't get het up again. Keep cool, Zuba, keep cool! Think of that dish water; it's gettin' cooler every minute."

The answer to this was an indignant snort followed by the bang of the door. Azuba had gone. Captain Daniel looked after her, smiled faintly, shook his head, and again turned his attention to the letter in his hand. He did not open it immediately. Instead he sat regarding it with the same haggard, hopeless expression which he had worn when he first read the firm's name upon the envelope. He dreaded, perhaps, as much as he had ever dreaded anything in his life, to open that envelope.

He was sure, perfectly sure, what he should find when he did open it. A letter from the legal representatives of Smith and Denton, the Boston hat manufacturers and dealers, stating that, unless the latter's account was paid within the next week, suit for the amount due would be instituted in the courts. A law suit! a law suit for the collection of a debt against him, Daniel Dott, the man who had prided himself upon his honesty! Think of what it would mean! the disgrace of it! the humiliation, not only for himself but for Serena, his wife, and Gertrude, his daughter!

He did not blame Smith and Denton; they had been very kind, very lenient indeed. The thirty-day credit originally given him had been extended to sixty and ninety. They had written him many times, and each time he had written in reply that as soon as collections were better he should be able to pay in full; that he had a good deal of money owed him, and as soon as it came in they should have it. But it did not come in. No wonder, considering that it was owed by the loafers and ne'er-do-wells of the town and surrounding country, who, because no one else would trust them, bestowed their custom upon good-natured, gullible Captain Dan. The more recent letters from the hat dealers had been sharper and less kindly. They had ceased to request; they demanded. At last they had threatened. And now the threat was to be fulfilled.

The captain laid the envelope down upon the open ledger, rose, and, going to the front of the store, carefully closed the door. Then, going to the door communicating with the other half of the store, he made sure that no one was in the adjoining room. He had a vague feeling that all the eyes in Trumet were regarding him with suspicion, and he wished to shut out their accusing gaze. He wanted to be alone when he read that letter. He had half a mind to take it to the cellar and open it there.

His fingers shook as he tore the end from the envelope. They shook still more as he drew forth the enclosure, a typewritten sheet, and held it to the light. He read it through to the end. Then, with a loud exclamation, almost a shout, he rushed to the side door, flung it open and darted across the yard, the letter fluttering from his fingers like a flag. The store was left unguarded, but he forgot that.

He stumbled up the steps into the kitchen. Azuba, a saucer in one hand and the dish towel in the other, was, to say the least, startled. As she expressed it afterward, "the everlastin' soul was pretty nigh scart out of her." The saucer flew through the air and lit upon the top of the cookstove.

"What--what--what--" stammered Azuba. "Oh, my land! WHAT is it?"

"Where's Serena?" demanded Captain Daniel, paying no attention to the saucer, except to tread upon the fragments.

"Hey? Oh, what IS it? Is the store afire?"

"No, no! Where's Serena?"

"She--she--what--"

"Where's SERENA, I ask you?"

"In her room, I cal'late. For mercy sakes, what--"

But the captain did not answer. Through dining-room, sitting-room, and parlor he galloped, and up the front stairs to the bedroom occupied by himself and wife. Mrs. Dott was standing before the mirror, red-faced and panting, both arms behind her and her fingers busily engaged. Her husband's breath was almost gone by the time he reached the foot of the stairs; consequently his entrance was a trifle less noisy and startling than his sky-rocket flight through the kitchen. It is doubtful if his wife would have noticed even if it had been. She caught a glimpse of him in the mirror, and heaved a sigh of relief.

"Oh, it's you, is it!" she panted. "My, I'm glad! For mercy sakes fasten those last three hooks; I'm almost distracted with 'em."

But the hooks remained unfastened for the time. Captain Dan threw himself into a chair and waved the letter.

"Serena," he cried, puffing like a stranded porpoise, "what--WHAT do you suppose has happened? Aunt Laviny is dead."

Serena turned. "Dead!" she repeated. "Your Aunt Lavinia Dott? The rich one?"

"Yes, sir; she's gone. Died in Italy a fortnight ago. Naples, I think 'twas--or some such outlandish place; you know she's done nothin' but cruise around Europe ever since Uncle Jim died. The letter says she was taken sick on a Friday, and died Sunday, so 'twas pretty sudden. I--"

But Mrs. Dott interrupted. "What else does it say?" she asked excitedly. "What else does that letter say? Who is if from?"

"It's from her lawyers up to Boston. What made you think it said anything else?"

"Because I'm not blind and I can see your face, Daniel Dott. What else does it say? Tell me! Has she--did she--?"

Captain Dan nodded solemnly. "She didn't forget us," he said. "She didn't forget us, Serena. The letter says her will gives us that solid silver teapot and sugar-bowl that was presented to Uncle Jim by the Ship Chandlers' Society, when he was president of it. She willed that to us. She knew I always admired that tea-pot and--"

His wife interrupted once more.

"Tea-pot!" she repeated strongly. "Tea-pot! What are you talking about? Do you mean to say that all she left us was a TEA-POT? If you do I--"

"No, no, Serena. Hush! She's left us three thousand dollars besides. Think of it! Three thousand dollars--just now!"

His voice shook as he said it. He spoke as if three thousand dollars was an unheard-of sum, a fortune. Mrs. Dott had no such illusion. She sat down upon the edge of the bed.

"Three thousand dollars!" she exclaimed. "Is that all? Three thousand dollars!"

"All! My soul, Serena! Why, ONE thousand dollars just now is like--"

"Hush! Do be still! Three thousand dollars! And she worth a hundred thousand, if she was worth a cent. A lone woman, without a chick or a child or a relation except you, and that precious young swell of a cousin of hers she thought so much of. I suppose he gets the rest of it. Oh, how can anybody be so stingy!"

"Sh-sh, sh-h, Serena. Don't speak so of the dead. Why, we ought to be mournin' for her, really, instead of rejoicing over what she left us. It ain't right to talk so. I'm ashamed of myself--or I ought to be. But, you see, I thought sure the letter was from those hat folks's lawyers, sayin' they'd started suit. When I found it wasn't, I was so glad I forgot everything else. Ah hum!--poor Aunt Laviny!"

He sighed. His wife shook her head.

"Daniel," she said, "I--I declare I try not to lose patience with you, but it's awful hard work. Mourning! Mourn for her! What did she ever do to make you sorry she was gone? Did she ever come near us when she was alive? No, indeed, she didn't. Did she ever offer to give you, or even lend you, a cent? I guess not. And she knew you needed it, for I wrote her."

"You DID? Serena!"

"Yes, I did. Why shouldn't I? I wrote her six months ago, telling her how bad your business was, and that Gertie was at school, and we were trying to give her a good education, and how much money it took and--oh, everything. When your Uncle Jim's business was bad, in the hard times back in '73, who was it that helped him out and saved him from bankruptcy? Why, his brother--your own father. And he never got a cent of it back. I reminded her of that, too."

Daniel sprang out of his chair.

"You did!" he cried again. "Serena, how could you? You knew how Father felt about that money. You knew how I felt. And yet, you did that!"

"I did. Somebody in this family must be practical and worldly-minded, and I seem to be the one. YOU wouldn't ask her for a cent. You wouldn't ask anybody for money, even if they owed it a thousand years. You sell everybody anything they want from the store; and trust them for it. You know you do. You sold that good-for-nothing Lem Brackett a whole suit of clothes only last week, and he owes you a big bill and has owed it for a year."

Her husband looked troubled. "Well," he answered, slowly, "I suppose likely I didn't do right there. But those Bracketts are poor, and there's a big family of 'em, and the fall's comin' on, and--and all. So--"

"So you thought it was your duty to help support them, I suppose. Oh, Daniel, Daniel, I don't know what to do with you sometimes."

Captain Dan looked very grave.

"I guess you're right, Serena," he admitted. "I ain't much good, I'm afraid."

Mrs. Dott's expression changed. She rose, walked over, and kissed him. "You're too good, that's the main trouble with you," she said. "Well, I won't scold any more. I'm glad we've got the three thousand anyway--and the tea-pot."

"It's a lovely tea-pot, all engravin' and everything. And the sugar-bowl's almost as pretty. You'll like 'em, Serena."

"Yes, I'll love 'em, I don't doubt. You and I can look at them and think of that cousin of Aunt Lavinia's spending the rest of her fortune. No wonder she didn't leave him the tea-pot; precious little tea he drinks, if stories we hear are true. Well, there's one good thing about it--Gertie can keep on with her college. This is her last year."

"Yes; I thought of that. I thought of a million things when I was racin' across the yard with this letter. Say, Serena, you've never told Gertie anything about how trade was or how hard-up we've been?"

"Of course not."

"No, I knew you wouldn't. She's such a conscientious girl; if she thought we couldn't afford it she wouldn't think of keepin' on with that college, and I've set my heart on her havin' the best start in life we can give her."

"I know. Ah hum! I wish she could have the start some people's daughters have. Mrs. Black was with me at the lodge room yesterday--we are decorating for the men's evening to-morrow night, you know--and Mrs. Black has been helping me; she's awfully kind that way. You'd think she belonged here in Trumet, instead of being rich and living in Scarford and being way up in society there. She and her husband are just like common folks."

"Humph! Barney Black IS common folks. He was born right here in Trumet and his family was common as wharf rats. HE needn't put on airs with me."

"He doesn't. And yet, if he was like some people, he would. So successful in his big factory, and his wife way up in the best circles of Scarford; she's head of the Ladies of Honor there as I am here, and means to get a national office in the order; she told me so. But there! that reminds me that I was going to meet her at the lodge room at ten, and it's half-past nine now. Do help me with these hooks. If I wasn't so fleshy I could do them myself, but I almost died hooking the others."

"Why didn't you call Zuba? She'd have hooked 'em for you."

"Azuba! Heavens and earth! She's worse than nobody; her fingers are all thumbs. Besides, she would talk me deaf, dumb and blind. She doesn't know her place at all; thinks she is one of the family, I suppose."

"Well, she is, pretty nigh. Been here long enough."

"I don't care. She isn't one of the family; she's a servant, or ought to be. Oh dear! when I hear Annette Black telling about her four servants and all the rest it makes me so jealous, sometimes."

"Don't make ME jealous. I'd rather have you and Gertie and this place than all Barney Black owns--and that means his wife, too."

"Daniel, I keep telling you not to call Mr. Black 'Barney.' He is B. Phelps Black now. Mrs. Black always calls him 'Phelps.' So does everybody in Scarford, so she says."

"Want to know! He was Barney Black when he lived here regular. Havin' a summer cottage here and a real house in Scarford must make a lot of difference. By the way, speakin' of Scarford, that's where Aunt Laviny used to live afore she went abroad. She owned a big house there."

"Why, so she did! I wonder what will become of it. I suppose that cousin will get it, along with the rest. Oh dear! suppose--just suppose there wasn't any cousin.

Suppose you and I and Gertie had that house and the money. Wouldn't it be splen-did? WE could be in society then."

"Humph! I'd look pretty in society, wouldn't I?"

"Of course you would. You'd look as pretty as Barney--B. Phelps Black, wouldn't you? And I--Oh, HOW I should love it! Trumet is so out of date. A real intelligent, ambitious woman has no chance in Trumet."

The captain shook his head. He recognized the last sentence as a quotation from the works of Mrs. Annette Black, self-confessed leader in society in the flourishing manufacturing city of Scarford, and summer resident and condescending patroness of Trumet.

"Well," he observed; "we've got more chance, even in Trumet, than we've had for the last year, thanks to Aunt Laviny's three thousand. It gives us a breathin' spell, anyhow. If only trade in the store would pick up, I--Hey! Good heavens to Betsy! I forgot the store altogether. Sam hadn't got back from breakfast and I left the store all alone. I must be crazy!"

He bolted from the room and down the stairs, the legacy forgotten for the moment, and in his mind pictures of rifled showcases and youthful Trumet regal-ing itself with chocolates at his expense. Azuba shrieked another question as her employer once more rushed through the kitchen, but again her question was unan-swered. She hurried to the window and watched him running across the yard.

"Well!" she exclaimed, in alarmed soliloquy. "WELL, the next time I fetch that man a letter I'll fetch the doctor along with it. Has the world turned upside down, or what is the matter?"

She might have made a worse guess. The Dott world was turning upside down; this was the beginning of the revolution.

CHAPTER II

Captain Dan's fears concerning the safety of his showcases were groundless. Even as he sprang up the steps to the side door of his place of business, he heard familiar voices in the store. He recognized the voices, and, halting momentarily to wipe his forehead with his handkerchief and to regain some portion of his composure and his breath, he walked in.

Gertrude, his daughter, was seated in his chair by the desk, and John Doane was leaning upon the desk, talking with her. In the front of the store, Sam Bartlett, the boy, who had evidently returned from breakfast, was doing nothing in particular, and doing it with his usual air of enjoyment. It was only when required to work that Sam was unhappy.

Gertrude looked up as her father entered; prior to that she had been looking at the blotter on the desk. John Doane, who had been looking at Gertrude, also changed the direction of his gaze. Captain Dan struggled with the breath and the composure.

"Why, Dad!" exclaimed Gertrude. "What is it?"

"What's the matter, Cap'n Dott?" asked Mr. Doane.

Daniel did his best to appear calm; it was a poor best. At fifty-two one cannot run impromptu hurdle races against time, and show no effects.

"Hey?" he panted. "Matter? Nothin's the matter. I left the store alone for a minute and I was in a kind of hurry to get back to it, that's all."

The explanation was not entirely satisfactory. Gertrude looked more puzzled than ever.

"A minute," she repeated. "Left it a minute! Why, John and I have been here fifteen minutes, and Sam was here when we came."

The captain looked at his watch. "Well, maybe 'twas a little more'n a minute," he admitted.

Master Bartlett sauntered up to take part in the conversation.

"I got here twenty minutes ago," he observed, grinning, "and you wasn't here then, Cap'n Dan'l. I was wonderin' what had become of ye."

Daniel seized the opportunity to change the subject.

"Anybody been in since you came?" he asked, addressing Sam.

"No, nobody special. Abel Calvin was in to see if you wanted to buy some beach plums for puttin' up. He said he had about a bushel of first-rate ones, just picked."

"Beach plums! What in time would I want of beach plums? I don't put up preserves, do I? Why didn't he go to the house?"

"I asked him that, myself, and he said 'twa'n't no use.'"

"No use! What did he mean by that?"

"Well, he said--he said--" Sam seemed suddenly to realize that he was getting into deep water; "he said--he said somethin' or other; I guess I've forgot what 'twas."

"I guess you ain't. WHAT did he say?"

"Well, he said--he said Serena--Mrs. Dott, I mean--was probably gallivantin' down to the lodge room by this time. Said 'twa'n't no use tryin' to get her to attend to common things or common folks nowadays; she was too busy tryin' to keep up with Annette Black."

This literal quotation from the frank Mr. Calvin caused a sensation. Captain Dan struggled to find words. His daughter laid a hand on his sleeve.

"Never mind, Dad," she said, soothingly. "You know what Abel Calvin is; you don't mind what he says. Sam, you shouldn't repeat such nonsense. Run away now and attend to your work. I'm sure there's enough for you to do."

"You--you go and clean up the cellar," ordered the irate captain. Sam departed cellarward, muttering that it wasn't his fault; HE hadn't said nothin'. Gertrude spoke again.

"Don't mind that, Dad," she urged. "Why, how warm you are, and how excited you look. What is it? You haven't spoken a word to John."

Her father shook his head. "Mornin', John," he said. "I beg your pardon. I ain't responsible to-day, I shouldn't wonder. I--I've had some news that's drivin' everything else out of my mind."

"News? Why, Dad! what do you mean? Bad news?"

"No, no! Good as ever was, and.... Humph! no, I don't mean that. It is bad news, of course. Your Great-aunt Laviny's dead, Gertie."

He told of the lawyer's letter, omitting for the present the news of the legacy. Gertrude was interested, but not greatly shocked or grieved. She had met her great-aunt but once during her lifetime, and her memory of the deceased was of a stately female, whose earrings and brooches and rings sparkled as if she was on fire in several places; who sat bolt upright at the further end of a hotel room in Boston, and ordered Captain Dan not to bring "that child" any nearer until its hands were washed. As she had been the child and had distinctly disagreeable recollections of the said hands having been washed three times before admittance to the presence, the memory was not too pleasant. She said she was sorry to hear that Aunt Lavinia was no more, and asked when it happened. Her father told what he knew of the circumstances attending the bereavement, which was not much.

"She's gone, anyhow," he said. "It's liable to happen to any of us, bein' cut off that way. We ought to be prepared, I suppose."

"I suppose so. But, Daddy, Aunt Lavinia wasn't cut off exactly, was she? She was your aunt and she must have been quite old."

"Hey? Why, let's see. She was your grandpa's brother's wife, and he--Uncle Jim, I mean--was about four years older than Father. She was three years younger'n he was when he married her. Let's see again. Father--that's your grandpa, Gertie--was sixty-five when he died and... Humph! No, Aunt Laviny was eighty-eight, or thereabouts. She wasn't exactly cut off, was she, come to think of it?"

Gertrude's brown eyes twinkled. "Not exactly--no," she said, gravely. "Well, Daddy, I'm sure I am sorry she has gone, but, considering that she has never deigned to visit us or have us visit her, or even to write you a letter for the past two years, I don't think we should be expected to mourn greatly. And," glancing at him, "I don't understand just what you meant by saying first that the news was good, and then that it was bad. There is something else, isn't there?"

Her father smiled, in an embarrassed way. "Well, ye--es," he admitted, "there is somethin' else, but--but I don't know as I didn't do wrong to feel so good over it. I--I guess I'll tell you by and by, if you don't mind. Maybe then I won't feel--act, I mean--so tickled. It don't seem right that I should be. Let me get sort of used to it first. I'll tell you pretty soon."

His daughter laughed, softly. "I know you will, Dad," she said. "You couldn't keep a secret in that dear old head of yours if you tried. Not from me, anyway; could you, dear?"

"I guess not," regarding her fondly. "Anyhow, I shan't try to keep this one. Well, this time to-morrow you'll be back at college again, in among all those Greek and Latin folks. Wonder she'll condescend to come and talk plain United States to us Cape Codders, ain't it, John."

John Doane admitted that it was a wonder. He seemed to regard Miss Dott as a very wonderful young person altogether. Gertrude glanced up at him, then at her father, and then at the blotter on the desk. She absently played with the pages of the ledger.

"Dad," she said, suddenly, "you are not the only one who has a secret."

The captain turned and looked at her. Her head was bent over the ledger and he could see but the top of a very becoming hat, a stray lock of wavy brown hair, and the curve of a very pretty cheek. The cheek--what he could see of it--was crimson. He looked up at Mr. Doane. That young man's face was crimson also.

"Oh!" said Captain Daniel; and added, "I want to know!"

"Yes, you're not the only one. We--I--there is another secret. Daddy, dear, John wants to talk with you."

The captain looked at Mr. Doane, then at the hat and the face beneath it.

"Oh!" he said, again.

"Yes. I--I--" She rose and, putting her arms about her father's neck, kissed him. "I will be back before long, dear," she whispered, and hurried out. Mr. Doane cleared his throat. Captain Dan waited.

"Well, sir," began the young man, and stopped. The captain continued to wait.

"Well, sir," began Mr. Doane, again, "I--I--" For one who, as Gertrude had declared, wished to talk, he seemed to be finding the operation difficult. "I--Well, sir, the fact is, I have something to say to you."

Captain Dan, who was looking very grave, observed that he "wanted to know." John Doane cleared his throat once more, and took a fresh start.

"Yes, sir," he said, "I have something to say to you--er--something that--that may surprise you."

A faint smile disturbed the gravity of the captain's face.

"May surprise me, hey?" he repeated. "Is that so?"

"Yes. You see, I--Gertie and I--have--are--"

Daniel looked up.

"Hard navigatin', ain't it, John?" he inquired, whimsically. "Maybe I could help you over the shoals. You and Gertie think you'd like to get married sometime or other, I presume likely. Is that what you're tryin' to tell me?"

There was no doubt of it. The young man's face expressed several emotions, relief that the great secret was known, and surprise that anyone should have guessed it.

"Why, yes, sir," he admitted, "that is it. Gertie and I have known each other for years, ever since we were children, in fact; and, you see--you see--" he paused once more, began again, and then broke out impatiently with, "I'm making an awful mess of this. I don't know why."

Captain Dan's smile broadened.

"I made just as bad a one myself, once on a time," he observed. "Just as bad, or worse--and I didn't know why either. There, John, you sit down. Come to anchor alongside here, and let's talk this thing over in comfort."

Mr. Doane "came to anchor" on an empty packing case beside the desk. As he was tall and big, and the box was low and small, the "comfort" was doubtful. However, neither of the pair noticed this at the time.

"So you think you want Gertie, do you, John?" said the captain.

"I know it," was the emphatic answer.

"So. And she thinks she wants you?"

"She says so."

"Humph!" with a sidelong glance. "Think she means it?"

"I'm trying to believe she does."

The tone in which this was uttered caused Captain Dan to chuckle. "'Tis strange, I'll give in," he remarked, drily. "No accountin' for taste, is there--Well," his gravity returning, "I suppose likely you realize that her mother and I think consider'ble of her."

"I realize that thoroughly."

"You don't realize it as much as you will some day, perhaps. Yes, we think Gertie's about right. She's a smart girl and, what's more, she's a good girl, and she's all the child we've got. Of course we've realized that she was growin' up and that-- Oh, good mornin', Alphy. Fine weather, ain't it. Lookin' for somethin', was you?"

He hurried out into the store to sell Mrs. Theophilus Berry, known locally as "Alphy Ann," a box of writing paper and a penholder. The transaction completed, he returned to his chair. John Doane, who had recovered, in a measure, from his embarrassment, was ready for him.

"Cap'n Dott," said the young man, "I know how you feel, I think. I know what Gertie is to you and how anxious you and her mother must be concerning her future. If I did not feel certain--practically certain--that I could give her a good home and all that goes with it, I should not have presumed to speak to her, or to you, concerning marriage. My business prospects are good, or I think they are. I--"

The captain held up his hand. "Er--er--John," he said, uneasily, "maybe you'd better tell about that part of it when Serena's around. She's the practical one of us two, I guess, far's money's concerned, anyway. I used to think I was pretty practical when I was on salt water, but--but lately I ain't so sure. I'm afraid--"

He stopped, began to speak again, and then relapsed into silence, seeming to forget his companion altogether. The latter reminded him by saying:

"I shall be glad to tell Mrs. Dott everything, of course. I have been with the firm now employing me for eight years, ever since I left high school. They seem to like me. I have been steadily advanced, my salary is a fairly good one, and in another year I have the promise of a partnership. After that my progress will depend upon myself."

He went on, in a manly, straightforward manner, to speak of his hopes and ambitions. Daniel listened, but the most of what he heard was incomprehensible. Increased output and decreased manufacturing costs were Greek to him. When the young man paused, he brought the conversation back to what, in his mind, was the essential.

"And you're certain sure that you two care enough for each other?" he asked. "Not just care, but care enough?"

"Yes."

"Well, then, I guess I ain't got much to say. There's one thing, though. Gertie's young. She ain't finished her schoolin' yet, and--"

"And you think she should. So do I. She wishes to do it, herself, and I should be the last to prevent her, even if I could. We have agreed that she shall have the final year at college and then come back to you. After that--well, after that, the time of our marriage can be settled. Gertie and I are willing to wait; we expect to. In a few years I shall have a little more money, I hope, and be more sure of success in life. I may never be a rich man, but Gertie's tastes and mine are modest. She does not care for society--"

The captain interrupted. "That's so," he said, hastily, "she don't. She don't care for 'em at all. Her mother has the greatest work to get her to go to lodge meetin's. No, she don't care for societies any more'n I do. Well, John, I--I--it'll come pretty hard to give her up to anybody. Wait till you have a daughter of your own and you'll know how hard. But, if I've got to give her up, I'd rather give her to you than anybody I know. You're a Trumet boy and I've known you all my life, and so's Gertie, for that matter. All I can say is, God bless you and--and take good care of my girl, that's all."

He extended his hand and John seized it. Then the captain coughed, blew his nose with vigor, and, reaching into his pocket, produced two battered cigars.

"Smoke up, John," he said.

At dinner, a meal at which Mrs. Dott, still busy with the lodge room decorations, was not present, Gertrude and her father talked it over.

"It comes kind of hard, Gertie," he admitted, "but, Lord love you, there's a heap of hard things in this world. John's a good fellow and--and, well, we ain't goin' to lose you just yet, anyhow."

Gertrude rose and, coming around the table, put her arms about his neck.

"Indeed you're not, dear," she said. "If I supposed my marriage meant giving you up, I shouldn't think of it."

"Want to know! Wouldn't think of John, either, I suppose, hey?"

"Well, I--I might think of him a little, just a tiny little bit."

"I shouldn't wonder. That's all right. You can't get rid of me so easy. After you two are all settled in your fine new house, I'll be comin' around to disgrace you, puttin' my boots on the furniture and--"

"Dad!"

"Won't I? Well, maybe I won't. I cal'late by that time I'll be broke to harness. Your mother's gettin' in with the swells so, lately, Barney Black's wife and the rest, that I'll have to mind my manners. There! let's go into the sittin'-room a few minutes and give Zuba a chance to clear off. Sam's tendin' store and his dinner can wait a spell; judgin' by the time he took for breakfast he hadn't ought to be hungry for the next week."

In the sitting-room they spoke of many things, of Gertrude's departure for school--she was leaving on the three o'clock train--of the engagement, of course, and of the three thousand dollar windfall from Aunt Lavinia. The captain had told that bit of news when they sat down to dinner.

"What is that cousin's name?" asked Gertrude. "The one who inherits all of your aunt's fortune?"

"Let's see. His name? I ought to know it well's I know my own. It's--it's Starvation, or somethin' like that. Somethin' about bein' hungry, anyhow. Hungerford, Percy Hungerford, that's it!"

Gertrude looked surprised.

"Not Percy Hungerford--of Scarford!" she cried. "What sort of a man is he? What does he look like?"

"Looked like a picked chicken, last time I saw him. Kind of a spindlin' little critter, with sandy complexion and hair, but dressed--my soul! there wasn't any picked chicken look about his clothes."

Gertrude nodded. "I believe it is the same one," she said. "Yes, I am sure of it. He came out to the college at one of our commencements. One of the girls invited him. He danced with me--once. They said he was very wealthy."

"Humph! All the wealth he had come from Aunt Laviny, far's I ever heard. He was her pet and the only thing she ever spent money on, except herself. And you met him! Well, this is a small world. Like him, did you?"

"No," said Gertrude, and changed the subject.

Before her father departed for the store and she went to her room to finish packing, she sat upon the arm of his chair and, bending down, said:

"Daddy, if you hadn't got this money, this three thousand dollars, do you know what I had very nearly made up my mind to do?"

"No, I'm sure I don't."

"I had almost decided not to stay at college, but to come back here and live with you and mother."

"For the land sakes! Why?"

"Because I was sure you needed me. You never told me, of course--being you, you wouldn't--but I was sure that you were troubled about--about things."

"Me? Troubled? What put that into your head? I'm the most gay, happy-go-lucky fellow in the world. I don't get troubled enough. Ask your mother if that ain't so."

"I shall not ask anybody but you. Tell me truly: Weren't you troubled; about the business, and the store? Truly, now."

Captain Dan rubbed his chin. He wished very much to deny the allegation, or at least to dodge the truth. But he was a poor prevaricator at any time, and his daughter was looking him straight in the eye.

"Well," he faltered, "I--I--How in time did you guess that? I--Humph! why, yes, I was a little mite upset. You see, trade ain't been first rate this summer, and collections were awful slow. I hate to drive folks, especially when I know they're hard up. I was a little worried, but it's all right now. Aunt Laviny's three thousand fixed that all right. It'll carry me along like a full sail breeze. You go back to school, like a sensible girl, and don't you worry a mite. It's all right now, Gertie."

"Honest?"

"Honest to Betsy!" with an emphatic nod.

He meant it; he really thought it was all right. The fact that he owed a thousand already and that the remaining two would almost certainly be swept into the capacious maw of the Metropolitan Store did not occur to him then. Daniel Dott was a failure as a business man but as an optimist he was a huge success.

"Then you're sure you can afford to have me go back for my last year?"

"Course I am. I couldn't afford to do anything else."

His absolute certainty stifled his daughter's doubts for the time, but she asked another question.

"And there's nothing that troubles you at all?"

"No-o." The captain's answer was not quite as emphatic this time. Gertrude smiled, and patted his shoulder.

"Daddy, dear," she said, "you're as transparent as a window pane, aren't you.

Well, don't worry any more. That will be all right pretty soon, too. Mrs. Black doesn't stay in Trumet all the year."

Her father gasped. That this child of his, whom he had always regarded as a child, should dive into the recesses of his soul and drag to light its most secret misgivings was amazing.

"What on earth?" he demanded.

"You know what I mean. I'm not blind. I can see. Mother is just a little carried away. She has heard so much about big houses and servants and society and woman's opportunity, and all the rest of it, that she has been swept off her feet. But it won't last, I'm sure. She isn't really discontented; she only thinks she is."

Daniel sighed. "I know," he said. "Fact is, I ain't up-to-date enough, myself, that's what's the matter. She's a mighty able, ambitious woman, your mother is, Gertie, and I don't wonder she gets to thinkin', sometimes, that Trumet is a kind of one-horse town. I like it; I AM one-horse, I suppose. But she ain't, and she ain't satisfied to be satisfied, like me. It's a good thing she ain't, I guess. Somebody's got to live up to the responsibilities of life, and--"

Gertrude laughed. "She said that, didn't she," she interrupted.

"Why, yes, she did. She says it every once in a while. How did you know?"

"I guessed. And I imagine Mrs. Phelps Black said it first. But there, Dad, be patient and.... Sh-sh! here's Mother now."

It was Serena, sure enough, breathless from hurrying, her hat a bit on one side, one glove off and the other on, but full of energy and impatience.

"I suppose you've had dinner," she exclaimed. "Well, all right, I don't care. I couldn't help being late, there was so much to do at the lodge rooms and nobody to do it right, except me. If Mrs. Black hadn't helped and superintended and--and everything, I don't know where we should have been. And those visiting delegates from Boston coming! I must get a bite and hurry back. Where's Azuba? Azuba!"

She was rushing in the direction of the kitchen, but her husband detained her.

"Hold on, Serena," he shouted. "Goin' back! What do you mean? You ain't goin' back to that lodge this afternoon, are you? Why, Gertie's goin' on the up-train!"

"I know, but I must go back, Daniel. Goodness knows what would happen if I didn't. If you had seen some of the decorations those other women wanted to put up, you would think it was necessary for someone with respectable taste to be there. Why, Sophronia Smalley actually would have draped the presiding officer's desk--MY desk--with a blue flag with a white whale on it, if I hadn't been there to stop her."

"Well, I--Why, Serena, you know Sophrony thinks a sight of that flag. Simeon Smalley, her father, was in the whalin' trade for years, and that flag was his private signal. She always has that flag up somewhere."

"Well, she shan't have it on my desk. Annette--Mrs. Black, I mean--said it was ridiculous. If such a thing happened in Scarford the audience would have hysterics. Would you want your wife to make a spectacle of herself, before those Boston delegates, standing behind a white whale, and a dirty white at that! Gertie, I shall be at the depot to say good by, but I must be at that lodge room first. I MUST. You understand, don't you?"

Gertrude said she understood perfectly and her mother hurried to the kitchen, where she ate lukewarm fried fish and apple pie, while Azuba washed the dishes and prophesied darkly concerning "dyspepsy." Gertrude went to her room to put the last few things in her trunks, and Captain Dan returned to the store, where he found the Bartlett boy pacifying a gnawing appetite with chocolate creams abstracted from stock.

At a quarter to three the captain was at the railway station, where he was joined by John Doane, who, his vacation over, was returning to Boston. After a five-minute wait Serena and Gertrude appeared. The latter had called at the lodge room for her mother and, during the walk to the station, had broken the news of her engagement.

Serena was not surprised, of course; she, like everyone else, had expected it, and she liked John. But she was a good deal agitated and even the portentous business of the lodge meeting was driven from her mind. She and Mr. Doane shook hands, but the young man felt very much like a thief, and a particularly mean sort of thief, as young men are likely to feel under such circumstances. Farewells were harder to say than usual, although Gertrude tried her best to seem cheerful, and the captain swallowed the lump in his throat and smiled and joked in a ghastly fashion all through the ceremony. Just before the train started, his daughter led him to one side and whispered:

"Now, Daddy, remember--you are not to worry. And, if you need me at any time, you will tell me so, and I shall surely come. You'll promise, won't you? And you will write at least once a week?"

The captain made both promises. They kissed, Serena and Gertrude exchanged hugs, and John Doane solemnly shook hands once more. Then the train moved away from the station.

Daniel and Serena walked homeward, Mrs. Dott wiping her eyes with a damp handkerchief, and her husband very grave and silent. As they passed the lodge building the lady said:

"I ought to go right back in there again. I ought to, but I just can't, not now. I--I want to be with you, Daniel, a time like this."

"Goodness knows I want you, Serena; but--but for mercy sakes don't call it a 'time like this.' Sounds as if we'd just come from the cemetery instead of the depot. We ain't been to a funeral; we're only lookin' for'ard to a weddin'."

In spite of this philosophical declaration the remainder of that afternoon was rather funereal for Captain Dan. He moped about the store, waiting half-heartedly upon the few customers who happened in, and the ring of the supper bell was welcome, as it promised some company other than his thoughts.

But the promise was not fulfilled. He ate his supper alone. Mrs. Dott had gone back to the lodge room, so Azuba said.

"I don't think she was intendin' to," remarked the latter, confidentially. "She said she guessed she'd 'lay down a spell'; said she was 'kind of tired.' But afore she got upstairs scarcely, along comes that Black automobile with that Irish 'shover man'--that's what they call 'em, ain't it?--drivin' it and her in the back seat, and he gets out and comes and rings the front door bell, and when I answer it--had my hands all plastered up with dough, I did, for I was makin' pie, and it took me the longest time to get 'em clean--when I answered it he said that she said she wanted to see her and--"

"Here! hold on, Zuba!" interrupted her bewildered employer. "'Vast heavin' a second, will you? You ought to run that yarn of yours through a sieve and strain some of the 'hes' and 'shes' out of it. 'He said that she said she wanted to see her.' Who wanted to see what?"

"Why, Barney Black's wife. She wanted to see Serena. So in she came, all rigged up in her best clothes and--"

"How do you know they were her best ones?"

"Hey? Well, they would have been MY best ones, if I owned 'em, I tell you that. I never see such clothes as that woman has! All trimmin' and flounces and didos, and--"

"Hi! steady there, Zuba. Keep your eye on the compass. You're gettin' off the course again. Annette--Mrs. Black, I mean--came to see Mrs. Dott; that's plain sailin' so far. What happened after that?"

"Why, they went off together in the automobile and Serena said to tell you she had to go to lodge, and she'd be back when she could and not to wait supper. That's all I know."

The captain finished his lonely meal and returned to the store, where he found Abel Blount's wife and their twin boys, aged eight, waiting to negotiate for rubber boots. The boots were for the boys, but Mrs. Blount did the buying and it was a long and talky process. At last, however, the youngsters were fitted and clumped proudly away, bearing their leather shoes in their hands. It was a dry evening, but to separate the twins from those rubber boots would have been next door to an impossibility.

"There!" exclaimed the lady, as she bade the captain good night, "that's done; that much is settled anyhow. I'm thankful I ain't got four twins, instead of two, Cap'n Dott."

Daniel, entering the sale in the ledger, was thankful also. If the lengthy Blount account had been settled he would have been still more so.

At nine o'clock he and Sam locked up, extinguished the lamps, and closed the Metropolitan Store for the night. Crossing the yard to the house, which he entered by the front door, he found Serena in the sitting-room. She was reclining upon the couch. She was tired, and out of sorts.

"Oh, dear!" she exclaimed, acknowledging her husband's greeting with a nod, "I am just about worn out, Daniel."

"I should think you would be, Serena. You've been makin' tracks between here and that lodge room all to-day and yesterday, too. I should think you'd be about dead."

"It isn't that. I don't mind the work. It's the thanklessness of it all that breaks me down. I give my time and effort to help the lodge, and what does it amount to?"

"Well, I--I give in that it don't seem to me to amount to much, 'cordin' to my figurin'. I don't care much for lodge meetin's and sociables and such, myself. I'd rather have one evenin' at home with you than the whole cargo of 'em."

This statement was frank, but it was decidedly undiplomatic. Serena sniffed contempt.

"Of course you would!" she said. "I don't get a bit of encouragement here at home, either. I should think you'd be proud to have your wife the head of the Chapter, presiding at meetings and welcoming the visiting delegates and--and all."

"I am," hastily. "I'm proud of you, Serena. Always have been, far's that goes. But I'm just as proud of you here in this sittin'-room as I am when you're back of that pulpit, poundin' with your mallet and tellin' Alphy Ann Berry to 'come to order.' Notwithstanding that you're the only one can make her come--or go, either-- unless she takes a notion. Why," with a chuckle, "it takes her husband half an hour to make her go home after meetin's over."

Mrs. Dott did not chuckle.

"You think it's a joke," she said. "I don't. It is the Berry woman and her kind that make me disgusted. I'm tired of them all. I'm tired of Trumet. I wish we were somewhere where I had an opportunity; somewhere where I might be appreciated."

"I appreciate you, Serena."

Serena ignored the remark. "I wish we had never settled here," she went on. "I'd leave in a minute, if I could. I'd like to be in with nice people, cultivated people, intelligent, up-to-date society, where I could have a chance to go on and be somebody. I'd like to be a leader. I could be. Annette says I would be in a city like Scarford. She says I 'have the faculty of the born leader.' All I lack is the opportunity."

Her husband sighed. He had heard all this before. Inwardly he wished Mrs. Black at Scarford, or China, or anywhere, provided it was not Trumet.

His wife heard the sigh. "There, Daniel," she said; "I won't be complaining. I try not to be. But," she hesitated, "there is one thing I'd like to ask, now that we've got your Aunt Lavinia's three thousand: Don't you suppose I could have some new clothes; I need at least two dresses right away."

"Why--why, I guess likely you could, Serena. Yes, course you can. You go see Sarah Loveland right off."

Miss Loveland was the Trumet dressmaker. At the mention of her name Serena shook her head.

"I don't want Sarah to make them, Daniel," she said. "Mrs. Black says the things she makes are awful old-fashioned; 'country,' she calls them."

Daniel snorted. "I want to know!" he exclaimed. "Well, I remember her husband when his ma used to make his clothes out of his dad's old ones. I don't know whether they was 'country' or not, but they were the dumdest things ever I saw. Country, huh! Scarford ain't any Paris, is it? I never heard it was."

"Well, it isn't Trumet. No, Daniel, if we could afford it, I'd like to have these dresses made up in Boston, where Gertie gets hers. Mrs. Black often speaks of Gertie's gowns; she says they are remarkably stylish, considering."

"CONSIDERIN'! What does she mean by that?"

"Don't be cross. I suppose she meant considering that they were not as expensive as her own. DO you suppose I could go to that Boston dressmaker, Daniel?"

Captain Dan's reply was slow in coming. He hated to say no; in fact, he said it so seldom that he scarcely knew how. So he temporized.

"Well, Serena," he began, "I--I'd like to have you; you know that. If 'twasn't for the cost I wouldn't hesitate a minute."

"But we have that three thousand dollars."

"Well, we ain't got all of it. Or we shan't have it long. I was footin' up what I owed--what the store owes, I mean--just now, and it come to a pretty high figure. Over twelve hundred, it was. That's GOT to be paid. Then there's Gertie's schoolin' and her board. Course, I never tell her we ain't so well off as we were. You and I agreed she shouldn't know. But it takes a lot of money and--"

Mrs. Dott sat up on the couch. Her eyes snapped. "Oh!" she cried; "money! money! money! It's always money! If only just once I had all the money I wanted, I should be perfectly happy. If I wouldn't GO IT!"

Steps sounded on the front porch, and the patent door bell clicked and clanged.

CHAPTER III

Next morning an astonishing rumor began to circulate through Trumet. It spread with remarkable quickness, and, as it spread, it grew. The Dotts had inherited money! The Dotts were rich! The Dotts were millionaires! Captain Daniel's brother had died and left him fifty thousand dollars! His brother's wife had died and left him a hundred thousand! It was not his brother's wife, but Serena's uncle who had died, and the inheritance was two hundred and fifty thousand at least. By the time the story reached Trumet Neck it seemed to be fairly certain that all the Dott relatives on both sides of the house had passed away, leaving the sole survivors of the family all the money and property in the world, with a few trifling exceptions.

Captain Dan, coming in for dinner,--one must eat, or try to eat, even though the realities of life have been blown away, and one is moving in a sort of dream, with the fear of awakening always present--Captain Dan, coming into the house for dinner, expressed his opinion of Trumet gossip mongers.

"My heavens and earth, Serena!" he cried, sinking into his chair at the table, "am I me, or somebody else? Do I know what I'm doin' or what's happened to me, or don't I?"

Serena, a transformed, flushed, excited Serena, beamed at him across the table.

"I should hope you did, Daniel," she answered.

"Well, if I do, then nobody else does, and if THEY do, I don't. I've heard of more dead relations this forenoon than I ever had alive. And yarns about 'em! and about you and me! My soul and body! Say, did you know you had a cousin-in-law in Californy?"

"I? In California? Nonsense!"

"No nonsense about it. You had one and he was a lunatic or a epileptic or an epizootic or somethin', and lived in a hospital or a palace or a jail, and he was worth four millions or forty, I forget which, and fell out of an automobile or out of a balloon or out of bed--anyhow, it killed him--and--"

"Daniel Dott! DON'T talk so idiotic!"

"Humph! that's nothin' to the idiocy that's been talked to me this forenoon. I've done nothin' for the last hour but say 'No' to folks that come tearin' in to unload lies and ask questions. And some of 'em was people you'd expect to have common sense, too. My head's kind of wobbly this mornin', after the shock that hit it last night, but it's a regular Dan'l Webster's alongside the general run of heads in this town. Aunt Laviny's will has turned Trumet into an asylum, and the patients are all runnin' loose."

"But WHAT foolishness was that about a cousin in California?"

"'Twa'n't foolishness, I tell you. You ask any one of a dozen folks you meet outside the post-office now, and they'll all tell you you had one. They might not agree whether 'twas a cousin or a grandmother or a step-child, or whether it lived in Californy or the Cape of Good Hope, but they all know it's dead now, and we've got anywheres from a postage stamp to a hogshead of diamonds. Serena, if you hear yells for help this afternoon, don't pay any attention. It'll only mean that my patience has run out and I'm tryin' to make this community short one devilish fool at least. There'll be enough left; he'll never be missed."

"Daniel, I never saw you so worked up. You must expect people to be excited. I'm excited myself."

The captain wiped his forehead with his napkin. "I ain't exactly a graven image, now that you mention it," he admitted. "But you and I have got some excuse and they ain't. Haven't they been in to see you; or did you lock the doors?"

"I have had callers, of course. Mrs. Berry was here, and Mrs. Tripp, and the Cahoon girls, and Issachar Eldredge's wife. The first four pretended they came on lodge business, and the Eldredge woman to get my recipe for chocolate doughnuts; but, of course, I knew what they really came for. Daniel, HOW do you suppose the news got out so soon? I didn't tell a soul and you promised you wouldn't."

"I didn't, neither. Probably that lawyer man dropped a hint down at the Manonquit House, and that set things goin'. Just heave over one seed of a yarn in most any hotel or boardin' house and you'll have a crop of lies next mornin' that would load a three-master. They come up in the night, like toadstools."

"But you didn't tell anyone how much your Aunt Lavinia left us?"

"You bet I didn't. I told 'em I didn't know yet. I was cal'latin' to hire a couple of dozen men and a boy to count it, and soon's the job was finished I'd get out a proclamation. What did you tell your gang?"

"I simply said," Serena unconsciously drew herself up and spoke with a gracious dignity; "I said they might quote me as saying it was NOT a million."

Azuba entered from the kitchen, heaving a steaming platter.

"There!" she exclaimed, setting the dish before her employers; "I don't know as clam fritters are what rich folks ought to eat, but I done the best I could. I'm so shook up and trembly this day it's a mercy I didn't fry the platter."

Yes, something had happened to the Dotts, something vastly more wonderful and surprising than falling heir to three thousand dollars and a silver tea-pot. When Captain Daniel shut up the Metropolitan Store the previous evening and started for the house, the bearer of the great news was on his way from the Manonquit House, where he had had supper. When Serena bewailed her fate and expressed a desire for an opportunity, he was almost at the front gate, and the ring of the bell which interrupted her conversation with her husband was the signal that Opportunity, in the person of Mr. Glenn Farwell, Junior, newest member of the firm of Shepley and Farwell, attorneys, of Boston, was at the door.

Mr. Farwell was spruce and brisk and businesslike; also he was young, a fact which he tried to conceal by a rather feeble beard, and much professional dignity of manner and expression. Occasionally, in the heat of conversation, he forgot the dignity; the beard he never forgot. Shown into the Dott sitting-room by Azuba, who, as usual, had neglected to remove her kitchen apron, he bowed politely and inquired if he had the pleasure of addressing Captain and Mrs. Daniel Abner Dott. The captain assured him that he had. Serena was too busy glaring at the apron and its wearer to remember etiquette.

"Won't you--won't you sit down, Mr. er--er--" began the captain.

Mr. Farwell introduced himself, and sat down, as requested. After a glance about the room, which took in the upright piano--purchased second-hand when Gertrude first began her music lessons--the what-not, with its array of shells, corals, miniature ships in bottles, and West Indian curiosities, and the crayon enlargement over the mantel of Captain Solon Dott, Daniel's grandfather, he proceeded directly to business.

"Captain Dott," he said, addressing that gentleman, but bowing politely to Serena to indicate that she was included in the question, "you received a letter from our firm about a week ago, did you not?"

Captain Dan, who had scarcely recovered from his surprise at his caller's identity, shook his head. "As a matter of fact," he stammered, "I--I only got it to-day. It came all right, that is, it got as far as the post-office, but the postmaster, he handed it over to Balaam Hamilton, to bring to me. Well, Balaam is--well, his underpinnin's all right; he wears a number eleven shoe--but his top riggin' is kind of lackin' in spots. You'd understand if you knew him. He put the letter in his pocket and--"

"Mercy!" cut in Serena, impatiently, "what do you suppose Mr. Farwell cares about Balaam Hamilton? He forgot the letter, Mr. Farwell, and we only got it this morning. That is why it hasn't been answered. What about the letter?"

The visitor did not answer directly. "I see," he said. "That letter informed you that Mrs. Lavinia Dott--your aunt, Captain,--was dead, and that we, her legal representatives, having, as we supposed, her will in our possession, and being in charge of her affairs--"

Mrs. Dott interrupted. Her excitement had been growing ever since she learned the visitor's name and, although her husband did not notice the peculiar phrasing of the lawyer's sentence, she did.

"As you supposed?" she repeated. "You did have the will, didn't you?"

"We had a will, one which Mrs. Dott drew some eight or nine years ago. But we received word from Italy only yesterday that there was another, a much more recent one, which superseded the one in our possession. Of course, that being the case, the bequests in the former were not binding upon the estate. That is to say, our will was not a will at all."

Serena gasped. She looked at her husband, and he at her.

"Then we--then she didn't leave us the three thousand dollars?" she cried.

"Or--or the tea-pot?" faltered Captain Dan.

Mr. Farwell smiled. He was having considerable fun out of the situation. However, it would not do to keep possibly profitable clients in suspense too long, so he broke the news he had journeyed from Boston to impart.

"She left you a great deal more than that," he said. "In the former will, her cousin, Mr. Percy Hungerford of Scarford, was the principal legatee. He was a favorite of hers, I believe, and she left the bulk of her property--some hundred and twenty thousand dollars in securities, and her estate at Scarford--to him. But last February it appears that he and she had a falling out. He--Mr. Hungerford--is, so I am told, a good deal of a sport--ahem! that is, he is a young gentleman of fashionable and expensive tastes, and he wrote his aunt, asking for money, rather frequently. The February letter reached her when she was grouchy--er--not well, I mean, and she changed her will, practically disinheriting him. Under the new will he receives twenty thousand dollars in cash. The balance--" Mr. Farwell, who, during this long statement, had interspersed legal dignity of term with an occasional lapse into youthful idiom, now spoke with impressive solemnity,--"the balance," he said, "one hundred thousand in money and securities, and the house at Scarford, which is valued, I believe, at thirty-five thousand more, she leaves to you, as her only other relative, Captain Dott. I am here to congratulate you and to offer you my services and those of the firm, should you desire legal advice."

Having sprung his surprise, Mr. Farwell leaned back in his chair to enjoy the effect of the explosion. The first effect appeared to be the complete stupefaction of his hearers. Those which followed were characteristic.

"My soul and body!" gasped Captain Dan. "I--I--my land of love! And only this mornin' I was scared I couldn't pay my store bills!"

"A hundred thousand dollars!" cried Serena. "And that beautiful house at Scarford! OURS! Oh! oh! oh!"

Mr. Farwell crossed his knees. "A very handsome little windfall," he observed, with condescension.

"We get a hundred thousand!" murmured the captain. "My! I wish Father was alive to know about it. But, say, it's kind of rough on that young Hungerford, after expectin' so much, ain't it now!"

"A hundred thousand!" breathed his wife, her hands clasped. "And that lovely house! Why, we could move to Scarford to-morrow if we wanted to! Yes, and live there! Oh--oh, Daniel! I--I don't know why I'm doing it, but I--I believe I'm going to cry."

Her husband rushed over to the couch and threw his arm about her shoulder.

"Go ahead, old lady," he commanded. "Cry, if you want to. I--I'm goin' to do SOMETHIN' darn ridiculous, myself!"

Thus it was that Fortune and Opportunity came to the Dott door, and it was the news of the visitation, distorted and exaggerated, which set all Trumet by the ears next day.

Azuba's clam fritters were neglected that noon, just as breakfast had been. Neither Captain Dan nor his wife had slept, and they could not eat. They pretended to, they even tried to, but one or the other was certain to break out with an exclamation or a wondering surmise, and the meal was, as the captain said, "all talk and no substantials." They had scarcely risen from the table when the doorbell rang.

Azuba heard it and made her entrance from the kitchen. She had remembered this time to shed the offending apron, but she carried it in her hand.

"I'm a-goin'," she declared; "I'm a-goin', soon's ever I can."

She started for the sitting-room, but the captain stepped in front of her.

"You stay right where you are," he ordered. "I'll answer that bell myself this time."

"Daniel," cried his wife, "what are you going to do?"

"Do? I'm goin' to head off some more fools, that's what I'm goin' to do. They shan't get in here to pester you to death with questions, not if I can help it."

"But, Daniel, you mustn't. You don't know who it may be."

"I don't care."

"Oh, dear me! What are you going to say? You mustn't insult people."

"I shan't insult 'em. I'll tell 'em--I'll tell 'em you're sick and can't see anybody."

"But I'm not sick."

"Then, I am," said Captain Dan. "They make me sick. Shut up, will you?" addressing the bell, which had rung the second time. "I'll come when I get ready."

He seemed to be quite ready that very moment. At all events he strode from the room, and his anxious wife and the flushed Azuba heard him tramping through the front hall.

"What--WHAT is he going to do?" faltered Serena; "or say?"

Azuba shook her head. "Land knows!" she exclaimed. "I ain't seen him this way since the weasel got into the hen-house. He went for THAT with the hoe-handle. And as for what he said! Well, don't talk to ME!"

But no riot or verbal explosion followed the opening of the door. The anxious listeners in the dining-room heard voices, but they were subdued ones. A moment later Captain Dan returned. He looked troubled.

"It's Barney Black and his wife," he answered, in a whisper. "I couldn't tell THEM to go to thunder. They're in the front room, waitin'. I suppose we'll have to see 'em, won't we?"

Mrs. Dott was hurriedly shaking the wrinkles out of her gown and patting her hair into presentable shape.

"See 'em!" she repeated. "Of course we'll see them. I declare! I think it's real kind of 'em to call. Daniel, do fix your necktie. It's way round under your ear."

They entered the parlor, Serena, outwardly calm, in the lead and her husband following, and tugging at the refractory tie.

Mrs. and Mr. Black--scanning them in the order of their importance--rose as they appeared. Mrs. Black was large and impressive, and gorgeous to view. She did not look her age. Her husband was not as tall as his wife, and did not look his height. Annette swept forward.

"Oh, my dear Mrs. Dott," she gushed, taking Serena's hand in her own gloved one. "We've just heard the news, Phelps and I, and we couldn't resist dropping in to congratulate you. Isn't it wonderful!"

Serena admitted that it was wonderful. "We can hardly believe it yet, ourselves," she said. "But it was real nice of you to come. Do sit down again, won't you? Daniel, get Mr. Black a chair."

Captain Dan and Mr. Black shook hands. "Sit down anywhere, Barney," said the former. "Anywhere but that rocker, I mean; that's got a squeak in the leg."

Mr. Black, who had headed for the rocker, changed his course and sank into an arm chair. The shudder with which his wife heard the word "Barney," and the glare with which Serena favored her husband, were entirely lost upon the latter.

"We had that rocker up in the attic till last month," he observed; "but Serena found out 'twas an antique, and antiques seem to be all the go now-a-days, though you do have to be careful of 'em. I suppose it's all right. We'll be antiques ourselves before many years, and we'll want folks to be careful of us. Hey? Ha! ha! ... Why, what's the matter, Serena?"

Mrs. Dott replied, rather sharply, that "nothing was the matter."

"The rocker isn't very strong," she explained, addressing Mrs. Black. "But it belonged to my great--that is, it has been in our family for a good many years and we think a great deal of it."

Mrs. Black condescendingly expressed her opinion that the rocker was a "dear."

"I love old-fashioned things," she said. "So does Mr. Black. Don't you, Phelps?"

"Yes," replied that gentleman. His love did not appear to be over-enthusiastic.

"But do tell us about your little legacy," went on the lady. "Of course we have heard all sorts of ridiculous stories, but we know better than to believe them. Why, we even heard that you were worth a million. Naturally, THAT was absurd, wasn't it? Ha! ha!"

Captain Dan opened his mouth to reply, but his wife flashed a glance in his direction, and he closed it again.

"Yes," said Serena, addressing Mrs. Black, "that was absurd, of course."

"So I told Phelps. I said that the way in which these country people exaggerated such things was too funny for anything. Why, we heard that your cousin had died--that is, I heard it was a cousin; Phelps heard it was an uncle. An uncle was what you heard, wasn't it, Phelps?"

"Yes," said Phelps. It was his second contribution to the conversation.

"So," went on Mrs. Black, "we didn't know which it was."

She paused, smilingly expectant. Again Captain Dan started to speak, and again a look from his wife caused him to change his mind. Before he had quite recovered, Mrs. Black, who may have noticed the look, had turned to him.

"Wasn't it funny!" she gushed. "I don't wonder you laugh. Here was I saying it was a cousin and Phelps declaring it was an uncle. It was so odd and SO like this funny little town. Do tell us; which was it, really, Captain Dott?"

Daniel, staggering before this point blank attack, hesitated. "Why," he stammered, "it was--it was--" He looked appealingly at Serena.

"Why don't you answer Mrs. Black?" inquired his wife, rather sharply.

"It was my Aunt Laviny," said the captain.

Mrs. Black nodded and smiled.

"Oh! your aunt!" she exclaimed. "There! isn't that funny! And SO characteristic of Trumet. Neither an uncle nor a cousin, but an aunt. What did you say her name was?"

"Laviny?"

"Yes, I know. Laviny--what an odd name! I don't think I ever heard it before. Was the rest of it as odd as that?"

Serena, who had been fidgeting in her chair, cut in here.

"It wasn't Laviny at all," she said. "That is only Daniel's way of pronouncing it. It is what he used to call her when he was a child. A--a sort of pet name, you know."

"Why, Serena! how you talk! She never had any pet name, far's I ever heard. You might as well give a pet name to the Queen of Sheba. She--"

"Hush! it doesn't make any difference. Her name, Mrs. Black, was Lavinia. She was Mrs. Lavinia Dott, and her husband was James Dott, Daniel's father's brother. I shouldn't wonder if you knew her. She has spent most of her time in Europe lately, but her home, her American home, was where you live, in Scarford."

This statement caused a marked sensation. Mrs. Black gasped audibly, and leaned back in her chair. B. Phelps evinced his first sign of interest.

"What!" he exclaimed. "Mrs. Lavinia Dott, of Scarford? You don't say! Why, of course we knew her; that is, we knew who she was. Everybody in Scarford did. Her place is one of the finest in town."

Serena bowed. Life, for her, had not offered many sweeter moments than this.

"Yes," she said, calmly, "so we understand. The place--er--that is, the estate--is a PART--" she emphasized the word--"a PART of what she left to my husband."

"Great Scott!" exclaimed Mr. Black. His wife said nothing, but her face was a study.

Captain Dan crossed his knees.

"I remember seein' that place after Uncle Jim first built it," he observed, reminiscently. "I tell you it looked big enough to me! I was only a young feller, just begun goin' to sea, and that house looked big as a town hall, you might say. Ho! ho! when I got inside and was sittin' in the front parlor, I declare I was all feet and hands! didn't know what to do with 'em.... Hey? did you speak, Serena?"

"I was only going to say," replied his wife, "that that was a good while ago, of course. You have been about the world and seen a great deal since. Things look different after we grow up, don't they, Mrs. Black?"

Annette's composure, a portion of it, had returned by this time. Nevertheless, there was an odd note in her voice.

"They do, indeed," she said. "I remember the Dott house, of course. It was very fine, I believe, in its day."

Her husband interrupted. "In its day!" he repeated. "Humph! there's nothing the matter with it now, that I can see. I wish I had as good. Why--"

"Phelps!" snapped Annette, "don't be silly. Mrs. Dott understands what I meant to say. The place is very nice, very attractive, indeed. Perhaps some might think it a bit old-fashioned, but that is a matter of taste."

"Humph! it's on the best street in town. As for being old-fashioned--I thought you just said you loved old-fashioned things. That's what she said, wasn't it, Dan?"

Mrs. Black's gloved fingers twitched, but she ignored the remark entirely. Daniel, too, did not answer, although he smiled in an uncertain fashion. It was Serena who spoke.

"I haven't any doubt it is lovely," she said. "We're just dying to see it, Daniel and I. I hope you can be with us when we do, Mrs. Black. You might suggest some improvements, you know."

"Improvements!" the visitor repeated the word involuntarily. "Improvements! You're not going to LIVE there, are you?"

"I don't know. We may. Now, Daniel, don't argue. You know we haven't made up our minds yet what we shall do. And Scarford is a beautiful city. Mrs. Black has told us so ever so many times. What were you going to say, Mrs. Black?"

The lady addressed looked as if she would like to say several things, particularly to her husband, who was grinning maliciously. But what she did was to smile, a smile of gracious sweetness, and agree that Scarford was beautiful.

"And so is the place, my dear Mrs. Dott," she added. "A very charming, quaint old house. But--you'll excuse my saying so, won't you; you know Phelps and I have had some experience in keeping up a city estate--don't you think it might prove rather expensive for you to maintain?"

Serena's armor was not even dented. "Oh," she said, lightly, "that wouldn't trouble us, I'm sure. Really, we've hardly thought of the expense. The Scarford place wasn't ALL that Aunt Lavinia left us, Mrs. Black."

"Indeed!" rather feebly, "wasn't it?"

"My goodness, no! But there! I mustn't talk about ourselves and our affairs any more. Have you seen the lodge rooms to-day? I must find time to run down there this afternoon for a last look around. I want this open meeting to go off nicely. Who knows--well, I may not have the care of the next one."

Azuba appeared in the doorway.

"The minister and his wife's comin'," she announced.

Mrs. Dott turned.

"The minister and his wife?" she repeated. "The bell hasn't rung, has it? How do you know they're coming here?"

"See 'em through the window," replied Azuba, cheerfully. "They was at the gate quite a spell. She was gettin' her hat straight, and he was helpin' her. Here they be," as the callers' footsteps sounded on the porch. "Shall I let 'em in?"

"Let them in! Why, of course! Why shouldn't you let them in?"

"Well, I didn't know. The way the cap'n was talkin' when you was havin' dinner, I thought--oh, that reminds me," addressing the horror stricken Daniel, "Sam was in just now and wanted you to come right out to the store. Ezra Taylor's there and he wants another pair of them checkered overalls, same as he had afore."

That evening when, having closed the Metropolitan Store at an early hour, the captain and his wife were on their way to the lodge meeting, Daniel voiced a feeling of perplexity which had disturbed his mind ever since the Blacks' call.

"Say, Serena," he asked, "ain't you and Barney Black's wife friends any more?"

"Why, of course we're friends. What a question that is."

"Humph! didn't seem to me you acted much like friends this afternoon. Slappin' each other back and forth--"

"Slappin' each other! Have you lost your brains altogether? What DO you mean?"

"I don't mean slappin' each other side of the head. 'Tain't likely I meant that. But the way you talked to each other--and the way you looked. And when 'twa'n't her it was me. She as much as asked you four or five times who it was that had died and you wouldn't tell, so, of course, I supposed you didn't want to. And yet, when she asked me and I was backin' and fillin', tryin' to get off the shoals, you barked out why didn't I 'answer her'? That may be sense, but I don't see it, myself."

Serena laughed and squeezed his arm with her own.

"Did I bark?" she asked. "I'm sorry; I didn't mean to. But it did make me cross to have her come sailing in, in that high and mighty way--"

"It's the same way she always sails. I never saw her when she didn't act as if she was the only clipper in the channel and small craft better get out from under her bows."

"I know, you never did like her, although she has been so kind and nice to me and to Gertrude. Why, we, and the minister's family, and Doctor Bradstreet's people, are the only ones, except the summer folks, that she has anything to do with."

The captain muttered that he knew it but that THAT didn't make him like her any better. His wife continued.

"I was a little put out by her to-day," she admitted. "You see, she was SO anxious to find out things, and SO sure we couldn't be very rich, and SO certain we couldn't keep up Aunt Lavinia's big house, that--that I just had to give her as good as she sent."

Daniel chuckled. "You did that all right," he said.

"But I wouldn't hurt her feelings--really hurt them--for the world. I like her and admire her, and I am sure she likes me."

"Humph! All right; only next time you get to admirin' each other I'm goin' out. That kind of admiration makes me nervous. I heard you admirin' Zuba out in the kitchen just before we left."

"Azuba makes me awfully out of patience. She won't do what I tell her; she will wear her apron to the door; she will talk when she shouldn't. Just think what she said about you when the minister called. It was just Providence, and nothing else, that kept her from telling the Blacks what you said and how you acted at dinner. That's it--laugh! I expected you'd think it was funny."

"Well, I give in that it does seem kind of funny to me, now, though it didn't when she started to say it. But you can't stop Zuba talkin' any more than you can a poll parrot. She means well; she's awful good-hearted--yes, and sensible, too, in her way."

"I can't help it. She's got to learn her place. Just think of having her up there at

Scarford, behaving as she does."

The captain caught his breath.

"Scarford!" he repeated. "At Scarford! Look here, Serena, what are you talkin' about? You didn't mean what you said to that Black woman about our goin' to Scarford to live?"

"I don't know that I didn't. There! there! don't get excited. I don't say I do mean it, either. Aunt Lavinia's left us that lovely house, hasn't she? We've got it on our hands, haven't we? What are we going to do with it?"

"Why--why, I--I was cal'latin' we'd probably sell it, maybe. We've got our own place here in Trumet. We don't want two places, do we?"

"We might sell this one, at a pinch. No, Daniel, I don't know what we shall do yet awhile. But, one thing I AM sure of--you and I will go to Scarford and LOOK at that house, if nothing more. Now, don't argue, please. We're almost at the meeting. Be sure you don't tell anyone how much money we've got or anything about it. They'll all ask, of course, and they'll all talk about us, but you must expect that. Our position in life has altered, Daniel, and rich folks are always looked at and talked over. Are your shoes clean? Did you bring a handkerchief? Be sure and don't applaud too much when I'm speaking, because last time I was told that Abigail Mayo said if she was married and had a husband she wouldn't order him to clap his hands half off every time his wife opened her mouth. She isn't married and ain't likely to be, but.... Oh, Mrs. Black, I'm SO glad to see you! It's real lovely of you to come so early."

Daniel Dott, as has been intimated, did not share his wife's love for lodge meetings. He attended them because she did, and wished him to, but he was not happy while they were going on. At this one he was distinctly unhappy. He saw Serena and Annette Black exchange greetings as if the little fencing match of the afternoon had been but an exchange of compliments. He saw the two ladies go, arm in arm, to the platform, where sat the "Boston delegates." He nodded to masculine acquaintances in the crowd, other captives chained, like himself, to their wives' and daughters' chariot wheels. He heard the applause which greeted Serena's opening speech of introduction. He heard the Boston delegates speak, and Mrs. Black's gracious response to the request for a few words from the president of our Scarford Chapter. He heard it all, but, when it was over, he could not have repeated a sentence of all those which had reached his ears.

No, Captain Dan was not happy at this, the most successful "open meeting" ever held by the Trumet Chapter of the Guild of Ladies of Honor. He was thinking, and thinking hard. Aunt Lavinia's will had changed their position in life, so Serena had said. She had said other things, also, and he was beginning, dimly, to realize what they might mean.

CHAPTER IV

SCARFORD!" screamed the brakeman, throwing open the car door. "Scarford!"

Mrs. Dott, umbrella in hand, was already in the aisle. Captain Dan, standing between the seats, was struggling to get the suitcase down from the rack above. It was a brand-new suitcase. Serena had declared that their other, the one which had accompanied them on various trips to Boston during the past eight years, was altogether too shabby. She had insisted on buying another, and, the stock in the store not being good enough, had selected this herself from the catalog of a Boston manufacturer. Her umbrella, silk with a silver handle, was new also. So was her hat, her gown and her shoes. So, too, was the captain's hat, and his suit and light overcoat. There was a general air of newness about the Dotts, so apparent, particularly on Daniel's part, that various passengers had nudged each other, winked, and whispered surmises concerning recent marriage and a honeymoon trip.

The suitcase, the buckle of which had caught in the meshes of the rack, giving way, came down unexpectedly and with a thump on the seat. The captain hurriedly lifted it. A stifled laugh from the occupants of adjacent seats reached Serena's ears.

"What is it?" she demanded impatiently. "Aren't you coming? Do hurry."

"I--I'm comin'," stammered her husband, thrusting his fist into the new hat which, as it lay on the seat, had received the weight of the falling suitcase. "I'm comin'. Go ahead! I'll be right along."

He pounded the battered "derby" into more or less presentable shape, clapped it on his head, and, suitcase in hand, followed his wife.

Through the crowd on the platform they passed, through the waiting room and out to the sidewalk. There Captain Dan put down the case, gave the maltreated hat a brush with his sleeve, and looked about him.

"Lively place, ain't it, Serena?" he observed. "Whew! that valise is heavy. Well, where's the next port of call?"

"We'll go to the hotel first. Oh, dear, it's a shame things happened so we had to come now. In another fortnight the Blacks would have been here and we could have gone right to their house. Mrs. Black felt dreadfully about it. She said so ever so many times."

The captain made no answer. If he had doubts concerning the depths of the Blacks' sorrow he kept them to himself. Picking up the suitcase, he stepped forward to the curb.

"Where are you going?" demanded his wife.

"Why, to the hotel. That's where you wanted to go, wasn't it?"

"Certainly; but how were you going? You don't know where it is."

"No, so I don't. But I can hail one of those electrics and ask the conductor to stop when he got to it. He'd know where 'twas, most likely."

"Electric" is the Down East term for trolley car, lines of which were passing and repassing the station. Daniel waved his disengaged hand to the conductor of the nearest. The car stopped.

"Wait a minute," said Serena quickly. "How do you know that car is going the right way?"

"Hey? Well, of course I don't know, but--"

"Of course you don't. Besides, we don't want to go in an electric. We must take a carriage."

"A carriage? A hack, you mean. What do we want to do that for?"

"Because it's what everyone does."

"No, they don't. Look at all the folks on that electric now. Besides, we--"

"Hi there!" shouted the conductor of the car angrily. "Brace up! Get a move on, will you?"

Mrs. Dott regarded him with dignity.

"We're not coming," she said. "You can go right along."

The car proceeded, the conductor commenting freely and loudly, and the passengers on the broad grin.

"Now, Daniel," said Serena, "you get one of those carriages and we'll go as we ought to. I know we've always gone in the electrics when we were in Boston, but then we didn't feel as if we could afford anything else. Now we can. And don't stop to bargain about the fare. What is fifty cents more or less to US?"

The captain shook his head, but he obeyed orders. A few minutes later they were seated in a cab, drawn by a venerable horse and driven by a man with a hooked nose, and were moving toward the Palatine House, the hostelry recommended by Mrs. Black as the finest in Scarford.

"There!" said Serena, leaning back against the shabby cushions, "this is better than an electric, isn't it? And when we get to the hotel you'll see the difference it will make in the way they treat us. Mrs. Black says there is everything in a first impression. If people judge by your looks that you're no account they'll treat you that way. But what were you and the driver having such a talk about?"

Captain Dan grinned. "I got the name of the hotel wrong at first," he admitted. "I called it the Palestine House instead of the other thing. The driver thought I was makin' fun of him. It ain't safe to mention Palestine to a feller with a nose like that."

The Palatine House was new and gorgeous; built in the hope of attracting touring automobilists, it was that dreary mistake, a cheap imitation of the swagger metropolitan article. Scarford was not a metropolis, and the imitation in this case was a particularly poor one. However, to the Dotts, its marble-floored lobby and gilded pillars and cornices were grand and imposing. Their room on the third floor looked out upon the street below, and if the view of shops and signs and trucks and trolleys was not beautiful it was, at least, distinctly different from any view in Trumet.

Serena gloried in it.

"Ah!" she sighed, "this is something like. THIS is life! There's something going on here, Daniel. Don't you feel it?"

Daniel was counting his small change.

"What say?" he asked.

His wife repeated her question, raising her voice to carry above the noises of the street.

"Feel it! Yes, yes; and hear it, too. How we're ever goin' to sleep with all that hullabaloo outside I don't know. Don't you suppose we could get a quieter room than this, Serena?"

"I don't want a quiet room. I don't want to sleep. I feel as if I'd been asleep all my life. Now, thank goodness, I am where people are really awake. What are you doing with that money?"

"Oh, just lookin' at it, while I can. I shan't have the chance very long, if the other folks in this town are like that hack driver. A dollar to drive half a mile in that hearse! Why, the whole shebang wa'n't worth more than two dollars, to buy. And then he had the cheek to ask me to give him 'a quarter for himself.'"

"Yes, that was his tip. We must expect that. Gertrude says she always has to tip the servants and drivers and such at college. Did you give it to him?"

"Who? Me? I told him I was collectin' for a museum, and I'd give him a quarter for the horse, just as it stood--or WHILE it stood. I said he'd better take the offer pretty quick because the critter looked as if 'twould lay down most any minute."

He chuckled. Serena, however, was very solemn.

"Daniel," she said, "I must speak to you again about your language. You've lived in Trumet so long that you talk just like Azuba, or pretty nearly as bad. You mustn't say 'critter' and 'wa'n't' and 'cal'late.' Do try, won't you, to please me?"

"I'll try, Serena. But I don't see what difference it makes. We DO live in Trumet, don't we?"

"We HAVE lived there. How long we shall--But there, never mind. Just remember as well as you can and get ready now for dinner."

Her husband muttered that he didn't see where the "getting ready" came in; he had on the best he'd got. But he washed his hands and brushed his hair and they descended to the dining-room, where they ate a 'table d'hote' meal, beginning with lukewarm soup and ending with salty ice cream.

They had left Trumet the previous evening, spending the night at Centreboro and taking the early morning train for Scarford. Two weeks had passed since the fateful visit of young Mr. Farwell, and, though the wondrous good fortune which had befallen the Dott family was still wonderful, they were beginning to accept it as a real and established fact. All sorts of things had happened during those two weeks. They had gone to Boston, where they spent the better part of two days with the lawyers, going over the lists of securities, signing papers, and arranging all sorts of business matters. Serena and the attorneys did the most of the arranging. Captain Dan looked on, understanding very little, saying "Yes" or "No" as commanded by his wife, and signing his name whenever and wherever requested.

After another day, spent in the Boston shops, where the new clothes were purchased or ordered, a process which Serena enjoyed hugely and her husband endured with a martyr's patience, they had paid a flying visit to the college town and Gertrude. They found the young lady greatly excited and very happy, but her happiness was principally on their account.

"I'm so glad for you both, Daddy," she told her father. "When I got Mother's letter with the news the very first thing I thought was: 'There! now Father won't have to worry any more about the old store or anything else. He can be comfortable and carefree and happy, as he deserves to be.' And you won't worry, will you, Dad?"

The captain seemed oddly doubtful.

"I shan't if I can help it," he said. "But I'm the most foolish chap that ever lived, in some ways, seems so. When the business was so I had to worry about it all the time I used to set up nights wishin' I didn't own it. Now that we're fixed so it don't make much difference whether I get a profit or not, I find myself frettin' and wonderin' how Nathaniel and Sam are gettin' along. I wake up guessin' how much they've sold since I've been away, and whether we're stuck on those canvas hats and those middy blouses and one thing or 'nother, same as I was afraid we'd be. I've only been away three days altogether, but it seems about a year."

Gertrude smiled and shook her head.

"Why don't you sell out?" she asked. "Or would no one buy? I presume that's it."

"No-o, that ain't it. I don't wonder you think so, but it ain't. Cohen--the fellow that owns the Emporium--was in only the day afore we left, hintin' around about my retirin' and so on. He didn't make any real bid for the business, but he as much as said he'd consider buyin' me out if I'd sell. Your mother, she'd give me fits if she knew it. She wants me to sell; but--but somehow I can't make up my mind to. I've been so used to goin' out to that store every mornin' and--and havin' it on my mind that somehow I hate to give it up. Seems like cuttin' my anchor rope, as you might say."

"I understand. I shall feel much the same, I know, when I graduate and my college work is over. I shall be lost for a time without it; or I should be if it were not for John and--and my other plans. But, whether you keep the store or not, you mustn't worry any more, Daddy dear. Nathaniel is a clever, able fellow; every one says so. You were fortunate to get him. Why don't you engage him permanently? With his experience, he might make a real success of the business. Who knows?"

He could not possibly make less of a success than the captain had made, that was fairly certain, although she did not say so. Nathaniel Bangs was a Trumet young man who had been getting on well with a little business of his own in Brockton, but who, owing to ill health, had been obliged to return to the Cape the year before. Then, health much improved, he was very glad of the opportunity to take charge of the Metropolitan Store during its owners' short absence. Serena had thought of him, and Serena had hired him.

Captain Dan's real reason for not selling out to the astute Mr. Cohen he had kept to himself. His wife's hints concerning Scarford and her discontent in Trumet were his reasons. These were what troubled him most. He liked Trumet; he liked its quiet, easy-going atmosphere; he liked the Trumet people, and they liked him. He had never been in Scarford, but he was certain he should not like the life there, the kind of life lived by the B. Phelps Blacks, at any rate. The Metropolitan Store was, he felt, an anchor holding him fast to the Cape Cod village. If he cut the anchor rope, goodness knows where he might drift.

On the very day of their return from the Boston trip Serena had begun to discuss the visit to Scarford, the visit of inspection to Aunt Lavinia's "estate." They must go, she said; of course they must go. It was their duty to do that, at least. How could they know what to do with the property until they saw it? To all Daniel's feeble objections and excuses she was deaf. Of course they could leave the house. Azuba would take care of that, just as she always did when they were away. As for the store, Nathaniel would be glad to remain as manager indefinitely if they wanted him. Surely he had done splendidly with it while they were in Boston.

He had. During the four days' absence of its proprietor the Metropolitan Store had actually sold more goods for cash than it had sold during any previous week that summer. Bangs was optimistic concerning its prospects. He was loaded with schemes and ideas.

"All you need is a little push and up-to-date methods, Cap'n," he said. "You must advertise a little, and let people know what you've got to sell. That's how I got rid of all that stale candy you had in the boxes behind the showcase. I knew the

Methodist folks had a Sunday school picnic on the slate for Tuesday. Kids like candy, but candy costs money. I got out all that stale stuff, put it up in bags at five cents apiece, and sent the bags and Sam here to the picnic. About every kid had ten cents or so to spend, and it didn't make any difference to him or her whether the candy was fresh or not, so there was enough of it. If a chocolate cream is harder than the rock of Gibraltar it lasts longer when you're eating it, and that's a big advantage to the average young one. Sam came back, sold out, and we've got four dollars and eighty cents right out of the junk pile, as you might call it. The kids are happy and so are we. There's a half-dozen dried-up oilskin coats in the attic that I've got my eye on. The Manonquit House crowd are going off on a final codfishing cruise tomorrow and I'll be on the dock with those coats at a dollar apiece when they sail."

"But--but those coats are old as Methuselah," faltered the captain. "They'll leak, won't they?"

"Not if it's fair weather, they won't. And, if it's rough, they're better than nothing. You can't expect a mackintosh for a dollar."

Daniel's method would have been to refuse selling the coats because they "wouldn't be much good in a no'theaster." When the codfishers returned, enthusiastic because, although it had "drizzled" for fifteen minutes, they had not gotten wet, he scratched his head and regarded his new assistant with awe. Mr. Bangs' services were retained, "for a spell, anyhow," and the captain's principal excuse for not visiting Scarford was knocked in the head. To Scarford they went, and at the Palatine Hotel in Scarford they now were.

The 'table d'hote' meal eaten, the next feature of Mrs. Dott's program was the visit to the Aunt Lavinia homestead. There was a caretaker in charge, so the Boston lawyers told them, and Serena had written him announcing the coming of the new owners. In spite of her husband's protestations, another carriage was hired for the journey. Daniel was strongly in favor of walking or going by trolley.

"Walkin'll be cheaper, Serena," he declared, "and pretty nigh as fast, to say nothin' of bein' more cheerful. A hack always makes me think of funerals and graveyards, and that skeleton of a horse looked like somethin' that had been buried and dug up. Let's walk, will you?"

But Serena would not walk.

"We must get used to carriages," she said. "We may ride in them a great deal from now on. And, besides, we needn't take a horse carriage. We shouldn't have taken one before. Get one of those new kind, the automobile ones. What is it they call them? Oh, yes--taxis."

The taxi gave no opportunity for complaint as far as slowness was concerned. After the first quarter of a mile dodge up the crowded street Captain Dan shouted through the window.

"Hi!" he hailed, addressing the driver. "Hi, you! You've made a mistake, ain't you? You thought we wanted to fly. We don't. Just hit the ground once in a while, so we'll know it's there."

After this the cab moved at a more reasonable speed and its occupants had an opportunity to observe the streets through which they were passing. The business district was being left behind and they were entering the residential section.

Mrs. Dott seized her husband's arm.

"Look!" she cried. "Look, Daniel, quick! Do you see that? That building there!"

"I see it. Some kind of a hall or somethin', ain't it?"

"Yes. And I'm quite sure, from what Mrs. Black said, that it is the hall where the Scarford Guild meets. Yes, it's just as she said it was. I'm SURE that's it. Oh, I'm glad I've seen it! Yes, and Mrs. Black said they lived not very far from the hall. Daniel! Daniel! ask the man if he knows where the Blacks live and if he can show us their house."

Captain Dan obediently made the inquiry.

"Who?" grunted the driver. "Which Black? Black and Cobb, the Wee Waist Corset feller? Sure! I know where he lives. I'll show you."

A few moments later the cab slackened its speed.

"There you are!" said the driver, pointing. "That's Black's house. Built two years ago, 'twas."

Serena and Daniel looked. The house was new and commodious, a trifle ornate in decoration, perhaps, and a bit mixed in architecture, owing to Mrs. Black's insisting upon the embodiment of various features which she had seen in magazines; but on the whole a rather fine house. To the Dotts, of course, it was a mansion.

"My!" said Serena, "to think of our knowing, really knowing, people who live in a house like that! Oh, dear!" with a sigh, "I almost wish I hadn't seen it until after we'd seen our own. We must try not to be disappointed, mustn't we?"

Captain Dan was surprised. "Disappointed?" he said. "Why, what do you mean? As I recollect Aunt Laviny's place, 'twas just as good as that, if not better. You said so yourself. You used to call it a regular palace."

"I know, but don't you think that was because we hadn't seen many fine houses then? I'm afraid that was it. You know Mrs. Black said it was old-fashioned."

"Humph! Barney--What's his name? Phelps, I mean--he said he wished his was as good. Don't you remember he did?"

"Probably he didn't mean it. I'm not going to expect too much, anyway. I'm going to try and think of it as just a nice old place, and then I shan't feel bad when I see it. I'm not going to get my expectations up or be a bit excited."

In proof of the sincerity of this determination, she sat bolt upright on the seat and looked straight before her. Her husband, however, was staring out of the window with all his might.

"Say!" he exclaimed, "this is a mighty nice street, anyhow."

"Is it? Is it really?" For a person not excited, Mrs. Dott's breathing was short and her fingers, tightly clasped in her lap, were trembling.

"You bet it is! Hey! Why, we're slowin' up! We're stoppin'."

The cab drew up at the curb and came to a standstill.

"Here you are," said the driver. "This is Number 180."

Daniel made no reply. Leaning from the window, he was staring with all his might. Serena's impatience got the better of her.

"Well? WELL?" she burst forth. "What does it look like? Do say something!"

The captain drew back into the carriage.

"My--soul!" he exclaimed presently. "Look, Serena."

Serena looked, and her look was a long one. Then, her face flushed and her eyes shining, she turned to her husband.

"Oh! Oh, Daniel!" she gasped. "It's as good as the Blacks', isn't it? I--I do believe it's better! Get out, quick!"

The caretaker, a middle-aged man with dark hair and mutton-chop whiskers, met them at the top of the stone steps leading to the front door. He bowed low.

"Good afternoon, ma'am," he said. "Good afternoon, sir. Mr. Dott, ain't it, sir? And Mrs. Dott, ma'am. My name is 'Apgood, sir. I was expecting you. Will you be so good as to walk in?"

He threw open the door and, bowing once more, ushered them into the hall, a large, old-fashioned hall with lofty ceiling and a mahogany railed staircase.

"I presume, sir," he said, addressing the captain, "that you and the madam would wish to 'ave me show you about a bit. I was Mrs. Dott's--the late Mrs. Dott's--butler when she resided 'ere, sir, and she was good enough to make me 'er caretaker when she went away, sir."

Captain Dan, rather overawed by Mr. Hapgood's magnificent manner, observed that he wanted to know, adding that he had heard about the caretaking from the lawyers "up to Boston." After an appraising glance at the speaker, Mr. Hapgood addressed his next remark to Serena.

"Shall I show you about the establishment, madam?" he asked.

Serena's composure was a triumph. An inexperienced observer might have supposed she had been accustomed to butlers and establishments all her life.

"Yes," she said loftily, "you can show us."

Mr. Hapgood was a person of wide experience; however, he merely bowed and led the way. Serena followed him, and Captain Dan followed Serena.

A large drawing-room, a library, a very large dining-room, five large bedrooms--"owners' and guest rooms," Mr. Hapgood grandly termed them, to distinguish from the servants' quarters at the rear--billiard room, bathroom, and back to the hall again.

"You would wish to see the kitchens, I suppose, ma'am," said Mr. Hapgood. "Doubtless Mr. Dott wouldn't care for those, sir. Most gentlemen don't. Perhaps, sir, you'd sit 'ere while the lady and I go through the service portion of the 'ouse, sir."

Daniel, who was rather curious to see the "service portion," partly because he had never heard of one before, hesitated. His wife, however, settled the question. She was conscious of a certain condescension in the Hapgood tone.

"Of course," she said lightly, "Cap'n Dott will not go to the--er--service portion. Such things never interest him. Sit here, Daniel, and wait. Now--" cutting off just in time the "Mister" that was on the tip of her tongue and remembering how butlers in novels were invariably addressed--"Now--er--Hapgood, you can take me to the--ahem--kitchens."

It was somewhat disappointing to find that the plural was merely a bit of verbal embroidery on the caretaking butler's part, and that there was but one kitchen, situated in the basement. However, it was of good size and well furnished with closets, the contents of which stirred Serena's housekeeping curiosity. The inspection of the kitchen and laundry took some time.

Meanwhile, upstairs in the dim front hall, Captain Dan sat upon a most uncomfortable carved teak-wood chair and looked about him. Through the doorway leading to the drawing-room--"front parlor," he would have called it--he could see the ebony grand piano, the ormolu clock, and the bronze statuettes on the marble mantel, the buhl cabinet filled with bric-a-brac, the heavy mahogany-framed and silk-covered sofa. There were oil paintings on the walls, paintings which foreign dealers, recognizing Aunt Lavinia's art craving as a gift of Providence--to them--had sold her at high prices. They were, for the most part, landscapes, inclining strongly to snow-covered mountains, babbling brooks, and cows; or marines in which one-third of vivid sunset illumined two-thirds of placid sea. Of portraits there were two, Uncle Jim Dott in black broadcloth and dignity and Aunt Lavinia Dott in dignity and black satin.

Captain Dan felt strangely out of place alone amid this oppressive grandeur. Again, as on the memorable occasion of his first visit to the house, he was conscious of his hands and feet. Aunt Lavinia's likeness, staring stonily and paintily from the wall, seemed to regard him with disapproval, almost as if she were reading his thoughts. If the portrait could have spoken he might have expected it to say: "Here is the person upon whom all these, my worldly possessions, have been bestowed, and he does not appreciate them. There he sits, upon the teakwood chair which I myself bought in Cairo, and, so far from being grateful for the gifts which my generosity has poured into his lap, he is wondering what in the world to do with them, and wishing himself back in Trumet."

Mrs. Dott and the caretaker reentered the hall.

"Thank you, Mr.--er--Thank you, Hapgood," said the lady. "That will be all for to-day, I think. We will go now. Come, Daniel."

Hapgood bowed. "You would wish me to stay 'ere as I've done, ma'am?" he asked.

"Yes. You may stay, for the present. Cap'n Dott and I will pay your regular wages as long as we need you."

"Thank you kindly, ma'am. And might I take the liberty of saying that if you decide to stay 'ere permanently, ma'am, and need a butler or a manservant about the place, I should be glad to 'ave you consider me for the position. I'm sure it would 'ave pleased the late Mrs. Dott to 'ave you do so, ma'am."

"Well," said the captain, with surprising promptness for him, "you see, Mr. Hapgood, as far as that goes we ain't intendin' to--"

"Hush, Daniel. We don't know what we intend. You know that our plans are not settled as yet. We will consider the matter, Hapgood. Good day."

"Good day, ma'am," said Hapgood. "Good day, sir."

He opened the big front door, bowed them out, and stood respectfully waiting as they descended the steps. The taxi driver, whom the captain had neglected to discharge or pay, was still there at the curb with his vehicle. Serena addressed him.

"The Palatine Hotel," she said, with great distinctness. "Come, Daniel."

They entered the cab. Captain Dan closed the door. The driver, looking up at Mr. Hapgood, grinned broadly. The latter gentleman glanced at the cab window to make sure that his visitors were not watching him, then he winked.

As the cab whizzed through the streets Serena gloated over the splendors of their new possessions. The house was finer than she expected, the furniture was so rich and high-toned, the pictures--did Daniel notice the pictures?

"And the location!" she cried ecstatically. "Right on the very best street in town, and yet, so the Hapgood man said, convenient to the theaters and the clubs and the halls. We saw the Ladies of Honor hall on the way up, Daniel, you remember."

Daniel nodded. "Yes," he admitted, "it's fine and convenient and all. We"-- with a sidelong glance at his wife's face--"we ought to get a good rent for it if we decide not to sell; hey, Serena?"

Serena did not answer. When they reached the hotel she left her husband to settle with the driver and took the elevator to their room. A few minutes later the captain joined her. He looked as if suffering from shock.

"My heavens and earth, Serena!" he exclaimed, "what do you suppose that tax hack feller had the cheek to--"

"Sshh! shh!" interrupted the lady, who was reclining upon the couch. "Don't bother me now, Daniel. I don't want to be bothered with common every-day things now; I want to think."

"Common! Everyday! My soul and body! if what that pirate charged me was everyday, I'd be in the poorhouse in a fortni't. Why--"

"Oh, don't! Please don't! Can't you see I am trying to realize that it's true and not a dream. That it has really happened--to ME. Please don't talk. Do go away, can't you? Just go out and take a walk, or something; just for a little while. I want to be alone."

Captain Dan slowly descended the stairs. The elevator, of course, would have been quicker, but he was in no hurry. If he must walk, and it seemed that he must, he might as well begin at once. He descended the stairs to the ground floor of the hotel and wandered aimlessly about through the lobby into the billiard room, and finally to a plate glass door upon which was lettered the word "Rathskeller."

What a Rathskeller might be he did not know, but, as there was another set of letters on the door and those spelled "Push," he pushed.

The Rathskeller was a large room, with a bar at one end and many little tables scattered about. At these tables men were eating, drinking and smoking. A violin, harp and piano, played by a trio of Italians, were doing their worst with a popular melody.

The captain looked about him, selected one of three chairs at an unoccupied table, and sat down. A waiter drifted alongside.

"What'll you have, sir?" inquired the waiter.

"Hey? Oh, I don't know. Give me a cup of coffee."

"Coffee? Yes, sir. Anything to eat?"

"No, I guess not. I've had my dinner."

"Smoke?"

"Well, you might bring me a ten-cent cigar."

The coffee and cigar were brought. Daniel lit the latter, took a sip of the former and listened to the music. This was not taking a walk exactly, but, so far as leaving his wife alone was concerned, it answered the purpose.

The room, already well tenanted, gradually filled. Groups of men entered, stopped to glance at the tape of a sporting news ticker near the bar, exchanged a word or two with the bartenders, and then selected tables. Several times the two vacant chairs at the captain's table were on the point of being taken, but each time the prospective occupants went elsewhere.

At length, however, two young men, laughing and talking rather loudly, sauntered through the room. One of them paused.

"Here are a couple," he said, indicating the chairs.

His companion, an undersized, dapper individual, whose raiment--suit, socks, shirt, shoes, hat and tie--might comprehensively be described as a symphony in brown, paused also, turned and looked at the chairs, then at the table, and finally at the captain.

"Yes," he drawled, regarding the latter fixedly, "so I see. Well, perhaps we can't do better. This place is getting too infernally common, though. Don't think I shall come here again. If it wasn't that they put up the best cocktail in town I should have quit before. All right, this will have to do, I suppose."

He seated himself in one of the chairs. His friend followed suit. The watchful waiter was on hand immediately.

"Good afternoon, gentlemen," he said, bowing obsequiously.

Neither of the young men acknowledged the bow or the greeting, although it was evident that the waiter was an old acquaintance. The symphony in brown did not even turn his head.

"Two dry Martinis," he said. "And mind that they ARE dry. Have Charlie make them himself. If that other fellow does it I'll send them back."

"Yes, sir. All right, sir. Will you have a bit of lunch with them, sir? Caviare sandwich or--"

"No."

"Shall I bring cigars, sir?"

"Lord, no! The last I had here nearly poisoned me. Get the cocktails and be lively about it."

The waiter departed. The young gentleman drew a gold cigarette case from his pocket.

"Here you are," he drawled, proffering the case. "Cigars!" with a contemptuous laugh. "They buy their cigars by the yard, at the rope walk. Fact, Monty; take my word for it."

"Monty" laughed. "That's pretty rough, Tacks," he declared.

"Oh, but it's so. You can actually smell the hemp. Eh? By gad, you can smell it now, can't you?"

Captain Dan was relighting the stump of his "ten-center" which had gone out. He had scarcely noticed the newcomers; his thoughts were far away from Scarford and the Palatine Hotel. Now, however, he suddenly became aware that his table-mates were regarding him and the cigar with apparent amusement. He smiled good naturedly.

"Been runnin' her too low," he observed. "Have to get up steam if I want to be in at the finish."

This nautical remark was received with blank stares. "Monty" turned his shoulder toward the speaker. "Tacks" did not even turn; he continued to stare. The arrival of the cocktails was the next happening of importance.

"I say, Tacks," observed Monty, leaning back in his chair and sipping his Martini, "how are you getting on? Made up your mind what to do?"

"No," shortly.

"Going to fight, are you?"

"No use. The confounded lawyers say I wouldn't have a show."

"Humph! Low-down trick of the old woman's, wasn't it, giving you the shake that way? Everybody thought you were her pet weakness. We used to envy your soft snap. Did you get the go-by altogether?"

"Pretty near. Got a little something, but it was precious little."

"Can you pull through on it?"

"'Twill be a devilish hard pull."

"Too bad, old man. But cheer up! You'll come out on top. Have another one of these things?"

"All right."

More Martinis were ordered. "Monty" and his friend lit fresh cigarettes. The former asked another question.

"Who are the lucky winners?" he inquired. "Some country cousins or other, I know that; but who are they?"

"Oh, I don't know. Yes, I know; but what difference does it make?"

"Isn't there a girl somewhere in the crowd?"

"Yes, but--" He broke off. Captain Dan was regarding him intently.

"Is there anything I can do to make you more comfortable, Uncle?" drawled "Tacks," with bland sarcasm.

Daniel was taken aback.

"Why," he stammered, "I--I don't know's there is."

"Shall I speak a little louder? Possibly that might help. Delighted to oblige, I'm sure."

This was plain enough, certainly. The captain colored. His confusion increased.

"I--I hope you don't think I was listenin' to you and your friend's talk," he protested hastily. "I wasn't. Why, if--if you two would like this table to yourself you can have it just as well as not. I can go somewhere else. You see, I was thinkin'-- when you spoke to me--I was thinkin' there was somethin' familiar about your face. Seemed as if I'd seen you somewhere before, that's all; and--"

The young gentleman in brown interrupted him. "You're mistaken," he said, "I was never there." Then, turning to his friend, he added, with an elaborate "Josh Whitcomb" accent: "Monty, 'taters must be lookin' up. All aour folks have come to town to spend their money."

Monty, upon whom, like his companion, the second cocktail--second in this particular sense--there had been others--seemed to be having some effect, laughed uproariously. Even the joker himself deigned to smile. Captain Dan did not smile. He had risen, preparatory to leaving the table; now he slowly sat down again.

"I guess I WAS mistaken," he said gravely. "I guess you're right about my not havin' seen you before. If I had I wouldn't have forgot where."

Monty evidently thought it his turn to be funny.

"You have a good memory, haven't you, Deacon?" he observed.

The captain looked at him.

"That don't necessarily follow, young man," he said. "There's some things you CAN'T forget."

There was a choking sound at the next table; a stout man there seemed to be having trouble in swallowing. Those with him looked strangely happy, considering.

"Tacks" frowned, pushed back his chair and stood up.

"Come on, Monty," he growled. "This place is going to the dogs. They let ANYTHING in here now."

Daniel turned to the stout man and his party.

"That's strange, ain't it?" he said in a tone of grave surprise. "I was just thinkin' that myself."

Then, his cigar smoked to the bitter end, he, too, rose, and, declining the invitations of the stout man and his friends to have something "because he had earned it," he walked out of the Rathskeller and took the elevator to the third floor.

He opened the door of the room gently and entered on tiptoe, for he thought it likely that Serena was taking a nap. She was not, however; on the contrary, she was very wide awake.

"Where have you been?" she demanded. "I've been waiting and waiting for you."

Daniel chuckled.

"I've been down below in a place they call the Rat Cellar, or some such name," he said. "The rats was there, two of 'em, anyhow. And I'd met one of 'em before. I know I have. I wish I could think who he was. A sort of--"

But Serena was not listening.

"Daniel," she interrupted, "it is all settled. I have made up my mind."

Her voice was tremulous with excitement. Captain Dan looked at her.

"Made up your mind?" he repeated. "I want to know! What about?"

"About our plans and our future, Daniel; my opportunity has come, the opportunity I was wishing for. It has been sent to me by Providence, I do believe--and it would be wicked not to take advantage of it. Daniel, you and I must move to Scarford."

The captain gasped.

"Why--why, Serena," he faltered. "What are you talkin' about? DON'T talk so! Move to Scarford! Give up Trumet and--"

"Trumet! Don't mention Trumet to me. Daniel Dott, you'll never get me back to Trumet again--to live there, I mean--never, never, NEVER!"

CHAPTER V

Captain Dan said--Well, it does not matter much what he said. He said a great deal, of course, during that evening and the next morning, and would have kept on saying it all the way to Trumet if his wife had not declined to listen.

"It is no use, Daniel," she declared calmly but firmly. "I have thought it all out and I KNOW it is the right thing for us to do. You will think so, too, one of these days."

"Durned if I will! I tell you, Serena--"

"Hush! you're telling everybody in the car, and THAT isn't necessary, at any rate. Now we won't argue any more until we get home. Then you can say your say; but"--with discouraging candor--"it won't change my decision a single mite. My mind is made up. A higher power than you or me has settled everything for us. We are going to Scarford to live, and we will go just as soon as we can get ready."

And go they did. The captain fought a stubborn battle, surprisingly stubborn and protracted for him, but he surrendered at last. Serena drove him from one line of entrenchments after the other, and, at length, when she had him in the last ditch, where, argument and expostulation unavailing, he could only say, "No! no, I won't, I tell you!" over and over again, she used her most effective weapon, tears, and brought him to terms.

"You don't care," she sobbed. "You don't care for me at all. All you care about is just yourself. You're willing to stay here in this awful place, you're willing to plod along just as you always have; and it doesn't make any difference about my wishes or my hopes, or anything. If you were like most husbands you'd be proud and glad to see me getting on in the world; you'd be glad to give me the chance to be somebody; you'd--"

"There! there! Serena, don't talk so. I'd do anything in this world to please you."

"Hush! hush! I should think you'd be ashamed to say such things. I should think you'd be AFRAID to say them, afraid something would happen to you--you'd be struck down or something. Oh, well! I must be resigned, I suppose. I must give in, just as I always do. I must be satisfied to be miserable and--and--Oh, what shall I do? What SHALL I do?"

Sobs and more sobs, frantic clutchings at the sofa pillows and declarations that she had better die; it would be better for her and ever so much better for everyone else if she were dead. No one would care.

Poor Daniel, distressed and remorseful, vaguely conscious that he was right, but conscience stricken nevertheless, hoisted the white flag.

"Hush, hush, Serena!" he pleaded. "Land sakes, don't say such things--please don't. I'll do anything you want, of course I will. I'll go to Scarford, if you say so. I was just--"

"I don't ask you to go there forever. I never have asked that. I only ask you to go there and live a while and just see how we like it. That was all I asked, and you knew it. But you won't! you won't!"

"Why, yes I will, too. I'll go--go next week, if you say so. I--I just--"

He got no further. Mrs. Dott, wet-eyed but radiant, lifted her head from the sofa pillow and threw her arms about his neck.

"Will you?" she cried ecstatically. "Will you, Daniel? I knew you would. You're a dear, good man and I love you better than all the world. We will be so happy. You see if we aren't."

The captain was no less doubtful of the happiness than he had ever been, but he tried to smile and to find comfort in the thought that she was happy if he was not.

He had written Gertrude telling of her mother's new notion and asking for advice and counsel. The reply, which came by return mail, did not cheer him as much as he had hoped.

"It was inevitable, I suppose," Gertrude wrote. "I expected it. I was almost certain that Mother would want to live in Scarford. Mrs. Black has been telling her all summer about society and club life and what she calls 'woman's opportunity,' and Mother has come to believe that Scarford is Paradise. You will have to go, I think,

Daddy dear. Perhaps it is just as well. Mother won't be satisfied until she has tried it, and perhaps, after she has tried it, she may be glad to come back to Trumet. My advice is to let her find out for herself, but, of course, if you feel sure it is wrong, then you must put your foot down, say no, and stick to it. No one can do that for you; you must do it yourself."

Which was perfectly true, as true as the other fact--namely, that Captain Dan could not "stick to it" in a controversy with his wife, having lost the sticking faculty years before.

But, oddly enough, there was one point upon which he did stick and refused to budge: That point was Azuba's going to Scarford with them. Mrs. Ginn's attitude when she was told of the family exodus was a great surprise. Serena, who broke the news to her, expected grief and lamentations; instead Azuba was delighted.

"Well, now!" she exclaimed. "Ain't that fine! Ain't that splendid! I always wanted to go somewhere's besides Trumet, and now I'm goin'. I always told Labe, my husband, that if there was one thing I was jealous of him about 'twas travelin'. 'You go from Dan to Beersheby,' I says to him, 'any time you want to.' 'Yes,' says he--this was the last time he was to home, three years ago--'Yes,' he says, 'and when I don't want to, too.' 'And I,' I says, 'I have to say stuck here in Trumet like a post in a rail fence.' 'You look more like the rail, Zuby,' he says--he's always pokin' fun 'cause I ain't fleshy. 'Don't make no difference what I LOOK like,' I says, 'here I be and I ain't never been further than the Brockton cattle show since I was ten year old.' But now I'm goin' to travel at last. My! I'm so tickled I don't know what to do. I'll start in makin' my last fall's hat over this very night. Say, it's a good thing you've got me to help in the goin' and the settlin', ain't it, Sereny--Mrs. Dott, I mean."

In the face of this superb confidence Serena, who had intended leaving Azuba behind, lacked the courage to mention the fact. And when she sought her husband in the store and asked him to do it, he flatly refused.

"What!" he said. "Tell Zuba Ginn we're goin' to cast her adrift! I should say not! Of course we can't do any such thing, Serena."

"But what can we do with her, Daniel? We might leave her here to take care of the place, I suppose, but that would only be for a time, until we find somebody to buy it. Of course we can't run two places, and we'll have to sell this one some time or other."

Daniel, to whom the idea of selling the home of which he had been so proud was unthinkable, ignored the question.

"You couldn't leave her here," he declared. "She wouldn't stay. Zuba's queer--all her tribe are and always was--but she's nobody's fool. She'd know right off you were tryin' to get rid of her. No, it may be all right enough to leave Nate Bangs in charge of the store, because he'd like nothin' better, but you can't leave Zuba in the house."

"Then what can we do with her?"

"Take her with us. She can do housekeepin' in Scarford same as she can here, can't she?"

"Take her with us! Why, Daniel Dott! the very idea! Think of Azuba in a place like that Scarford mansion! Think of her and that dignified, polite Hapgood man together! Think of it!"

The captain seemed to find the thought amusing.

"Say, that would be some fun, wouldn't it?" he chuckled. "I'd risk Zuba, though. He wouldn't do the Grand Panjandrum over her more'n once. I'd risk her to hold up her end."

"What do you think the B. Phelps Blacks would say if they saw Azuba trotting through the grand front hall with her kitchen apron on?"

The mention of the name had an odd effect upon the captain. He straightened in his chair.

"I don't care what they say," he declared. "I don't care what the Blacks would say, nor the Yellows nor the Blues either. If they don't like it they can stay in their own front halls and lock the door. Look here, Serena: Zuba Ginn has been with us ever since Gertie was born; she took care of her when she had the scarlet fever, set up nights and run the risk of catchin' it herself, and all that. The doctor told us that if it hadn't been for Zuba and her care and self-sacrifice and common sense Gertie would have died. She may be queer and hard to keep in her place, as you call it, and a regular walkin' talkin' machine, and all that. I don't say she ain't. What I do say is she's been good enough for us all these years and she's good enough for me now. She ain't got any folks; her husband is as queer as she is, and only shows up once in two or three years, when he happens to think of it. She ain't got any home but ours, and nobody else to turn to, and I won't cast her adrift just because I've got more money than I did have. I'd be ASHAMED to do it. No, sir! if Zuba Ginn wants to go to Scarford, along with us, she goes, or I don't go myself."

He struck the desk a violent blow with his clenched fist. Serena regarded him with astonishment. It had been a long time since she had seen him like this, not since the old seafaring days.

"Why--why, Daniel," she faltered, "I didn't mean to make you cross. I--I only thought.... Of course, she can go with us if you feel that way."

"That's the way I feel," said her husband shortly. Then, as if suddenly awakening and with a relapse into his usual manner, he added, "Was I cross? I'm real sorry, Serena. Say, don't you want some candy? Nathaniel's just openin' a new case from Boston. Hi, Sam! Sam! bring me a pound box of those Eureka chocolates, will you?"

Serena did not again suggest Azuba's remaining in Trumet. Neither she nor Captain Dan referred to the subject again. Mrs. Dott was, to tell the truth, just a bit frightened; she did not understand her husband's sudden outbreak of determination. And yet the explanation was simple enough. So long as he was the only sufferer, so long as only his own preferences and wishes were pushed aside for those of his wife or daughter, he was meekly passive or, at the most, but moderately rebellious; here, however, was an injustice--or what he considered an injustice--done to someone else, and he "put his foot down" for once, at least.

So, upon the fateful day when, preceded by a wagonload of trunks and bags and boxes, the Dotts once more drove through Scarford's streets to the mansion which was to be their home--permanently, according to Serena; temporarily, so her husband hoped--Azuba accompanied them. And Azuba was wildly excited and tirelessly voluble. Even Captain Dan, the long-suffering, grew weary of her exclamations and chatter at last.

"Say, Zuba," he remonstrated, "is this an all-day service you're givin' us? If it is, I wish you'd take up a collection or somethin', for a change. Mrs. Dott and I are gettin' sort of tired of the sermon."

"Why--why, what do you mean? I was only just sayin' I never see so many folks all at once since that time I was at the Brockton cattle show. I'll bet there's a million right on this street."

"I'll take the bet. Now you start in and count 'em, and let's see who wins. Count 'em to yourself, that's all I ask."

Azuba, with an indignant toss of the "made-over" hat, subsided for the time. But the sight of the Aunt Lavinia mansion, with Mr. Hapgood bowing a welcome from the steps, was too much for her.

"Oh!" she burst forth. "Oh! you don't mean to tell me THAT'S it! Why, it's perfectly grand! And--and there's the minister comin' to call already! Ain't it LOVE-LY!"

That night, as they sat down for the first meal in the new abode, a meal cooked by Azuba and served by the light-footed, soft-spoken, deft-handed Hapgood, Serena voiced the exultation she felt.

"There, Daniel," she observed, beaming across the table at her husband, "now you begin to appreciate what it means, don't you. NOW you begin to see the difference."

Captain Dan, glancing up at the obsequious Hapgood standing at his elbow, hesitated.

"Yes, sir?" said Mr. Hapgood anxiously. "What is it you wish, sir?"

"Nothin', nothin'. Why, yes, I tell you: You go out and--and buy me a cigar somewhere. Here's the money."

"Cigar, sir? Yes, sir. What kind do you--"

"Any kind; only get it quick."

Then, as the door closed behind the dignified Hapgood, he added:

"I've got three cigars in my pocket now, but that doesn't matter. I had to send him after somethin'! Say, Serena, is it real necessary to have that undertaker hangin' over us ALL the time? Every time he looks at me I feel as if he was takin' my measure. Has EVERY meal got to be a funeral?"

There was no doubt that the captain noticed the difference. He noticed it more the following day, and more still on each succeeding one.

The next evening the Blacks called--called in state. A note from Mrs. Black, arriving by the morning's post, announced their coming. Serena noted the Black stationery, its quality and the gilded monogram, and resolved to order a supply of her own immediately. Also she bade her husband don his newest and best. She did the same, and when Captain Dan, painfully conscious of a pair of tight shoes, entered the drawing-room he found her already there.

"My!" he exclaimed, regarding her with admiration, "you do look fine, Serena. Is that the one the Boston dressmaker made?"

"Yes. I'm glad you like it."

"Couldn't help likin' it. I can't hardly realize it's my wife that's got it on. Walk around and let me take an observation. Whew! I always said you looked ten years younger than you are. THAT rig don't spell forty-five next January, Serena."

Mrs. Dott sniffed.

"Don't remind me of my age, Daniel," she protested. "It isn't necessary to tell everyone how old I am."

"All right. Nobody'd guess it, anyhow. But how funny you walk. What makes you take such little short steps?"

"I can't help it. This dress--gown, I mean--is so tight I can hardly step at all."

"Have to shake out a reef, won't you? How in the world did you get downstairs--hop?"

"Hush! Don't be foolish. The gown is no tighter than anyone else's. It's the style, Daniel, and you and I must get used to it. Are those your new shoes?"

"They certainly are. Do they look as new as they feel? I walk about the way you do, Serena. Bein' in style ain't all joy, is it?"

"It's better than being out of it. And, Daniel, please remember not to say 'ain't.' I've asked you so many times. We have our opportunity now and so must improve ourselves. You're not keeping store in the country any longer. You are a man of means, living among cultivated society people, and you must try to behave like the ladies and gentlemen you will be called upon to associate with."

"Humph!" doubtfully. "I don't know as I could behave like a lady if I tried. As for the gentleman, if you mean Barney Black--"

"I mean B. Phelps Black. Don't you dare call him Barney to-night. If you do I shall be SO mortified. Hush! Here they are. Very well, Hapgood. You may show them in."

Even Serena's new gown, fine as it was and proud as she had been of it, lost something of its glory and sank into a modest second place when Annette appeared. Mrs. Black had dressed for the occasion. Also, she had insisted upon her husband's dressing.

"What in blazes must I climb into a dress suit for?" demanded that gentleman grumpily. "Going to call on Dan Dott and his wife. You don't expect Dan to be wearing a dress suit, do you? He never wore one in his life."

"It doesn't make any difference what he wears. I want you to go in evening dress."

"But, confound it, Annette, we've been calling on those people all summer."

"THAT was in the country; this is not. Don't you SEE, Phelps? Can't you understand? Those Dotts have come here to live. I did all I could to prevent it, but--"

"WHAT?" Mr. Black interrupted with an amazed protest. "Did all you could to prevent it! Why, you used to preach Scarford to Serena Dott from morning till night. You were always telling her how much better it was than Trumet. I don't believe she would ever have thought of coming here if it hadn't been for you."

Annette stamped her foot impatiently. "Don't you suppose I know it?" she demanded. "That was when I never imagined there was any chance of their really coming. But now they have come and we've got to be with them to some extent. We've GOT to; we can't get out of it. That is why I want them to see how people of our class dress. I can't TELL her that her clothes are a sight, as country as a green pumpkin, but I can show her mine, and she's clever enough to understand. And you can show her husband. Not that that will do much good, I'm afraid. HE is the real dreadful part of the thing. Goodness knows what he may say or do at any time!"

Phelps grinned. Nevertheless, he donned the dress suit.

Mrs. Black had another reason, one which she did not mention, for making this, their first, call upon the Dotts in their new home a ceremonial occasion. It was true that they would be obliged to associate with these acquaintances from the country more or less; the commonest politeness required that, considering all that had gone before. But she meant there should be no misunderstanding of the relations between the families. In Trumet she had made Mrs. Dott her protegee because it was her nature to patronize, and Serena had not resented the patronage. Now circumstances were quite different; now the Dotts possessed quite as much worldly wealth as the Blacks, but Annette did not intend to let Serena presume upon that. No, indeed! She intended, not only by the grandeur of her raiment and that of her husband, but by her tone and manner, to make perfectly plain the fact that the acquaintanceship was still a great condescension on her part and did not imply equality in the least.

But this lofty attitude was destined to be shaken before the evening was over. The first shock came at the very beginning, and Mr. Hapgood was responsible for it. Annette had referred, during the Trumet acquaintanceship, to her "staff of servants," and had spoken casually of her cook and second girl and laundress and "man," as if the quartette were permanent fixtures in the Black establishment. As a matter of fact, the only fixtures were the cook and second girl. The laundress came in on Mondays and Tuesdays to do the washing and ironing, and the "man" acted as janitor's helper at the factory three days of the week. The chauffeur was but a summer flourish; B. Phelps drove his own car eight months in the year.

So when the door of the Dott mansion was opened by a butler--and such a dignified, polite, imposing butler--Mrs. Black's soul was shaken by a twinge of envy. The second shock was Serena's appearance and the calm graciousness of her demeanor. The Boston gown was not as grand, as prodigal of lace and embroidery, as was the visitor's, but it was in the latest fashion and Serena wore it as if she had been used to such creations all her life. Neither was she overawed or flurried when her callers entered. Serena had read a good deal, had observed as much as her limited opportunities would allow, and was naturally a clever woman in many ways.

"Why, how do you do, Mrs. Black?" she said. "It's so good of you to come. And to bring Mr. Black, too. You must take off your things. Yes, you must. Hapgood, take the lady's wraps. Daniel!"

The captain, who, not being used to butlers and lacking much of his wife's presence of mind, had started forward to assist with the wraps, stopped short.

"Yes, Serena?" he faltered.

"Can't you ask Mr. Black to sit down?"

"Hey? Why, course I can. I judged he was goin' to sit down anyway. Wasn't figgerin' to stand up all the evenin', was you, Bar--er--Phelps?"

"No," replied Mr. Black. To prove it he selected the most comfortable chair in the room.

"I had such a time to get Phelps to come," declared Annette, sinking, with a rustle, into the next best chair. "He wanted to see you both, of course, and to welcome you to Scarford, but he is SO busy and has so many engagements. If it isn't a directors' meeting it is a house committee at the club, or--or something. You should be thankful that your husband is not a man of affairs and constantly in demand. It was a club meeting to-night, wasn't it, Phelps, dear?"

"'Twas a stag dinner," observed Mr. Black. "Say, Dan, I'll have to take you to one of 'em some time. It's a good bunch of fellows and we have some of the cleverest vaudeville stunts afterward that you ever saw. Last week there were a couple of coons that--"

"Phelps!" Annette interrupted tartly, "you needn't go into details. I don't imagine Captain and Mrs. Dott will be greatly interested. What a charming old room this is, isn't it? SO quaint! Everything looks as if it had been here a hundred years."

Before Serena could frame a reply to this back-handed compliment the unconscious B. Phelps removed the greater part of its sting by observing:

"That butler of yours looks as if he had been here a thousand. I felt as if George the First was opening the door for me. He's a star, all right. Did he come with the place?"

Mrs. Dott explained that Hapgood was one of Aunt Lavinia's old servants. "She thought the world of him. Daniel and I feel perfectly safe in leaving everything to him. Auntie found him somewhere abroad--working for a lord or a count or something, I believe--and brought him over. He is pretty expensive, his wages, I mean, but he is worth it all. Don't you think so?"

Yes, Mrs. Black found it much more difficult to patronize than she expected, and Serena was correspondingly happy. But the crowning triumph came later. The doorbell rang, and Hapgood entered the drawing-room bearing a tray upon which were several cards. He bent and whispered respectfully.

Mrs. Dott was evidently surprised and startled.

"Who?" she asked.

Hapgood whispered again.

Serena rose. "Yes, of course," she said nervously. "Yes, certainly. I declare, I--"

"What's up?" asked her husband, his curiosity aroused. "Nothin' wrong, is there? What's that he's bringin' you on that thing?"

He referred to the cards and the tray. His wife, who had caught a glimpse of Mrs. Black's face, fought down her nervousness and announced with dignified composure.

"Some more callers, that's all, Daniel," she said. "Oh, you mustn't go, Mrs. Black. You know them, I'm sure. I've heard you speak of 'em--of them often. It's"--

referring to the cards--"the Honorable Oscar Fenholtz and Mrs. Fenholtz. Ask them right in, Hapgood. Daniel, get up!"

Daniel hurriedly obeyed orders. Mr. Black also rose.

"The Fenholtzes!" he observed in a tone of surprise. "Say, Dan, I didn't know you knew them. Annette didn't say anything about it."

Annette hadn't known of it; her expression showed that. The Honorable and Mrs. Fenholtz were Scarford's wealthiest citizens. Mr. Fenholtz was proprietor of a large brewery and was an ex-mayor. His wife was prominent socially; as prominent as Mrs. Black hoped to be some day.

Hapgood reappeared, ushering in the new arrivals. The Honorable Oscar was plump and florid and good-natured. He wore a business suit and his shoes were not patent leathers. Mrs. Fenholtz was likewise plump. Her gown, in comparison with Annette's, or even Serena's, was extremely plain and old-fashioned.

She hastened over to where Serena was standing and extended her hand.

"How do you do, Mrs. Dott?" she said pleasantly. "Welcome to Scarford. You and I have never met, of course, but I used to know Mrs. Lavinia Dott very well indeed. And this is Mr. Dott, I suppose. How do you do? And here is my husband. Oscar, these are our new neighbors."

Mr. Fenholtz and the captain shook hands. Captain Dan felt his embarrassment disappearing under the influence of that hearty shake.

"I suppose you scarcely expected callers--or calls from strangers--so soon," went on Mrs. Fenholtz. "But, you see, I hope we shan't be strangers after this. I couldn't bear to think of you all alone here in this great house in a strange place, and so I told Oscar that he and I must run in. We live near here, only on the next corner."

"I said you would be having your after-dinner smoke, Mr. Dott," explained the Honorable, with a smile and a Teutonic accent. "I said you would wish we was ouid instead of in; but Olga would not have it so. And, when the women say yes, we don't say no. Eh; what is the use?" He chuckled.

Captain Dan grinned. "That's right," he said. "No use for the fo'mast hand to contradict the skipper."

Mrs. Black stepped forward.

"How do you do, Mrs. Fenholtz?" she said with unction.

"Dear me!" exclaimed Serena. "I--I'm forgetting everything. But you know Mr.

and Mrs. Black, don't you, Mrs. Fenholtz?"

Mrs. Fenholtz turned.

"How do you do, Mrs. Black?" she said. Her tone lacked the enthusiasm of Annette's.

"Hello, Black," said her husband. "What are you doing here? I thought you would be at the club, listening to the--what is it?--the cabaret. Py George, my wife says I shall not go any more! She says it is no place for a settled man so old as I am. Ho! ho! Yet I tell her the stag dinner is good for the beer business."

Before B. Phelps could answer, Mrs. Black spoke.

"He wanted to go, Mr. Fenholtz," she declared. "But he felt, as I did, that our first duty was here. Captain and Mrs. Dott are old friends of ours. We meet them every year at the Cape; we have a summer home there, you know."

Fenholtz seemed interested. "That is so," he said. "I forgot. Dott, are you one of those Cape Cod skippers they tell me about? I am glad of it. I have got a boat myself down in Narragansett Bay. One of those gruisin' launches, they call them. But this one is like the women, it will gruise only where and when it wants to, and not where I want to at all. There is something the matter with the engine always. I have had egsperts--ah, those egsperts!--they are egsperts only in getting the money. When they are there it will go beautifully; but when they have left it will not go at all. I wish you could see it."

Captain Dan was interested, too.

"Well," he said, "I'd like to, first rate. I've got a boat of my own back home; that is, I used to have her. She was a twenty-five foot cat and she had a five-horsepower auxiliary in her. I had consider'ble experience with that engine. Course, I ain't what you'd call an expert."

"I am glad of that. Now I will explain about this drouble of mine."

He went on to explain. In five minutes he and the captain were head over heels in spark plugs and batteries and valves and cylinders. Mr. Black endeavored to help out with quotations from his experience as a motorist, but his suggestions, not being of a nautical nature, were ignored for the most part. After a time he lost interest and settled back in his chair.

Meanwhile the three ladies were engrossed in other matters. Mrs. Fenholtz asked to be shown the house; she had not seen it for a long time, she said, and was much interested. Annette suddenly remembered that, she also was "mad" to see it. So Serena led a tour of inspection, in which Mr. Hapgood officiated as assistant pilot and superintendent of lighting.

After the tour was at an end, and just before the party descended to the drawing-room, Mrs. Fenholtz turned to Serena and said:

"Mrs. Dott, are you interested in club matters; in women's clubs, I mean?"

Serena's answer was a prompt one.

"Indeed I am," she said. "I have always been interested in them. In fact, I am president of the Trumet Chapter; that is, I was; of course, I resigned when I came here."

Mrs. Fenholtz looked puzzled.

"Trumet Chapter?" she repeated.

"Why, yes, the Chapter of the Guild of the Ladies of Honor. The order Mrs. Black belongs to."

"Oh!" in a slightly different tone. "Oh, yes, I see."

"I'm terribly interested in THAT," declared Serena enthusiastically. "If you knew the hours and hours I have put in working for the Guild. It is a splendid movement; don't you think so?"

"Why--why, I have no doubt it is. I don't belong to it myself. I was thinking of our local club, our Scarford women's club, when I spoke. I thought perhaps you might care to attend a meeting of that with me."

"I should love--" began Serena, and stopped.

Mrs. Black, who was standing behind Mrs. Fenholtz, was shaking her head. The last-named lady noticed her hostess' hesitation.

"But of course," she went on, "if you are interested in the Ladies of Honor you would no doubt prefer visiting a meeting of theirs. In that case Mrs. Black could help you more than I. She is vice-president of the Scarford Branch, I think. You are vice-president, aren't you, Mrs. Black?"

Annette colored slightly.

"Why--why, yes," she admitted; "I am."

Serena was surprised.

"Vice-president?" she repeated. "Vice-president--I--I--must have made a dreadful mistake. I introduced you as president at that Trumet meeting. I certainly thought you were president."

Now, as a matter of fact, if Mrs. Black had not specifically said that she was president of the Scarford Chapter, she had led her acquaintances in Trumet to infer that she was; at all events, she had not corrected Serena's misapprehension on the night of the meeting. She hastened to do so now.

"Oh, no!" she said. "I noticed that you made a mistake when you introduced me, but, of course, I could hardly correct you publicly, and, when it was all over, I forgot. I am only vice-president, just as Mrs. Fenholtz says."

Mrs. Fenholtz smiled. "Well, I am not even an officeholder in our club," she said, "although I was at one time. I have no doubt you will prefer to be introduced by a vice-president rather than a mere member; and I am sure Mrs. Black is planning for you to attend one of the Guild meetings, so I mustn't interfere."

Annette was visibly flurried. The Scarford Chapter was the one subject which she had carefully avoided that evening. But between it and the Woman's Club there was a bitter rivalry, and, although she had not been at all anxious to act as sponsor for her friend from the country, now that Mrs. Fenholtz had offered to do so and had placed the responsibility squarely on her shoulders, she could not dodge.

"Why--why, of course," she said. "That was understood. We have had so many things to talk about this evening that I had really forgotten it, my dear Mrs. Dott. I had indeed! When," she hesitated, "when could you make it convenient to attend one of our meetings? Of course I know how busy you are just now in your new home, and I shall not be unreasonable. I shouldn't, of course, expect you to attend the NEXT meeting."

"Oh," said the unconscious Serena, "I'm not so busy as all that. I could go to the next meeting just as well as not. I should love to."

They entered the drawing-room, to find Captain Dan and the Honorable Oscar still deep in the engine discussion and Mr. Black sound asleep in his chair. Roused by his indignant wife, he drowsily inquired if it was time to get up, and then, becoming aware of the realities of the situation, hastily explained that he had been thinking about business affairs and had forgotten where he was.

"Going, Annette, are you?" he asked.

Annette tartly observed that she was going, and added that she judged it high time to do so. Mrs. Fenholtz said that she and her husband must be going, also.

"But we shall hope to see a great deal of you and Mr.--I should say Captain Dott," she said. "You must dine with us very soon. I will set an evening and you mustn't say no."

"That is right," said Mr. Fenholtz heartily. "Captain, some of these days you and I will take a gouple of days and go down and look at that boat. If she does not go then, we will put an 'egspert' in her and sink them both. What?"

Altogether, it was a wonderful evening. The only fly in the ointment was Azuba, who appeared just as the visitors were at the door, to announce that "that foolhead of a grocer's boy" hadn't brought the things she ordered and what they was going to do for breakfast she didn't know.

"I could give you b'iled eggs," she added, "but Captain Dan'l made such a fuss about them we had yesterday that I didn't dast to do it without askin' you. I wanted to have some picked-up fish, but they didn't keep none but the hashed-up kind that comes in pasteboard boxes, and I'd just as soon eat hay as that."

On the way home Mrs. Black divided her discourse into two parts, one a scorching of her husband for falling asleep and making her ridiculous before the Fenholtzes, and the other a sort of irritated soliloquy concerning "those Dotts" and the way in which they had been loaded upon her shoulders.

"I did my best to keep the Guild out of the conversation," she said, "but that Fenholtz woman had to drag it in, and now, of course, I've got to take that Dott person to the next meeting and introduce her to everybody, and I suppose I shall have to see that she is made a member. Oh, dear! I almost wish I had never seen Trumet."

B. Phelps grunted. "Humph!" he said. "If the Fenholtzes take them up I don't see what you've got to kick about. You've been trying to get in the Fenholtz set yourself for the last three years. Maybe you can do it now."

CHAPTER VI

The Scarford Chapter of the Guild of the Ladies of Honor was not as large a body as Mrs. Black in the exuberance of her Trumet conversation had led Serena to think. In reality, its membership was less than a hundred. It was formed in the beginning by a number of seceders from the local Women's Club, who, disappointed in their office-seeking ambitions and deeming the club old-fashioned and old-fogyish in its ideas, had elected to form an organization of their own. They had affiliated with the national order of the Ladies of Honor, chiefly because of the opportunity which such a body offered for office holding and notoriety. The members were not drawn from the oldest families of Scarford nor from those whose social position was established. They were chiefly the wives and daughters of men who had made money rather suddenly; would-be geniuses whose genius had not been recognized as yet; women to whom public speaking and publicity were as the breath of their nostrils; extravagants and social climbers of all sorts.

The purposes of the organization, outside those specified in the constitution of the parent body, were rather vague. Ex-Mayor Fenholtz expressed a rather general opinion when he said:

"The Ladies of Honor? Sure! it is a place where the women go who think their husbands don't appreciate them. If I was one of those husbands I should appreciate their having that place. They might stay at home if they didn't. That would be a galamity."

The ladies of the Scarford Chapter made it a point to be always abreast of the times. Theirs was not a suffrage organization because, as many of them said, the belief in suffrage was so common nowadays. Their motto was "Advancement." Just what sort of advancement seemed to make little difference.

The next meeting--that is, the meeting to which Serena had been invited--

was one of the few at which men were permitted to be present. The Blacks called at the Dott mansion with the car, Mr. Black not acting as driver this time, and the journey to the hall was made in that vehicle. It was not a lively journey, so Captain Dan thought. He and B. Phelps occupied the folding seats facing the two ladies and Mr. Black maintained a gloomy silence all the way. As for Annette and Serena, they talked and talked upon subjects miles above the head of the captain. Mrs. Black did most of the talking; Serena was content to listen and pretend to understand.

"This is to be an open meeting, Mrs. Dott," said Annette graciously. "You see, we have open meetings, just as you do in Trumet, although I doubt if you find much resemblance between the two. You'd scarcely expect that, would you? Ha! ha! It is a good thing," she added, addressing the occupants of the carriage in general, "for these husbands of ours to be shown occasionally what their wives are capable of. Here is our Chapter building. Phelps, give Mrs. Dott your arm."

The Chapter building proved to be not quite up to Serena's expectation. It was a building, of course, but the Chapter occupied only two or three rooms on the third floor, the other floors being occupied by offices of various sorts. The largest room, that which Mrs. Black dignified by the title of "Assembly Hall," was partially filled when they entered. Some sixty women of various ages, with a sprinkling of men among them, occupied the chairs on the floor. Upon the speakers' platform half a dozen ladies in radiant attire were chatting volubly with another, an imposing creature in crimson silk, who surveyed the audience through a gold lorgnette, and whose general appearance reminded Daniel of one of the stuffed armchairs in the parlor of their new home.

"That is Mrs. Cornish, the speaker of the evening," whispered Annette. "She is one of our most brilliant members."

"Yes," replied Dan'l, to whom the information had been imparted, and upon whom the crimson silk had made an impression; "yes, she--she does look sort of--sort of brilliant."

"But I thought the Chapter was larger than this," said the puzzled Mrs. Dott. "I thought Scarford had one of the largest Chapters."

"Oh, no, not the largest, merely one of the best. Our motto always has been quality not quantity. And now will you excuse me? They are waiting for me on the platform. I will see you when the open meeting is over. Phelps, find good seats for

Mr. and Mrs. Dott."

She bustled away to the platform. The gloomy B. Phelps found seats for the guests and himself and sank heavily down beside them. Daniel, who had been gazing about him with curiosity, whispered a question.

"What do they do at these things, Barney--Phelps, I mean?" he asked. "Are they like lodge meetings at home? This is my first trip here, you know."

"Humph!" grunted his companion. "You're in luck."

"Talk, don't they?"

"Talk! Good Lord! Say, Dan, if I get to sleep and you notice Annette looking this way, nudge me, that's a good fellow."

He settled himself in his chair and closed his eyes. Daniel turned to his wife.

"Serena," he murmured. "Say, Serena, don't you think it is a queer-lookin' crowd? Seems to me I never saw such clothes or so many different kinds of hair. Look at that woman's skirt. It's tore all up one side."

"Sshh! Don't speak so loud. That's the latest style."

"What! THAT? Well, I--"

"Sshh! It's the latest style, I tell you. Haven't you seen the fashion magazines? All the new dresses are made that way."

"Yours ain't."

"Well, I--I'm not as young as that woman is."

"You wouldn't wear a thing like that if you were as young as Gertie; and she wouldn't either, not if I saw it first. I never saw such folks as these at Trumet."

"Of course you didn't. Trumet isn't Scarford. We are in society now, Daniel. We mustn't show our ignorance."

"Humph! I'd rather show my ignorance than--Hello, the doin's are goin' to commence."

The Chapter president, a Mrs. Lake, advanced to the desk, smote it fiercely with a gavel and demanded order. The hall, which had been buzzing like a colony of June bugs, gradually grew still. Then Mrs. Lake opened the meeting. She delivered a short speech. Mrs. Black, in lieu of the secretary, who was absent, read the minutes. Then there were motions and amendments and excited calls for recognition from "Madam President." It was livelier than Daniel had expected.

But soon the woman in crimson silk was introduced. Mrs. Cornish bowed in recognition of the gloved applause, and proceeded to talk... and talk... and talk....

At first Captain Dan endeavored to pay strict attention to the address. Its title was "The Modern Tendency," and the tendency in this case seemed to be to say as much as possible about nothing in particular.

Daniel found his attention wandering and his eyes closing. They opened at intervals as the applause burst forth, but they closed between bursts. The tremendous enthusiasm at the end, however, awoke him for good, and he remained awake until the close of the "open meeting," a marked contrast to Mr. Black, who slumbered to the finish.

When it was over Annette descended from the platform and came hurrying to them.

"How did you enjoy it, Captain Dott?" she purred.

Daniel rather dubiously admitted that he guessed 'twas first rate, far's he could make it out. His wife was enthusiastic; she affirmed that it was splendid.

"I'm sure we couldn't help enjoying it, Mrs. Black," she said. "Everyone of us. Didn't you enjoy it, Mr. Black?"

"Sure!" replied Phelps promptly. "Great stuff!"

His wife swooped upon him like a swallow on a fly.

"You?" she snorted contemptuously. "You didn't hear a word of it. I only hope Mrs. Cornish wasn't watching you, as I was. And now," she added, turning to Serena, "comes the other part, the important part. Captain Dott, there is to be a short business meeting in a few minutes, and men are, of course, excluded. Phelps, will you have James drive Captain Dott home? You had better go with him, and then come back again and wait for us. Captain Dott, I am going to borrow your wife for a short time."

Daniel, not knowing exactly what to say, said nothing. Phelps seized his arm and led him down to the carriage. The driver received his instructions and the homeward ride began.

"I say, Barney," observed Daniel, after waiting for his escort to volunteer a word or two, "are all their meetings like that?"

Mr. Black snorted. "No," he declared; "some are a d----d sight worse."

It was after eleven when Serena returned. Her face was flushed and shining with excitement. She did not wait to remove her hat, but rushed into the parlor where her husband sat in lonely magnificence. The solicitous Hapgood, who had happened in every few minutes to see if his employer "wished anything," had been ordered to "go aloft and turn in." The tone in which the order was given made an impression and Hapgood had obeyed.

"Oh, Daniel!" she cried. "What do you think? I've been made a member of the Chapter!"

Captain Dan should perhaps have been enthusiastic. If he was, he suppressed his feelings wonderfully.

"Have you, Serena?" he observed. "I want to know!"

He listened while his wife dilated upon the wonderful happenings at the meeting and the glorious consequences which she felt sure were to follow. Just before putting out the light he asked one more question.

"That--that Mrs. Lake?" he said. "She's a grass widow, ain't she--isn't she, I mean?"

"Yes, what of it?"

"Oh, nothing. Only I thought you were kind of prejudiced against--against--"

"I've had a good many prejudices, I suppose, like other people. But Mrs. Lake's husband was a brute; Mrs. Black told me so. He must have been, for she is perfectly lovely. I've met them all, and they are ALL lovely. They're going to call and--and everything. Oh, Daniel, this means so much to us!"

Captain Dan turned out the gas.

"Yes, Serena," he said slowly. "I shouldn't wonder if it did."

The calls began the very next afternoon. Mrs. Black, having made up her mind that the taking of the Dotts under her wing was a necessity, made a virtue of that necessity and explained to her fellow members of Scarford Chapter that Serena and Daniel were really very nice people. "A little countrified, of course. You must expect that. But they are very kind hearted and immensely wealthy--oh, immensely." She was kind enough to add that Serena was quite an exceptional person and an advanced thinker, considering her opportunities. "The club people were going to take them up, and so I felt that we should get in first," she explained. "If they should prove to be impossible we can drop them at any time, of course."

In making this explanation she did not mention the Fenholtzes, and yet if it had not been for the call of the Honorable Oscar and his wife it is extremely doubtful if Serena would have become a member of Scarford Chapter so soon. Also it is doubtful if the little dinner given by the Blacks to Mr. and Mrs. Dott would have taken place within the week. At that dinner Captain Dan wore his first dress suit. He bought it ready made at one of the Scarford shops and it fitted him remarkably well, considering. What he could not do, however, was to feel at ease in it.

"Good land, Serena!" he said, when the dressing was completed and they were about to start for the dinner, "don't pick at me so everlastin'ly. Don't you suppose I know I look as stiff and awkward as if I'd froze? You won't let me put my hands in my pockets, and all I can do is hang 'em around loose and think about 'em, and this blessed collar is so high I can't scarcely get my chin over it. I'm doin' my best, so don't keep remindin' me what I look like all the time."

"I don't care what you say, Daniel," declared his wife. "The clothes are just what you ought to wear, and if you would only forget them for a little while you would look all right."

"But I can't forget. I know the clothes are all right. It's me that's all wrong. My red face stickin' over the top of this collar looks like a fireman's shirt on a white fence. I tell you I ain't used to this kind of thing. I wasn't born to it and it don't come natural to me."

"Neither was Mr. Black 'born to it,' but he has got used to it and so can you if you will try."

"Oh, I'll try. But I'm beginnin' awful late in life. I know you'll be ashamed of me, Serena. You ought to have a different husband."

"I don't want a different one. I wouldn't change you for anybody. But I do think you ought to try and help me as much as you can. My chance has just come; I am only just beginning and I mean to go on and improve myself and our position in life all I can. All I ask you to do is not to hold me back by complaining."

The "little dinner" was not as little as it might have been. Annette had taken pains to make it as elaborate and as costly an affair as she could. This was not solely on the Dotts' account. She had invited Mr. and Mrs. Fenholtz and the impression was to be made upon them, if possible. But, unfortunately, the Fenholtzes did not attend. Mrs. Fenholtz wrote that she had a prior engagement and sent regrets, just as she had previously done on the occasions of Mrs. Black's other "little" functions.

However, the leading lights of Scarford Chapter attended and the display of gowns and coiffures was more varied and elaborate than at the open meeting. Serena, seated at the right hand of B. Phelps, was in her glory. She felt that at last she was in touch with the real thing. Daniel, sandwiched between Annete and Mrs. Lake, was not as happy. The necessity of forgetting his clothes and remembering his grammar was a heavy burden. His conversation was limited to "Yes" and "No" and "I shouldn't wonder," and after a time the ladies ceased in their efforts to make him talk and carried on an animated dialogue across his shirt front.

After dinner there was music and bridge. Daniel was fond of music, but most of the songs, sung by a thin young lady with a great deal of hair and a decollete gown, were in a language which he did not understand, and the piano solos seemed to him to be made up of noise and gymnastics with very little melody. He watched Serena, however, who, in turn, was watching Mrs. Lake and the rest; when they applauded, she applauded and the captain followed suit.

Bridge was an unknown quantity to both of them, and they sat and looked on while Mrs. Black made it "without" and found fault with her partner when they lost. The thin young lady, who had obliged with the vocal selections, asked the captain if he played "nullos." Daniel, who was not sure whether "nullos" was a musical instrument or a game, replied that he wasn't sure, but he didn't think he did; after which he retired into the corner to avoid further questioning.

They reached home about two o'clock, and the captain fell sound asleep in the taxi and had to be shaken into consciousness when the machine reached the Dott door.

"My soul, Serena," he said, when they were upstairs in the bedroom, "don't those folks ever go to bed? There was stuff enough to eat at that dinner to last the average family through three meals. Time I had finished the ice cream I was ready to curl up like a cat in front of the fire; but the rest of them seemed to be just startin' in to be lively. Are we goin' to keep this up very long? If we are, I'll have to sleep in the daytime, like a fo'mast hand on night lookout."

"But wasn't it splendid?" explained his wife. "Weren't they cultivated, brilliant people? You and I never went to anything like THAT dinner before, Daniel Dott."

The captain admitted that they never did. "Could you make anything out of that game they were playin'?" he asked. "What was it they called it?"

"Bridge. No, I couldn't, but I'm going to. I'm going to learn it just as soon as I can. Mrs. Black says everybody plays it now."

Her husband chuckled. "Those that don't play it had better not try," he observed. "Judgin' from what I saw to-night, if they do try they get into trouble. That Lake woman was givin' that poor little bald-headed fellow she was playin' with fits most of the time. Whenever they won she patted herself on the back, and when they didn't she said it was his fault. He ought to have 'echoed' or hollered back--or somethin'. One time she put down a card and he put another kind of a one on it, and she glared at him and said, 'Havin' no clubs?' and he had one that he'd forgot. He spent the next ten minutes beggin' her pardon, but 'twas a good thing SHE didn't have a club. She'd have used it on him if she had. He was all shriveled up like a frostbitten cranberry when they got through."

After they were in bed he said, "Serena, what was that black stuff they had on the toast at the beginnin' of that supper? Looked like tar, but it tasted kind of salty and good."

"Don't say supper, Daniel. It was a dinner. All city people have dinner at night. That was caviar on the toast. I've read about it. It comes from Russia."

Silence for a moment. Then Captain Dan said reflectively, "Caviar? Caviar, eh? I've heard of that somewhere before; where was it? Yes, yes, I know. 'Twas a caviar sandwich the waiter asked that young fellow I met in the Rat Cellar to have. I never found out who that young fellow was, and yet I know I've met him somewhere before. I wish I could remember where it was. My memory is failin' me, I guess; must be gettin' old. Can't you remember, Serena?"

But his wife bade him stop talking and go to sleep.

The next day there were more calls, and Serena was asked to attend a committee meeting as a guest. She attended it and returned more full of Chapter enthusiasm than ever. She announced that she might be asked to prepare a paper to be read before the Chapter, and that she intended to study and prepare for it. Study and prepare she did, and, between dodging callers, or helping to entertain them, and keeping out of his wife's way while she was busy with the encyclopedias which she had taken from the library, the captain began to feel somewhat deserted. Hapgood's company was too stately to be congenial, and Daniel sought refuge in the kitchen, where Azuba, as usual, was always ready to talk.

Azuba was brimming over with the novelty of city life. She had been to the theater once already since her arrival, and to the moving picture show three times.

"Don't talk to ME," she said. "If them pictures ain't the most wonderful things that ever was, then I *don't know.* I never expected to see such sights--soldiers pa-radin', and cowboys a-ridin', and houses a-burnin', and Indians scalpin' 'em! I was so worked up I hollered right out."

"I should think you would. An Indian scalpin' a house is enough to make any-body holler."

"They didn't scalp the house; what sort of foolishness would that be--the idea! They scalped the folks IN the house. That is, they would have scalped 'em, only along come the cowboys wavin' pistols and hurrahin'--"

"Could you hear 'em hurrah?"

"No, but I could see 'em. And the way they went for them Indians was a cau-tion. And--Oh, say, Captain Dott, there was one set of pictures there made me think of you. 'Twas all about some people that wanted to go into society. She had a para-lyzed father and they had a child, a real pretty girl, and, would you believe it, they commenced to neglect their child and go off playin' cards and dancin' and carousin' around, and the child was took down sick and the poor paralyzed grandfather--"

"Grandfather? Thought you said it was a father."

"'Twas the WOMAN'S father--the child's grandfather. Well, anyhow, the poor thing had to take care of it, and the nurse went to sleep and the father come home and found her dyin'--"

"Who, the nurse?"

"No, no, the child. The nurse wa'n't sick; but the child was terrible sick."

"What was the matter with the child; paralysis, too?"

"I don't know what was the matter with it. 'Tain't likely 'twas paralysis. You get me so mixed up I shan't know what I AM sayin' pretty soon. Well, anyhow, what happened was that the child's mother and father neglected it on account their fashionable goin's-on, and the child up and died. 'Twas the most affectin' thing. There was the child a-dyin', and the mother and father cryin', and the old grandfa-ther goin' all to pieces--"

"All to pieces! That's worse than paralysis. Hold on a minute, Azuba! Was all this in the picture?"

"Yes."

"And you paid to see it?"

"Course I paid to see it. They wouldn't let me in for nothin', 'tain't likely."

"Well, seems to me you've made a mistake. If cryin' and misery is what you want, I don't doubt you can find a lot of funerals to go to for nothin'. But what was there about all this mess of horrors that made you think of me?"

"Oh, I don't know, unless the way you and Mrs. Dott are goin' in for society in Scarford. Course your child is grown up, so that's different, though, ain't it?"

"Yes, and there isn't any paralysis in the family, so far as I know. That's a mercy. Don't you get paralysis, Azuba. If you do, it will take you longer to get breakfast than it does now."

"That's all right. You ought to be thankful you've got me to get breakfast. If I wa'n't here you'd have to get it yourself, I cal'late. Your wife's too busy these days, and that Hapgood man wouldn't do it. I know that."

Relations between the butler and Azuba were already somewhat strained. He considered her a rude and interfering person and she considered that he would bear watching.

"He's always recommendin' folks for us to trade with," she told Captain Dan. "What business is it to him who we trade with?--unless he gets a little somethin' for himself out of it. He won't do it more than once--not if I catch him at it. Don't talk to me about that Hapgood! I wouldn't trust one of them foreigners, anyhow."

The invitation to dine with the Fenholtzes came about a week after the dinner at the Blacks'. Daniel, who opened the letter containing the invitation, was very much pleased. He liked the Fenholtzes at first sight and felt sure he should like them better on further acquaintance. But when Serena came back from the lodge meeting--the first regular meeting which she had attended since becoming a member--she received the news rather coldly.

"When is it they want us?" she said. "Next Tuesday night? Well, we could go, I suppose, but I don't believe we shall. Mrs. Lake said something about coming around that evening to help me read my paper and criticise it."

The captain was surprised and troubled. "She could come some other time, couldn't she? I think 'twas real kind of the Fenholtzes to ask us. Seems to me we ought to go. You and I haven't even been to pay back that call yet."

"I know it. I've meant to, but I've been so busy. Besides, I don't know whether it is worth while or not. The Fenholtzes have got a great deal of money, but all the Chapter people say they are sort of back numbers."

However, she decided to accept the invitation, and they went in state. But the state was largely on their part. The dinner was a very simple affair compared to the elaborate spread of the Blacks, and the two or three people whom they met were quite different from Mrs. Lake and her friends. Captain Dan enjoyed himself hugely. He sat next to Mrs. Fenholtz at the table, and her quiet conversation on everyday subjects he could understand. Before the dinner was over he was thoroughly at ease, and when later on, in company with the Honorable Oscar and the male guests, he sat smoking in the library, he found himself spinning yarns and joking as freely as if he had been in the back room of the Metropolitan Store in Trumet. The shouts of laughter from the library could be heard in the parlor, and Serena grew nervous.

"Your husband must be very entertaining," said Mrs. Fenholtz. "I haven't heard Mr. Fenholtz laugh so heartily in a long time."

Mrs. Dott was fearful that Daniel might be making himself ridiculous. She didn't mention her fears. Her own remarks were delivered with a great deal of dignity, and she quoted Mrs. Black and the encyclopedia often. On the way home she took her husband to task.

"What in the world were you talking about with those men?" she demanded. "I never heard such a noise as they made. I do hope you didn't forget yourself."

The captain rubbed his chin. "I don't know but what I did forget myself, Serena," he replied. "I know I had a good time and never thought about my clothes after the first ten minutes. Could you hear 'em laughin'? I was tellin' em' about Azuba's goin' to the movin' pictures then."

His wife was shocked. "And Azuba is our cook," she said, "and they know it. I don't know what sort of servants they think we have. They must think you're pretty familiar with them."

"Good land, Serena! I've been familiar with Zuba all my life. If I was to put on airs with her she'd take me down in a hurry."

Mrs. Dott sighed. "I'm afraid you did forget yourself," she declared. "I think if you could hear what the Fenholtzes are saying about us now you'd be ashamed. I'm sure I should."

And at that very moment Mr. Fenholtz was saying: "That man Dott is all right. I have not laughed so for years. And he has common sense, too. I like him."

His wife nodded. "So do I," she said; "and I think I should like Mrs. Dott, too, if she had not been spoiled by Annette Black and the rest of those foolish women she associates with. I don't mean to say that Mrs. Dott is completely spoiled yet, but she will be soon, I'm afraid, unless I can make her realize that she is beginning all wrong here in Scarford. If she could only have gone to the Woman's Club first I think she might understand, but now I'm afraid it's too late."

At the next meeting of the Chapter Serena read her paper. She mounted the platform with fear and trembling. She left it exalted and triumphant. The paper had been applauded and she had been congratulated by her fellow members. Annette was enthusiastic and Mrs. Lake and the other leaders equally so. Stories of the "vast" wealth inherited by the Dotts had been circulated freely, and these, quite as much as the wonderful paper, were responsible for Serena's bound into popularity.

But the popularity was there, and the unconscious Serena believed it to be real. That meeting was the beginning of her obsession. Thereafter she talked chapter and society and opportunity and advancement, and ate them and drank them, too--at least the meals--those at home--seemed to the captain to be made up of very little else. Their evenings alone together became few and fewer. When they were not entertaining callers they were calling. Captain Dan actually began to feel at home in his evening clothes; a good deal more than he did in his night clothes, so he told his wife. Breakfast, which, in the beginning of their Scarford residence, had been served at seven-thirty, was now an hour later, and even then Daniel frequently ate alone.

Then came the reception idea. Annette--she and Mrs. Dott were calling each other by their Christian names now--had dropped the hint concerning it. She had said that a good way in which to repay social obligations was by doing it all at once, by giving a dinner, or reception, or a tea, to which everyone should be invited. Serena decided that the reception was perhaps the better, all things considered. And so preparations for the reception began. There was to be a collation, and when this item of information was imparted to Azuba the kitchen became a maelstrom of activity in which Captain Daniel could no longer find rest and refuge.

"But, Zuba," he remonstrated, "what do you think's comin' here; a drove of hyenas? You've cooked enough already to victual a ship halfway across the ocean. These folks eat sometimes at home. You don't think they're comin' here to make up for six months' starvation, do you?"

"Don't talk to me!" was all the satisfaction he got. "I've heard about what they had to eat over there at Barney Black's, and I don't mean for folks to say that they went hungry when they come here. Don't say another word. I don't know now whether it was a cup full of sugar or a pinch of salt I put in, or the other way 'round. Cookin'! Don't talk to ME."

The captain found it practically impossible to talk to anybody. Hapgood was busy; Serena was busier, and Azuba was busiest of all. Wherever he went he seemed to be in the way, and when he fled for walks up and down the streets the crowds of strange faces made him feel lonelier than ever. On the evening before that upon which the reception was to be held he returned from one of these walks to find Serena in tears.

"Why, good gracious sakes!" he exclaimed. "What's the matter?"

"Matter!" sobbed his wife. "Oh, dear me! Everything is the matter! I'm so tired I don't know what to do, and Annette and Mrs. Lake were coming here to-morrow to help me, and now they can't come. They'll be at the reception, of course, but they can't come before; and there's so much to get ready and I don't know whether I'm doing it right or not. What SHALL I do!"

Daniel shook his head. "Seems to me I'd do the best I could and let it go at that," he advised. "If they ain't satisfied I'd let 'em stay the other way. I wish I could help you, but I don't know how."

"Of course you don't. You don't have any sympathy for the whole thing, and I know it. I feel it all the time. You haven't any sympathy for ME."

The captain sighed. He had a vague feeling that he could use a little sympathy himself, but with characteristic unselfishness he put that idea from his mind.

"I guess what you need is a manager," he said. "Somebody that's used to these sort of things that could help you out. I wish I knew where there was one."

Hapgood appeared and announced that dinner was served. Serena hurriedly dried her eyes and they descended to the dining-room. Just as they were about to take their seats at the table the doorbell rang. Hapgood left the room and returned a few moments later bearing a card on a tray. Serena took the card, looked at it, and then at her husband. Her face expressed astonishment and dismay.

"Why, Daniel!" she exclaimed under her breath. "Why, Daniel! WHO do you suppose is here?"

Her husband announced that he didn't know. He took the card from her hand and looked at it. It was a very simple but very correct card, and upon it in old English script was the name "Mr. Percy Hungerford."

Daniel's face reflected the astonishment upon his wife's.

"My soul!" he muttered. "Percy Hungerford! Why, that's--that's the cousin; the one Aunt Laviny cut out of her will; the one that would have had all this place and all the money if we hadn't got it. I thought he was in New York somewhere. Black said he was, and now he's here. What in the world does he want?"

Mrs. Dott rose. "I don't know," she gasped. "I can't imagine. But I suppose we must see him. We've got to. Did you ask him to wait, Hapgood?"

Hapgood bowed respectfully. "Mr. Hungerford is in the drawing-room, ma'am," he said.

To the drawing-room moved Serena, followed by her husband.

"Good evening, Mr. Hungerford," said the lady, with a partially successful attempt at calmness. "How do you do? My husband and I--"

She paused. The expression on Mr. Hungerford's face was an odd one. She turned to Daniel, and his expression was odder still. He was standing in the doorway gazing at the visitor, his eyes opening wider and wider.

Mr. Percy Hungerford was the young man whom his friend had addressed as "Tacks," the young man with whom Captain Dan had exchanged repartee in the Rathskeller of the Palatine Hotel.

CHAPTER VII

Of the two men, Mr. Hungerford was the first to recover presence of mind. Presence of mind was one of the qualities upon which he prided himself, and it was a very awkward situation to which he could not rise. For just an instant the color rushed to his cheeks as he recognized the captain and saw that the latter recognized him. Then:

"Why, how do you do, Captain Dott?" he said. "By Jove, this is extraordinary, isn't it! Strange that relatives shouldn't know each other when they meet. How do you do?"

He stepped forward with extended hand. Captain Dan, who had expected almost anything but this bland cordiality, scarcely knew what to say or do. He took the proffered hand mechanically and dropped it again.

"Well!" he stammered. "Well!--I declare I--I didn't expect to--"

He paused. Mrs. Dott, who had been watching this scene in bewilderment, spoke before he could finish his sentence.

"Why, what is it?" she asked. "Have you--"

Mr. Hungerford smiled. "Your husband and I have met before," he explained. "Just a casual meeting and we weren't aware of each other's identity. I'm afraid I was not as cordial as I might have been on that occasion, Captain. I was a bit tired and rather out of sorts. I hope you'll forgive me, I'm sure."

Daniel hesitated; then he smiled.

"Why, I guess I can forgive my half if you can yours," he said slowly.

Before the puzzled Serena could ask another question the visitor turned to her.

"I'm sure you must be very much surprised to see me here," he said. "I'm somewhat surprised to be here myself. I've spent a greater part of the past month in New

York and have only just returned--that is, to stay. I fully intended to call before, and should if I had been in town. How are you getting on? How do you like the dear old place? Ah!" with a sigh, as he seated himself and looked about him, "how familiar it all seems!"

The Dotts looked at each other. Serena sank into a chair. Captain Dan remained standing.

"Does it?" said the former rather feebly.

"Indeed it does. One almost expects to see Auntie coming in at the door. Dear old Auntie! I can scarcely realize that she has gone."

Again Serena looked at Daniel and he at her. This was so strange, so different from the attitude which a disappointed legatee might be expected to assume that neither of the pair knew exactly how to reply. But Mr. Hungerford did not appear to notice the look or the hesitation.

"This house seems like home to me," he said. "I've spent so many happy hours here. When old Hapgood opened the door for me I almost ordered him to take my bags to my room. Really I did. That would have been droll, wouldn't it?"

He laughed languidly. Serena admitted that it would have been droll. Captain Dan remained silent as before.

"Are--are you stopping at the hotel?" queried Mrs. Dott.

"Not yet. In fact, I'm not really stopping anywhere. I've just arrived. I must be hurrying back to dinner, I suppose, but I couldn't resist coming here first. It seemed the natural thing to do."

Voices were heard in the hall. One of the voices was Azuba's; she was informing Mr. Hapgood that if that soup didn't go back on the stove pretty soon it might just as well be on ice. The words were distinctly audible, and Serena colored. Mr. Hungerford rose.

"I'm sure I must be keeping you from your own dinner," he said. "Don't let me do that for the world."

"Why--why--" faltered Serena. She looked appealingly at Daniel, and the latter's instinctive hospitality asserted itself. He had disliked the young man "Tacks" when he met him in the Rathskeller. Now that "Tacks" had become Mr. Percy Hungerford, Aunt Lavinia's cousin and his own distant relative, the dislike was only partially abated. But to turn him away from the door hungry seemed wrong somehow.

"Hadn't you better--" he began.

"Have dinner with us?" finished his wife.

Mr. Hungerford protested.

"Oh, I couldn't think of it," he declared. "No doubt you have guests--"

"Oh, no, we haven't. We're all alone and it would be no trouble at all. We should like to have you stay. Shouldn't we, Daniel?"

"Sartin, no trouble at all," said Daniel heartily. "Like to have you first rate."

"Well, if you insist. It is a frightful imposition--I shouldn't think of it, of course, but--well, thank you so much."

So Hapgood received orders to lay another plate, and Mr. Hungerford, still murmuring protests, suffered himself to be conducted to the dining-room.

All through the meal the captain regarded him with puzzled curiosity. That he had come to the house merely for a friendly call he could scarcely believe. He had heard little or nothing of the conversation between Hungerford and his friend at the table in the Rathskeller, and yet the attitude of the former on that occasion had not indicated a temperament likely to forgive "dear Aunt Lavinia" so freely or to display such angelic cordiality toward those who had come into possession of her property. But the cordiality remained unchanged, and the visitor, so far from bearing a grudge toward his more fortunate relatives, continued to treat them as though they were near and dear friends, and do everything in his power to relieve their constraint and to make himself agreeable. The dinner ended and they adjourned to the drawing-room, with Captain Dan's mental question "What in the world is this young chap really up to?" still unanswered.

Serena had asked herself that same question when the caller first came, but now she was beginning to be ashamed of her suspicions and to think them unfounded. Mr. Hungerford was agreeable; there was no doubt of that. Also he was good-looking, in an effeminate sort of way, and his conversation was fluent and cultured. He led Serena into speaking of the Chapter and her work there, and he displayed a knowledge of and an interest in that Chapter and its members which was very gratifying.

The coming reception was mentioned, and the visitor's interest in that was more gratifying still. It was evident that receptions and society functions generally were matters of every day, or every night, occurrence to him. He asked Mrs. Dott who was to assist her in receiving, and when she answered the question his approval of the selections was unqualified. He suggested one or two little ideas which he said might add to making the affair a success. Serena welcomed the suggestions as a starving man might welcome a meal.

"That'll be lovely," she said, "and we can do it just as well as not. And I had thought of having some bridge or something afterwards; but Annette--Mrs. Black, I mean--didn't seem to think bridge would be just the thing after a reception. And there's music; I know we really ought to have music, and I had meant to have somebody play the piano. But the woman I wanted can't come, and now I don't know what to do. What would you think about that, Mr. Hungerford?"

Mr. Hungerford suggested hiring one or two professional musicians. "A violinist, or harpist, or both, perhaps," he said. "Music is always, as you say, a great addition to such affairs, Mrs. Dott. I happen to know of a young fellow who plays exceptionally well, and his sister is really a very accomplished performer on the harp. Of course they should be engaged in merely a professional capacity. They are not persons who would mingle with our set, but they're not at all objectionable, really."

The diplomatic phrasing of this remark had its effect. It indicated that Mrs. Dott's "set" was an exclusive one and, incidentally, that the accomplished and polished Mr. Hungerford considered his host and hostess as social equals.

"There!" exclaimed Serena. "I think that will be just fine. And you are the first one, Mr. Hungerford, to think of it. Do you suppose you could get these--these--er--persons you speak of to come and play for us?"

"I think so. I have befriended the young man in various ways, and he is, if you will excuse my saying so, under some obligations to me. I should be glad to make the attempt if you wish it, Mrs. Dott."

"Cost somethin', won't it?" observed Captain Dan casually. Mr. Hungerford regarded him with well-bred surprise.

"Why, of course," he said, "there will be some expense. I think fifty dollars will cover the bill. The usual rate for musicians of their class is somewhat higher."

There was no doubt that the captain was surprised. "Fifty DOLLARS!" he repeated. "Why--"

His wife interrupted. "That will be all right, Mr. Hungerford," she said. "That will be quite satisfactory."

"Of course, there are many whom you can obtain for less, and, if you feel that that figure is too high, I shall be glad to try elsewhere. I have had little experience outside of the best, but--"

Serena interrupted again. "We don't want anybody but the best," she declared, emphatically. "Be still, Daniel. This isn't Trumet."

Daniel drew a long breath. "There ain't much doubt of that," he observed. "But, all right, Serena, if you and Mr. Hungerford think it's all right, I guess it is. I'm more used to hirin' sailors than I am folks to play the harp."

"Music," went on Mr. Hungerford, "is almost a necessity, in these days, when everyone dances. Is this a formal reception, or had you intended clearing a floor for dancing, Mrs. Dott?"

Mrs. Dott had not intended any such thing; she had not thought of it. But she concealed the fact from her visitor with remarkable presence of mind.

"Oh, of course!" she said.

The conversation continued, a conversation limited to Mr. Hungerford and his hostess, while Captain Dan remained a silent and amazed listener. The young gentleman was invited to attend the reception, Serena making many apologies for the informality of the invitation, and the guest expressing himself as delighted.

"Of course," he said, "I wouldn't intrude for the world, but I don't feel like an intruder in this house, where I have spent so many happy hours. Feeling as I do, I'm going to make another suggestion which, under different circumstances, might be considered an impertinence. I am at leisure to-morrow--in fact, all this week--and if there is anything that I can do to help you and Cousin Daniel, in this matter of the reception or any other, I shall be at your service. I do hope you will permit me to help and that you will not consider me presuming in offering to do so."

It was quite evident that the offer was very welcome. Mrs. Dott accepted it with enthusiasm and called upon her husband to confirm the acceptance. He did so, but with less warmth, and it was agreed that the obliging Mr. Hungerford should drop in the next morning after calling upon his protege, the violinist. A half hour later he said "Good-night," and departed.

"There!" said Serena. "If that isn't Providence, then I don't know. And it only goes to show how one person can misjudge another without knowing anything about him. I've always had a prejudice against that Mr. Hungerford simply because of what you told me of meeting him years ago, and now I don't think I ever met a kinder, nicer young man. Did you, Daniel?"

The captain hesitated. "I--I," he stammered, "well, Serena, I will give in that he seemed nice and obligin' enough to-night, but you see there's just one thing that--"

Serena turned on him. "Yes, I know," she said. "There's always 'one thing' about everybody that I like. He's smart and bright and well dressed and polite. He's a gentleman! and a different kind from any that we've ever met. That makes YOU suspicious, of course."

"Now you know it isn't that; but--but--"

"But what?"

There was more hesitation on the captain's part. He had intended to tell of the meeting at the Rathskeller; then he remembered the young man's explanation and apology and thought better of it. He and "Cousin Percy" might have another interview on the morrow. Meanwhile, he would keep still, particularly as his wife seemed to have forgotten their caller's reference to the meeting. He finished his sentence in another way.

"But I don't see what he came here for," he said.

"He came here to see us. And, I think, considering how he was treated in Aunt Lavinia's will, it was awfully nice of him to come at all. And, as for helping me out on that reception, he's been a perfect godsend already. I should THINK you would appreciate it."

Before the next day was over, and long before the first of the evening's guests arrived, the services of the new-found friend of the family were appreciated even by the reluctant Daniel. Mr. Hungerford came early and proceeded immediately to make himself useful. He had seen the violinist, and the latter and his sister had promised to be on hand. He took Hapgood in charge and superintended the arranging of the drawing-room and the library for the reception and the dancing. When the messenger from the florist came with the flowers which Serena, acting upon the suggestion of Mrs. Lake and Mrs. Black, had ordered, he saw that they were placed in exactly the right positions for effect. Being urged to stay for lunch, he stayed.

And his conversation during the meal was so fluent, so aristocratic in flavor, and yet so friendly, that Serena became more and more taken with him. With the captain he was not quite as much at his ease. But he did his best to be agreeable, and Daniel, still vaguely suspicious, found nothing tangible upon which to base distrust. There was so much to be done in the afternoon that, acting upon a hint so delicate that it could scarcely be called a hint, Mrs. Dott urged him to send to the hotel for his bag and stay at their home overnight. He accepted and was even busier than he had been during the forenoon session. He was never so busy as to perform manual labor with his own hands--he never stooped to that extent--but he managed to convey the impression of being always ready and always helpful.

To say that Mrs. Black and Mrs. Lake were, upon their arrival, surprised to find him there would be expressing their feelings far too mildly. They knew Mr. Hungerford, but, heretofore, that gentleman had moved in circles other than their own. It is true that he belonged to the same club as did Mr. Black, but Mr. Hungerford's friends had been younger, the ultra-fashionable set, the set which Annette had characterized as "rather fast" but which, because of its money and society connections, she secretly envied. To find him here, an associate and friend of the people she had called "countrified," was most astonishing. She wondered, but she could not help being impressed, and her attitude toward her dear friend Serena was never so gushingly cordial. As for Mr. Hungerford, he greeted the Chapter representatives with condescending urbanity. When the reception began, somehow or other, Cousin Percy was in the receiving line.

Captain Dan, uncomfortably starched and broad-clothed, received likewise, but his remarks to those who pressed his hand and murmured compliments were rather commonplace and very much alike; this consisted principally of "How d'ye do's" and "Glad to see you's"; and it was only when the Honorable and Mrs. Fenholtz came that he appeared to remember anything else. It was evident that Mr. and Mrs. Fenholtz were as surprised as the rest to see Mr. Hungerford there. The Honorable, seizing an opportunity when the captain was for a moment alone, whispered in his ear.

"Where did he come from?" he asked, with a jerk of the head in Cousin Percy's direction.

"Him?" replied Daniel. "Oh, he came last night."

"Is that so? Is he a friend of yours?"

"Well, he ain't--isn't exactly a friend, I guess. He's a sort of relation, a nephew of Aunt Laviny's."

"Oh, oh, I see--I see."

There was something in the tone which caused Captain Dan to ask a question in return.

"Know him, do you?" he inquired.

"Yes, I know him, but--it is all right, Olga; I'm coming."

He passed on to make room for another assortment of new arrivals, lady members of the Chapter, and Daniel's curiosity remained unsatisfied.

After the reception proper, came a social and, to Daniel, very uncomfortable hour, and then Mr. Hungerford, who seemed to have taken upon himself the position of master of ceremonies, suggested dancing.

Of all the captain's society experiences so far, this was the most amazing. He had danced in his younger days, it is true, but his were dances of quite another variety. Quadrilles and Virginia reels he was acquainted with, but tangos and Bostons and all the infinite varieties of the one-step were to him revelations, and revelations of a kind which caused him to gasp. He saw middle-aged matrons dipping and hopping and twisting about the room in company with middle-aged, stout, red-faced men who looked as if on the verge of apoplexy. He saw Mr. Hungerford laboring dutifully to pilot a woman of forty through the sinuosities of the "hesitation waltz," and when the lady, who was inclined toward plumpness, had collapsed into an armchair, he sought out her late partner and vented his feelings.

"For the land sakes!" he demanded; "what did you do that for?"

"Do what?" inquired Mr. Hungerford, himself as fresh and unwilted as an Easter lily.

"Why, that--to her. Look at her, she's pretty nigh gone! She ain't caught more than two breaths in the last minute and a half. I've been watchin' her."

Cousin Percy condescended to smile. "It's her own fault," he observed. "She said she was dying to learn the 'hesitation' and asked me to teach it to her."

"Well, she ought to be satisfied. If she was dyin' before, she's pretty near dead now. Why didn't you stop sooner? She all but capsized a dozen times in the last two or three turns you and she took around the room."

Percy's smile became broader. "That is all part of the dance," he explained. "Watch this couple here."

Daniel watched as directed. The couple were a young man and a girl about Gertrude's age. They were doing the "hesitation" with the hesitancy emphasized.

"My soul!" muttered the captain. "Where's that girl's mother? Somebody ought to tell her."

Hungerford smiled once more. "That was her mother I was dancing with," he said.

"Good Lord!" exclaimed Daniel. It was the only comment he made. He watched the rest of the dancing in silence.

The collation followed the dancing, and Azuba and Mr. Hapgood served it, assisted by four waiters who, at Mr. Hungerford's suggestion, had been hired for the occasion. The butler's serving was done with grace and elegance, not to mention dignity. Azuba served as if the main object to be attained was to provide each guest with as much food as possible in the shortest possible time. She was arrayed in a new black gown, worn under protest, for her own idea had been to wear her Sunday dress, a vivid purple, with trimmings which, for color and variety, looked "like a patchwork tidy," as Captain Dan expressed it. Also, under still greater protest, she wore a white apron and cap.

"I feel like my grandmother doin' dishes," Azuba declared when Mrs. Dott brought the cap and apron to her and insisted on a dress rehearsal. "The old woman lived to be ninety-five and wore a cap for all the world like this one for thirty year. She had some excuse for wearin' it--it hid the place where her hair was thin on top. But I ain't bald and I ain't ninety-five neither. And why in the world you want me to put an apron on in the parlor, I don't see. You've been preachin' at me to leave one off till I was just rememberin' to do it, and now you want me to put it on again."

"Not this kind of an apron, Azuba. Mrs. Black's maids wear aprons like that, and so do Mrs. Fenholtz's. It's the proper thing and I expect you to do it."

"Humph! All right. Land knows I don't want to be improper. But I'd just like to ask you this: Does that Fenholtz hired help have to wear black clothes like this dress?"

"Yes, always."

"Well, then I suppose I'll have to do the same, but I hope they don't feel as much like bein' in mournin' as I do. I thought this reception thing was supposed to be a good time, but when I looked at myself in the glass just now, all I could think of was the Trumet post-office draped up for President McKinley's funeral. I suppose it's style, so it'll have to be. But if Labe, my husband, should see me now, he'd have a shock, I guess. Cal'late he'd think he was dead and I'd got word of it afore he did."

But the food was good and the guests seemed to enjoy it. Some of them seemed to enjoy Azuba, and Mr. Fenholtz was observed by the indignant Serena to laugh heartily every time the transformed maid-of-all-work addressed him.

As they were leaving he said to Captain Dan: "Captain, that maid of yours is a wonder. If you ever want to get rid of her, let me know. I thought Mrs. Fenholtz and I had tried every variety of servant, but she is something fresh."

Daniel grinned. "She's fresh enough, if that's all you want," he admitted. "That's the main trouble with her, accordin' to my wife. I like her myself. She reminds me of home."

The Honorable shook his hand. "Home is a good thing to remember," he said earnestly, "and a bedder thing not to be ashamed of. You are not ashamed of your home and you do not forget it. That is why I like you. Good night!"

Somehow this remark pleased the captain greatly, but when he repeated it to Serena, she did not seem pleased.

"I don't know what we shall do with that Azuba," she said. "She mortifies me to death, and yet you won't let me get rid of her."

Her husband did not answer. In the matter of Azuba he was as determined as ever. Amid the new life into which he had been thrown, head over heels, the housekeeper was the one familiar substantial upon which he could rely. He was used to her, her conversation, and her ways. As he had said, she reminded him of home, his real home, the home from which he was drifting further and further every day.

Next morning Serena was suffering from headache and had breakfast in her room. Mr. Hungerford, also, did not descend to the morning meal. Daniel wrote a long letter to Gertrude, describing the reception, after his own fashion, but taking care to seem as cheerful as ever. He did not feel cheerful, but there was nothing to be gained by troubling his daughter, as he reasoned.

Mr. Hungerford remained through that day and the next day and the next. At the end of that time he sent for his trunks and settled down to make the Dott house his home, for "a short season," he said. This, of course, was done only after much protest on his part and strenuous urging on the part of Serena. Cousin Percy had taken her fancy at the very beginning of their acquaintance, and his conduct since then had strengthened that liking tremendously.

"Of course he can stay," she said in conversation with her husband. "Why, Daniel, I don't know what I should do without him. His coming was a special Providence, just as I told you. Just see how he helped at that reception. It would never have been the success it was if it hadn't been for him. And see how he's helped me since. He knows just what is right and proper for people in our station to do; he's been in society all his life. He's educated and he has helped me with my paper for the next meeting of the Chapter so much already. There's no reason why he can't be here; we've got plenty of room. And it will only be while he's on his vacation, anyway."

Daniel rubbed his chin. "I know," he admitted; "so he says. But how long a vacation is it goin' to be?"

"How do you suppose I know that? I haven't asked him, it isn't likely."

"No, I didn't suppose you had; but it seems kind of funny he hasn't told you himself. What's it a vacation from? What's he do for a livin'? Anything but run receptions?"

"That's it--sneer! He does a great many things. He is interested in literary work, so he says. He writes for a living, I suppose that means."

"Humph! Has he got any answer?"

"Answer? Answer to what?"

"Why, to his writing. Has the livin' sent him word 'twas on the way, or anything like that? I don't want to be mean, Serena. You know well enough I ain't stingy. But I can't quite make that young fellow out. Why did he come here, anyway? that's what sticks in my mind. What sort of a chap is he? You know what that lawyer man said about him. Nigh as I could make out from that, he thought he was a kind of high-toned loafer, sportin' round on his aunt's money. Why does that kind of a fellow come to live along with us? WE ain't sports."

"Will you EVER remember not to say 'ain't'? He came here because he isn't that kind of a fellow at all. He explained about that. It seems that he and that young upstart of a Farwell, the lawyer, had had some words and Farwell had a grudge against him. He thinks it was largely owing to those lawyers' influence that Aunt Lavinia treated him as she did in her will. But he doesn't hold any grudge. I never heard anybody speak more forgiving or kind than he did about the whole affair. I declare, it was positively affecting! He told me about his life and about how he was all alone in the world; how he had never had to earn much--never having been brought up to it--but that now he was trying to do his best. I felt so sorry for him, and that was one of the reasons why I thought we, the only relations he has, ought to be kind and show him hospitality at least. I never thought you were inhospitable, Daniel."

"I ain't, Serena. That is, I mean I are--am not. But--but--Well, I'll tell you. I haven't told you before, although I meant to, but he and I met once since we've been in Scarford. I told you about the meeting, but I didn't know then who I met. Now I--"

"I know. He told me about that, too. He was the one you met at the hotel that afternoon. He said he was ashamed of his behavior that day, that he was tired, out of sorts, and discouraged. He thought you had been listening to what he and his friend had been saying, and it made him cross. He said that he apologized when he first came to the house, and I remember that he did, and he asked me whether I thought any further apology was necessary. I said no, of course it wasn't."

"Well, I don't suppose it is. But--well, there was somethin' else. It seemed to me that afternoon at the Rathskeller that he and that chum of his had been drinkin'."

"Drinking? Do you mean that they were intoxicated?"

"No, not exactly that; but they had a couple of cocktails while I was there."

"Is that all? Oh, dear me! Daniel, you are SO old-fashioned. Your ideas don't change a single mite. In Trumet a cocktail is a dreadful thing; but here it isn't. Why, everybody drinks a cocktail before dinner. The Blacks always have them. There were cocktails at that dinner at their house."

"I know there was, but I didn't see you drinkin' yours, Serena."

His wife hesitated. "No," she admitted rather reluctantly, "I didn't. I've been temperance all my life and somehow I couldn't bring myself to do it. I hope Annette didn't think it was bad manners, but I just couldn't somehow. Perhaps I ought to have tried--"

"Tried! My soul and body, Serena! Don't talk that way. If I see you startin' in to drink cocktails I shall begin to think the world's comin' to an end. SOMETHIN' will come to an end right then and there, I'll tell you that! The first cocktail you drink will be the signal for me to clear decks for action. There's some things I WON'T stand, and that's one of 'em!"

"There, there! Don't get excited! I shan't begin at my time of life. But I shan't be narrow, either. I don't want you to be. If all you've got against Cousin Percy is that he drinks a cocktail once in a while I think you'd better get over it as soon as you can. He does help me, Daniel, in my Chapter work and all the rest of it, and I'd like to have him stay here at present. Now won't you be nice and obliging, same as you usually are, and let him stay, for my sake? You will, won't you, dear?"

Captain Dan said that he would, and yet he said it with considerable inward reluctance. There was no real reason why he should have distrusted Percy Hungerford. At least he could think of none in particular. His distrust was based upon generalities and a knowledge of human nature acquired during his years of knocking about among men. His wife's words made an impression. If what she said was true, his conscience told him that he should be kind and generous in his attitude toward the literary person. But--well, the "but" was still there.

It was his intention to seek out Fenholtz and ask a few questions concerning Cousin Percy, but the opportunity did not offer itself, and shortly after the reception the Fenholtzes left for the South, where they were to spend the winter. So that source of information was cut off.

During the next fortnight the captain's sense of desertion and of being almost a stranger in his own house grew stronger than ever. There were more callers and more calls to return; there were more bridge parties and teas. His wife astonished him by announcing that she was going to take lessons in bridge and that Mr. Hungerford had found a teacher to perfect her in that branch of knowledge.

"Of course," she said, "it will cost quite a little, but Cousin Percy says there's no use having a teacher at all unless you have a good one, and three dollars a lesson isn't too much, because you learn so quickly from an expert. I was sure you would be willing for me to take the lessons, Daniel."

Daniel shook his head. "I'm willin' for you to do most anything that pleases you, Serena," he said, "but three dollars a lesson for learnin' how to play cards seems to me a pretty good price. If it was me I should feel as if 'twas doubtful whether I'd get as much out of it as I put in. That's what Ezra Small, back home, said when he put his sprained foot in a plaster cast. Ezra said he never expected to get more than half his foot back, because the way that plaster stuck he cal'lated it would hang on to the rest. I should feel the same way about the three dollars for a bridge lesson."

"Oh, no, you wouldn't after you had taken a few. You'll like it then."

"I, like it! Good Heavens, you don't mean--"

"I meant that you're going to take lessons, too, of course. You must learn to play bridge--everybody plays it. And you used to like cards."

"I used to like high-low-jack, and I could manage to take a hand at euchre without raisin' too big a disturbance; but I never could learn that bridge and play it with those women friends of yours--never in this world. More'n that, I don't intend to try."

And he positively refused to try in spite of his wife's pleading. However, he consented to the employment of the bridge teacher for her and, thereafter, two hours of each alternate afternoon, Sundays excepted, were spent by Mrs. Dott and two other female students in company with a thin and didactic spinster who quoted Elwell and Foster and discoursed learnedly concerning the values of no-trump hands. The lessons were given at the Dott home and Mr. Hungerford was an interested spectator. Daniel, who was not interested, and felt himself in the way, moped in his own room or went upon more of the lonely walks about town.

Chapter meetings and Chapter activities occupied more of Serena's time. There were "open" meetings occasionally and these Captain Dan seldom attended. Mr. Hungerford acted as his wife's escort and seemed to enjoy it, in his languid fashion. Chapter politics began now to have their innings. There was to be a national convention of the Ladies of Honor, a convention to be held in the neighboring city of Atterbury, and Scarford Chapter was to send delegates. Mrs. B. Phelps Black, who aspired to national honors, was desirous of being one of these delegates, but so were many others, and Mrs. Black's candidacy was by no means unopposed. She called upon Serena for help, and into the fight in aid of her friend Serena flung herself, heart and soul.

There were meetings, and more meetings, and letter writing, and canvassing of voters. Here again, Daniel was of no use. Cousin Percy's experience--he seemed to have had all sorts of experience--helped amazingly. Mr. Hungerford's willingness to help in all things where no particular labor was concerned was most astonishing. By this time he was as much a member of the Dott household as Serena herself-- more than the captain, who began to feel that he was not a member at all. Even bridge was side-tracked for the more absorbing political game, and evening after evening Captain Dan spent alone. Occasionally Mr. Hungerford kept him company, but his was company not too congenial. It is true that the young man was agreeable enough, but he and the captain found nothing in common to talk about, and Cousin Percy usually gave up the attempt at conversation rather early and fell asleep upon the sofa or went out on little excursions of his own to which Daniel was not in- vited.

Mr. Hungerford smoked a good deal, and it was Daniel's cigars that he smoked. His vacation seemed no nearer the end than it had when he first came. The shrewd Azuba informed the captain that she guessed it was "one of them vacations that didn't have any end, but was all beginnin'." Her employer reproved her for speak- ing in this way of a friend of the family--he felt it was his duty to do that--but the rebuke was a mild one.

One night, or rather one morning, for it was nearly two o'clock, he was awak- ened by a series of violent shakes, and opened his eyes to find his wife bending over him. She had been out, attending a special meeting of the Chapter, and had hastened upstairs without stopping to take off her wraps.

"Daniel, Daniel, wake up!" she cried.

The captain groaned. "Hey! what is it?" he asked sleepily. Then, with a little more interest, "Is the house afire?"

"No, no, but do wake up and listen. I've had the greatest honor done me. You will hardly believe it. The delegates to the Atterbury Convention were elected to- night. Annette Black is one--I just KNEW she'd win--and Mrs. Lake is another, and who do you suppose is the third?"

Captain Dan sat up in bed. "Not you?" he shouted.

"Yes, I. And, more than that, I was the one selected to read a paper there. An- nette expected to do that, but, when it came to the vote, my last paper, the one I read Thursday night, the one Cousin Percy helped me so in preparing, was selected over all the rest. The vote was nearly two to one. I am to read it on the second day of the Convention. Isn't it wonderful! Annette was so jealous she hardly said good-night to me. But I don't care. There, Daniel Dott! aren't you proud of your wife?"

There was a little hesitation in her husband's manner, and yet he tried his best to be enthusiastic. "Oh, yes," he said, "but then I was proud of you before, Serena. But--but what does this mean? Have you and I got to traipse way over to Atterbury?"

"Not you. You're not going. None of the men are. This is a women's convention. Men are not invited."

"I know. But I've got to go there with you. You ain't goin' off travelin' by yourself."

"I'm going with the other Chapter delegates; we will travel together."

"I want to know! How long are you goin' to be gone?"

"I'm not sure. Three or four days probably."

"And I've got to stay here alone?"

"Why, you won't be alone. Cousin Percy will be here, and there's Azuba."

"Yes, and that everlastin' Hapgood, I suppose. Say, Serena, have you GOT to go?"

"Got to? Why, I WANT to! It's an honor. Don't you want me to go?"

"Why--why, I suppose I do; but--but--"

"But, what? Oh, you DON'T want me to go! I can see--and I thought you'd be so glad!"

She was almost in tears. Daniel's sensitive conscience smote him once more. "Land sakes!" he protested. "Of course I want you to go, Serena! I wouldn't have you do anything else for the world. I--I was just kind of lonesome, that's all. I get that way sometimes, lately. Seems as if you and I don't see as much of each other as we used to. Do you think it's all worth while?"

"Worth while! Why, Daniel Dott!"

"There, there! don't take on. I guess it is. I suppose you know best about such things. But I get kind of blue settin' around here thinkin', without you to talk to; and Gertie isn't here. You see, I miss you both."

"Yes, I suppose you do. Well, after this convention is over I shall have a little more time, I hope. And Gertie will be home pretty soon. It's almost time for her

Christmas vacation."

"Yes, I know it is. I was thinkin' that to-day. My! we'll be glad to see her, won't we?"

"Of course we will. But, do you know, Daniel, I've been so busy that I almost forgot about Christmas and Gertie's vacation and everything. It was Cousin Percy that reminded me of it."

"Reminded you of what?--of Christmas?"

"No, of course not--of Gertie's vacation. He said that she was coming and that he should be glad to make her acquaintance."

"HE said so? How did he know? I never told him."

"I don't remember that I did, either. But I suppose I must have. Anyhow, he knew. He is very much interested in Gertie and how she was getting on at college and all that. I saw him looking at her photograph that very day of the reception. He knew that it was she, without being told."

"Humph! He seems to know a lot. But, there! I recollect now--Gertie said she met him at college. Well, Serena, I won't complain any more. You can go to Atterbury if you want to. I'll get along all right."

And to Atterbury Mrs. Dott went. It was the first time since the old sea-going days that Captain Dan and his wife had been separated longer than twenty-four hours. He saw her off on the train and then moped drearily back to Aunt Lavinia's mansion, which he was now beginning to hate, and, seating himself in the library, tried to find interest in a novel. He did not find it, however, and went to bed early. Cousin Percy, who was out that evening, did not retire early. Next morning he seemed to have little appetite for breakfast, and was less agreeable than usual.

The three days passed somehow. The wanderer was to return on Thursday morning, but she did not. Instead came a telegram, reading as follows:

"Meeting and paper great success. Send immediately one of my latest photographs. Serena."

The puzzled Daniel sent the photograph preceded by a telegram of his own which read:

"When are you coming home? Why don't you write? Have been worried about you. Answer."

The answer was delayed still another day. When it came, it was in the shape of a very short note stating that Saturday was the date of return. Serena wrote that she was having a lovely time. She would tell him all about it when she got back. "And," she added, "I am sending you by this mail copies of the Atterbury paper. Please show it to any of the Chapter members whom you may meet."

Captain Dan unfolded the paper and gazed at the page marked with blue pencil. Here, under black headlines, which screamed the success of the convention of the Ladies of Honor, was a horrible blotted outrage resembling a stout negress peering through a screen door and labeled, "Mrs. Serena Sarah Dott, of Scarford, whose brilliant paper scored the success of the meeting." It was only by a process of deduction that Daniel realized the thing to be a reproduction of the photograph he had sent. He glanced hurriedly over the account of the meeting, catching here and there phrases like "Mrs. Dott's forte is evidently platform speaking"--"clear thought, well expressed"--"tumultuous applause." He felt that he ought to read the account from beginning to end, but also that he could not. Azuba, however, when it was shown to her, had no such feeling. She bore it to the kitchen, read it all, and returned to crow vaingloriously.

"Well, there now, Captain Daniel!" she exclaimed. "Ain't it wonderful! Ain't it grand! Ain't you a lucky man to have a wife as notorious as she's gettin' to be! I swan to man, if it ain't--"

The captain interrupted her. "Azuba," he said, rather testily for him, "if you use that word again I don't know as I won't make you eat a dictionary. My wife may be famous and she may be a platform speaker, but I'm blessed if I'll have her notorious, not if I can help it."

"But she is notorious, ain't she? Look at her right there in the newspaper, with all that piece about her in print! I wish Labe could read such a piece in the paper about me. Why, what ails you, Daniel Dott? Just look at that photograph!"

Captain Dan rose. "Yes," he said drily, "I've been lookin' at it. That's part of what ails me."

On Saturday he was at the station to meet his wife. Serena was inwardly jubilant, although, because of the presence of Mrs. Lake and Annette, she tried to appear dignified and calm. But when she and her husband were alone on their way to the house her jubilation burst forth.

"Oh, it was a wonderful success!" she declared. "I declare, I wish you might have been there. The way they applauded! And the entertainment they gave me! And the reporters after interviews! And the things the women of the other Chapters said! Oh, Daniel, it was splendid!"

Lunch was a mere formality on her part. She talked incessantly, while Cousin Percy and her husband listened. Mr. Hungerford's congratulations were hearty. His praise was as close to fulsome flattery as it could be and not overstep the mark.

Daniel offered congratulations, too. He was glad that his wife had succeeded, but the pleasure was solely because of her happiness. He was not as happy on his own account. Several remarks which Serena had made seemed to prophesy that the excursion to Atterbury was but the beginning.

All that afternoon Mrs. Dott spent in her room. She was going to be very busy, she said, and she must not be interrupted. It was only just before dinner that the captain found a moment for an uninterrupted interview. He entered the room to find her seated at the writing table, her fingers ink-stained, and the table covered with closely written sheets of manuscripts. She looked up when he appeared.

"Oh," she said, "I'm so tired! I've written steadily all the afternoon. My report had to be ready, and there was so much to say."

Daniel regarded her gravely. "You look tired, Serena. You're doin' altogether too much of this sort of thing. You ought to stop, or you'll be sick. Now, you just rest a while. My, it does seem good to have you back again! We can have an evening together now. I'll tell you what we'll do: You tell Hungerford you're tired and then come right up here, and I'll come, too. Then we can sit and talk. I've got so much to say to you."

But Serena shook her head. "No, Daniel," she said. "I can't talk to-night."

"Then don't; I'll do the talkin'. Land's sakes! it'll be enough just to look at you. I don't feel as if I'd seen you for a hundred years."

Another shake of the head. "I'm sorry, Daniel, but I can't be with you at all to-night. I must present my report to the Chapter and I shall probably not be home till very late."

Daniel sprang from his chair. "Serena Dott!" he cried. "Do you mean to tell me that you're goin' out to that Chapter thing again TO-NIGHT! after bein' away from me all this time! Why, you've just got home!"

"I can't help it, Daniel. I must present my report. It's my duty to do it. The

Chapter expects me and I must be there."

"Expects you! I expected you, didn't I? And, by the everlastin', I think I had a right to expect you! I'm your husband, ain't I? Seems to me I am entitled to a little of your society."

"I can't help it, Daniel. The Chapter--"

Captain Dan's feelings got the better of his prudence. "Damn the Chapter!" he shouted. "I wish you and I had never heard of it, nor anybody that belongs to it."

The instant after the words left his lips he would have given a good deal to recall them, but it was too late. His wife slowly rose.

"Daniel Dott!" she gasped. "Daniel Dott! You--YOU--why--my husband talking to me like that! My own HUSBAND! the man of all men that I expected would be proud of me! The man who should be proud and glad that I have found my lifework--speaking to me like that! Oh! oh! what shall I do! How CAN I bear it!"

She fell back into the chair, her head sank upon her arms over the manuscript of the precious report, and she burst into a storm of sobs.

Daniel was as much overcome as she. He hurried to her side and in an agony of remorse bent over her.

"There, there, Serena," he pleaded. "Don't do so. I didn't mean it. It kind of--"

He would have put his arms about her but she pushed them away.

"And swearing at me," she sobbed. "And using language that--"

"I didn't mean to swear, Serena. I never swore at you before in my life. I didn't mean to this time. It just seemed to come out all of itself. Please forgive me, won't you? Please?"

But Serena was not ready to forgive. The sleepless nights and days of wild excitement had thrown her nerves into a state where it needed but the slightest jar to break them completely. She sobbed, and choked, and gasped, her fingers clutching at her hair. Daniel, hanging over her, tried in vain to put in a word.

"Please, Serena," he kept saying. "Please."

Suddenly the sobs ceased. Serena's hands struck the desk and she rose so abruptly that her husband had scarce time to get out of her way.

"Serena," he cried.

But Serena cut him short. "Go away," she commanded. "Go away and leave me. I don't want to speak to you again."

"But, Serena--"

"Go away. Don't come near me again to-night. Go, go, GO!"

And Daniel went, slowly, reluctantly. He was scarcely past the sill, his hands still upon the knob of the door, when that door was closed from within with a slam. He made one more effort to speak, but he heard the key turn and his wife's voice commanding him to go away. He descended the stairs to the library and threw himself into a chair. Mr. Hungerford, smoking one of his host's cigars and reading the evening paper, looked at him curiously and asked what was the matter.

Daniel turned on him. "Nothin'," he roared. "Nothin', do you hear?" Then he rushed from the library to the hall, seized his hat and coat from the rack and hurried out of the house. He walked and walked, but if, upon his return, anyone had asked him where he had walked he could not have told them. This was the first serious quarrel that he and his wife had had during their married life.

It was half-past seven when he returned and found Azuba fidgeting in the dining-room. It was Mr. Hapgood's free evening and he had left early.

"For mercy sakes!" Azuba demanded. "Where have you been?"

"Out!" was the gloomy rejoinder. "Where's the rest of the folks?"

"Gone to Chapter meetin'."

"Both of 'em?"

"Yes. It was an open meeting and Mr. Hungerford went along, too. Where are you goin' now? Don't you want anything to eat? It's been waitin' for you for an hour."

"Let it wait; I don't want it."

He walked from the room. Azuba gazed after him open-mouthed.

"Well!" she soliloquized in a voice loud enough for the captain to hear. "Well, if anybody'll tell me what's the use of gettin' all het up cookin' vittles in this house, then I'd like to have 'em do it. Here I've worked and worked and fussed and fussed to get dinner and nobody's ate a mouthful but one, and he's the one that gets it for nothin'. I never saw such doin's. Don't talk to ME!"

Captain Dan didn't talk to anybody. He sat alone in the library, miserable and downhearted. After a while Azuba came and announced that she guessed she'd get a mouthful of fresh air, if she wasn't needed. Receiving no answer, she apparently considered the request granted and the captain heard the back door shut. Still the captain sat in the library, a huddled, pathetic heap in the armchair, gazing at vacancy. Occasionally he sighed.

The doorbell rang. Aroused from his doleful reverie by the sound, Daniel jumped from his chair and, going to the hall, shouted for Azuba. Then he remembered that Azuba was not on the premises and answered the ring himself. He had forgotten to push the button of the porch light and, peering out into the dark, he could see only that the person standing upon the top step was a woman. A carriage had drawn up at the curb and the driver was unloading a trunk from the rack.

"Good evenin'!" said Daniel.

The answer was a surprise. There was a laugh, and then a pair of arms were thrown about Captain Dan's neck and a girlish voice said: "Good evening! Is THAT all you've got to say to me? Why, Daddy, you dear old goose, don't you know me?"

Daniel's answer was a shout that might have been heard at the next corner.

"What!" he roared. "GERTIE! Good land of love! Where'd you come from?"

CHAPTER VIII

But aren't you glad to see me, Daddy?" asked Gertrude. They were in the library. The trunk had been carried upstairs and the young lady had assured her father over and over again that she really didn't want any dinner, as she had eaten on the dining car during the journey from Boston.

The captain, who had scarcely taken his eyes off her since her arrival at the house, drew a long breath.

"Glad to see you!" he repeated. "I never was more glad to see anybody in MY life. How'd you happen to come so soon? We weren't expectin' you for a week."

"I hadn't expected to come, but I changed my mind. Now tell me all about yourself. How are you, and how's Mother? And how are you getting on? Mother has gone to the Chapter meeting, you say. Did she go alone?"

"No, she didn't go alone. That--Cousin Percy went with her."

"Cousin Percy? Oh, you mean Mr. Hungerford. Do you call him Cousin Percy? How funny!"

She seemed much amused. Her father smiled, but it was a rather sheepish smile.

"'Tis kind of funny, I suppose," he admitted. "I don't know as he really is a cousin. Fact is, I guess he ain't any real relation."

"Of course he isn't. He was Aunt Lavinia's second cousin, or something like that, but she was only your aunt by marriage. I don't see why you should speak of him as 'Cousin Percy.' Did he ask you to?"

"No-o; I don't know as he did. But, you see, he always calls your mother Cousin Serena and me Cousin Daniel, and--and--well, I guess we've kind of got into the habit. Your mother began it and, now that he's been here so long, I've caught the disease, I shouldn't wonder."

"Long! Why, he hasn't been here more than a month, has he?"

"Hey? No; no; now that you mention it I don't suppose he has. But it seems a lot longer than that to me."

He sighed. Gertrude regarded him keenly. Unconscious of the regard he sat there, lost in thought, apparently forgetful of her presence. She reminded him by saying:

"Why does it seem longer?"

He started and looked up.

"Hey? Why?" he repeated. "Oh, I don't know. So many things have happened, I guess."

"What kind of things?"

"All kinds. But there--tell me about yourself. How's college? And how's John? Land sakes! I ain't said a word about John, and he's about as important as anything on earth just now, or he ought to be. Guess you think I'm a selfish old pig, not to ask about him before this. How is he?"

"You couldn't be selfish if you tried, Daddy. You never knew how to be. John is well and very busy. He sent his love to you and Mother, and he hopes to run down here before very long and spend a few days with us."

"Does, hey? That's good. I suppose YOU don't hope he'll come. Ha! ha! no, of course not. He's doin' all the hopin'."

"Well, perhaps not all. But there, Daddy, don't waste time talking of John or me. I want to hear about you and about Mother, and how you like living in Scarford."

"Why, I wrote you all about that."

"Yes, I know you did, but I want to hear more, lots more. And I want to see the house. Just think, I haven't seen it at all. Now, Daddy, you must show me all the rooms right away. We can talk as we go. Come on."

She led the way and Daniel followed. The house was shown from top to bottom. Gertrude asked many questions, the majority of which seemed to have little to do with the new establishment and more with the life which her parents had spent in it. Captain Dan answered these questions in the intervals between rooms, and his answers were less guarded than they might have been under different circumstances. At length the young lady ceased to question, and the tour of inspection was finished in silence on her part.

When they returned to the library, the captain, who had been waiting for some expression of approval from his daughter, suddenly blurted out:

"Well, why don't you say somethin', Gertie? Don't you like it?"

Gertrude, seated in the easy chair, her elbow resting on the chair arm and her chin supported by her hand, answered promptly.

"No," she said, "I don't like it at all."

"What! Don't LIKE it? Don't like this house? Well, for mercy sakes!"

"Oh, not the house; I like that well enough. I liked our old one quite as well--but never mind that now. The house is all right. It is the rest of it that is all wrong. I don't like that."

"The rest of it? What do you mean?"

Gertrude did not answer. Instead she raised her head and looked at him. It was a long look and a steady one, and the captain found it hard to bear. He fidgeted for a moment and then blurted out:

"Well, what is it? Why are you starin' at me like that?"

The stare continued.

"What is it?" demanded Daniel. "What does ail you, Gertie? Or is it me?"

His daughter nodded. "Yes," she said, "it is you. Why don't you tell me all about it, Daddy? I have a right to know. Why don't you tell me?"

"Tell you? Tell you what?"

"You know. Why don't you tell me? You have told me so much already that you may as well make a clean breast of it. Why, you silly old Dad, what do you suppose brought me here a week ahead of my vacation? Why do you think I came?"

"Why do I think--? Why--why, you came because you wanted to see your mother and me, I suppose. That's reason enough--or I flattered myself that 'twas. I thought you was as anxious to see us as we was to see you."

"So I was; but that wasn't reason sufficient to make me leave my work at college before the term was over, leave it for good, very likely. I came because I was sure you needed me. And your letters made me sure."

Daniel gasped. His letters had been triumphs of diplomatic evasion, so he considered. He had been so careful to write nothing of his troubles, to leave out everything which should hint at his disturbed state of mind. He had taken pains to express, in each epistle, his contentment and happiness, had emphasized them. And now--

"My letters!" he exclaimed. "My letters made you think--made you sure--"

"Yes; your letters and mother's. Hers were full of all sorts of things, the very things that you never mentioned. She didn't say she was having a good time here, but it was plain enough that she was. You said it in every letter--that you were having the good time, I mean--but it was perfectly plain that you weren't. And her last letter was so short--she was so busy with the Atterbury preparations that she could not write more, she said--and yours was so very, very long, and SO full of lonesomeness--"

Her father interrupted. Lonesomeness was the very thing he had tried to keep out of that letter.

"Gertrude Atwell Dott!" he shouted. "How you talk! I never wrote a word--"

"Yes, you did. It was all there, between the lines. I could read it, for you and I have been acquainted a good many years. As soon as I received that letter I made up my mind to come at once. Since I have been here I have asked a good many questions, and you have answered them. But I didn't need the answers. Just to look at you was enough. You are miserable, Daddy dear, and, because you are you, you won't admit it. But you've got to; you've got to tell me the whole story. I want to know all about everything."

The wind was taken completely out of Daniel's sails. He could only sit there, guilt written plainly upon his face, and stammer frantic protestations.

"No, no," he declared. "It ain't so. You're all wrong, Gertie. You're way off the course. The idea of you sayin' your mother was neglectin' me."

"I didn't say it. You have said it a dozen times, but I haven't."

"I said it? I never. Your mother is a fine woman, Gertie; as good a woman as ever was."

"I know that. And she would not neglect you wilfully for the world. But she has not had experience. She takes people and things at their face value. She doesn't understand--Why are you smiling? Is it so funny?"

Captain Dan rubbed the smile from his lips. In spite of his perturbation he had been amused for the moment.

"Why," he observed, "I don't know as 'tis, but--but--well, I couldn't help wonderin' how old you'd got to be in the last couple of months, Gertie. You talk as if you was the grandmother and your ma and I were young ones just out of school. About how much experience have YOU had, young lady? now that we're speakin' of it."

Gertrude's earnestness was too real to be shaken by this pertinent inquiry.

"I have had a good deal," she declared. "One can get a lot of experience in college. There are as many kinds of character there, on a small scale, as anywhere I know. I have seen girls--but there! this is all irrelevant, away from the subject. You ARE neglected, Daddy; you are lonely and miserable. Now, I want you to tell me all about it."

But her father had, in a measure, recovered his composure, and he declined to tell. He had been longing for a confidant, and here was the one he had longed for most; but his sense of loyalty to Serena kept him silent.

"There's nothin' to tell," he vowed stoutly. "I'm all right. You're dreamin', Gertie."

"Nonsense! I shall lose patience with you pretty soon, and I don't want to. Judging by what I have seen and learned so far, I am likely to need a great deal of patience in this house, and I can't waste any. Mother has gone head over heels into this precious Ladies of Honor work of hers, hasn't she?"

"We-ll, she's terrible interested in it, of course; but she's so smart anyhow, and here in Scarford she's got the chance she's been lookin' for."

"And she is very much in society here, isn't she?"

"Yes. That's natural, too, with her smartness and all."

"What kind of society is it?"

"Hey? What kind? Why, it's the genuine gilt-edged kind, I should say. I never saw such clothes, nor such dinners, nor dances. It--"

"Hush! Yes, I can believe all that. You wouldn't be likely to see them--in Trumet. And I can believe in the gilt; the genuine part is what I am most doubtful of. Mrs. Black is as influential with Mother as ever, isn't she?"

"Yes. She and Serena bein' such close friends, it--"

"I know. Tell me, Daddy, are the rest of Mother's friends like the Blacks?"

"Pretty much. They're all the same tribe--that is, I mean they're all brilliant, fashionable folks."

"I see. What sort of friends have YOU made?"

This was straight from the shoulder and the captain was somewhat staggered.

"Well," he admitted, after a slight pause, "I--I ain't made so dreadful many friends, Gertie. Most of the men here are--are kind of different from me, seems so. They belong to clubs and such, and they're out a lot nights. I don't care for goin' out much; I've always been a great home body--you know that, Gertie. I don't doubt, if I joined the club and went to 'stag' dinners and so on, I'd have more friends. It ain't their fault, you know, it's me."

"Yes, it always is you, isn't it, Daddy? No one else is to blame, of course. Well, I'm very glad I came when I did. How many evenings have you spent alone, as you were spending this one?"

"Not a great many. I just--"

"Why didn't you go to the Chapter to-night? It must have been an open meeting, otherwise Mr. Hungerford couldn't have gone. Why didn't you go with Mother?"

Here was the one question Daniel had dreaded most. To answer it truthfully meant telling of the quarrel between Serena and himself. He could not tell that, not even to his daughter.

"I--I didn't feel like goin', somehow," he faltered.

"That's strange. I knew that you were not particularly interested in the Chapter--at least you never were in Trumet--but I never knew you to stay at home when Mother asked you to go with her. Did she ask you?"

"Now--now, Gertie, 'tain't likely I--I--"

"Never mind; you needn't answer. Tell me more about this new relative of ours, 'Cousin Percy.' Do you like him, now that you really know him?"

"Why--why, yes, I like him all right enough, I guess. Course he and I are different, in some ways; but, then, he's younger by a good many years."

Gertrude nodded slowly. "I see," she said. "You've made up your mind not to tell me anything, haven't you, Daddy? You wouldn't hurt anyone's feelings for the world, and you are afraid I may blame Mother. Well, I am not going to blame anyone yet. And I am not going to quiz you any longer. But I came home to find out things, and I am going to find out. If you won't help me, I must help myself."

Her father leaned forward and patted her hand.

"Now--now, Gertie," he pleaded nervously, "don't be foolish. Everything's all right, I tell you. Don't go stirrin' up any trouble. I am so tickled to have you here I don't know what to do. Let's be contented with that. Let's just be happy together. Don't--Hello! here comes the Chapter folks now, I guess. Maybe your mother won't be glad to see you! Oh, Serena, who do you think is here? I'll bet you'll be some surprised!"

There was no doubt of the surprise; neither was there any doubt as to Serena's joy at seeing her daughter. An outburst of greetings and questions and explanations followed. Gertrude explained that she had had an opportunity to leave college a week earlier than the end of the term and had availed herself of it.

"I just had to see you and father," she declared. "I couldn't wait any longer. I've been telling father so; haven't I, Daddy?"

She accompanied this question with a glance which Captain Dan recognized as a warning. He nodded.

"Yes," he said.

Serena suddenly remembered that the family was not alone.

"Oh!" she exclaimed. "What have I been thinking of? Your coming home like this, Gertie, has made me forget everything else. Cousin Percy--Why, where is Cousin Percy?"

Mr. Hungerford, who, from motives of delicacy or other reasons, had stepped back into the hall, where he could see and hear without being too conspicuous, now made his appearance.

"Gertrude," said Mrs. Dott, "this is our cousin, Mr. Percy Hungerford. You've heard him spoken of. Oh, yes--why, you and he have met. I remember now, so you have."

Mr. Hungerford bowed.

"I had the pleasure of meeting Miss Dott one evening a year or two ago," he observed politely. "No doubt she has forgotten me, however, by this time."

Gertrude shook her head.

"Oh, no," she said. "I remember you very well, indeed. How do you do, Mr. Hungerford?"

The young gentleman announced that he was quite well. He made a move as if to shake hands, but as there was no corresponding move on Miss Dott's part, he put his hand in his pocket instead.

"That evening--the evening of the college dance--is one of my pleasantest rec-ollections," he observed. "I made some delightful acquaintances there. I am ashamed to say that I have forgotten the names of the young ladies, but forgetfulness is one of my failings."

"He meets so many people," cut in Serena, by way of apology.

Gertrude smiled. There was a mischievous twinkle in her eye.

"I'm sure he hasn't forgotten us all," she declared. "He could not be so ungallant as that."

"He didn't forget you, anyway," declared Daniel. "He knew your photograph just as soon as he laid eyes on it."

"Oh, thank you, Daddy. You've saved my self-respect. But I was not referring to myself. There are others whom I am sure Mr. Hungerford has not forgotten. Isn't that true, Mr. Hungerford?"

Cousin Percy appeared somewhat disconcerted.

"Why," he stammered, "I don't understand. I can't recollect--"

"Can't you! Oh, that is dreadful! Do you correspond with so many young ladies that you can't remember their identity? Oh! oh! and Margaret was SO proud of those letters! Really, Mr. Hungerford!"

She shook her head. Her eyes were brimming over with fun. Cousin Percy's cheeks had lost something of their aristocratic pallor. Margaret Babcock, the daugh-ter of a well known glass manufacturer, had been one of the list of feminine ac-quaintances whom he had honored with long distance familiarity. She was an im-pressionable young person and her papa was very wealthy. The correspondence had broken off when her mother discovered one of the letters. Mrs. Babcock had definite views concerning her daughter's future, and Mr. Hungerford was not in-cluded in the perspective. The latter had forgotten, for the moment, that he met Miss Babcock at the college dance; therefore he was confused.

But the confusion was short-lived. He recovered quickly.

"I BEG your pardon, Miss Dott," he said with a laugh. "I had forgotten Miss Babcock. Poor Margaret! She was of an age when letters, especially masculine let-ters, are delightfully wicked. Forbidden fruit, you know. She asked me to write, and I was foolish enough to do so. I presume my humble epistles furnished harmless amusement for the class. Very glad to have contributed, I'm sure."

"You did contribute. We all enjoyed them so much--especially Margaret. She is a year older than I, Mr. Hungerford."

Serena, who, like the captain, did not understand a great deal of all this, decided to change the subject. She did not address her husband--she had not spoken to him since the scene in the room upstairs--but the exaltation and triumph which the evening just passed had brought to her soul now burst forth. She began to describe the Chapter's meeting and to tell of her great success at Atterbury, and the enthusiastic reception by the Scarford members of her report. Mr. Hungerford seized the opportunity to deprive the family of his society. He was rather tired, he explained, had a bit of writing to do before retiring, and, if they would excuse him, would go to his room. Being excused, with reluctance on Mrs. Dott's part and silence on the part of Gertrude and her father, he said good-night and withdrew.

"And now, Mother," said Gertrude, "tell me more about yourself, and about the Chapter, and the friends you have made, and everything. Father has told me a little, and your letters and his have told me more, but I want to know it all. I am very much interested."

Serena did not need to be asked twice. She told a great deal, warming to her subject as she proceeded. She told of their arrival in Scarford, of the kindness shown by the Blacks and Mrs. Lake and the rest. "Wonderful women, Gertie! brilliant, intellectual, advanced thinkers, every one of them. Not much like Abigail Mayo and the rest at Trumet."

She told of their adventures in society, of the Blacks' dinner, of the reception, of her bridge lessons. Gertrude listened, saying nothing, but watching both her parents intently as the narrative proceeded.

Daniel, fidgeting in his chair, waited, nervously expectant, for the protest which he felt sure his daughter might make at any moment. But no protest came. Only once did the young lady interrupt, and then it was to ask a question.

"I suppose Daddy enjoys all this as much as you do, Mother?" she said. "Doesn't he?"

Mrs. Dott's expression changed. The radiant joy, which had illumined her face as she described her progress at bridge, faded, and she seemed on the verge of tears.

"Don't, Gertie," she begged. "Don't ask me about your father, please. Enjoy it?

No, he doesn't enjoy it at all. He has no sympathy for my aims and ambitions. He takes no pride in my advancement. To-night--only this very night, he said to me-- Oh, I can't tell you what he said! Don't ask me, please."

Captain Dan almost slipped from his chair in the agony of justification.

"I never meant it, Gertie," he declared. "It just happened, I don't know how. I'll leave it to you; I'll leave it to anybody, if--"

For the first time his wife noticed his presence.

"Leave it to anybody!" she repeated wildly. "You'll leave it to anybody! I wish you would! I wish you could hear what people think of it. Why, Cousin Percy said--"

For the second time since lunch the captain forgot to be prudent.

"Cousin Percy said!" he shouted. "He said! Do you mean to say you told him-- THAT? What business was it of his, I'd like to know? What did he say? If he says it to me, I'll--I'll--"

Gertrude motioned him to stop.

"There! there!" she commanded. "Daddy, be quiet. Mother, you're tired out. You must go to bed. I'll go up with you, and we can talk while you are getting ready. Daddy will wait here. Come, Mother, come."

She led the sobbing Serena from the room. Captain Dan, his feelings divided between deep contrition at his own behavior and anger at Mr. Hungerford's interference in the affairs of himself and wife, obeyed orders and remained where he was.

It was a long wait. He smoked a cigar half through, lighting it three times in the process. When it went out for the fourth time he dashed the stump into the fireplace and took to pacing up and down the room. This reminded him of other days, days when he had paced the deck of his three-master, counting the hours which separated him from his wife and his home. He thought of the welcome he had always received when he reached that home. Oh, why--WHY had he ever retired from the sea? That was where he belonged; he was of some use in the world there. With a groan he stopped pacing and went out into the hall to listen for sounds from above. He heard the low murmurs of voices, the voices of his wife and daughter, but he could not distinguish words. Back he went to the library and lit another cigar. These cigars cost three times what his old Trumet brand had cost, but he got not a hundredth of the enjoyment from them.

Twelve o'clock struck before Gertrude re-entered the library. She entered quietly and, walking over to her father's chair, laid a hand on his shoulder. He looked up at her in mute appeal.

"It's all right, Daddy," she said. "You can go up now."

"But--but she--is she--"

"She has forgiven you, I think. You must be very kind to her."

"Kind to her? Kind! Why, Gertie, I never meant to be anything else. I wouldn't have--"

"Of course you wouldn't. Oh, Daddy, if you weren't the very worst diplomat in all this world this wouldn't have happened. Why didn't you tell me all about it? Why didn't you write me the truth long, long ago? If I had only come sooner! If I had only known! Oh, WHY did you let things reach this state? Why didn't you stop it?"

"Stop it? Stop what?"

"Oh, everything. Don't you remember that I told you to send for me if you needed me? To send at any time and I would come? And don't you remember that I wrote you if you felt this moving to Scarford was wrong to say no and stick to it? Why didn't you do that?"

"Why, I--I--Serena, she was so set on comin' and all that, that--"

"I know. You needn't tell me. And yet, in a way, it seems strange. I remember some things Laban Ginn, Azuba's husband, told me about you and your ways aboard ship; he said your crews obeyed every order you gave as if it was what he called 'Gospel.' You, and no one else, was master there. However, that is not pertinent just now. Run along to bed, there's a dear."

Daniel obediently rose.

"But what are you goin' to do, Gertie?" he asked.

"I don't know what I am going to do. First of all I am going to see and find out for myself. Then I shall decide. One thing seems certain: I shall not go back to college."

"Not go back! Not go back to college? Why, it's your last term! What'll your mother say? What'll John say?"

Gertrude's lips closed tightly and she gave a determined toss of her head.

"John will say what I say, I think," she declared. "As for Mother--well, what she says won't make any difference, not at present. Good-night, Daddy. Now don't worry, and," she repressed a smile, "be very careful and, if you must express your opinion of the Chapter, do it in the back yard or somewhere out of hearing. Good-night."

She kissed him and he went slowly and fearfully upstairs. Serena's attitude of reproachful and self-sacrificing forgiveness he met with meek repentance and promises not to offend again. He got into bed, worn out and troubled, but with a ray of hope in his bosom, nevertheless. Gertie had come home; Gertie was going to do something or other, he did not know and could not guess what. At any rate she was with him, and he could see her every day. Perhaps--perhaps--still wondering perhapses he fell asleep.

Next morning at breakfast the young lady seemed to be in good spirits and, except for Serena's absence--Serena had breakfast in her room, a proceeding which was apparently developing into a habit--the meal was to Daniel quite like one of the happy breakfasts of Trumet days. Mr. Hungerford marred the captain's pleasure somewhat by joining the pair before they left the table, and to him Gertrude was surprisingly cordial and communicative. Cousin Percy, who had been, at first, rather on his guard, soon thawed and became almost loquacious. Gertrude and he found a kindred taste for pictures and art in general, and before the captain's second cup of coffee was disposed of Mr. Hungerford had invited Miss Dott to accompany him to a water-color exhibition at a neighboring studio. Gertrude said she thought she might accept the invitation, if the exhibition was to remain for a few days.

"Is the artist a friend of yours?" she asked casually.

"Oh, no," was the languid answer. "He's a queer old gink--old chap, I mean--whose work is quite the go about here recently. Some very decent people have taken him up, I believe. He's worth meeting, so I'm told, as a curiosity. I've seen only two or three of his paintings, but they're really not bad. Some of the fellows at the club were talking about him the other night. I think you'd enjoy the exhibition, Miss Dott."

"I'm sure I should. I should like to see the pictures and the--er--gink as well. Thank you very much, Cousin Percy."

When they were alone, Captain Dan turned to his daughter in puzzled amazement.

"What did you call him 'Cousin Percy' for?" he demanded. "Thought you thought your mother and I callin' him that was funny; you said you did."

Gertrude laughed. "Did I?" she replied. "Well, perhaps I think so still."

Whatever she may have thought, it did not prevent her continuing to be very cordial to the newly discovered relative. He and she were together a good deal during the day. She seemed to really enjoy his society. The remainder of the time she spent with her mother. Captain Dan scarcely saw her except at luncheon and dinner. Once he found her in the kitchen talking with Azuba, and on another occasion she and Mr. Hapgood were in conversation, but for her father she could spare only odd moments. The captain did not know what to make of it. When, taking advantage of a fleeting opportunity, he asked her she only laughed.

"I am very busy, Daddy," she said. "You mustn't bother."

"Bother! Well, I like that! How long since my company was a bother to you, Gertie? It never used to be."

"It isn't now, and you know it. But, as I say, I am very busy. Business first, pleasure afterwards."

"Humph! I'm glad I'm a pleasure, even if it's the kind that comes after everything else. What have you and your ma been talkin' about upstairs for the last hour?"

"A great many things--society and the Chapter and--oh, all sorts."

"Want to know! What were you and Azuba talkin' about?"

"About household matters and the people IN the house."

"People in the house! What people?"

"You and mother and Mr. Hun--that is, Cousin Percy--and Hapgood."

"That's all there is, except yourself. What was you and Hapgood havin' a confab on; more household matters?"

"Yes, in a way. Daddy, have Mr. Hungerford and Hapgood known each other long?"

"I guess so. He was Aunt Laviny's butler for a good many years, and Percy was a regular visitor there. What made you ask that?"

"Feminine curiosity, probably. Has our cousin many friends here in Scarford?"

"Why, he seems to know 'most everybody; everybody that's in what he and your mother call society, that is."

"But has he any intimate friends? Have you met any of them?"

"I met one once. He seemed to be pretty intimate. Anyhow, they called each other by their first names. Ho! ho! that whole thing was kind of funny. I never wrote you about that, did I?"

He told of the meeting in the Rathskeller. Gertrude evinced much interest.

"What was this friend's name?" she asked.

"'Monty,' that's all I heard. Queer name, ain't it--isn't it, I mean. But it ain't any queerer than 'Tacks'; that's what he called Hungerford."

"Has this 'Monty' called here? Has he been here at the house?"

"No-o, no, he hasn't. I caught a glimpse of him at the club, that time when I went there with Barney--Godfreys! it's a good thing Serena didn't hear me say that--with Phelps Black, I mean."

"Daddy, sometime when you have an opportunity, ask Mr. Black about this Monty, will you?"

"Sartin, if you want me to. But what do you care about Percy Hungerford's friends?"

"I don't--about his friends."

With which enigmatical remark she moved away to join Cousin Percy, who had just entered the room.

During the next three days, Daniel's feeling that his daughter was neglecting him grew stronger than ever. Her "business," whatever it might be, occupied practically all her time, and the captain and she were scarcely ever alone. He was disappointed. He had regarded her coming as the life preserver which was to help him through the troubled waters to dry land, and so far he was as helplessly adrift as before. Serena had forgiven his profane expression concerning her beloved Chapter, that was true, but Serena also was "busy" during the days and evenings, and at bedtime she was too tired to talk. Gertrude was with her mother a great deal, and with Cousin Percy almost as much. They visited the water-color exhibition together, and would have gone on other excursions if the cousin had had his way. Daniel did not like Mr. Hungerford. He had grown to tolerate him because Serena liked him so much, and declared him such a help in her literary and political labors, but the captain had found secret comfort in the belief that his daughter did not like him any better than he did. Now it looked as if she was beginning to like him, after all. And there was no doubt whatever that Cousin Percy liked her.

Gertrude's apparent interest in her mother's social and Chapter affairs was another disquieting feature of the situation, as Daniel viewed it. Mrs. Black and Mrs. Lake called one afternoon and to them the young lady was cordiality itself. They talked "Chapter," of course, and to her father's horror Gertrude talked it, too. Being invited to attend the next meeting she announced that she should be delighted to go.

"You didn't mean it, did you, Gertie?" pleaded the captain, when Serena had escorted the guests to the door. "You didn't mean you was figgerin' to go to that devilish--to that Chapter?"

"Hush! Yes, of course I meant it."

"But--but YOU!"

"Hush! Daddy, don't interfere. I know what I'm about."

Daniel was doubtful. If she had known she surely would not think of going. And yet, on the evening of the meeting, go she did. The meeting was a protracted one, and, on their return, Serena, finding the lower rooms apparently deserted, went upstairs. Gertrude was about to follow, but a figure stepped from the shadows of the library and detained her.

"Why, Daddy!" she exclaimed. "What are you doing up at this hour?"

"Sh-sh!" in an agitated whisper. "Don't let your mother hear you. I--I've been waitin' for you, Gertie. I just had to talk to you. Come in here."

He led the way into the library.

"Don't say anything," he whispered; "that is, don't say very much. Serena'll be wantin' to know where I am in a minute. Gertie, what are you up to? WHY did you go to that Chapter?"

"Hush, Daddy, hush! It is all right."

"All right! Yes, I know it's all right so far. That's what your mother used to say, back in Trumet, when she first started in. You begin by sayin' it's all right and pretty soon it IS all right. It ain't all right for me--it's all wrong. Why did you go to that meetin'?"

"I went because I wanted to see for myself. And I saw."

"Yes, you saw. And you heard, too, I'll bet you. Well, did you like it?"

"LIKE it! Daddy, tell me: There is another Woman's Club in Scarford, isn't there? This can't be the only one."

"No, it ain't. I believe there's another. A different one--a sensible one, so I've heard tell. Mrs. Fenholtz--you've heard me speak of her, Gertie; she's a fine wom-an--she belonged to the other one. She wanted Serena to join, but Annette Black had her innin's first, and after that 'twas all off."

"I see, I see."

"You see; but what are you goin' to do? Are you goin' to any more of them blessed meetin's?"

"I may. I probably shall. Daddy, dear, you must trust me. It is all right, I tell you."

Ordinarily this would have been enough. But to-night it was not. Captain Dan had spent some troubled hours since dinner and his nerves were on the ragged edge.

"All right!" he repeated impatiently. "Don't say that again. Is it all right for you to be gettin' into the same mess your mother is in? Is it all right for you to be talkin' about society and Chapters and--and I don't know what all? I did trust you, Gertie. I said so. I told Serena so this very afternoon. She was talkin' about Cousin Percy, she's always praisin' him up, and she said you liked him just as much as she did. He was a cultivated, superior young man, she said, and you recognized it. I laughed at her. I says, 'That's all right,' I says, 'but I wouldn't take too much stock in that. Gertie knows what she's up to. She's got some plan in her head, she told me so. She may pretend--'"

His daughter interrupted him.

"Father!" she exclaimed indignantly. "Why, Daddy! did you tell Mother THAT?"

"Course I did! Why not? It's so, ain't it? What is the plan, Gertie? What are you up to? You are pretendin', aren't you? Don't tell me you ain't! Don't tell me--"

"I shan't tell you anything. You don't deserve to be told. I'm out of patience with you, altogether. You deserve to be miserable. You'll spoil--But there! good-night."

"Gertie! Gertie! hold on. Don't--"

Serena's voice sounded at the head of the stairs.

"Gertie!" she called. "Who is it you're talking with? Is your father there? Why doesn't he come to bed?"

"He's coming, Mother, right away. So am I. Good-night, Daddy."

The next forenoon, as Azuba was blacking the stove, Gertrude entered the kitchen.

"Good-morning, Azuba," she said. "Are you alone?"

"Yes, yes, I'm alone."

"Where is Hapgood?"

"Land knows! Upstairs, lookin' out for that Hungerford man's clothes, I guess likely. He waits on that young critter as if he was the Prince of Wales. Well, you went Chapterin' and advancin' last night, I understand. What did you think of it?"

"Think? I thought--Oh, Azuba!"

"Yup. It's 'oh, Azuba,' I guess. That's what I've been sayin' to myself for quite a spell. I'd have said it to your pa, too, if it would have done any good."

"It wouldn't. We mustn't say a word to him, or anyone else."

"I know. And yet, when I think of the way things are goin' at loose ends I have the shakes. Do you know what it's costin' to run this place the way it's run? I know. And I know, too, that nobody else seems to know or care. Your pa trusts everything to his wife, and she trusts everything to that Hapgood. She can't be bothered, she says, and Hapgood's such a capable buyer. Capable! he'll be rich as well as capable if it keeps on, and the rest of us'll be capable of the poorhouse. And there's Serena's health. She's gettin' more nervous all the time, and just wearin' herself out with her papers and conventions and politics and bridge and society. My land! Don't talk to me! And it ain't no use to talk to her. There's got to be somethin' more'n talk."

Gertrude nodded.

"So I think," she affirmed. "Azuba, I have a scheme. It may be the best idea in the world and it may be the worst, but I am going to risk it. And you must help me. Will you?"

"Sartin sure I will!"

"And you won't tell a soul, not a living soul?"

"Not one, livin' or dead. You needn't look at me like that. I swan to mercy, I won't tell anybody."

"Good! Then listen."

Azuba listened, listened in silence. When her young mistress ceased speaking she shook her head slowly.

"Well," she observed, "it looks some like hoppin' out of the fryin' pan into the fire, but, even if it turns out that way, perhaps it's just as well to be roasted as fried. Humph! no, 'twon't do to tell anybody. I shan't, and you mustn't."

"I don't intend to."

"Um! Not even John Doane?"

"Well," doubtfully, "I may tell John later on. But I shall wait to tell him, I shan't write. He'll have to trust me, too."

"So he will. Fur's that goes, it's a good thing for men folks to learn to trust us women. If Labe, my husband, hadn't trusted me all these years, he'd have done some worryin', I cal'late. All right, Gertie, I'm with you till the last plank sinks. But," with a chuckle, "I'm kind of sorry for your pa. The medicine may cure us all in the end, but it'll be a hard dose for him to take, won't it?"

CHAPTER IX

Captain Dan's foundations were slipping from beneath him. His daughter's return had seemed to him like the first ray of sunshine breaking through the clouds and presaging the end of the storm. Now, it began to look as if the real storm was but beginning. Gertrude was apparently contracting the society and Chapter disease. Gertrude, upon whose good sense and diplomacy he had banked so heavily, was rapidly losing that sense. So far from influencing her mother to give up the "crazy notions" which were, Daniel firmly believed, wrecking their home and happiness, she was actually encouraging and abetting these notions.

The young lady was certainly spending a great deal of time with her mother and her mother's friends. When Mrs. Black and Mrs. Lake called for consultations concerning Chapter affairs, Gertrude took part in these consultations. Daniel, peeping into the library, saw the four heads together over the table, and heard his daughter's voice suggesting this and that. Invitations to various social functions came, and it was Gertrude who urged acceptance of these invitations. Captain Dan's pleas for quiet evenings together at home went for nought.

"You needn't go, Daddy," said Gertrude. "Mother and I know you don't care for such things. She and I can go without you."

"Go without me? The idea! Look pretty, wouldn't it, to have you two chasin' around nights all by yourself, without a man to look after you!"

"Oh, Cousin Percy will go with us. He is always obliging that way. Cousin Percy will go, I am sure."

The captain was equally sure. Cousin Percy was altogether too willing to go anywhere, at any time, provided Miss Dott went also. This very obvious fact did not add to Daniel's peace of mind. Rather than have his family escorted by its newest member, he resolved to sacrifice his own inclinations and go himself.

Miss Canby--the blonde young woman who played the piano at the Black home on the night of the dinner--issued invitations for an "At Home" in her apartments. All the Dott household--Mr. Hungerford included--were invited. Mrs. Black, who came to call, was enthusiastic. Her jealousy of Serena, which had manifested itself on the night of the latter's appointment as an Atterbury delegate, had apparently disappeared. She was again the dear friend and counselor, with all the old cordiality and a good deal of the old condescension.

This condescension, however, was confined to Serena and Captain Dan. Toward Cousin Percy she was extremely polite, but never patronizing, perhaps because that gentleman was so languidly at ease in her presence. He listened to her conversation with apparent interest, but his answers, gravely delivered, were at times a trifle sarcastic. She seemed to be a bit afraid of Cousin Percy, afraid and somewhat suspicious.

To Gertrude she was gushingly friendly, overwhelmingly so, and the friendship was, to all outward seeming, returned. Daniel, who had gathered from his daughter's previous remarks that she disliked the great Annette, was surprised and dismayed.

"For goodness sakes, Gertie," he demanded, "what did you kiss her for? Anybody'd think she was somebody near and dear that you hadn't laid eyes on for ten years. And she was here only yesterday. Do you love her so much you have to hug her every time you see her?"

Gertrude laughed. "Do you think I do?" she asked.

"I don't know what to think. It's a mighty sudden love, that's all I've got to say. Do you want her here ALL the time?"

"Well, when she is here I know where she is."

"So does anybody within hearin'. I never saw such a change in a person as there is in you. And all inside of a week. You used to go out of the room when that Black woman came into it. Now you kiss her when she comes."

"No, Daddy; I kiss her when she goes."

With which puzzling statement the interview ended.

B. Phelps accompanied his wife when the latter called to discuss the Canby invitation. His coming was unusual, the Dotts had seen comparatively little of him since their arrival in Scarford. Daniel was glad he came. Black and he were not altogether congenial; the captain would not have chosen him as an intimate; but at least there would be someone present with whom he could exchange a word. As B. Phelps did not care for Chapters and "At Homes" any more than he did, there was that bond between them.

Mr. Hungerford was, for a wonder, not in when the callers came. He went out very little nowadays, except when Miss Dott and her mother went; then he was always ready to go.

Annette declared that the Canby "At Home" was certain to be a most unusual affair. "So--er--well, so different," she explained. "Miss Canby is a very unusual woman, a unique woman, and her affairs are always as unique as she is. So truly Bohemian. I adore Bohemians, don't you, Gertrude?"

Gertrude said she did. "I don't know that I've met a great many," she added, "but I'm sure they must be very enjoyable."

"Oh, they are! And Miss Canby is one. The very first time I attended a gathering at her home I said to myself: 'THIS is true Bohemianism.'"

Captain Dan was astonished.

"Why!" he exclaimed, "Miss Canby's folks came from Down-East somewheres--Bangor, Maine, I think 'twas. She told me so, herself."

The remark was received in various ways, by various individuals. Serena frowned; Gertrude bit her lip; B. Phelps Black burst into a roar of laughter.

"I did not mean my statement literally, Captain Dott," explained Annette in gracious toleration. "But when people are independent and free from the usual conventionalities, as Miss Canby is, we speak of them as Bohemians. It is an--er--a term among artists and musicians, I believe."

Daniel understood little or nothing of this. He understood perfectly well, however, that he had blundered somehow, a glance at his wife's face told him that. Gertrude smiled at him kindly and observed: "Father is like myself, his acquaintance in Bohemia has been limited."

Captain Dan muttered that he guessed likely that was so, adding that he had an Armenian steward once who was a pretty good fellow. Then he subsided. Serena took up the conversation, changing the subject to the ever fruitful one of her beloved Chapter. In a moment the two ladies were deep in a discussion concerning the election of National officers for the Legion, an election which was to take place in Boston a few months later. Gertrude joined in the discussion, a proceeding which her father noticed with apprehension.

Mr. Black accepted an invitation to smoke, and he and Captain Dan went into the library. After the cigars were lighted, B. Phelps, lowering his voice so as not to be heard in the adjoining room, said suddenly:

"Dan, is that daughter of yours going off her head like the rest of the females?"

Daniel was indignant.

"Off her head!" he repeated. "Gertie! She's as smart and sensible a girl as ever lived. I say so, even if she is my daughter. What are you talkin' about?"

Mr. Black waved his hand. "Keep your hair on, Dan," he counselled pleasantly. "I like Gertrude, always have. I always thought she was as sensible as she is pretty, and that's saying something. But what has got into her since she got here in Scarford? You used to tell me she didn't care anything for society and all the rest of it; now she seems to be as daffy as her--well, as my wife, if you like that better."

"Daffy! See here, Barney Black, I--"

"Hush! Don't begin to yell or we'll have that hen convention in the parlor down on us. I'm not finding any fault with your daughter. I'm only talking for her good and yours. What does she care about this confounded Chapter foolishness?"

"She don't care nothin' about it."

"Doesn't she? She seems to be mighty interested in that talk they're having in there now. And she was as joyful as the rest of 'em over this Canby woman's 'At Home.'"

The captain was quite aware of the apparent joy; and Gertrude's growing interest in her mother's Chapter and its members was too obvious to be denied. Nevertheless, he tried to deny it.

"Oh, that's nothin'," he declared. "She and Serena have always been plannin' together over things, and this Chapter's like the rest, that's all. As for the 'At Home,' why--why--well, Gertie's young, and young folks generally like a good time."

"A good time! Great Scott! Have you ever been to that Canby apartment and seen the crowd that--No, of course you haven't. Dan, if my wife heard me she'd take my head off, but you're an old friend of mine and I like your daughter. Listen to me: Don't let Gertrude go to that 'At Home' if you can help it."

"Don't let her! How am I goin' to help it?"

"I don't know. Keep her in the house. Lock the door and hide the key. I would. If she was my daughter I'd--I'd chloroform her. Hanged if I wouldn't!"

Captain Dan's indignation was rapidly changing to alarm.

"See here, Barney," he demanded, "what are you tryin' to say, anyhow? What's wrong with this Miss Canby? Out with it."

"Nothing's wrong with her, so far as I know. And yet there isn't anything right. She's good enough, I guess, and she can play the piano like a streak, but she's a fool. She and the gang she is with are bleached-haired, frowzy-headed idiots, who hope they are Bohemians--whatever that is. They like to do what they call unusual things; they like to shock people--think it's smart. Don't let your wife or Gertrude--Gertie, especially--get in with that crowd. They don't belong there. And there's something else."

He hesitated. Daniel, trembling with anxiety, urged him to continue.

"What is it?" he begged. "What is the somethin' else?"

"Oh, nothing. It isn't my business anyhow. I ought to keep still."

"Keep still! After sayin' as much as you have? You go ahead or I'll shake it out of you one word at a time. Heave ahead now! I'm waitin'."

"Well, then, don't get mad. Remember I'm saying it merely as a friend. Is Gertie engaged to be married?"

"Sartin she is. To a fine fellow, too. What of it?"

"Why, this: If she is engaged why is she trotting about with this precious cousin of yours--this Percy Hungerford?"

Captain Dan started violently. He had asked himself that very question many times during the week which had just passed. To have someone else ask it, however, was too much. He bristled up like an angry cat.

"By Godfreys!" he sputtered, "what do you mean? Do you mean to hint--"

"I'm not hinting anything. Be quiet, or I'll stop right here. What do you know about Hungerford, anyway? Why is he here at your house?"

"Here! Why--why, he's here 'cause we asked him to stay. He's on his vacation and he's just makin' us a visit. As to knowin' anything about him, what do you mean by that? Do YOU know anything about him?"

"Not much. Neither does anyone else; that's the queer part of it. While old lady Dott--your Aunt Lavinia--occupied this house, he was here a good deal. He didn't do anything then, except to be a general high-flyer around town with a few chums like Monty Holway, who is another gay young bird with money. After Mrs. Dott went abroad to live, he left Scarford and went to Providence a while; after that to Boston and New York, and various places. He had the reputation of being something of a sport, and in with a fast set. Now, all at once, he comes back here and settles down on--with you and your wife. What did he do that for?"

"I--I don't know. He didn't intend to settle. Says he didn't, anyway. As for bein' a sport--well, he's told us about that, told Serena the whole yarn. He owned up that he never took life very seriously while Aunt Laviny lived; had plenty of money and didn't have to. But now it's different. He's realized that he must work, same as other folks, and he's doin' it. He works for some magazine or other, doin' what he calls literary work."

"Humph! What magazine is it?"

"I don't know. I never asked."

"Well, all right. I tell you, honestly, Dan, there's a feeling that he is working you and the family for easy marks. You give him a good home and plenty to eat and smoke and it's a pretty soft thing for him. As to work--Humph!"

Daniel hesitated now. He had had faint but uneasy suspicions along this very line, although these, like other suspicions and misgivings, he had kept to himself. And Serena was such a firm believer in Cousin Percy; at the least hint against that young gentleman she flew to arms. The captain remembered this and his strong sense of loyalty to his wife caused him to remonstrate. He shook his head.

"No, no," he said, "you're wrong there, Barney, sure you are. Why, Percy has done a lot of writin' and such since he's been here. He goes to his room 'most every afternoon to write, and he's helped Serena with her Chapter papers and speeches more than you could imagine. As for Gertie's trottin' around with him, that's just foolishness. She's gone to picture shows and such when he asked her to, but that's only because she likes such things and wanted company her own age. It's all foolishness, I tell you. If anybody says 'tain't, you tell 'em I say they're lyin'. By Godfreys! if they say it to me I'll--"

"There! there! Keep your hair on, I tell you."

"'Tis on, what there is left of it. But, Barney, what sort of talk have you been givin' me? If Hungerford ain't all right, how is it that he knows so many folks in this town? How is it that he's invited everywhere, to all sorts of places, into everybody's houses? Invitations! Why, he gets more'n we do, and," with a sigh, "land knows that's enough, nowadays."

B. Phelps grunted contemptuously. "It is easy enough to get invitations," he observed. "When you've been in this town as long as I have you'll know that any young fellow, who is as good looking and entertaining as he is, will be invited to all sorts of things. The girls like him, so do their mothers--some of them. But there! I may be all wrong. Anyhow, I mustn't stay with you any longer or Annette'll be suspicious that you and I are knocking her dashed Chapter. I've told you this for your own good. Gertrude's a bully girl; I always liked her--wished a good many times I had a daughter like her. I should hate to see her get in wrong like--well, like some people you and I know. You keep her at home as much as you can. Good Lord, man!" with sudden vehemence, "do you want your house to get to be an empty d----d hole, only fit to sleep in, like--like--Yes, Annette, I'm coming."

This conversation remained in Captain Dan's head for days. It disturbed him greatly. Several times he made up his mind to speak to Serena concerning it, but each time he changed his mind. He even thought of writing a note to John Doane, urging the latter to run down to Scarford for a few days, but he was fearful that to do this might be a mistake. John would tell Gertrude, and she might not like it. Besides, Gertrude had said that she expected John to come before very long. So Daniel did nothing further than to remonstrate mildly concerning the acceptance of Miss Canby's invitation. As he gave no reason for his objection, other than the general one that he was tired and did not care about it, his remonstrances were unheeded. He need not go unless he wished, said Serena, she and Gertrude and Cousin Percy could go and he could stay at home and rest. Gertrude said the same. When the evening came, the whole family went, the captain included.

Annette had characterized the gifted Miss Canby as unusual, and the social affairs given by her as unique. After the first half hour in the "Bohemian" apartments, Daniel would have agreed with her, although his opinion might have been more emphatically expressed. Miss Canby WAS unusual, her apartments were unusual, and the "Bohemians" there gathered most unusual of all.

Gertrude, strolling about in the company of a young gentleman--not a Bohemian, but, like herself, merely a commonplace guest--found her father seated in a corner, sheltered by a Japanese screen and an imitation palm, and peering out at the assembled company with a bewildered expression on his face.

"Well, Daddy," she asked, "are you having a good time?"

Daniel, who had not noticed her approach, started and looked up.

"Hey?" he asked. "A good time! My soul and body! Yes, I'm havin' a good time. I haven't had a better one since I went to the sideshow at the circus. Who's that long-legged critter with the lay-down collar and the ribbon necktie? That one over there, talking to the woman with the hair that don't match. What ails him?"

Gertrude looked and laughed. "That is Mr. Abercrombie, the poet," she said. "Nothing ails him; he is a genius, that's all."

"Humph! That must be bad enough, then. What--"

He stopped. His daughter's escort had caught his attention. The young man's face was familiar.

"Why!" he faltered, "isn't this--"

"This is Mr. Holway, Daddy. I wanted you to meet him."

Her tone was quite serious, but there was an odd expression in her eye. Mr. Holway, blond, immaculate and blase, bowed. Then he, too, started.

"Eh!" he exclaimed. "Why, by Jove!"

Captain Dan nodded. "Yes," he observed, quietly. "Well, I'm much obliged to you, Gertie, but Mr. Holway and I have met before."

Gertrude's surprise, real or assumed, was great.

"Have you?" she cried. "Why, how odd! When?"

Mr. Holway, himself, answered. He seemed confused and his explanation was hurriedly given.

"Your father and I met one afternoon at--at the Palatine," he stammered. "I--I should have known. Tacks told me, but--but I had forgotten. I'm ashamed of my part in that, Mr. Dott. I really am. I owe you an apology. I hope you--I hope--"

Captain Dan nodded. "All right," he said briefly. "Don't say any more about it."

"But--but I hope you and Miss Dott won't--won't think--"

"We won't. I won't, anyway. I stopped thinking about it long ago. Well, Gertie, what have you been doin'? 'Most time to go home, is it?"

"Time to go home? Why, Daddy, we've just got here. We haven't been here an hour yet."

"Haven't we? I want to know! Seemed a good deal longer than that to me. All right, don't you worry about me. I can stand it, I guess. Where's your mother and--and Cousin Percy?"

"Mother is in the next room with Mrs. Lake and some more of the Chapter members. Cousin Percy is--Oh, here he comes now."

Hungerford appeared, strolling in their direction. He seemed surprised when he saw his relatives in company with Mr. Holway.

"Hello, Monty!" he said. "You here? How are you?"

The two young men shook hands. Gertrude smiled upon them both.

"Father and Mr. Holway were renewing acquaintanceship," she observed, cheerfully. "It seems that they have met before."

Cousin Percy's acknowledgment of this statement was a brief "Oh, indeed!" He and his friend exchanged glances.

"The--er--performance is about to begin, I believe," announced Mr. Hungerford. "Our hostess has--er--reluctantly consented to be led to the piano. Shall you and I adjourn to the next room, Cousin?"

Gertrude shook her head.

"Oh, thank you," she said, "but Mr. Holway has been telling me the most interesting stories about Scarford and the people in it, and I want to hear the rest. He is dreadfully sarcastic; I should not listen, I know, but I want to. Come, Mr. Holway."

She moved away, the flattered "Monty" in her wake. Mr. Hungerford gazed after them. He appeared not altogether pleased.

"Very sociable, chatty chap, that friend of yours, I should judge," observed Captain Dan drily.

"Um-hm!" grunted Cousin Percy. "Been chatting to you, has he?"

"No-o, not much this time. But you remember I've had the pleasure before."

Mr. Hungerford doubtless remembered; he looked as if he did. Then he, too, strolled away. The captain, left alone, indulged in a quiet chuckle.

Miss Canby's rendition on the piano, of what she was pleased to call "A sweet little thing of Tschaikovsky's--one of my favorites," was enthusiastically applauded, and she obliged with another, and still another. Then Mr. Abercrombie was prevailed upon to read one of his own outpourings of genius, a poem called "The Tigress," in which someone, presumably the author, described the torments involved in his adoration of a feminine person with "jetty brows and lambent eyes," whose kiss was like "a viper's sting" and who had, so to speak, raised the very dickens with his feelings. He read it with passionate fervor, and Captain Dan, listening, decided that the Tigress must be a most unpleasant person.

However, judging by the acclaim of the rest of the audience, she was a huge success, and the poet was coaxed into reading again, this time something which he had labeled "Soul Beams," and in which "love" rhymed with "dove" and "heart" with "dart" and "bliss" with "kiss" in truly orthodox fashion. Mr. Abercrombie's poetic gems were not appreciated by the mercenary and groveling minions who edited magazines, but here, amid his fellow Bohemians, they were more than appreciated, a fact which their creator announced gratified him more than he could express. And yet, he seemed to have little difficulty and less hesitation in expressing most things.

Daniel was not enthusiastic over the poems. He could not understand a great deal of them, but he understood quite enough. When B. Phelps Black winked at him from his seat at the other side of the room, he did not return the wink, although he knew perfectly well what it meant.

The poems were bad enough, according to his figuring, but when Miss Beatrice Dusante tripped into the circle to slip and twist and slide and gyrate in "one of her delightful Grecian dances," he found himself looking about for a convenient exit. Discovering none he remained where he was and blushed for the company.

The Bohemians, however, did not blush; neither, to his amazement, did Serena, who looked on and applauded with the rest. He found some comfort in the absence of his daughter, who was not among the seated guests, but, at last, even this comfort was dispelled. He caught a glimpse of Gertrude, still accompanied by the attentive Mr. Holway, standing in the back row. He tried to catch her eye and, by frowns and shakes of the head, to indicate his disapproval of the dance and her presence as a witness. He did not succeed in attracting her attention, but when, a moment later, she and her escort moved off, he was somewhat relieved. Gertrude looked as if she did not care for Miss Dusante's dancing any more than he did. Mr. Hungerford, also, did not appear interested. He was looking at Miss Dott and "Monty," and there was a frown on his face.

Upon their return, after they were together in the library at home, Daniel's shocked indignation burst forth.

"Well!" he declared, "that's enough. That's the limit, that is! What kind of a gang IS that, anyway?"

His wife regarded him with astonishment. Gertrude, after one glance at his face, turned and walked to the other side of the room, where she busied herself with a book on the table. Cousin Percy smiled broadly.

"Gang!" repeated Serena. "Gang! Why, what are you talking about, Daniel?"

"I'm talkin' about that gang at that Canby woman's place to-night. I never saw such a brazen gang anywhere. Haven't they got ANY respectability? How'd they come to let that dancin' thing in there? Couldn't they see her before she got in? Couldn't they stop her? Why--"

Serena interrupted. "Stop her!" she repeated. "How could they stop her? She was an invited guest."

"Who invited her? That's what I want to know. Who invited her?"

"Miss Canby, I suppose. She is a friend of hers."

"A friend! A FRIEND!"

"Yes. Now, Daniel, don't be silly. I know what you mean, and I must say I sympathize with you just a little. Annette explained to me afterwards though, so I suppose it is all right. Annette says that this Miss Dusante's dancing is all the rage now. She has made a study of the ancient Grecian dances and she does them everywhere. She is paid high prices for it, too."

"I don't doubt it. I should think she'd want to be. Did you see the way she was dressed? I never--"

"Hush, Daniel! That was the old Greek costume. Miss Canby told me all about it; the old Greeks used to dress like that."

"They did! Then it didn't take 'em long. Brazen thing! Why!" with a sudden turn upon his daughter, "Gertie--Gertie Dott, stop fussin' with that book and listen to me. You were there; I saw you lookin' on. YOU didn't like that Greek dancin', did you?"

Gertrude hesitated. Her cheeks were red and, for a moment, she seemed to find it difficult to speak. Then, after a quick look at her mother, she answered, calmly:

"Like it! Why not, Daddy? It is all the rage, just as Mother says, and it is certainly graceful. I rather think I should like to learn it myself. I understand Miss Dusante gives lessons."

Daniel's mouth opened and remained open. Cousin Percy stared at the speaker. Even Serena, defender of the dances of the ancient Greeks, looked shocked.

"Why, Gertie!" she cried. "Gertie! You! the idea!"

"Why not, Mother?"

"Why not! I should think you would know why not. I never heard you speak like that before."

"I never saw any dances like those before. I have heard about them, of course, but I never saw them. We never did--you or father or any of us--a great many things that we are doing now. We are learning all the time; that's what you told me, Mother. I never went to a Bohemian 'At Home' before."

Serena's eyes snapped. "Well, you'll never go to another one," she declared, "if it's going to have this effect on you."

The young lady smiled. "Why, of course I shall," she cried. "I want to learn, just as you do, Mother. And I mean to. Good-night!"

She left the room and they heard her ascending the stairs. Daniel and Serena looked at each other. Cousin Percy looked at them both.

Captain and Mrs. Dott had a long talk before retiring. The captain derived some satisfaction from the talk; it seemed to him that their daughter's declaration of independence had startled Serena somewhat. She even went so far as to admit that, in spite of Mrs. Black's explanations and gracious commendations, she, herself, had not been impressed by Miss Canby's guests. She and Gertrude would have an interview in the morning, she declared.

Captain Dan waited hopefully for the result of that interview. The hope was crushed when Serena reported to him.

"It is all right, Daniel," said Mrs. Dott. "I guess Gertie didn't really mean what she said about taking lessons of the Dusante woman. She thought the dances graceful, and they were, of course. But Gertie is older now--yes, she is older, and she expects to have her own way more than she has had it. She said a lot of things to me, things that she hasn't said before. It seems that when she first came home she was inclined to think I had exaggerated when I wrote her about the lovely people here in Scarford, and the Chapter, and the brilliant women in it. Now, she sees I was right. She has helped me a good deal already with my Chapter work, and she means to do more. She is going to join the Chapter herself. She--why, what's the matter?"

Daniel had made a choking noise in his throat; he appeared to be strangling.

"Noth--nothin'," he gasped. "Nothin' much. I'm all right. But--but you said-- why, how can Gertie join the Chapter? She ain't goin' to stay here. She's goin' back to college soon as her vacation's over."

Serena shook her head. There was just a shade of doubt, almost of trouble, in her voice as she answered.

"No-o," she said, "no, Daniel, she isn't. She isn't going back any more. She thinks it isn't necessary."

"Not necessary! Why, how you talk, Serena! Not necessary to finish out her last term! What do you mean? One of the things that troubled me most, back there in Trumet before we was rich, was that I might not afford for her to finish out at that college, and now, when I can, she ain't goin'. I say she is. I say she's got to."

"I don't believe that will make any difference, Daniel. She seems to have made up her mind. I'm kind of sorry, I must say, but she is obstinate. She says it is so much more interesting here that she is going to stay. You can talk to her, if you want to, but I don't think it will do any good."

Serena was right; although Captain Dan did talk to his daughter his arguments and persuasions were quite useless.

"No, Daddy," said Gertrude, "I am going to stay right here. I told you that if I were needed I should come home. I have come home and I am needed. I shall not go back. It is only the last half term, anyway."

"Yes, but then's when the girls have all their best times, all the dances and--and entertainments and society times. You said so. Do you want to miss all those?"

Gertrude smiled. "Oh," she observed, "I expect to have a great many 'society times,' as you call them, right here in Scarford. There seems to be no lack of them, and Mother is decidedly in the swim. It's no use, Daddy; my mind is made up. Don't you worry, it is all right."

"Well--well, I--I must say--See here, are you really going to join that Chapter thing?"

"Yes."

"You are! After all you said--"

"Yes, no matter what I may have said."

"By--by time! I don't know what to do with you. I--I set a lot of store by you, Gertie. I kind of banked on you. And now--"

Gertrude's expression changed. She patted his cheek.

"Keep on banking on me, Daddy dear," she whispered, "perhaps I'm not altogether hopeless, even yet."

But her father, for once, refused to believe her.

"I don't like it," he declared. "And other folks don't like it, either. Why, Barney Black got after me only the other day about you. He wanted to know why you--you, an engaged girl--was cruisin' around so much with this Cousin Percy of ours. He thought 'twas queer. I said--"

Gertrude rose to her feet. Her arm was snatched from the captain's shoulder so quickly that he jumped.

"Daddy!" she cried, her cheeks blazing, "do you mean to say that you have been discussing me with--with Mr. Black?"

"I didn't start it, he did. He said--"

"I don't care what he said. Oh, the impertinence of it! And you listened! listened and believed--"

"I didn't say I believed it."

"You did believe it, though. I can see you did. I shan't try to comfort you any more. You deserve all that is coming to you. And," with a deliberate nod, "it is coming."

"Comin'! It's HERE! Gertie, there's another thing: What about John? What do you think John would say if he knew you weren't goin' back to college?"

Gertrude looked at him. Her lips twitched.

"Oh," she said, mischievously, "as to that--well, Daddy, you see, he DOESN'T know it."

That afternoon Daniel wrote a letter. He said nothing to anyone, not even Serena, about the letter, but wrote it in the solitude of the library and posted it with his own hands. Just before sealing the envelope he added this postscript: "Whether you come or not, don't tell a soul that I wrote you this. And, if you do come, just let them think it was all on your own hook. THIS IS IMPORTANT."

On Saturday evening there was to be a meeting of the Chapter, and on Tuesday Serena returned from committee with the joyful news that Gertrude was to be admitted to membership at that meeting. The young lady expressed herself as delighted. Cousin Percy extended congratulations. Captain Dan said nothing. Later, he visited Azuba in the kitchen, and there he received another shock.

Azuba was not, as usual, busy with her cooking or scrubbing. She was seated in a chair by the window, reading a paper. She looked up as he entered, but immediately resumed her reading. The captain waited for her to speak. As a general thing he did not have to wait.

"Hello, Zuba," he hailed.

Azuba turned a page of the paper. She did not answer.

"Hello!" he hailed again. "What's the matter, Zuba? Gone into a trance, have you?"

"Hey?" Azuba did look up then, but at once looked down again. "Hey?" she repeated. "No, I ain't in no trance. I'm readin', that's all."

"I should think that was enough, if it fixes you so you can't speak to anybody. Must be mighty interestin' readin'."

"Hey? Interestin'? I guess 'tis interestin'! It's more'n that, it's upliftin', too. I'm just beginnin' to realize what I am."

"That so? Well, what are you?"

"I'm a woman, that's what I am."

She made the declaration with the air of one imparting news of a startling discovery. Daniel laughed.

"Is that so!" he exclaimed. "Well, well! I want to know! I always suspected it, Zuba, but I'm glad you told me, just the same. Does it say so in that paper?"

Azuba rose from her chair. She did not laugh; she was intensely serious.

"It says a lot of things," she announced, "a lot of things I never thought of afore. I don't mean that exactly. I've thought of 'em, but I never knew how to make anything out of my thoughts. I just kept thinkin' and let it go at that. Now, I'm beginnin' to realize. I'm a woman, I am, a free woman. That paper is for free women. Have you read it, Cap'n Daniel?"

Captain Dan took the paper which she extended to him at arm's length. He recognized it immediately. It was "The Woman's Voice," official organ of the National Guild of Ladies of Honor. Serena was a subscriber.

He glanced at the paper and tossed it on the table.

"Yes," he said shortly, "I've read some of it."

Azuba seized the discarded journal as if it were a precious treasure, a thing to be treated tenderly and with reverence.

"Some of it!" she repeated. "Humph! I'd read all of it, if I was you. 'Twould do the men good if they was made to read every number ten times over. It's a wonderful paper. It's opened MY eyes, I can tell you that."

It had, apparently, opened her mouth as well, although to do that required no great urging at any time. She went on to preach the glories of the "Voice," and concluded by reading an editorial which, like Mrs. Lake's addresses at Chapter meetings, contained a great many words and, to the captain's mind, little understanding.

He listened, fidgeting impatiently, to perhaps two-thirds of the editorial, and then he interrupted.

"Hold on! Heave to!" he ordered. "For the land sakes, Zuba, what's set you goin' like this? Are YOU goin' to--to--"

"To what? Am I goin' to what?"

"Are you goin' to 'advance' or whatever you call it? What ails all you women, anyway?"

"What ails us? Hain't I been readin' you what ails us?"

"You've been readin' a whole lot, but I've heard it all before. You want to be 'free'! Confound it, you ARE free, ain't you? You want to take your place in the world! Why, you've had the front place ever since Eve got Adam to eat the apple. She was skipper of that craft, wasn't she! And us men--most of us, anyhow--have been fo'mast hands ever since. What is it you want? Want to vote? Go ahead and vote. I'M willin'."

But Azuba laughed scornfully.

"Vote!" she repeated. "I don't care whether I vote or not."

"Then what do you want?"

"We want--" Azuba hesitated, "we want--what this paper says we want. And," with determination, "we're goin' to have it."

"All right, have it, then! Meantime, let's have dinner. It's pretty nigh half-past five, and the table ain't set. And," with a sniff, "there's somethin' burnin' somewheres, I smell it."

This statement had an effect. Azuba dropped the precious paper and sprang to open the oven door.

"Well!" she declared, "it's all right. 'Twas that cranberry pie, and 'twas only beginnin' to scorch. It's all right."

"Glad to hear it. Now, say, Zuba, you take my advice; you're a practical, sensible woman, I always said so. Don't you get to be silly, at your age."

It was an impolitic remark. Azuba bristled.

"At my age!" she repeated. "Humph! I ain't so much older than some folks in this kitchen, nor in the rest of the house, either. What do you mean by silly?"

"I mean--I mean--well, I mean don't you get to joinin' lodges and readin' papers and racin' out every night in the week to somethin' or other. It ain't worth while. It's silly--just silly."

"Oh, is it! Well, other women do it. Your wife's been doin' it ever since we got here. And now Gertie's startin' in. You always made your brags that she was about as sensible, smart a girl as ever drawed breath. I ain't got money; nobody's left ME a cart load of dollars and a swell front house. But I've got rights and feelin's. I'm a woman, a free woman, and if it ain't silly for Mrs. Dott and Gertie to want to advance and--and so on, I cal'late 'tain't silly for me either. Perhaps you'd like to have me tell Serena that you said she was silly. Shall I?"

Daniel did not answer, but his look was answer sufficient. Azuba smiled triumphantly.

"Practical," she sneered. "No, Cap'n Daniel, I ain't been practical so far, but I'm goin' to be. I'm a-goin' to be. You watch me."

Her employer's guns were spiked. He marched out of the kitchen, slamming the door viciously. The library was tenanted by Cousin Percy, who was taking a nap on the lounge. Upstairs, Gertrude was helping her mother with a "report" of some kind. Hapgood, the butler, was in the hall, and he bowed respectfully.

"Yes, sir," he said. "Did you wish anything, sir?"

"No," snarled Captain Dan, and went out for a walk. This was the last straw. If Azuba was going crazy the situation was hopeless indeed. And he had received no reply to his letter.

Hapgood, left alone in the hall, grinned, strolled into the library and, regardless of Mr. Hungerford's presence, filled his pockets with cigars from his employer's box. Downstairs, in the kitchen, Azuba was busy getting dinner. At intervals she burst out laughing.

That evening Mr. "Monty" Holway called.

CHAPTER X

Mr. Holway's call was, ostensibly, a call upon the Dott family in general, but it was to Gertrude that he addressed most of his conversation. The young lady was very affable and gracious. She expressed herself as glad to see him, and she appeared to be. "Monty" was a voluble person, and he talked a great deal, although a critic might possibly have considered his remarks more remarkable for quantity than quality. In the presence of Captain Dan he appeared a trifle ill at ease, a fact which the captain attributed to circumstances attending their first meeting. Serena seemed somewhat surprised at the call. She regarded her daughter and Mr. Holway with an odd expression, and, so it seemed to her husband, was apparently dissatisfied or disturbed. At all events she said little and, when addressed, answered absent-mindedly.

Mr. Hungerford was the most surprised of all. He had been out, and when, returning, he found his friend in the drawing-room, his greeting was not too cordial. Mr. Holway also seemed embarrassed, and a bit on his guard.

"Hello, Tacks!" he said, rising and extending his hand.

Cousin Percy did not see the hand, or, if he saw it, did not offer his own.

"Hello," he said, gruffly. Then, after a quick glance at the quartette in the drawing-room, he pulled forward a chair and, without waiting for an invitation, seated himself.

"How goes it?" inquired Monty.

"All right enough. Oh--er--Gertrude, I've found out about that recital affair. It is next Wednesday afternoon. I have arranged for us to go. Rather difficult business to manage, at such a late date, but I managed to pull it off."

Gertrude smilingly declared that she was much obliged. "I don't know, of course," she added, "what Mother's plans for that day may be, but if she is not busy

I'm sure we shall be pleased to go. Thank you for thinking of us."

Mr. Hungerford hesitated. "Well," he said, "to tell you the truth, I had supposed that Mrs. Dott might be rather busy. It is your committee meeting afternoon, isn't it, Mrs. Dott? and so I arranged for only two. Awfully stupid of me, I know."

"Oh, that will be all right. You and Mother can go, then. I don't mind at all. Really, I don't. And Mother is so fond of music. It is all right, Mother," turning to Serena, who had been about to speak, "you can go just as well as not. You must. Never mind the committee meeting; I'll act as your substitute there."

Cousin Percy was not overcome with joy; at least, he managed to restrain his ecstasy. Mr. Holway volunteered a word.

"Is it the Wainwright Recital you are talking about?" he inquired, eagerly. "That's all right. I can get cards for that. It's a cinch. I'll see that you go, Miss Dott. By George! I'll--I'll go myself. Yes, I will, really. We'll all go."

This prompt suggestion should have cleared the air. Somehow it did not. Mr. Hungerford merely grunted. Gertrude shook her head.

"No," she said, "I think, perhaps, I had better not go, after all. But it is ever so nice of you to offer, Mr. Holway. You and Cousin Percy can take Father and Mother. That will be splendid."

"Don't bother about me," put in Daniel, hastily. Recitals were almost as distasteful as Chapter meetings or "At Homes" to his mind.

"It won't be any bother, I'm sure," declared Gertrude. "Will it, Cousin Percy? Will it, Mr. Holway?"

Both the young gentlemen murmured their pleasure at the prospect of acting as escorts to the elder members of the Dott family. Serena said she would "see about it," she couldn't say for certain whether or not she would be able to attend the recital. Captain Dan said nothing.

The conversation dragged somewhat after this. "Monty" and Mr. Hungerford addressed the greater portion of their remarks to Gertrude, only occasionally favoring Serena and Daniel with a word or question. To each other they were very uncommunicative. At last, however, after Mr. Holway had given a very full account of a "dinner dance" which he had recently attended, "a very exclusive affair, only the best people, you know," Percy, who had been listening impatiently, turned toward him and drawled:

"I remember that dance. Beastly tiresome, I judged it would be, so I sent regrets. I heard you enjoyed yourself, old chap. Said I imagined so, considering your company. By the way, that must be getting quite serious, that affair of yours. When may we expect the announcement?"

Holway colored. His usual facility of speech seemed to have deserted him.

"Announcement!" he stammered. "Announcement! What--what--"

His friend laughed.

"Oh, it's all right, old man," he observed. "Don't get excited. She's a charming girl. No one blames you."

"Monty" continued to sputter. Gertrude was all excitement.

"Oh, how interesting!" she said. "Do tell us about her, Mr. Holway. Do I know her?"

"Know her!" Mr. Holway's indignation was intense. "I--I don't know her myself. He's just guying, Miss Dott. He--he thinks because he--he is so confoundedly fascinating, and has so many--so many--

"Oh, that reminds me, Tacks," turning upon the smiling Hungerford, "I saw a friend of yours yesterday. She looked quite desolate, quite broken-hearted, my word she did. You were a little cruel there, weren't you, my boy? Just a bit cruel. Everyone expected--"

He did not finish the sentence, but his expression indicated that much was expected. It was Cousin Percy's turn to color.

"Don't be an idiot, Monty," he snapped. "That is, more of an idiot than you can help. Don't mind him, Gertrude; he has an amazing idea of repartee, that's all."

Serena volunteered a remark concerning the weather just then. She observed that it might be raining, it had looked that way before dinner. Mr. Holway possibly considered that a hint was involved; at any rate, he rose and announced that he must be going. Gertrude begged him not to hurry, they had all enjoyed his call so much, she said. Cousin Percy suddenly declared that he would accompany his friend on his way, a walk would do him good. Monty expressed no enthusiasm at the prospect of company, but the pair left the house together.

After they had gone, Daniel turned to his wife.

"Humph!" he observed, "what sort of talk do you call that? I thought those two were chums; and yet I didn't know but they was goin' to fight one spell. It's a good thing you hove in that about the rain when you did, Serena."

Serena was grave. "Gertie," she inquired, "did you ask that young man to call here?"

Gertrude was the picture of surprised innocence.

"Ask him to call?" she repeated. "Mr. Holway, do you mean? I don't know. I think not. Why?"

"WHY?" Captain Dan almost shouted it. His wife motioned him to be quiet.

"Hush, Daniel," she said. "You know why, Gertie, as well as I do. You are engaged to be married."

Gertrude smiled. "Of course I am," she answered. "What of it?"

"What OF IT?"

"Hush, Daniel, hush! Engaged girls, Gertie, are not supposed to have young men calling upon them."

"Oh," with a shrug. "I don't know that he was calling on me. He did not ask for me when he came. And you and Daddy were here all the time. Besides, merely because I am engaged isn't any reason why I should retire from the world altogether, is it? Mrs. Lake says--"

Daniel struck the table with his fist.

"Mrs. Lake!" he shouted. "Mrs. Lake don't live with her husband. She's a grass widow, that's what she is."

"She is one of Mother's dearest friends, and any friend of Mother's should be good enough for me."

The captain choked. "You--you talk to her, Serena," he stammered; "I can't."

Serena looked more troubled than ever.

"Gertie," she faltered, "if Mrs. Lake has been advising you--to--to--"

"She hasn't advised me at all. Now, Mother, what IS the use of all this? If I have learned anything from you and your Chapter friends it is to be broad-minded and independent. If Mrs. Lake is not a living example of independence, who is?"

Serena could not seem to find an answer at the moment. Her husband tried again.

"Gertie Dott," he declared, "I--I don't know what to make of you, all at once. And John Doane wouldn't either. If John knew--"

Gertrude interrupted. "That's enough, Daddy," she said, firmly. "I am quite willing John shall know; when I am ready I shall tell him. He is a dear, good fellow, in his way, but--"

She hesitated. Her parents asked a question in concert.

"But what?" they demanded.

"Why--why, nothing of importance. But I am learning here in Scarford. My opportunity has come, just as yours did, Mother. I am a free woman and I shall not be a slave--a SLAVE to any man."

With which remark, a quotation from a paper read at the most recent Chapter meeting, she walked from the room. Her astonished parents looked at each other. Daniel was the first to speak.

"My soul and body!" he gasped. "What--what--Serena, did you hear what she said? That about John? That he was a good fellow--in his way? In his WAY! My soul and body!"

Serena shook her head.

"I--I don't believe she meant it, Daniel," she said. "I'm sure she didn't. She's just a little carried away, that's all. All this society--this altered social position of ours--has turned her head the least bit. She didn't mean it. I'll have another talk with her pretty soon."

"I should say you'd better. Serena, do you know what I've done? Done on my own hook, I mean. I've written--"

He paused. The disclosure which, on the impulse of the moment, he had been about to make was, for him, a serious one. He had written the letter "on his own hook," without telling his wife of his action. What would she say if he told her now, so long afterward?

"You've done? What have you done?" asked Serena sharply.

The captain still hesitated. Before his mind was made up the front door opened and Cousin Percy made his appearance. He entered the hall quickly, and to Mr. Hapgood--who hastened from somewhere or other to take his coat and hat--he said nothing, except to snarl a comment on the butler's slowness. He did not speak to the Dotts either, but tramped savagely up the stairs. His face, as seen by the electric light, was flushed and frowning.

Serena turned to her husband.

"How cross he looked," she said, wonderingly. "I never saw him so before.

What do you suppose has happened?"

Speculation concerning Cousin Percy's evident perturbation caused her to forget the disclosure Captain Dan had been about to make. By the time she remembered to ask about it the captain had decided not to tell. He fabricated some excuse or other, and the excuse was accepted, to his great relief.

None of the Dott household attended the Wainwright recital. Mr. Holway called on Wednesday, just after luncheon, to say that he had obtained the necessary cards, but his kindness went for nought. He stayed, so it seemed to Daniel, a good deal longer than was necessary, and Mr. Hungerford, who remained in the room every moment of the time, evidently thought so, too. So did Serena. Gertrude, however, was very cordial, and again begged the visitor not to hurry.

Saturday evening was that of the Chapter meeting, the meeting at which Gertrude was to be made a member. That forenoon Azuba electrified her mistress by expressing an ardent desire to become a member also. Her wish was not received with enthusiasm.

"Why, what do you want to do that for, Azuba?" asked Serena in amazement.

"Why shouldn't I want to? You're a member, ain't you? Gertie's goin' to be a member to-night, ain't she?"

"Yes. But--but--"

"Well, but what?"

"I didn't know you were interested in such things. You never were when we lived in Trumet."

Azuba dismissed the past with a scornful sniff and a wave of the hand.

"Trumet!" she repeated. "Trumet ain't nothin'. Nobody's anything in Trumet. We're in Scarford now, and Scarford's a progressive, up-to-date place. We've all changed since we've been here, and I'm changin' much as anybody. I've been hearin' your papers, when you read 'em to Gertie and the cap'n, and I've been readin' 'The Voice,' too. Yes ma'am, I've read it and I've found out what a back number I've been. But, I ain't goin' to be so no more. I'm goin' to be as up-to-date as the next one, even if I do have to wash dishes for a livin'. Serena--Mrs. Dott, I mean--I'd like first rate to join that Chapter of yours. You put my name in to-night and maybe it can be voted on next meetin'."

"But--but, Azuba, are you sure you know what it means? Do you think your husband would want you to--"

"My husband! What's he got to do with it? If we free women have got to be slaves to our husbands it's a pretty state of things, I must say. You don't ask your husband every time you go to meetin' whether he likes it or not. No, ma'am, you don't! You're above that, I cal'late. And I shan't ask Labe neither--even if he was where I could ask him, which he ain't. Husbands! Don't talk to me about husbands! THEY don't count."

Serena said that she would see what could be done and hurried away to discuss the new development with the family.

"Of course she can't join," she declared. "It is ridiculous. The idea! I supposed she had more sense."

Daniel chuckled. "So did I," he observed, "until she got shoutin' independence to me the other day. But it looked then as if she'd got it bad. All right, Serena, if Zuba Jane Ginn is goin' to make speeches at your Chapter meetin's, I'll go any time. You won't have to ask me but once."

He laughed aloud. His wife was vexed.

"Of course you think it's a great joke," she said. "Anything that makes trouble for me is a joke to you. She can't join. What do you suppose Annette and Mrs. Lake and the rest would say if I proposed my servant girl as a member? Do stop being silly, if you can. What are you grinning at now?"

Captain Dan, repressing his grin with difficulty, explained that he was thinking of what they would say. Serena, giving him up in disgust, turned to her daughter.

"Gertie," she begged, "why don't you say something? Azuba can't join that Chapter and you know it."

Gertrude shook her head.

"I suppose, she can't," she replied. "And yet, I'm afraid, Mother, that you will find that fact rather hard to explain to her. Azuba doesn't consider herself a servant, in the ordinary sense, at all. She feels, I think, that she is a friend of the family. And she has a right, of course, to improve and advance in every way. I am very much pleased to know she is so ambitious."

"Ambitious! Azuba Ginn! What does she know about progress or advancement? Who put such ridiculous ideas in her head?"

"Perhaps I did. She and I have had some long talks on the subject. She asked questions and it was duty--and my privilege--to answer them. I am very hopeful of Azuba. She is my first convert. I shall help her all I can."

"Help her! Help her to what? To be too high and mighty for her place? Help her to be dissatisfied with her station in life?"

"Yes; why not? None of us should be satisfied, short of the very highest. Why, Mother, if you had been satisfied we might all be stagnating in Trumet."

Serena abandoned the argument. She refused to mention Azuba's desire for advancement again. Several times during the day Captain Dan saw her regarding her daughter with the same odd, doubtful look that she had worn when Mr. Holway made his first call.

After dinner that evening Gertrude and Serena hastened upstairs to dress for the Chapter meeting. Mr. Hungerford, after expressing his regret that the gathering was not to be an "open" one and he, therefore, would not be permitted to see Miss Dott become one of the elect, went out. When he first became a member of the household it was his custom, on occasions of this kind, to remain in the library as "company" for Captain Dan. Now, however, he seldom did this. The captain did not mind; he preferred his own society to that of Cousin Percy.

Just as the ladies descended the stairs the doorbell rang. Hapgood answered the ring, and the voice which replied to his polite query concerning the caller's name was a familiar one.

"Why!" exclaimed Serena, "it is--isn't that--"

"It's John!" cried Gertrude. "Why, JOHN!"

Mr. Doane pushed past the butler and entered the hall. His glance took in the group at the foot of the stairs, but it lingered upon only one member of it.

"Gertie!" he said, and stepped forward. Captain and Mrs. Dott looked the other way; Hapgood gave his attention to the closing of the door.

A moment later the young man was ready to shake hands with the less important inhabitants of the mansion. He did so heartily.

"My!" he exclaimed, "but I'm glad to see you all. It seems a hundred years since I did see you. How are you?"

Serena answered. Captain Dan, his first surprise over, seemed nervous.

"We're real well," declared Serena. "And it seems awfully good to have you here. Gertrude and I--"

Gertrude interrupted.

"But, John," she said, "how did you happen to come so unexpectedly? I didn't know--you didn't write me a word about it."

"I didn't know it, myself. That is, I wasn't sure of it. You know our junior partner, Mr. Griffin, has been very ill--I wrote you that. He is very ill even yet, but he is a little better, and so I grabbed the opportunity. I should have come before, just as soon as--"

He paused. Daniel, in the background, was grimacing and shaking his head.

"As soon as what, John?" asked Gertrude.

"As soon as--as soon as I could. You're glad I came, aren't you; even if it was rather sudden?"

"Of course I am. You know it."

Her tone was hearty enough, and yet Mr. Doane seemed to find something lacking in it. Serena, too, looked quickly at her daughter.

"Of course she's glad," she declared. "So are we all. But what are we thinking of? Take off your things. Where's your trunk? Have the man bring it right in."

"There isn't any trunk. There's a bag outside there, that's all. My visit is likely to be a very short one. If I should have a wire that Mr. Griffin was worse it might be shorter still. I should have to go at once. But we won't worry about that. Dinner? No, thank you, I have dined."

Captain Dan ushered the newcomer into the drawing-room. John exclaimed at the grandeur of the apartment.

"Whew!" he whistled. "You're fine, aren't you? Gertie wrote me how grand you were and I have been anxious to see the new house. Gertie--why, Gertie! what is it?"

Gertrude was standing in the doorway. She looked perplexed and troubled. John noticed, for the first time, that she was wearing her coat and hat.

"Were you going out?" he asked.

Gertrude hesitated. Serena answered for her.

"Gertie and I were going out," she said. "It is Chapter night and she was going to be made a member. But you won't go now, of course, Gertie. I'll go--John will excuse me, I know--and you can join at the next meeting. It will be all right, I think. It will have to be, of course."

But Gertrude still hesitated. Her father was surprised.

"Why, Gertie!" he cried. "What are you standin' there for? 'Tain't likely you'll go to that meetin' now that John's come all the way from Boston to see you. Tell him you ain't goin'."

The young lady was plainly much disturbed. She looked at Mr. Doane and it was evident that she wanted to say something very much indeed. What she did say, however, was a surprise to everyone.

"I--I ought to go, John," she faltered. "It is a very important meeting. I can't tell you--now--how important it is."

John's disappointment showed in his look, but his answer was prompt.

"Then go, by all means," he said. "I'll go with you, if I won't be in the way."

But this self-sacrificing proposal was dubiously received by both the ladies. Serena shook her head.

"I'm afraid you couldn't do that, John," she said.

"It isn't an open meeting, and men are not admitted. But Gertie doesn't need to go."

"Yes, I do, Mother."

"No, you don't. I'll explain to Mrs. Lake and the rest. Of course you won't go and leave John here alone."

"Daddy will be with him and I shall hurry home as soon as I can. I must go, John; I really must. I will explain why later. If I had only known that you were coming! If you had only written me! WHY did you come without writing?"

Captain Dan, fearful of the answer, and indignant at his daughter's conduct, burst into protest.

"You ought to be glad he's come, anyhow," he declared. "I cal'late he thought--I don't care, Serena, I've said 'cal'late' all my life, and I can't help forgettin' once in a while--I suppose John thought he'd surprise you, Gertie. And now you're goin' to clear out and leave him, just on account of that--that Chapter of yours. You never used to be crazy about Chapters. You used to poke fun at 'em. You did and you know it. But since you've got here to Scarford--I can't help it, Serena; I'm mad clean through. Can't YOU tell that girl to stay to home where she belongs?"

"Gertie," began Serena, again; but her daughter would not listen.

"Don't, Mother!" she cried, "you are wasting time. We shall be late, as it is. John knows that my going is necessary, or I should not do it. He trusts me to that extent, I hope."

"Of course," said Mr. Doane heartily. "Run along and don't say any more about it. Come back as soon as you can, that's all. Shan't I come after you? I can wait outside until the thing is over."

"No; I don't intend to wait until it is over. Mother and I can take a cab. Come, Mother."

Serena reluctantly led the way to the hall. Hapgood opened the door.

"One moment, Mother," said Gertrude. She left Serena on the step and hurried back to the drawing-room. Captain Dan and John were standing there in silence.

"Daddy," said the young lady, "I think I left my pocketbook upstairs in my room. Will you get it for me?"

The captain ran to the stairs. Gertrude stepped quickly over to her lover.

"John," she whispered, "you will forgive me, won't you, dear? I MUST go. It will spoil everything if I don't. You see--why, Daddy! you haven't found that pocketbook so soon!"

Daniel had reappeared in the doorway.

"I sent Hapgood for it," he announced. "It's a good thing to make him work once in a while. What's the use of my runnin' errands when I pay him wages to run 'em for me? He'll be down in a minute."

Gertrude did not seem pleased. "Oh!" she exclaimed. "Well, never mind. Why! here is the pocketbook in my bag, after all. Good-by, John. I will hurry back. You and Daddy will have a lot to talk about, I know. Good-by."

The door closed behind her. Captain Dan stepped to the foot of the stairs.

"Found it yet?" he shouted.

Hapgood answered from above.

"No, sir, not yet."

"Then keep on lookin' till you do. It's a good excuse to keep him out of the way," he explained, turning to Mr. Doane. "He makes me nervous, hangin' around and lookin' at me. I never was brought up to a butler and I can't get used to this one. Come on into the sittin'-room--library, I mean. The furniture ain't so everlastin' straight up and down there and there's somethin' to smoke--or there ought to be, if Cousin Percy ain't smoked it first. Come on, John."

In the library, with lighted cigars and in comfortable easy chairs, the two men looked at each other.

"Well, John," began the captain, "you--you come, didn't you?"

"Yes, of course. I should have come as soon as I got your letter, but I couldn't get away. I was going to tell you that."

"Yes," drily, "I know you was. If I hadn't cut across your bows, you would. Whew! if you had I guess likely there'd have been somethin' doin'. If Gertie or Serena knew I wrote you that letter I'd stand to lose what hair I've got left. Didn't I write you not to mention that letter to a livin' soul?"

"You did. But I couldn't understand why. What is all this secrecy, anyhow? And what is troubling you about Gertie?"

"Well, now, I don't know as there's anything."

"Humph! I judged there was a little of everything. What is the matter? Out with it.

"Well--we-ell--you see--you see--"

"I don't see anything, Captain Dott."

"You saw how she was set on goin' to that Chapter meetin', didn't you? You saw that?"

"Yes, but what of it?"

"What of it? What OF it? Did she ever use to want to go to such things? Down in Trumet did she ever want to go? I bet she didn't! But now she does. And she's goin' to join the thing--join it, herself! As if one loon--I mean as if one Chapter member in the family wasn't enough. I thought when Gertie come home she'd probably keep her ma from goin' off the course altogether. I thought, with her level head, she'd swing us back into the channel again. But she didn't--she didn't. John, Gertie's got the Chapter disease worse than her ma ever had it, I do believe. You've got to talk to her, John, that's what you've got to do--talk to her."

John laughed. He did not take the situation very seriously. If Gertrude wished to become interested in the Chapter, he was willing she should. She probably had a good reason for it. Her insisting upon attending a meeting on the very evening of his arrival was odd--it did not seem like her--but she doubtless had a good reason for that, too.

"Why don't you talk to her yourself, Captain?" he asked.

"Me! Me talk to her! I have, and what good has it done? She won't listen to me any more. I don't mean she ain't kind to me and lovin' and all that--she wouldn't be Gertie if she wasn't that--but when it comes to Chapter business she's all on her ma's side."

"Why not talk to her mother, then?"

Daniel straightened in his chair. "To Serena!" he repeated. "Talk against Chapter to Serena! John, you don't know what you're sayin'. One time--just one--I did talk that way. I biled over and I damned that Chapter and the gang in it, cussed 'em in good plain United States. But I'll never do it again. Once was enough."

He was so very serious that his companion fore-bore to laugh.

"Why?" he asked.

"Why! John, you ain't married or you wouldn't ask that. I'm a peaceable body and I like peace in the house. More'n that, I hate to go 'round feelin' like a sneak thief. That one damn made me miserable for two days. I never swore to Serena afore and I never will again. She was all cut up over it and in a way she was right. No, swearin' aboard ship is one thing--I've had mates that couldn't navigate without it--but ashore in your own house, to the women folks you care for, it don't go. I can't talk to Serena about that Chapter--not even if I'm left alone ALL the time, same as I'm left to-night."

John nodded. He thought that, at last, he had reached the milk in the cocoanut. Captain Dan, with his love for home and his hatred of lodges and societies, had refused to be interested in his wife's pet hobby, and felt himself neglected and forsaken. He had brooded upon it, and this outburst and the letter he had written were the consequences.

"Oh, well," he said. "I shouldn't worry. The Chapter here is a large one and Mrs. Dott is interested in it. The interest will wear off when it gets to be an old story."

"Wear off! With Gertie goin' it harder than her mother ever thought of?"

"Oh, Gertie doesn't mean it."

"She DON'T! She don't! Perhaps you don't think she means it when she goes to every 'tea' and 'recital' and 'at home' and crazy dido from here to Beersheba and back. Is THAT goin' to wear off? Chasin' around with Cousin Percy and that Holway and land knows who?"

"What? Captain Dott, you're making mountains out of mole hills. Gertie isn't that kind."

"That's what I said. That's what I used to think. It's this Scarford that's doin' it. It's this Scarford and the society crowd we've got in with. Annette Black--Barney Phelps's wife--is in society, and so's the Lake woman and that Canby piano pounder and that Dusante--my Godfreys! you ought to have seen her, John! She was the brazen thing. Dancin' around! And all hands sittin' lookin' at her as if she was a Sunday School. Everybody! Serena and Gertie and that Holway man and all. And Gertie up and says she might like to dance that way. She! And Cousin Percy laughin' because she said it."

"Hold on! Wait a minute, Captain. I never saw you so excited. What about this Cousin Percy of yours? He's living here with you, I know that; but what sort of a chap is he? And Holway--who is Holway?"

Daniel went on to explain who Holway was. Also he spoke of Mr. Hungerford and his ways and his intimacy with the family, particularly Gertrude. For weeks the captain had been wanting to talk to someone about these things and, now that he had that opportunity, he made the most of it. He spoke of his own loneliness, and of Serena's infatuation for society, of Gertrude's coming and the great change in her, of the gay life in Scarford, and of his daughter's apparent love for it. He gave his opinion of Hungerford and of Holway, the latter's friend. When John asked questions which implied a belief that the situation was not really as bad as the narrator thought it, Captain Dan, growing warmer and more anxious to justify himself, proceeded to make his statements stronger. He quoted instances to prove their truth. Serena was crazy on the subjects of Chapter and Chapter politics and fashion and money and society, and Gertrude was getting to be even worse. It wasn't any use to talk to her. He had tried. He had told her she was engaged and ought to be more careful. He wasn't the only one who thought so. Barney Black had said the same thing. He quoted from Mr. Black's conversation.

John Doane listened, at first with the smile of the disbeliever, then with more and more uneasiness. He trusted Gertrude, he believed in her, she was not a flirt, but if these stories were true--if they were true--he could not understand. He asked more questions and the answers were as non-understandable. Altogether, Captain Dan, with the best intentions in the world, and with the happiness of his daughter and John uppermost in his mind, succeeded in laying a mine which might wreck that happiness altogether.

At last something--perhaps the expression on his visitor's face--caused him to feel that he might have said too much. He hastened to rectify the mistake.

"Of course you mustn't think Gertie ain't all right, far's you're concerned, John," he said. "She is--I--I'm dead sure she is. But, you see--you see--You do see, don't you, John?"

Mr. Doane did not answer. He seemed to be thinking hard.

"You see, John, don't you?" repeated Captain Dan.

"Yes, I suppose I do."

"And you know Gertie's all right--at heart, I mean? You mustn't be jealous, nor anything of that kind."

John laughed. "Don't talk nonsense," he said curtly.

"No, I won't. But--er--what are you thinkin' about?"

"Nothing. Humph! I can't understand--"

"Neither could I. That's why I wrote you. You see why I wrote you, don't you, John?"

"Yes--yes, I see why I wrote me; but--but I can't see why she didn't. She hasn't written me a word of all this."

And then the captain, in his anxiety to explain, made another indiscreet remark.

"Well," he observed, "I suppose likely she was afraid you might think that, now she had money--more money than she ever had before, I mean--and was in a different, a higher-toned crowd than she had ever been, that--that--well, that she was likin' that crowd better than the old one. She might have thought that, you know, mightn't she?"

Mr. Doane did not answer. Daniel had made a pretty thorough mess of it.

"Of course," went on the captain, "as far as Cousin Percy is concerned--"

John stirred uneasily. "Cousin Percy be hanged!" he snapped. "That's enough of this foolishness. Let's change the subject. How is Nate Bangs getting on with the store at home?"

The Metropolitan Store at Trumet was the one thoroughly satisfactory spot on the checkered map of Daniel Dott's existence at the present time. Nathaniel Bangs was making a success of that store. He reported each week and the reports showed increasing business and a profit, small as yet, but a profit nevertheless.

So the captain was only too glad to speak of the store and did so. John appeared to listen, but his answers and comments were absent-minded. He accepted a fresh cigar, at his host's invitation, but he permitted it to go out.

At half-past ten the doorbell rang. Daniel sprang to his feet.

"Here they are!" he declared. "Gertie come home early, just as she said she would. That's 'cause she wanted to see you, John. Hi!" shouting at Mr. Hapgood, who had long since given up the search for the missing pocketbook and had been dozing upstairs, "Hi! you needn't mind. Go aloft again! Go below! Go somewhere! We don't need you. I'll let 'em in, myself."

The butler, looking surprised, obeyed orders and went--somewhere. The captain flung open the door.

"Well!" he hailed. "Here you are! And pretty early for Chapter night, too. We're waitin' for you, John and I. Shall I pay the cab man?"

Serena, the first to enter, answered.

"No," she said, "he is already paid."

"That so? Did you pay him, Serena? Thought that was my job usually. I--" Then, in a tone go entirely different that John Doane, in the drawing-room, noticed the change, he added, "Oh! oh! I, see."

"Come in," went on Serena. "Come right in, Cousin Percy."

She entered the drawing-room, followed by Gertrude and--Mr. Percy Hungerford. Captain Dan, remaining to close the door, came last.

"John," said Serena proudly, "we want you to meet our cousin, Mr. Hungerford. Percy, this is John."

John and Hungerford exchanged looks. The latter gentleman extended a gloved hand. "Charmed," he observed.

John expressed pleasure at the meeting. The pair shook hands.

"So--so Cousin Percy came home with you, did he?" inquired Daniel. "That was kind of unexpected, wasn't it?"

Mr. Hungerford himself answered.

"Why," he declared, "not altogether, on my part I hoped for the pleasure. It seemed rather rough for Miss Dott and her mother to come alone, and so I hung about until the affair was over."

"He had a carriage all ready for us," declared Serena. "It was so thoughtful of him."

"Not at all. Great pleasure, really."

Gertrude made the next remark.

"We did not need a carriage," she said. "Or, if we did, we could easily have gotten one. Cousin Percy need not have troubled."

"John offered to come for you," said Daniel. "So did I. We'd have both come, but you wouldn't have us. Wouldn't accept our invitation, would they, John? Gave us to understand they didn't like our company."

"Cousin Percy did not wait for an invitation," explained Serena. "He just came. He is so thoughtful."

Gertrude looked annoyed. She had been regarding Mr. Doane.

"Mother," she said sharply, "don't be silly. We did not ask for an escort and we didn't need one. The whole thing was quite unnecessary and unexpected. Come, Mother, do take off your things. Oh, I'm so glad to get home."

The ladies retired to remove their wraps. John made a move to go to their assistance, but Mr. Hungerford, attentive as usual, got ahead of him.

"Well, Daddy dear," said Gertrude, as they re-entered, "what have you and John been doing while we were away? I suppose you've had a long talk?"

Daniel colored. He looked at Mr. Doane, who, in spite of himself, colored also, and was tremendously annoyed because he did so.

"Yes," said the captain hastily. "Yes, we talked. We talked, didn't we, John?"

"We did," affirmed John.

"I'm sure you did. And what about?"

"Oh--oh, about everything. How did the Chapter doin's go off? You're a member now, I suppose, Gertie?"

"Yes," was the brief reply, "I am a member."

"Um-hm! Well, I hope you're satisfied--I mean I hope you'll like it. Didn't make a speech, did you? Ha! ha!"

Gertrude did not answer. Serena, to her husband's surprise, appeared vexed.

"But she did though, by Jove!" exclaimed Cousin Percy. "She did, and I'm told it created a great sensation. Miss Canby told me about it as I was waiting for you to come out, Gertrude. She said you gave them a brand-new idea. Congratulations,

Gertrude. Wish I might have heard it. Something about the privileges of the Chapter being extended to the hoi polloi, wasn't it?"

The new member of Scarford Chapter looked more annoyed than ever.

"I spoke of the Chapter's advantages being extended," she said, "that's all."

"And enough, too," cried her mother, impatiently. "Quite enough, I should think. If I had known you were going to do that, I should have stayed at home. It was that foolish Azuba who put the notion in your head. You'll be proposing her name next, I suppose. The idea!"

Daniel burst into a roar of laughter.

"What do you think of that, John?" he cried. "Zuby Jane makin' speeches! There's advancement for you, ain't it?"

John smiled, but rather faintly. He had scarcely taken his eyes from Cousin Percy's aristocratic presence. The latter gentleman turned to him.

"Well--er--Mr.--Mr. Doane," he observed carelessly, "how do you like Scarford, as far as you've seen it?"

John replied that he had seen very little of it.

"You will find it a bit different from--er--what is it? Oh, yes, Trumet. You'll find it a bit different from Trumet, I imagine."

"No doubt. I can see that already."

"But John doesn't come from Trumet," explained Serena; "that is, not now. He is in business in Boston."

Cousin Percy seemed surprised. He favored the visitor with another look. "Indeed!" he drawled. He did not add "He doesn't look it," in words, but his manner expressed just that.

Daniel caught his wife's eye. "Well, Serena," he observed, with a meaning wink, "I guess likely you're tired, ain't you? Time to go aloft and turn in, I should say."

Serena nodded. "Yes," she answered. "Gertrude, you and John will excuse us, won't you? John, Captain Dott and I will see you in the morning. Good-night! Good-night, Cousin Percy."

"Good-night!" said Mr. Hungerford.

"You'll excuse us, John, I'm sure," went on Serena. "Of course you and Gertie will want to talk, and," with a slight pause and a glance at Percy, "we will only be in the way. Come, Daniel."

Captain Dan paused in the doorway. "Ain't you tired, too, Cousin Percy?" he inquired.

It was a fairly broad hint, but Mr. Hungerford did not take it.

"Oh, no," he replied; "not at all. Good-night, Captain."

He seated himself on the sofa. Daniel, frowning, followed his wife upstairs.

The conversation which ensued was confined almost altogether to Hungerford and Gertrude. John Doane had little to say, and less opportunity to say it. Each remark made by the young lady was answered by Percy, and that gentleman talked almost incessantly. His remarks also were of a semi-confidential nature, dealing with happenings at various social affairs which Gertrude and he had attended, and hints at previous conversations and understandings between them. John began to feel himself an outsider. After a time he ceased trying to talk and relapsed into silence.

Gertrude noticed the silence and, seizing a moment when her entertaining cousin had paused, perhaps for breath, said, almost sharply:

"John, why don't you say something? You haven't spoken for five minutes."

John said very little, even in reply to this accusation.

"Haven't I?" he observed. "Well, what shall I say?"

"You might say something, considering that you and I haven't seen each other for so long."

Mr. Hungerford rose. "I hope I haven't interfered," he announced. "Didn't mean to intrude, I assure you. Beg pardon--er--Doane."

John did not answer. Gertrude also rose.

"Good-night, Cousin Percy," she said, with a gracious smile. "Thank you so much for the carriage and your escort."

"Quite welcome. Pleasure was mine. Goodnight, Gertrude. Oh, by the way, I believe you and I are to go over that paper of your mother's tomorrow. She asked my advice and said you would assist, I think. I shall look forward to that assistance. Good-night, Doane. Glad to have met you, I'm sure."

He strolled out. Upon reaching his room he discovered that his cigar case was empty. Hapgood not being on hand and, feeling the need of a bedtime smoke, he tiptoed down the stairs and through the back hall into the library. The room was dark, but sufficient light shone between the closed curtains of the drawing-room to enable him to locate Captain Dan's box. Silently and very slowly he refilled the case.

John Doane and Gertrude, alone at last, looked at each other. The former was very solemn. Gertrude, quite aware of the solemnity, but not aware of its principal cause--her father's impolitic disclosure of his apprehensions concerning herself-- was nervous and a bit impatient.

"Well, John," she asked, after a moment's wait, "aren't you going to say anything to me even now?"

John tried his best to smile. It was a poor attempt.

"Why, yes," he said slowly, "I came all the way from Boston to see you and talk to you, Gertie. There is no reason why I shouldn't say--whatever there is to say, I suppose."

Gertrude looked at him. The tone in which this speech was delivered, and the speech itself--the first part of it, especially--amazed and hurt her. Incidentally, her temper having been sorely tried already that evening by Mr. Hungerford, it made her angry.

"All the way from Boston," she repeated. "Well, I never knew you to complain in that way before. I'm sorry to have caused you so much trouble."

"It wasn't a trouble, Gertie. You know I would go around the world for you."

"Then why speak of coming all the way from Boston? Whose fault was it, pray? Did I ask you to come?"

And now, John, who had been fighting his own temper for some time, grew angry.

"You did not," he declared. "But I judge it was time I did."

"Indeed! Indeed! Why?"

"Well--well, for various reasons. Of course, had I known my coming would interfere with your--your precious Chapter affairs and--"

"John, I had to go to that meeting. If you had written you were coming I shouldn't have gone. I should have made other arrangements. But you didn't write."

"I wrote every day."

"Yes, but you did not write you were coming here."

"I didn't think it was necessary. You wrote every day, too, but you didn't write- -you didn't write--"

"What?"

"A good many things that--that I have learned since I came here."

"Indeed! What things? How did you learn them?"

"I--" John hesitated. To bring Captain Dan's name into the conversation would be, he felt, disloyal. And it would surely mean trouble for the captain. "I--I learned them with my own eyes," he declared. "I could see. Gertie, I can't understand you."

"And I don't understand you. I told you, at the only moment we have had together, I told you then that I would explain about the Chapter. I said that I must go or everything would be spoiled. You very nearly spoiled it by coming as you did."

Mr. Doane's expression changed. It had softened when she reminded him of the whispered word in the drawing-room. The last sentence, however, brought his frown back again.

"Well!" he exclaimed. "Well--humph! that's easily remedied. I came in a hurry and I can go the same way."

"John! John, what do you mean? How can you speak so to me! Would you go away now that--that--"

"You wouldn't miss me so much, I should imagine. Cousin Percy will be here, and you and he seem to be very confidential and friendly, to say the least."

Gertrude gasped. She was beginning to understand, or imagined that she was. She laughed merrily.

"John! Why, John!" she cried. "You're not jealous! YOU!"

John looked rather foolish. "No-o," he admitted doubtfully, "I'm not jealous. Of course I'm not, but--"

"But what? Don't you trust me, John? Don't you?"

"Of course I do. You know I do, but--See here, Gertie, you said you were going to explain--to explain something or other. Do it, then. I think I am entitled to an explanation."

But Gertrude's merriment had vanished. Her eyes flashed.

"I shall not explain," she said. "You don't trust me. I can see you don't."

"I do. I do, Gertie, really; but--but--"

"But you don't. You think--you think--oh, I don't know WHAT you think! No, I shall not explain, not now, at all events. Good-night!"

She hastened from the room. John ran after her.

"Gertie," he cried, "you're not going? You're not going to leave me in this way, without a word? I do trust you. I only said--"

"It wasn't what you said; it was the way you said it. I am going. I am shocked--yes, and hurt, John. I shall not speak to you again to-night. To-morrow perhaps, if you beg my pardon and I am really sure you do trust me, I may tell you--what I was going to tell. But not now. I--I didn't think you would treat me so."

She put her handkerchief to her eyes and hurried up the stairs. John, standing irresolute on the lower step, hesitated, fighting down his own pride and sense of injury. That moment of hesitation was freighted with consequence. Then:

"Gertie," he cried, hastening after her, "Gertie, wait! I do beg your pardon. I'm sorry. I didn't mean--"

But it was too late. Gertie's chamber door closed. John went slowly up to his own room, the room to which the butler had carried his bag. A few minutes after he had gone the curtains between the library and drawing-room parted and Mr. Hungerford appeared. He was very cautious as he, too, ascended the stairs. But his expression was a pleasant one; there was no doubt that Cousin Percy was pleased about something.

CHAPTER XI

Captain Dan stirred uneasily. In his dream he had navigated the Bluebird, his old schooner, to a point somewhere between Hatteras and Race Point light. It was night all at once, although it had been day only a few minutes before, and Azuba, who, it seemed, was cook aboard the Bluebird, was washing breakfast dishes in the skipper's stateroom. She was making a good deal of noise about it, jingling pans and thumping the foot of the berth with a stick of stove wood. The captain was about to remonstrate with her when Serena suddenly appeared--her presence on the schooner was a complete surprise--to ask him if he had not heard the bell, and why didn't he come into the house, because dinner was ready. Then Azuba stopped pounding the foot of the berth and began to thump him instead.

"Don't you hear the bell?" repeated Serena. "Wake up! Daniel! Daniel!"

Daniel stirred and opened his eyes. The Bluebird had vanished, so had Azuba, but the thumps and jingles were real enough.

"Hey?" he mumbled, drowsily. "Stop poundin' me, won't you?"

"Pounding you! I've been pounding and shaking you for goodness knows how long. I began to think you were dead. Wake up! Don't you hear the bell?"

Daniel, still but two-thirds awake, rolled over, raised himself on his elbow and grunted, "Bell! What bell?"

"The door bell. Someone's at the door. Don't you hear them?"

Captain Dan slid out of bed. His bare feet struck the cold floor beneath the open window and he was wide awake at last. The room was pitch dark, so morning had not come, and yet someone WAS at the door, the front door. The bell was ringing steadily and the ringer was varying the performance by banging the door with his feet. The captain fumbled for the button, found and pressed it, and the electric light blazed.

"For mercy sakes!" he grumbled, glancing at his watch hanging beside the head of the bed, "it's quarter past one. Who in time is turnin' us out this time of night?"

Serena, nervous and frightened--she, too, had been aroused from a sound sleep--answered sharply.

"I don't know," she snapped. "It's something important though, or they wouldn't do it. Hurry up and find out, can't you? I never saw such a man!"

Her husband hastened to the closet, found his slippers and bathrobe--the latter was a recent addition to his wardrobe, bought because his wife had learned that B. Phelps Black possessed no less than three bathrobes--and shuffled out into the hall. The bell had awakened other members of the household. A light shone under the door of John Doane's room, and from Gertrude's apartment his daughter's voice demanded to know what was the matter.

Daniel announced that he didn't know, but cal'lated to find out, and shuffled down the stairs. The lights in the hall and drawing-room were still burning, Gertrude and John having forgotten to extinguish them. Captain Dan unlocked the front door and flung it open. A uniformed messenger boy was standing on the steps.

"Telegram for John Doane," announced the boy. "Any answer?"

Daniel seized the proffered envelope. "How in time do I know whether there's any answer or not?" he demanded pettishly. "I ain't read it yet, have I? Think I've got second sight? Why in the nation didn't you ring up on the telephone, instead of comin' here and routin' out the neighborhood?"

The boy grinned. "Against the rules," he said. "Can't send telegrams by 'phone unless we have special orders."

"Well, I give you orders then. Next time you telephone. Hold on a minute now. John! oh, John!"

Mr. Doane, partially dressed, his coat collar turned up to hide the absence of linen, was already at the head of the stairs, and descending.

"Coming, Captain Dott," he said. "For me, is it?"

"Yes. A telegram for you. What--good land, Gertie! you up, too?"

Gertrude, in kimono and cap, was leaning over the rail. "What is it?" she asked quickly.

John announced, "A wire for me," he said. "I'm afraid--" He tore open the envelope. "Yes, I thought so. Mr. Griffin is worse and they want me at once. Every minute counts, they say. I must go--now. When is the next train for Boston, Captain?"

Daniel was very much flustered. "I don't know," he stammered. "There's a time-table around on deck somewheres, but--you ain't goin' now, John? To-night?"

"Yes, I must."

Gertrude hastened to find the time-table. John turned to the messenger.

"Know anything about Boston trains?" he asked.

"Yup. Two-twenty express through from New York. That's the next."

John stepped to the drawing-room and looked at the clock. "I can get it, I think," he announced. "I must. If I can get a cab--"

"I'll 'phone for one. But--but, John, you hadn't ought to--"

"Any answer?" demanded the messenger boy, intent on business.

"Yes. Say that I am leaving on the two-twenty. On the two-twenty. Got that, have you?"

"Sure, Mike! Prepay or collect?"

"I'll--I'll pay it, John." Captain Dan reached under his bathrobe. "Hey!" he exclaimed. "I declare I forgot I didn't have on--All right, John, I'll pay it. You go get ready."

Mr. Doane was on his way to his room. Daniel hurried after him, a difficult progress, for the slippers and bathrobe made hurrying decidedly clumsy. He located his trousers and the loose change in their pockets, explaining the situation to Serena as he did so. He and his wife descended the stairs together. The captain paid the messenger and hastened to telephone for the cab.

When the vehicle arrived, John was ready. His farewells to Daniel and Serena were hurried ones.

"I'm awfully sorry I can't stop longer," he declared. "I really shouldn't have come at all, under the circumstances. I--"

He paused. Gertrude was standing by the door. She was very grave and her eyes looked as if she had not slept. John went over to her; he, too, was grave.

"Gertie," he faltered, "Gertie--"

Serena interrupted. "Daniel!" she said, "Daniel!"

The captain looked at her. She frowned and motioned with her head. The light of understanding dawned in her husband's eyes.

"Hey? Oh, yes!" he cried hastily. "Come into the front room, Serena, just a minute. I want to speak to you."

They entered the drawing-room together. Gertrude and John were alone. For a moment neither spoke. Then the young man, bending forward, whispered: "Gertie," he asked anxiously, "aren't you--haven't you anything to say to me?"

"I thought, perhaps, you had something to say to me, John."

"I have. Gertie, I--"

There was a sound from above. Cousin Percy Hungerford, fully dressed and debonnair as always, was descending the stairs.

"What's the row?" he drawled. "I heard the racket and decided the house must be on fire. What's up?"

Whatever else was "up" it was quite plain John was sorry that Mr. Hungerford was up because of it. His tone was decidedly chilly as he answered.

"A wire for me," he said shortly. "I'm called to Boston at once."

"Really! How extraordinary! It wasn't a fire then, merely a false alarm. Sorry to have you go, Doane, I'm sure."

He spoke as if he were the host whose gracious pleasure it had been to entertain the guest during the latter's stay. John resented the tone.

"Thanks," he said crisply. "Gertie, I--I hope--"

He hesitated. It was not easy to speak in the presence of a third person, particularly this person. Cousin Percy did not hesitate.

"Gertie," he observed, "your--er--friend is leaving us at the wrong time, isn't he? There's so much going on this coming week. Really, Doane, you're fortunate, in a sense. Miss Dott and I are finding the social whirl a bit tiresome; you will escape that, at least."

Captain Dan appeared at the entrance to the drawing-room.

"I say, Hungerford! Percy!" he hailed impatiently.

Mr. Hungerford did not seem to hear him. He was regarding Miss Dott with anxious concern.

"Really, Gertrude," he said, "I shouldn't stand by that open door, if I were you. You have a slight cold and for--all our sakes--you must be careful. Step inside, I beg of you."

His begging was so tender, so solicitous, so intimate. John Doane's fists clenched.

"Hi!" It was the cabman calling from the street. "Hi! we've only got twelve minutes to catch that train."

John turned, involuntarily, toward the door. Gertrude, startled by the cabman's voice and aware of the need of haste, stepped to one side. Cousin Percy chose to put his own interpretation upon her movement.

"Thank you, Gertrude," he said feelingly. "That's better; you will be out of the draft there. Thank you."

John Doane, who was still hesitating, hesitated no longer. He seized his bag.

"Good-by, all," he said, in a choked voice. "Good-by, Captain Dott."

He strode through the doorway. Gertrude, for a moment, remained where she was. Then she followed him.

"John!" she cried, "John!"

John, half way down the steps, halted, turned, and looked up at her.

"Good-by, Gertie," he said.

"But, John, are you--aren't you--"

She stretched out her hands. Mr. Hungerford, pushing by the captain and Serena, stepped in front of her.

"Here, you!" he shouted, addressing the cabman; "what are you thinking about? Why don't you take the gentleman's bag?"

The driver sprang to get the bag, incidentally he seized his prospective passenger by the arm.

"Come on!" he shouted. "Come on! We'll miss the train. Ten to one we've missed it, anyhow."

"Oh, DO hurry, John!" cried Serena, anxiously. "You WILL miss it. You MUST go!"

And Mr. Doane went. The cab rattled away up the street, the old horse galloping, the driver shouting, and the whip cracking. Daniel drew a long breath.

"Well!" he said slowly, "he's gone. Yes, sir, he's gone, ain't he."

Serena turned on him.

"Yes, he's gone," she observed sarcastically, "but he isn't going very fast. Why in the world didn't you order an electric cab instead of that Noah's Ark? Half the neighbors have been waked up and they'll see it. How many times must I tell you? You NEVER learn!"

"Well, now, Serena--"

"Don't talk to me! Don't! My nerves are all of a twitter. I--I--oh, do let me go to bed! Gertie--why, Gertie, where are you going?"

Gertrude was on her way to the stairs. She did not appear to hear her mother's question.

"Gertie!" cried Serena again.

There was no answer. The young lady hurried up the stairs and they heard her chamber door close. Cousin Percy shrugged his shoulders.

"Too bad our friend was called away so suddenly," he observed. "Very much of a surprise, wasn't it? Too bad."

No one replied, not even Serena, who was not wont to ignore the comments of her aristocratic relative. Her next remark was in the nature of an order and was addressed to her husband.

"Come! Come! Come!" she said fretfully. "Do come to bed!"

Daniel, pausing only to extinguish the lights, obeyed. Mr. Hungerford, with another shrug and a covert smile, preceded him up the stairs. As the captain was about to enter his bedroom, a voice, which sounded as if the speaker was half asleep, called from the third floor.

"Is there anything I can do, sir?" asked Hapgood. "I 'ave just been aroused, sir."

Daniel turned. Here was a heaven-sent vent for his feelings.

"Do!" he repeated. "Anything you can do? Yes, there is. Shut your door and turn in."

"But, sir--"

"And shut your head along with it!"

There were some inmates of the Dott mansion who, probably, slept peacefully the remainder of that night, or morning. Cousin Percy doubtless did, also Mr. Hapgood. Azuba, sleeping at the rear of the house, had not been awakened at all. But neither Captain Dan or Serena slept. Mrs. Dott's nerves kept her awake, and the combination prevented Daniel from napping. Nerves were a new acquisition of Serena's; at least she had never been conscious of them until recently. Now, however, they were becoming more and more in evidence. She was fretful and impatient of trifles, and the least contradiction or upset of her plans was likely to bring on fits of hysterical weeping. It was so in this case. Daniel, trotting for smelling salts and extra pillows and the hot water bottle, was not too calm himself. His plans, the plans founded upon John Doane's remaining in Scarford for a time, had been decidedly upset. He pleaded with his wife.

"But I don't see what ails you, Serena," he declared. "John's gone, that's true enough, but you didn't know he was comin'. He was here, a little while, and that's some gain, ain't it? I don't see--"

"See! You wouldn't see if your eyes were spyglasses. Oh, dear! why does everything have to go wrong with me? I thought when John came that Gertie--"

"Yes. That Gertie what?"

"Oh, nothing, nothing! Oh, my poor head! It aches so and the back of it feels so queer. Where are the pillows? Can't you get me another pillow?"

"Sure I can! You've got three already, but I can fetch another. It's all this society business that's breakin' you down, Serena. That everlastin' Chapter--"

He was sorry as soon as he said it, but said it had been. He spent the next hour in explaining that he did not mean it.

Serena was not on hand at breakfast time. Neither was Gertrude. That young lady came into the library at ten o'clock, looking pale and worn and with dark circles under her eyes. She had a thick envelope in her hand.

"Daddy," she said, "will you post this for me?"

Her father looked up from the pile of papers on the writing table before him. He, too, appeared somewhat worried.

"Sartin," he announced promptly. "I've got a stack of stuff for the postman, myself. Bills and checks they are, mostly. Serena usually attends to the house bills, but she's kind of under the weather this morning. Say, Gertie," gravely, "it costs a sight to run this place, did you know it?"

"I suppose it does."

"You bet it does! Why, I never realized--But there, I suppose likely these bills are heavier than usual. I suppose they are. Good land! if they ain't! But, of course they are. I'll ask Serena about 'em by and by, when she's better. Give me your letter, Gertie, I'll mail it."

"You won't forget?"

"Not a mite. I'll put it right here with the others and give 'em to the postman when he comes. Humph! it's to John, isn't it? You're pretty prompt in your writin', ain't you? But that's natural; I remember when I used to write your mother twice a day. It's a wonder she stood it and kept her health, ain't it. Ha! ha!"

He chuckled and turned back to his bills and the checkbook. Gertrude left the room.

Captain Dan wrote and enclosed and affixed stamps. The pile of envelopes on the table grew steadily larger. Mr. Hungerford entered, seeking the cigar box.

"Good-morning," he observed, cheerfully.

Daniel looked up, grunted, and went on with his work. Cousin Percy smiled. A querulous voice called from the second floor.

"Daniel!" called Serena. "Daniel, where are you? Why don't you come up? I am all alone."

The captain sprang to his feet, "Comin'! Serena!" he shouted. "Comin'!"

He hurried out. Mr. Hungerford, left alone, helped himself to a cigar and strolled about the room. The pile of letters on the table caught his attention. Idly he turned the envelopes over, examining the addresses. All at once his interest became less casual; one of the written names had caught his attention.

Five minutes later the postman rang the doorbell. Captain Dan ran downstairs, entered the library, seized the letters from the table and hastened to hand them to the carrier.

"Daddy!" called Gertrude from above, "did you post my letter?"

"Sure!" was the prompt answer. "Just gave it to the mail man. It's on the road now."

Serena's "nerves" were in much better condition the following day, and her spirits likewise. Gertrude, however, was still grave and absent-minded and non-communicative. Toward Mr. Hungerford in particular she was cool and distant, answering his chatty remarks and solicitous inquiries concerning her health with monosyllables, and, on several occasions, leaving the room when he entered it. This state of affairs was even more marked on the second day after Mr. Doane's abrupt departure, and still more so on the third. She seemed nervously expectant when the postman brought the mail, and depressed when each consignment contained no letter for her. On the fourth day this depression was so marked that her father asked the cause.

"What ails you, Gertie?" he inquired. "You look as if you just come from a funeral. What's wrong?"

Gertrude, who was standing by the window, looking out, answered without turning her head.

"Nothing," she said shortly.

"Well, I'm glad of that. I thought you was troubled in your mind about somethin'. Ain't frettin' about John, are you?"

His daughter looked at him now, and the look was a searching one.

"About--Why should I fret about him, pray?" she asked slowly.

"I don't know. I thought maybe his goin' away so sudden was a sort of disappointment to you. 'Twas to the rest of us. Hey? Did you say somethin'?"

"No."

"Oh, I thought you did. Well, you mustn't be disappointed, Gertie. You see, business is business. John did what he thought was right and--"

"Daddy, do be still. I do not intend to trouble myself about--him. Don't talk to me, please. I don't feel like talking."

Daniel talked no more, at that time, but he wondered, and determined to ask Serena her opinion when the opportunity came.

It did not come immediately. A new development in Chapter politics was occupying Mrs. Dott's mind, a development so wonderful and so glorious in its promise that that lady could think or speak of little else. Mrs. Lake's term as president of Scarford Chapter was nearing its end. Annette Black, the vice-president, would have been, in the regular course of events, Mrs. Lake's successor to the high office. But Mrs. Lake and Annette, bosom friends for years, had had a falling out. At first merely a disagreement, it had been aggravated and developed into a bitter quarrel. The two ladies did not speak to each other. Annette announced her candidacy in meeting, and the very next day Mrs. Lake came to Serena with an amazing proposition.

The proposition was this: Mrs. Lake, it seemed, wished to become secretary of the National Legion. In order to do this--or to become even a prominent candidate--it was necessary for her to have the support of the officers of her own Chapter. If

Mrs. Black was elected president she most decidedly would not have this support.

"That woman is a cat," she declared, "a spiteful underhanded cat. After all I have done for her! Why, she never would have been vice-president if it had not been for me! And just because she heard that I said something--something about her that was perfectly true, even if I did not say it--she broke out in committee and said things to me that--that I never shall forget, never! She shan't be president. I have as many friends as she has and I'll see to that. Now, my dear Mrs. Dott, I am counting on you--and your daughter, of course--as among those friends. We must select some woman for the presidency who will command the respect and get the votes of all disinterested members. Miss Canby wants the office, but she is too closely identified with me to be perfectly safe. But our party--I and my friends, I mean--have been considering the matter and we have decided that a dark horse-- that is what the politicians call it--a dark horse is bound to win. We must get the right kind of dark horse. And we think we have it--him--her, I mean. YOU shall be our candidate. YOU shall be president of Scarford Chapter."

Serena gasped.

"Me?" she cried, forgetful, for once, of her carefully nurtured correctness of speech. "Me? President?"

"Yes, you. You are liked and respected by every member. You are known to be rich--I mean cultured and progressive and broad-minded. We can elect you and we will. Isn't it splendid? I'm SO proud to be the one to bring you the news!"

There was one strong qualification possessed by Mrs. Dott which the bearer of good news omitted to mention. Serena was supposed to be Annette Black's most devoted friend. Announcement of her candidacy would have the effect of splitting the Black party in twain. Mrs. Lake and her followers were very much aware of this, although their spokeswoman said nothing about it.

"You'll accept, of course," gushed Mrs. Lake. "Of course you will. I shall be so proud to vote and work for you."

Serena hesitated. The honor of being president of her beloved Chapter was a dazzling prospect. And yet--and yet--

"You will, won't you?" begged the caller.

"No," said Serena. "No, Mrs. Lake, I can't. I could not run against Annette Black. She is my best and dearest friend. If it were not for her I should not have come to

Scarford at all. It would be treachery of the meanest kind. No, Mrs. Lake, I am not that kind of a friend. No."

"But--"

"Please don't speak of it again. I am ashamed even to hear you. Let's talk of something else."

But Mrs. Lake did not want to talk of anything else. She urged and argued and pleaded in vain. Then she began to lose her temper. The parting was not cordial.

And then came Mrs. Black, herself. She, somehow or other, had learned of the offer to be made Serena. When she found that the latter had refused that offer because of loyalty to her, she fairly bubbled over.

"You dear!" she cried, embracing her hostess. "You dear, splendid thing! It was what I expected; I knew you'd do it; but I'm SO happy and SO grateful. I never shall forget it--never. And whenever I can prove my loyalty and devotion to you, be sure I shall do it."

Serena was touched and gratified, but there was just a shade of disappointment in her tone as she answered.

"I know you will," she said. "Of course, I had rather be president of Scarford Chapter than anything else in the world, but--"

And then Annette had an idea. She clasped her hands.

"You shall be," she cried. "You shall be. Not this term, but the next--the very next. This term I shall be president, and you--YOU shall be vice-president. With you as our candidate we can beat that Canby creature to death. Oh, lovely! It is an inspiration."

And on that basis it was settled. The opposing tickets were Black and Dott against Canby and a lady by the name of Saunderson, another of Mrs. Lake's "dear friends." The Chapter was racked from end to end. Politics became the daily food of its members.

For Serena it was almost the only food. She was too busy to eat, except at odd times and hurriedly, and she slept less than ever. Her nervousness increased and she lost weight. Daniel was worried concerning her health and would have mentioned his worriment to Gertrude had not that young lady's mental state and behavior worried him almost as much.

Gertrude, for the first week after John Doane's departure, was depressed and silent and solemn. Once, her father found her in her room, crying and when he anxiously asked the reason she bade him go away and leave her, so sharply and in a tone so unlike her, that he went without further protestation. He did, however, go to Serena for advice.

"Oh, I don't know," said Serena impatiently. "She misses John, I suppose. She thought he was going to stay and he didn't, and she was disappointed. Don't bother me! Don't! I've checked this voting list over three times already and it has come out different each time. I'm so tired and headachy and nervous I think I shall die. Sometimes I don't care if I do. Go away."

"But, Serena, there's--there's somethin' queer about Gertie and John. I don't believe she's heard from him since he left. I don't believe she has."

"Then, why doesn't she write and find out what is the matter? Perhaps he's sick."

"Maybe so, but perhaps she don't want to write. Perhaps she's waitin' for him to do it."

"He can't write if he's sick, can he? Why don't she telegraph him?"

"That would be just the same, the way she may look at it."

"Then wire him yourself, why don't you? Oh, please go away--PLEASE. I'll speak to her, Daniel, when I get time; I was going to. But just now I--oh, my POOR head!"

Daniel made up his mind to telegraph Doane that very afternoon, but he did not. A happening in the household prevented him. Mr. Hapgood was summarily discharged.

Azuba was responsible for the affair. Serena was out--"committeeing" as usual--Gertrude was with her. Mr. Hungerford, also, was absent. Captain Dan, in the library, dolefully musing in an arm chair, heard a violent altercation in the kitchen. As it did not cease, but became more violent, he hastened to the scene.

Azuba was standing in the middle of the kitchen, her back against the table, facing the butler. Mr. Hapgood's face was red, his fists were clenched, and he was shaking one of them under the housekeeper's nose.

"Give it to me!" he ordered. "'And it over now, or I'll bash you good and 'ard."

Azuba merely smiled. "You'll bash nobody," she declared. "You're a thief, that's what you are--a low-down thief. I've always cal'lated you was one, ever since I laid eyes on you; now I know it. Don't you dare shake your fist at me. If my husband was here he'd--"

Hapgood interrupted, savagely consigning the Ginns, both male and female, to a much hotter place than the kitchen. Captain Dan strode into the room.

"Here!" he said sharply. "What's all this? You," addressing Hapgood, "what, do you mean by shakin' your fist at a woman?"

Mr. Hapgood's bluster collapsed, like a punctured toy balloon. He cringed instead.

"W'y, sir," he pleaded, "it wasn't anything. I lost my temper a bit, sir, that's all. She"--with a malignant snarl at Azuba--"she's got a letter of mine. She stole it and won't give it up. I was angry, sir, same as any man would 'ave been, and I forgot myself. Make 'er 'and over my letter, sir."

The captain turned to the defiant Mrs. Ginn.

"Have you got a letter of his, Zuba?" he demanded.

Azuba laughed. "I have," she declared, "and I'm glad of it. I've been waiting to get somethin' like it for a long spell. Stealin'! HE accuse anybody of stealin'! Here, Daniel Dott, you read that letter. Read it and see who's been doin' the stealin' around here."

She extended the letter at arm's length. The butler made a snatch at it, but Captain Dan was too quick. He unfolded the crumpled sheet of paper. It bore the printed name and address of one of Scarford's newer and more recently established grocers and provision dealers, and read as follows:

EDWARD H. HAPGOOD,

SIR:--Our order clerk informs us that you expect a higher percentage of commission on goods ordered by your household. We do not feel that we should pay this. While we, being a new house, were willing, in order to obtain your business, to allow a fair rate of commission to you for putting it in our way, and while, during the past three months, we have paid such commission, we do not feel--

Daniel tossed the note on the floor. He marched to the door leading to the back yard and threw it open. Then he turned to the butler.

"See that door?" he inquired, pointing toward it. "Use it."

Hapgood did not seem to comprehend.

"Wh-what, sir?" he faltered.

"Use that door. Get out! Out of this house, and don't you dare show your nose inside it again. Here!" stepping to the rack behind the open door. "These are your--duds--aren't they? Take 'em and get out. Quick!"

He threw an overcoat and hat at the astonished man-servant, who caught them mechanically.

"Get!" repeated the captain.

Hapgood apparently understood at last. His usual expression of polite humility vanished and he glowered malevolently.

"So I'm fired, am I?" he demanded. "Fired, without no notice or nothin'. 'Ow about my two weeks' wages? 'Ow about square treatment? 'Ow about my things upstairs? I've got rights, I 'ave, and you'll find it out. Blame your eyes, I--"

He darted through the doorway just in time. Captain Dan was on the threshold.

"You can send for your things upstairs," said the captain. "They'll be ready--either up there or on the sidewalk. Now, my--hum--thief," with deliberate and dangerous calmness, "I'm comin' out into that yard. If I was you I'd be somewhere else when I get there. That's my advice."

The advice was taken. Mr. Hapgood was in the street by the time his employer reached the gate. Bolting that gate, Daniel walked back to the kitchen.

"Thank you, Zuba," he said quietly. "You've only confirmed what I suspected before, but thank you, just the same."

Azuba was regarding him with a surprise in which respect was strongly mingled.

"You're welcome," she said drily. "It's good riddance to bad rubbish, that's what I call it. But," her surprise getting the better of her judgment, "I must say I ain't seen you behave--I mean--"

She stopped, the judgment returning. But Captain Dan read her thoughts and answered them.

"He's a man," he said shortly, "or an apology for one. I know how to deal with a MAN--his kind, anyway."

Azuba nodded. "I should say you did," she observed. "Well, if you'd like to hear the whole yarn, how I come to suspect him and all, I can tell you. You see--"

But Daniel would not listen. "I don't want to hear it," he said. "Tell Serena, if you want to, when she comes home. I've got too much else on my mind to bother with swabs like him. If he should try to come back again you can call me, otherwise not. I ain't interested."

And yet, if he could have seen and heard his ex-butler just at that moment, he might have been interested. Hapgood, on the next corner, out of sight from the Dott home, had met and waylaid Mr. Percy Hungerford. To the latter gentleman he was telling the story of his discharge. Cousin Percy seemed disturbed and angry.

"It's your own fault," he declared. "You ought to have been more careful."

"Careful! 'Ow should I know the fools was going to write a letter? I told 'em not to. And 'ow did I know the old woman--blast 'er--was watchin' me all the time? And now I've lost my job, and a good soft job, too. You've got to get it back for me, Mr. 'Ungerford; you've got to 'elp me, sir."

"I'll help you all I can, of course, but I doubt if it will do any good. I can't stand talking with you here. Drop me a line at the club, telling me where you are, and I'll let you know what turns up. Oh, say, have any more letters come for--you know who?"

"No, that was the only one, sir. But a telegram came this morning."

Mr. Hungerford started. "A telegram?" he repeated. "For her?"

"Yes, sir. And from 'im, it was, too."

"Did she get it?"

Mr. Hapgood winked. "It was 'phoned up from the telegraph office, sir," he said, "and I answered the 'phone. 'Ere's the copy I made, sir."

He extracted a slip of paper from his pocket. Cousin Percy snatched the slip and read the penciled words. Hapgood smiled.

"Looks good, don't it, sir," he observed. "'Frisco's a long way off."

Hungerford did not answer. He tore the paper into small pieces and tossed them away.

"Well," he said, after a moment, "good by and good luck. Let me know where you are and meanwhile I'll see what can be done for you. Good by."

He was moving off, but his companion stepped after him.

"Just a minute, sir," he said. "Could you 'elp me out a bit, in the money way? I'm flat broke; the old 'ayseed chucked me without a penny; 'e did, so 'elp me."

Cousin Percy looked distinctly annoyed.

"I'm pretty nearly broke myself," he declared, impatiently.

"Is that so, sir, I'm sorry, but I think you'll 'ave to 'elp me a bit. I think--I think you'd better, Mr. 'Ungerford, sir."

Hungerford looked at him. The look was returned. Then the young gentleman extracted a somewhat attenuated roll of bills from his pocket, peeled off two and handed them to his companion.

"There you are," he replied. "That's all and more than I can spare, just now. Good by."

"Good by, sir--for now. And thank you kindly."

Captain Dan, for all his prompt handling of the thieving butler and his professed ability to deal with men--Mr. Hapgood's kind of man--awaited the return of his wife and daughter with considerable uneasiness. Hapgood, in his capacity as trained, capable, aristocratic servant, had been a favorite of Serena's. The captain dreaded telling his wife what, in the heat of his anger, he had done. But his dread was needless. Serena's mind was too much occupied with politics and political ambition to dwell upon less important matters.

"I suppose it is all right," she said. "If he was a thief he should be discharged, of course. No doubt you did right, Daniel, but we shall miss him dreadfully. I don't know where we can get another butler like him."

Daniel gasped. "Good land of love!" he cried; "we don't WANT another like him, do we! I should hope we didn't."

"I don't mean another thief. Oh, dear me! Why do you pick me up in that way? One would think you took a delight in worrying me all you could. Get me a cup of tea. I want it right away. My nerves are all unstrung. Gertie--"

But Gertie had gone to her room; she spent the greater part of her time there now. Her mother sighed.

"She's gone," she declared. "Just when I need her most, of course. I can't see what has got into her for the last few days. She was so interested in the Chapter. Even more than I, I began to think. And yet, at the committee meeting this afternoon--the most important meeting we've had; when we were counting the votes which we can be sure of and those that are doubtful, she scarcely said a word. Just sat there and moped. I don't know what is the matter with her."

Daniel nodded. "I think I do," he said. "It's John. Somethin's the matter between her and John. If he had only stayed here! If he would only come back!"

"Then for mercy sakes get him back! Telegraph him. You said you were going to."

Captain Dan rose. "I will," he declared. "I'll do it right now, this minute. Not till I see you to your tea, Serena," he added, hastily. "I'll tell Zuba about that first, of course."

He sent the telegram within the hour. It was an inquiry concerning Mr. Doane's whereabouts, his employer's health, how he was getting on, and when he--John--was to return to Scarford. The answer arrived, via telephone, about eight that evening. It was a surprising answer.

"Doane gone to San Francisco on business of the firm," it said. "Left at midnight yesterday."

It was signed by the senior partner. Serena had gone out, of course; she was scarcely ever in now, but Gertrude, having finished dinner, was in her room as usual. Her father hurried up the stairs.

"Gertie," he cried, entering without knocking, "Gertie, what do you suppose I've just found out? It's the most astonishing news. John is--he has--Why, you'd never guess!"

Gertrude, who was sitting in the rocking chair by the window, showed her first sign of interest. At the mention of the name she turned quickly.

"What?" she cried, in a startled voice. "What? Is it--is it bad news? He isn't--isn't--"

"No, no! No, no! He's all right. Don't look like that, you scare me. John's all right; that is, I suppose he is. But he--Here! read it yourself."

Gertrude took the paper upon which he had written the message. She read the latter through; read it and reread it. Then she turned to her father.

"But I can't understand," she faltered. "I can't--I can't understand. He didn't send this himself. He has gone to San Francisco; but--but this is signed by someone else. What does it mean?"

Daniel was frightened. It was time to explain, and yet, considering his daughter's look and manner, he was afraid to explain.

"You see," he stammered, "well, you see, Gertie, that's an answer, that is. John didn't send it, he'd gone. But, I presume likely they thought my telegram ought to be answered, so--"

Gertrude interrupted. "Your telegram?" she repeated. "YOUR telegram? What telegram?"

"Why, the telegram I sent to John. I knew you hadn't heard from him, and I thought probably--"

"Wait--wait a minute. Did YOU send a telegram to--to him?"

"Yes; sure I did. I--"

"What did you say?"

"I said--why, I said that you--we, I mean--was wonderin' about him and--and missin' him and when was he comin' back here. That's about what I said. I wrote it in a hurry and I don't remember exactly. That's about it, anyhow. Why, what's the matter?"

Gertrude had risen.

"You said that!" she cried. "You--without a word to me--said--you begged him to come back! Begged him! on your knees! to--to--"

"No, no! I never got on my knees. What would I do a fool thing like that for, when I was sendin' a telegram? I just asked--"

"You just asked! You said that I--I--And this was your answer! THIS!"

She dashed the message to the floor, covered her face with her hands and threw herself upon the bed. Daniel, aghast and alarmed, would have raised her but she pushed him away.

"Oh!" she cried. "The shame of it! Don't touch me! Please don't touch me!"

"But, Gertie--what on earth?"

"Don't touch me. Please don't touch me. Just go away, Daddy. Go and leave me. I mustn't talk to you now. If I do, I shall say--Please go. I want to be alone."

Daniel went. That he had made another blunder was plain enough, but just now he was too hurt and indignant to care a great deal.

"All right," he said shortly; "I'm goin'. You needn't worry about that. That's about all the orders I get nowadays--to go away. I ought to be used to it, by this time. I'm a fool, that's what I am, an old worn-out, useless fool."

He slammed the door and descended the stairs. He had been in his accustomed refuge, the library, for perhaps twenty minutes, when the bell rang. He waited for Hapgood to answer the ring and then, suddenly remembering that the butler had departed, answered it himself.

Mr. Monty Holway smiled greeting from the steps.

"Good evening, Captain Dott," he said. "Is Miss Dott in?"

Daniel hesitated. "Yes," he said, "she's in, but--"

"May I see her? Will you be good enough to give her my card?"

The captain took the card.

"Ye-es," he said, "I'll give it to her, but--but--Well, you see, she ain't feelin' very well this evenin' and I don't know as she'll want to see anybody."

Gertrude herself called from the head of the stairs.

"Who is it, Daddy?" she asked. "Someone for me?"

"It's--er--Mr. Holway."

"Oh, is it!" The tone was one of delighted surprise. "Ask him to come in, Daddy. I'll be right down."

She came almost immediately. She greeted the caller with outstretched hand.

"I'm so glad to see you, Mr. Holway," she said. "I was lonely. It was nice of you to come."

She was pale, and the dark circles under her eyes were more apparent than ever, but the eyes themselves were shining brightly. She was gay and, for her, extremely vivacious. Mr. Holway looked gratified and happy. Captain Dan looked astonished and bewildered.

CHAPTER XII

The bewilderment and astonishment remained with the captain for some time, just as his daughter's apparent light heartedness remained with her. Holway's call was longer than usual, lasting until Serena, escorted by Mr. Hungerford, returned from Mrs. Black's, where they had been discussing the all-important election. Hungerford and his friend greeted each other with a marked lack of warmth; in fact, they scarcely spoke. Serena was too tired to talk, but Gertrude talked enough for all. She chatted and laughed with almost feverish gaiety until the caller, after many false starts and with evident reluctance, finally tore himself away. Then her manner changed, she was silent and thoughtful and, soon afterward, said goodnight and went up to her room.

Captain Dan forebore to trouble his wife with the news of the telegram announcing John Doane's departure for the West, and the reception of that news by Gertrude. After hearing Serena's complaints of her "nerves" and weariness, he decided that there was trouble sufficient for that night. But the next morning he spoke of it. Serena was surprised, of course, and worried likewise.

"You're right, Daniel," she said, "I am afraid you're right. She and John must have had some disagreement. I suppose it is only a lover's quarrel--young engaged people are always having foolish quarrels--and they always get over them and make up again. But, oh, dear! why did they quarrel just now? Haven't I got enough on my mind without fretting about them? Well, I'll talk to Gertie this very forenoon."

She did, but the talk was unsatisfactory. When Daniel, waiting anxiously to learn what had taken place, questioned her she shook her head.

"I can't make Gertie out," she declared pettishly. "She acts so queer. Doesn't want to talk about John at all. Says it is all right, and why should I worry if she doesn't? And she is so different, somehow. She was willing enough to discuss my chances for the vice-presidency. She asked twenty questions about that and declares she is going to help me. And yesterday, when I wanted her to help, she didn't take any interest. I never saw such a change. And she is so--so fidgety and--and nervous and high-spirited and silly. She laughed at nothing and kept jumping up and walking about and sitting down again. I declare! it made ME jumpy just to look at her."

Gertrude's conduct was certainly surprising. It caused Captain Dan to feel "jumpy" more than once. Her determination to help her mother in the campaign she put into immediate practice. She called Cousin Percy into council, borrowed Serena's list of Chapter members, and the pair spent hours checking that list together. Then Gertrude announced that she was going to make some calls. She made them and returned, exultant.

"I think I have made two converts this afternoon," she said. "I am almost sure they will vote for you, Mother. You and I must go to Mrs. Black's to-night and talk it over with her. We MUST; it is very important."

Serena, who had hoped for an early bedtime, expressed weariness, and protested, but her protests were overruled. They went to the Blacks' and Captain Dan and Mr. Hungerford went, also. Annette was delighted to see them. Mr. Black succeeded in repressing his joy.

"For the Lord's sake, Dan!" he exclaimed, when, he and the captain were alone, "isn't there EVER going to be any let-up to this tom-foolery? Are these women of ours going stark crazy?"

Daniel gloomily replied that he didn't know.

"You're worse off than I am," continued B. Phelps. "There's two lunatics in your family and only one in mine. Your daughter's just as bad as her mother, every bit--worse, if anything. But, it seems to agree with HER. I never saw her so lively or so pretty either. Humph! your pet cousin there is badly gone, or I'm no judge. Well, you remember what I told you about him."

Daniel nodded. He was too depressed for words.

"All right, it's your funeral, not mine. But, say! there's one ray of hope. The whole crowd may be licked to death in this election. If they are, my wife says she'll resign from the Chapter and never speak to one of the bunch again. It sounds too good to be true, but it may be. It's enough to make a fellow hop in and do some political work himself--for the other side. What?"

The political work continued, mornings and afternoons, evenings and far into the nights. Serena was in it, Gertrude was in it, and Cousin Percy and Mr. Holway were in it because she was. Monty's calls were of frequent occurrence. Mr. Hungerford and his erstwhile chum did not speak to each other at all now. But at receptions and teas and dances and musicals and committee meetings one or the other was on hand at Miss Dott's elbow. And Gertrude was very gracious to them both; not more to one than the other, but exceptionally kind and agreeable to each.

The social affairs were of almost as frequent occurrence as the political meetings. Gertrude accepted all invitations and urged her mother to accept.

"You must, Mother," she declared. "Now is the time when you can't afford to offend or neglect anyone. You may need their votes and influence."

"But, Gertie," pleaded poor, tired Serena, "I can't go everywhere."

"You must. If this vice-presidency is worth all the world to you, as you say it is, you must sacrifice everything else to get it."

"But, I can't! I'm almost worn out. I--I--oh, sometimes I feel almost willing to give it all up and go back to--to--almost anywhere, even Trumet, if I could rest there."

"You don't mean that, Mother."

"No; no, of course I don't."

"Because if you do, why--well, that is different. If you WANT to go back to dead and alive old Trumet--"

"I don't. I--I wouldn't for anything. I shouldn't think you, of all people, would hint at such a thing. You! When I have climbed so high already; when our social position has become what it is. You! talking of going back to Trumet."

"I'm not. You mentioned it; I didn't. I'm having a beautiful time. I just love our social position. The Blacks and the Kellys and--er--that Miss Dusante! Oh, I adore them. I wouldn't leave such cultured people for anything. And you enjoy it so, Mother. You look so happy."

Was there a trace of sarcasm in this outburst? Serena was, for the moment, suspicious. She tried her hardest to look very happy indeed.

"I am happy, of course," she declared.

"I know it. And we want to keep on being happy, don't we. So we must not decline anyone's invitation. We must go, go, go, all the time."

"But some of the invitations are from people I scarcely know at all. And some I don't like."

"That makes no difference. They may be of value to you in your campaign, or socially, or somehow. Don't you see, Mother? In politics or society one wishes to advance, to climb higher all the time. And to do that one must use one's acquaintances as rounds in the ladder. Use them; get something from them; pretend to love them, no matter whether you really hate them or not. They may hate you, but they want to use you. That's part of the game, Mother."

This was worldly advice to be given by a young lady scarcely out of college. And it sounded so unlike Gertrude. But, then, Gertrude had changed, was changing more and more daily.

"We don't entertain enough," went on the adviser. "We should be giving some affair or other at least once a week. Invite everybody you know--everyone but the Lake crowd, of course. I'll make out a list of eligibles to-day and we'll give an 'At Home' next week."

"But, Gertie--the expense. It costs so dreadfully. We're not rich; that is, not very rich."

"No matter. Everyone thinks we are. If they didn't, most of them would cut us dead to-morrow. We must pretend to be very rich. I'll make out the list. Mr. Holway will help me. He is coming to call this evening."

Serena looked more troubled than ever.

"Gertie," she said earnestly, "I think I ought--yes, I am going to warn you against that Mr. Holway. I don't like your having him call or being seen in his company."

"You don't! I am surprised. I'm sure he is very polite and agreeable. He belongs to the best club and he dresses well, and as to society--why, he is in the very heart of it; our kind of society, I mean."

"I know, I know. But--well, Cousin Percy doesn't speak well of him. He says he is a very fast young man."

Gertrude bit her lip. "Did Percy say that!" she exclaimed. "How odd! Why, Monty--I mean Mr. Holway--said almost the same thing about him. And I KNOW you like Cousin Percy, Mother."

Mrs. Dott scarcely knew how to answer. As a matter of fact she did not like their aristocratic relative quite as well as she had at first. There were certain things about him, little mannerisms and condescensions, which jarred upon her. He was so very, very much at home in the family now; in fact, he seemed to take his permanent membership in that family for granted. He had ceased to refer to himself as being on a vacation, and, as for his "literary work," he appeared to have forgotten that altogether.

But these were not the real reasons for Serena's growing dislike and uneasiness. She hinted at the real reason in her next remark.

"I don't think," she said, "I don't think, Gertie, that you and he should be so much together. You are engaged to be married, you know, and John--"

Gertrude interrupted. She ignored the mention of Mr. Doane's name.

"Oh, Cousin Percy is all right," she said lightly. "He's good company. Of course he may be something of a sport, but that is to be expected. The trouble with you and me, Mother, is that we are too old-fashioned; we are not sporty enough."

"GERTIE!" Serena's horror was beyond words.

Gertrude laughed. "But that can be mended," she went on. "Mother, you should learn to drink cocktails and tango. I think I shall. Everybody's doing it, doing it, doing it!"

Humming this spirited ditty, which the street pianos had rendered popular, and smiling over her shoulder at her mother, she "one-stepped" from the room. Serena put both hands to her head. Her "nerves" were more troublesome than ever the remainder of that day.

There were enough troubles to rack even a healthy set of nerves. The domestic situation was decidedly complicated. No successor to the departed Hapgood had, as yet, been selected. Mr. Hungerford was partially responsible for this. At first, when told of the butler's misbehavior and its consequences, he had expressed sorrow, but had advised forgiveness and the reinstallation of the discharged one. The crime was, after all, not so very serious. Most butlers exacted commissions from tradespeople, so he had been told. Of course it was all wrong, a pernicious system and all that, but they did do it. And many employers winked at the system. Hapgood was an exceptional fellow, really quite exceptional. Aunt Lavinia had treated him as one of the family, almost. Captain Dan, to whom these statements were made, was stubbornly indignant. He wouldn't wink at a thief, and he wouldn't fire him and then hire him over again, either. If "that everlastin' sneak showed his white-washed face on the premises again, he'd have that face damaged." All the captain hoped for was a chance to inflict the damage.

So Cousin Percy, finding Daniel obdurate, tried his influence upon Serena, whom he regarded, and justly, as the real head of the house. But Serena, too, refused to consider Mr. Hapgood's re-employment. She had talked with Azuba, and Azuba had declared that she should leave in "just about two-thirds of a jiffy" if the butler came back. "When he comes into my kitchen," she said, "I get out. I should hate to quit the folks I'd worked for the biggest part of my life, but there's some things I won't stand. He's one of 'em. Don't talk to me about HIM!"

Mr. Hapgood was not re-engaged nor forgiven, and Hungerford kindly volunteered to find a competent successor. He would make some inquiries among his friends, the right sort of people, he said, and his manner indicated that the said people were accustomed to employing butlers in droves.

Azuba, therefore, was left with all the domestic cares upon her hands. These hands were quite competent, had they been disengaged, but just now they were full. Azuba was "advancing," just as she had proclaimed to Captain Dan that she intended to do. She read "The Voice" and kindred literature a great deal, and quoted from her readings at every opportunity. Denied admittance to the Chapter, in spite of Gertrude's efforts in her behalf--Gertrude had warmly advocated the formation of a Servants' Branch--she had made search on her own hook and suddenly announced that she had found what she was looking for. This, so she affirmed, was an organization called "The Free Laborers' Band," and it met in a hall somewhere or other, though no one but its members seemed to know just where that hall was. Serena made inquiries, but neither servants nor mistresses had ever heard of the "Band." Gertrude, when she heard of it, at first seemed to be much amused, and laughed heartily. Then she became very grave and declared it a splendid thing and that she was delighted because Azuba had found her opportunity. She was entitled to that opportunity, as was every free woman, and certainly neither Gertrude or her mother, being "free women" themselves, must offer objection or permit mere household drudgery to interfere.

So Azuba "advanced" and preached and went out at night and occasionally during the day. Gertrude and Serena went out all the time, when they were not entertaining themselves. Life became a never-ending round of politics and society functions, followed by, on Mrs. Dott's part, sleepless nights and "nerves" and fretful worriment concerning Gertrude. Gertrude did not appear to worry. She grew gayer and more gay, more careless in her manner and more slangy in her speech. Mr. Holway continued to call and Cousin Percy to dance solicitous attendance. John Doane's name was never mentioned in his fiancee's presence. She would not speak, or permit others to speak, of him.

And then Mr. Holway ceased to call. His final call was a lengthy one, and he and Gertrude were alone during the latter part of it. The following day Daniel met him on the street and was barely recognized. The captain was not greatly troubled at the slight--he did not care greatly for the lively Monty--but he was surprised. When he mentioned the meeting to his daughter the young lady smiled, but offered no explanation. Her father did not press the point. As Holway came no more and it became apparent that he was not coming, the captain was satisfied.

Gertrude's strange behavior alarmed and troubled him, but his wife's ill health and her worn, weary expression alarmed him more. He was actually frightened concerning her.

"Oh, Serena," he begged, "what makes you do it? It isn't worth it. You're killin' yourself. Let's give it up and go somewhere and rest. The Queen of Sheba's job ain't worth it, let alone just bein' vice-president of Scarford Chapter."

But Serena shook her head. "I can't give it up, Daniel," she declared hysterically. "I--I think I would if I could. I really do. Sometimes I feel as if I would give up everything just to be at peace and happy and contented again."

"You bet!" with enthusiasm. "So would I. And we were contented at Trumet, wasn't we? That is, I was; and you was enough sight better contented than you are now."

"I know, I know. But I can't give it up, Daniel. Don't you see? I can't! I mustn't think of myself at all. See how loyally Annette and the rest have stood by me. Their splendid loyalty is the one thing that makes it worth while. I must keep up and fight on for their sakes. I must be as true to them as they are to me. Would they desert me for anything? No! And I shan't desert them. I am going to be elected. I know it. After that, after the election is over, I may--I might, perhaps--"

"You might go somewhere with me and have a good, comfortable time. All right, we will. And Gertie can go, too."

The mention of her daughter's name seemed to be more disturbing than all the rest. Serena burst into tears.

"She wouldn't go, Daniel!" she cried. "You know she wouldn't. She--she is going crazy, I do believe. She is wild about society and bridge--she told me only yesterday she wasn't sure that playing for money was wrong. All my friends and her friends did it and why shouldn't we? And she dances all these dreadful new dances and uses slang and--and--oh, she is--I don't know WHAT she will be if this keeps on. Why does she do it? WHO is responsible?"

Daniel did not answer. He had a feeling that he could, without moving from his chair, lay a hand upon the person chiefly responsible, but he kept that feeling to himself.

"She'd go, if we wanted her to," he affirmed stoutly.

"No, she wouldn't."

"By time! she would. You and I would make her. I couldn't do it alone, I know that, but if you'll say the word and stand by me she'll go, if I have to--to give her ether and take her while she's asleep. Say the word, that's all I want you to do."

Serena did not say the word, not then. She continued to moan and wring her hands.

"She's all wrong, Daniel!" she cried. "She does wrong things. She is with--with Cousin Percy too much. He and she are getting to be altogether too friendly. She has dropped John for good, I'm afraid. Oh, suppose she should--"

The captain's anger burst forth at this expression of his own secret dread.

"Suppose she should marry that Hungerford, you mean!" he cried. "She won't! She won't! She's too sensible, anyway; but, if she should, I--I'd rather see her dead. Yes, sir, dead!"

"So had I. But Cousin Percy--"

"D--n Cousin Percy!"

For once his profanity met with no rebuke. Serena did not appear to notice it.

"He is not the right sort of man for her," she declared. "He is polite and aristocratic and he has helped us in society; but he is dissipated and fast, I'm sure of it. He has been out a great deal lately and comes home late, and I have heard him come up the stairs as if--as if--Oh, WHY did you insist on his staying here, living here with us?"

"Why did I--Humph! Well, that's all right. That's all right, Serena. You back me up in that, too, and he'll go out a sight quicker than he came in. I'll see that he does. He'll fly. I can handle MEN even yet--though I don't seem to be good for much else."

But Mrs. Dott wouldn't hear of it. They couldn't PUT him out, she declared; think of the scandal! No, no, no! The interview ended by the captain's dismissal and Serena's getting ready for that evening's committee meeting.

It developed that Azuba's "Band" met on that same evening. Gertrude and her mother had gone--they were to dine with the committee at Annette's--and when Daniel, at seven o'clock, shouted for his dinner, no dinner was ready.

"I can't stop to fuss with dinner," said Azuba firmly. "I've got to get ready for my Band meetin'. All the afternoon I've been fussin' with my speech--I'm goin' to speak to-night--and now it's time for me to change my clothes. I'm sorry, Cap'n Dott; I never neglected you afore; but this time I've got to. There's plenty to eat in the ice-chest and you must wait on yourself. No use to talk! I ain't got time to listen."

Captain Dan was furious. This was a trifle too much.

"You get that dinner!" he roared. "Get it, or you'll never get another meal in this house!"

"Won't I? Why not? Mrs. Dott said I might go to this meetin'. She'll understand."

"By time, Zuba Ginn, I'll discharge you! I will! I don't care if you have been with us since Methusalem's time. You old foolhead! At your age--"

"I'm no older than your wife, Dan'l Dott. And you can't discharge me, neither. I wouldn't go. I'm no Hapgood. I've got rights and I'll stand up for 'em. You ain't the boss, I guess. If Serena discharges me, all right; but she won't. There! don't talk to ME. I've got other fish to fry."

She marched up the back stairs. Daniel sprang after her, but she closed the door in his face. For a moment he hesitated. Then he turned back and, re-entering the kitchen, began to pace up and down, his hands in his pockets.

He strode from the sink to the back door, wheeled and strode back again. There was an odd expression on his face. He frowned, muttered to himself, whistled, smiled, and once broke into a short laugh. But, as he continued the pacing, gradually the frown and smile disappeared and his expression became one of grim determination. His lips closed, his eyes puckered, and his stride lengthened. His heels struck the oilcloth with sharp, quick thumps. If one of his former shipmates, a foremast hand on the schooner Bluebird, could have seen him then, that foremast hand would have interpreted his behavior as a forerunner of trouble. He would have known that the "old man" was making up his mind to a definite course of action and that, having made it up, he would keep to that course so long as he could see or breathe.

And that interpretation would have been correct. Captain Dan was desperate. He had made up his mind to fight, to "put his foot down" at last. Serena's ill health, Gertrude's conduct, the aggravating insolence of Cousin Percy, all these had helped to spur him to this pitch. And now came Azuba's open rebellion and her declaration that his command amounted to nothing, that he was not the "boss." It was true, that was the humiliating fact which stung. He was not the boss; he was not even cabin boy, and he knew it. But, to be openly told so, and by his cook, was a little too much. The worm will turn--at least we are told that it will--and Daniel Dott was turning.

He jerked his hands from his pockets and opened his mouth.

"Azuba!" he roared. "You, Zuba, come here!"

Azuba did not answer. She was in her room at the top of the house and, of course, did not hear the shout. Before the captain could repeat it someone knocked at the back door.

The knock was no hesitating, irresolute tap. It was an emphatic, solid thump. Daniel heard it, but, in his present state of mind, was in no mood to heed.

"Zuba!" he repeated. "Zuba Ginn, are you comin' here or shall I come after you? ZUBA!"

The back door was merely latched, not locked. Now it was thrown open, a heavy step sounded in the entry and a voice, a man's voice, said, in a shout almost as loud as the captain's, "Yes, Zuba; that's what I was cal'latin' to say, myself. Who--why, hello, Cap'n Dan! How are you?"

Daniel turned. A man had entered the kitchen, a big man, wearing a cloth cap, and carrying in one hand a lumpy oilcloth valise. He tossed the valise to the floor, grinned, and extended a hand.

"Well, Cap'n Dan," he observed, "you look as natural as life. I must have changed, I cal'late. Don't you know me?"

The captain's eyes were opening wider and wider. "Labe!" he exclaimed; "Laban Ginn! Where in the world did you come from?"

The person who had so unceremoniously entered the kitchen was Azuba's husband, mate of the tramp steamer.

CHAPTER XIII

For the land sakes! Laban Ginn!" repeated Daniel.

Mr. Ginn grinned cheerfully. He was six feet tall, or thereabouts, and more than half as wide. His hair and beard were grayish red and his face reddish brown. He was dressed in the regulation "shore togs" of a deep sea sailor, blue double-breasted jacket, blue trousers and waistcoat, white "biled" shirt, low collar--celluloid, by the look--and a "made" bow tie which hung from the button by a worn loop of elastic. His hands were as red as his face and of a size proportionate to the rest of him. He seized the captain's hand in one of his, crushed it to a pulp, and returned the remains to the chief mourner.

"Well, say," he cried, his grin widening, "that feels natural, don't it? Last time you and me shook hands was over three years ago. How are you? Blessed if it ain't good to see you again."

Captain Dan was slowly regaining his equilibrium.

"Same to you, Labe," he returned heartily. "But--but, by Godfreys, you're the last person I expected to see just now."

"Yep, I shouldn't wonder."

"Sit down, sit down. Humph! Does Azuba know you're comin'?"

"No, not yet."

"Well, sit down and I'll call her. She's here with us, of course."

"Sartin she is. Where else would she be? I knew she was here; heard you hailin' her just as I made port at the back door. Set down?" He threw himself into a chair, which groaned under the pressure. "Sure, I'll set down! Feels kind of good to drop anchor when you've been cruisin's long as I have. No, Zuby don't know I'm comin'. Last time I wrote her was from Mauritius. I've been to clink and gone since. She WILL be surprised, won't she? Ho! ho! Did I leave the hatch open? Here, let me shut it."

But Daniel himself shut the "hatch," that is to say, the back door. He was on his way to the stairs, but Mr. Ginn detained him.

"Hold on a shake, Cap'n," he said. "I ain't hardly seen you yet. Let's have a look at you." Crossing his legs--his feet were like miniature trunks--he added, "How are you, anyway?"

Daniel replied that he was fair to middling.

"Sit still and make yourself comfortable, Labe," he went on. "I'll tell Zuba you're here."

"What's your hurry? Give me a chance to catch my breath. I lugged that dunnage bag," indicating the valise, "from the depot up here, and I feel as if I'd strained every plank in my hull. Ought to go into dry dock and refit, I had. I landed in Philadelphy a week ago," he continued. "Quit the old steamer for good, I have. Me and the skipper had some words and I told him where he could go. Ho! ho! I don't know whether he went or not; anyhow, I started for Trumet. Got there and found you'd come into money and had moved to Scarford and was livin' with the big-bugs. Some house you've got here, ain't it! Soon's I see it I headed for the back door. 'A first cabin companion like that's no place for me,' I says. Ho! ho! Besides, I cal'lated to find Zuby Jane out in the fo'castle here. Didn't expect to locate you, though, in this end of the ship. How's it seem to be rich? Ain't got fat on it, have you."

Daniel, amused in spite of his recent ill temper, shook his head.

"Not yet," he answered. "So you've been ashore a week and your wife doesn't know it? Why didn't you write to her from Philadelphia?"

"Oh, I don't know. Zuby and me's got an understandin' about that, and other things. There's nothin' like havin' a clear understandin' to make married folks get along together. We write letters, of course, but we don't write very often. I'm li'ble to be 'most anywheres on the face of the earth, and it makes me fidgety to think there's letters chasin' me round and I ain't gettin' 'em. I say to Zuby, 'Long's you don't hear from me you'll know I'm all right, and long's I don't hear from you I'll know the same. We'll write when we feel like it. I'll come home as often as I can, and when I come I'll fetch you my share of the wages.' That's our understandin' and it's a good one. We ain't had a fight since we was spliced; or, if we have, I always stop it right off--stop her part, I mean. Where IS the old gal, anyhow?"

"She's up in her room, I presume likely."

"Oh, is she? Well, she'll be down in a jiffy. If she ain't I'll go up and give her a surprise."

"I'll call her, if you give me a chance."

"No, no, you needn't. No 'special hurry. She's waited for three years; cal'late ten minutes more won't hurt neither of us. Had your supper yet?"

Daniel smiled grimly. "Not yet," he replied.

"Then she'll be down to get it, of course. I shan't stop her; I'm empty as a rum bottle four days out of port. You folks eat late, don't you?"

"Sometimes."

"I should think so. What's Zuby doin' up in her room this time of night?"

"She said she was goin' to change her clothes."

"Oh, yes, yes; I see. Well, 'twon't take her long. If I went up I'd only hold her back, and I want my supper. Let's have a smoke, Dan, while we're waitin'."

He patted one pocket after the other and finally located a chunky, battered pipe, which he proceeded to fill with shavings from a black plug. Daniel watched him. A new idea was dawning in his mind, an idea which seemed to afford him some pleasurable anticipation. Mr. Ginn looked up from his tobacco shaving.

"Now, tell me about all this money of yours," he commanded. "I didn't hear nothin' else at Trumet; that and your wife's gettin' to be commodore of some woman's lodge or other was all they talked about. Hey? Why, where's your pipe? Ain't you goin' to smoke? I've got plenty terbacker."

Daniel looked dubious. "I guess not, Labe," he said. "Zuba--well, the fact is, Zuba doesn't like people to smoke in her kitchen."

Laban's face expressed astonishment. "She don't!" he cried. "She don't? How long since?"

"Oh, almost ever since she came here. It is one of her new ways."

"'Tis, hey? Well, I like the old ones better, myself. Never you mind her ways; trot out your pipe and light up. I--"

He was interrupted by his companion, who made a flying jump toward the stove. The teakettle was boiling over.

"Let it bile," commented Mr. Ginn. "'Tain't your funeral, is it? You ain't supposed to boss the galley. That's the cook's business, not the skipper's."

But Daniel carefully removed the kettle to a place of safety.

"It's my business to-night," he said. "I'm gettin' my own supper."

Mr. Ginn straightened in his chair. "You be?" he exclaimed. "You BE? What for? Ain't there no women folks in the house? Ain't Zuby--why, you said--"

"I know I said, but what I say don't seem to amount to much. You see, Labe, your wife has got some of what MY wife calls advanced ideas. She belongs to some kind of a lodge herself, and this is their meetin' night. Just before you came Zuba made proclamations that I could cook my own supper. She said she couldn't stop to do it; she'd be late to the meetin' if she did."

Laban's mouth opened. The pipe fell from it, scattering sparks like a Roman candle, and bounced upon the spotless floor of the kitchen. Daniel would have picked it up, but his visitor intervened. He put one mammoth foot upon the sparks and, leaning forward, demanded instant attention.

"For thunder sakes, Dan Dott!" he cried. "Never mind that pipe; let it alone. For thunder sakes, tell me what you're talkin' about? Zuby--Zuby Jane Ginn racin' to lodges and tellin' you--YOU--to cook your own meals! Go on! You're loony."

"Maybe I am, Labe, but it's so."

"It's so? And you let it be so? I don't believe it. What do you mean? How long has it been so?"

Captain Dan proceeded to tell of his housekeeper's conversion to progress and advancement. He did not suppress any of the details; in fact, he magnified them just a bit.

"She's a free woman, so she says, Labe," he said, in conclusion. "And a free woman has a right to be free."

"Is that so! That's what she says, hey? And you let her say it? Why, you--you--" He hesitated, hovering between candid expression and the respect due an ex-skipper of a three-master. "Wh-what do you have such goin's on in your house for?" he demanded. "What makes you let the gang afore the mast run over you this way? Why don't you--who's that upstairs; your wife?"

"No, my wife is out. I shouldn't wonder if that was Zuba. She's on her way to the door, probably."

"She is, hey? Call her down here. Sing out to her to come down. Hi!" as the captain stepped to the stairs, "don't say nothin' about me."

Daniel, suppressing a grin, shouted up the stairs.

"Zuba!" he called. "Zuba, come down here a minute."

Azuba answered, but in no complacent tone. "Don't bother me, Cap'n Dott," she protested. "I'm late as 'tis."

"Just a minute, Zuba, that's all. One minute, please."

Mr. Ginn snorted at the "please." They heard the housekeeper descending. At the bottom step she sniffed loudly.

"I do believe it's tobacco smoke!" she exclaimed. "Cap'n Dott, have you been smokin' in my kitchen?"

She entered the room, waving an indignant arm. She was dressed in her Sunday best, bonnet and all.

"What!" she began, and then, suddenly aware that her employer was not alone, turned to stare at his companion. "Why!" she exclaimed; "who--oh, my soul! LA-BAN!"

"Hello, Zuby!" roared her husband, rising to greet her. "How be you, old gal?"

Before she could speak or move he seized her in his arms, squeezed her to him, and pressed a kiss like the report of a fire-cracker upon her cheek. "How be you, Zuby?" he repeated.

"Oh, Labe!" gasped Azuba. "Labe!"

"I'm Labe, all right. No doubt about that.... Well, why don't you say somethin'? Ain't you glad to see me?"

Azuba looked as if she did not know whether she was glad or not; in fact, as if she knew or realized any little of anything.

"Labe!" she said again. "Laban Ginn! When--WHERE did you come from?"

"Oh, from all 'round. Trumet was my last port and I made that by way of Malagy and Philadelphy. But I'm here, anyhow, and that's somethin'. My! it's good to see you. You look as natural as life. Set down and let's look at you."

The housekeeper sat down; she appeared glad of the opportunity. Her husband faced her, grinning broadly.

"Just as handsome as ever; hey, old lady," he observed. "And look at the duds! Say, you're rigged up fine, from truck to keelson, ain't you, Zuby! Never seen you rigged finer. A body would think she knew I was comin', wouldn't they, Cap'n Dan?"

Daniel did not answer, although he seemed much interested in the situation. Azuba drew a hand across her forehead.

"I DIDN'T know it," she declared emphatically. "Indeed, I didn't! Why didn't you write me, Laban Ginn?"

"Write! Write nothin'! I wanted to surprise you. But there, there! Don't set around in that rig any longer. Makes me feel as if you'd come to call on the parson. Take off your coat and bonnet and let's be sociable. And while we're talkin' you turn to and get supper. I'm pretty nigh starved to death. So's the cap'n; he said so."

Mrs. Ginn looked at Captain Dan. There was a twinkle in his eye. Azuba noticed that twinkle.

"Laban," she stammered, "I--I--I CAN'T stay here and get supper to-night. I can't."

Laban was tremendously surprised--at least he pretended to be.

"Can't!" he repeated. "Can't stay here, when I've just got home?"

"No, I can't. If I had known you was comin' 'twould have been different. But I didn't know it."

"What difference does that make? Zuby, don't make me laugh; I'm too hungry for jokin'. Take off your bonnet, now; take it off."

"I mustn't, really, Labe. It's lodge night and they expect me. I--"

"Take off your bonnet!"

"I can't! ... Well, I will, for just a minute." The last sentence was added in a great hurry, for her husband showed signs of preparing to remove the headgear with his own hands. She placed the bonnet on the table and fidgeted in her chair, glancing first at her employer and then at the clock. Captain Dan was smiling broadly.

"That's fine!" exclaimed Mr. Ginn. "Now you look like home folks. Now she'll get us some supper, won't she, Cap'n?"

Again Daniel did not answer, but his smile, as Azuba interpreted it, was provokingly triumphant. Her lips closed tightly.

"I can't get any supper to-night, Laban," she declared firmly. "I just can't. I'm awful sorry, bein' as you've just got home, but you'll have to forgive me. I'll explain when you and me are alone."

"Explain? Explain what?"

"Why--why--" with another look, almost vindictive, at the grinning captain, "what my reason is. But I can't tell you now--I can't."

"That's all right. I don't care about explainin's. You can explain any old time; just now, me and the cap'n want our supper."

"I shan't get your supper. I told Cap'n Dott I couldn't before I went upstairs. I'm goin' out."

"No, no, you ain't. Quit your foolin', old lady. I'm gettin' emptier every minute. So are you, ain't you, Cap'n?"

Daniel hesitated, looked at his housekeeper's face, and burst into a roar of laughter. That laugh decided the question. Azuba rose.

"Don't talk to me," she snapped. "I'm sorry, but it serves you right, Laban, for comin' home without sendin' me word; and just at the wrong time, too. Give me that bonnet."

She reached for the bonnet, but her husband reached it first. "'Tain't much of a bonnet, anyhow, Zuby," he said. "Now I look at it closer I don't think it's becomin' to your style of complexion. Some day I'll buy you another."

"Give me that bonnet, Laban Ginn!"

"I don't like to see that bonnet around, Zuby. Let's get it out of sight quick."

His wife sprang at the bonnet, but he barred her off with an arm like a fence-rail, removed a lid from the stove, put the unbecoming article in on the red-hot coals, and replaced the lid. "There!" he said, "that helps the scenery, don't it? Now let's have supper."

Captain Dan laughed again. For an instant Azuba stared, white-faced, at the cremation of the bonnet. Then she darted to the door. "I'll go now," she cried, "if I have to go bareheaded! I'll show you! Let go of me!"

Mr. Ginn had thrown an arm about her waist. She pulled his hair and gave him some vigorous slaps on the cheek, but he smiled on. "You want to get supper, Zuby," he coaxed. "I know you do. You just think it over now. It's too noisy out here to do much thinkin'. Where's a nice quiet place? Oh! this'll be first rate."

He bore her, kicking like a jumping-jack, across the kitchen to the closet where the pans and cooking utensils were kept. "Think it over in there, Zuby," he said calmly, shutting the door and planting himself in a chair against it. "That's a fine place to think. Now, Cap'n, you and me can have our smoke, while she's thinkin' what to give us to eat; hey?"

Judging by the thumps and kicks and screams inside the closet the housekeeper's thoughts were otherwise engaged.

"You let me out, Labe Ginn!" she screamed. "Cap'n Dott, you make him let me out!"

Daniel, weary from laughing, could only gasp.

"I can't, Zuba!" he answered, choking. "I can't! It ain't my affair. I couldn't interfere between husband and wife. You're a free woman, Zuba, you know. You ought to be advanced enough by this time to fight your own battles."

"That's right, Zuba," counseled Mr. Ginn. "Fight 'em out in there. You can be just as free in there as you want to. Have some of my terbacker, Cap'n?"

Captain Dan declined. The prisoner continued to thump and kick and threaten. Her jailer refilled and lighted his pipe.

"Thought over that bill of fare, Zuby?" he shouted, after a time.

More thumps and threats; tears as well. Daniel began to feel pity instead of triumph.

"Hadn't you better, Labe," he began. Mr. Ginn waved him to silence.

"How about supper, Zuby?" he called. "Oh, all right, all right. I don't know as I'm as hungry as I was, anyway. Appetite's kind of passin' off, I cal'late. You stay in there and think till mornin', and we'll have it for breakfast."

Silence--actual silence--for a moment. Then Azuba asked, in a half-smothered but much humbler voice, "Oh, Labe! WON'T you let me out?"

"Sure thing--if you've thought up that supper for me and Cap'n Dan'l."

"But I did so want--oh, if I could only tell you! It was SO necessary for me to go to that meetin'. You've spiled everything, and just as 'twas goin' so nice. What Gertie'll say I don't know."

Daniel developed a new interest.

"Gertie?" he repeated. "Hush, Labe! wait a minute. What's Gertie got to do with it?"

"Nothin', nothin'. Oh, Labe, PLEASE."

"Well, I tell you, Zuby: it's close to nine now, and that's too late for you to be cruisin' out to meetin's. Sorry you have to miss the speeches and things, but--Say, I tell you what I'll do. If it's a sermon you want I'll preach you one, myself. Make it up while you're settin' the table. Ready to come out and be good? That's right. Now,

I bet you she's thought up somethin' that'll make our mouths water, Cap'n."

The crestfallen housekeeper emerged, blinking, from her thinking place. She removed her coat and, without even a glance at her employer, proceeded to adjust the dampers of the stove. Captain Dan rose from his chair.

"I'm afraid I can't stop to have supper with you, Labe," he said. "I've got an--an errand to do outside, myself. I'll eat at a restaurant or somewhere. You'll stay here to-night, of course. I'll see you in the mornin'. Good-night! Good-night, Zuby!"

Azuba did not reply. Laban shouted protests. What was the sense of going just when supper was being made ready at last? Daniel, however, did not stay to listen. He climbed the back stairs to the hall, put on his overcoat and hat and went out. He had been too tender-hearted to remain in the kitchen and gloat, or appear to gloat, over a "free woman's" humiliation. Nevertheless, he astonished the waiter at the restaurant where he ate dinner by bursting into laughter at intervals, and with no obvious cause. The waiter suspected that the old gentleman from the country had been drinking, and the size of the tip he received helped to confirm his suspicion.

His dinner eaten, Captain Dan walked slowly home. Unlocking the front door with his latchkey he tiptoed through the hall and listened at the head of the back stairs. There was a steady murmur of voices in the kitchen. He heard a bass grumble from Mr. Ginn and Azuba's shrill reply. Then the pair burst into a laugh. Evidently some sort of understanding on a peaceful basis had been reached. Still chuckling, the captain went up to his bedroom, removed his outer garments and his shoes, put on his bathrobe and slippers, and settled himself, with the evening paper, to await his wife's return. He resolved to be awake when she did return; he had news for her. Filled with this resolution, he read for three-quarters of an hour steadily, then at intervals between naps, and at last dropped into a sound sleep, the paper in his lap.

Gertrude and Serena came home at a surprisingly early hour. Not that the committee meeting was over; it was not. In fact, the elaborate dinner spread before her supporters by the grateful Mrs. Black had scarcely reached its last course when Gertrude suddenly rose from the table and hastened to her mother's side. She had been watching the latter with increasing anxiety all the evening.

"What is it, Mother?" she asked. "What is it?"

Serena, sitting with her elbow on the table, her hand to her forehead, and her untasted ice before her, looked up in a bewildered way.

"What--why, what do you mean, Gertie?" she stammered. "What--I don't think I understood you."

"What is the matter, Mother?" repeated Gertrude. "Don't you feel well?"

Still Mrs. Dott did not seem to understand. She tried to smile, but the vague uncertainty of the smile caused even Annette, who had been deep in discussion of a plan for securing the vote of a still doubtful member, to cease speaking and regard her guest with surprise.

"What is it, Mother?" urged Gertrude. "You look so strange. Are you ill?"

Serena gazed at her for a moment, rose, stood looking about in the same hesitating, uncertain manner, and then, throwing her arms about her daughter's neck, burst into hysterical sobs.

The alarmed guests clustered about them, asking questions, exclaiming, and offering suggestions.

"What IS it?" demanded Annette. "My DEAR! What IS it?"

Serena, still clinging to Gertrude, continued to sob.

"I--I don't know," she moaned. "I--I feel so strange. I'm--I'm tired, I guess. I'm--I'm worn out. I--oh, Gertie, take me home. Take me home--please."

"Yes, yes, Mother, dear. We will go home at once. Come."

She led her into the next room. Annette, hastening with a glass of wine and the smelling salts, caught the young lady's arm.

"She isn't going to be ill, seriously sick, is she?" she demanded. "You don't think she is. It would be dreadful if she was."

Gertrude shook her head.

"I don't know," she answered. "I certainly hope not. Will you call a carriage, Mrs. Black?"

"Yes, yes, I'll call one right away. Oh, I hope she isn't going to be sick. It would be dreadful--just now. The election is only two weeks off, and without her I--we should be almost certain to lose. I know we should. Oh, Serena, DEAR! you WON'T be sick, will you? for my sake!"

It did not seem to occur to the agitated Annette that her friend might not care to be ill, for her own sake. But it was evident that Gertrude was thinking just that. The young lady's tone was sharp and decidedly cold.

"She is tired out," she said. "She has worn herself out working for her--for her friends, Mrs. Black. Will you call the carriage?"

"Yes, yes. They are calling it now. I'm so sorry the chauffeur--or--or Phelps--is out. If he--if they were not you could use our car. But, oh, Serena--"

Serena looked up. She was calmer now, she had heard, and loyally she answered.

"Don't worry, Annette," she said. "I am not going to be sick. I won't. You can depend on me. Oh, Gertie, I'm SO tired! My poor head!"

The carriage came and she and Gertrude were driven home. Annette did not offer to accompany them. It was such an important meeting and there were so many things to talk about, she explained. She would call the very next day. Serena thanked her; Gertrude said nothing.

Serena seemed better on the way home. When they reached the house she announced bravely that she was all right again; all she needed was a night's rest, that was all. Gertrude insisted on accompanying her to her room. They found Daniel asleep in the chair, and to him his daughter explained the situation. The captain was too greatly disturbed to think of his "news," the news of Mr. Ginn's arrival and Azuba's subjection.

"You get right into bed, Serena," he ordered. "Gertie, you call the doctor."

But his wife would not hear of the doctor. "Nonsense!" she declared. "I don't need any doctor. I want to go to bed. I'm tired--tired. I won't see the doctor or anybody else. Go, Gertie, please go. Your father will be with me. Please go! I am all right now."

Gertrude went, but she whispered to the captain that she would wait in the library and, if they needed her, he was to be sure and call.

In the library she took a book--one of Aunt Lavinia's legacies--from the shelf and tried to read, but that was impossible. She could not read, she could only think, and thinking was most unpleasant. Her conscience was troubling her. Had she been wrong? Had she gone too far? She had meant well, her plan had seemed the only solution of the family problem, but perhaps she had made a mistake. She loved her mother devotedly. Oh, if anything serious should happen--if, because of her, her mother should be ill--if--if she should. She could not think of it. She would never forgive herself, never. It had been all wrong from the beginning, and she had been wicked and foolish. It had cost her so much already; her own life's happiness. And yet--and yet, she had meant to do right. But now, after that misunderstanding and consequent sacrifice, if her mother should--

She broke down and was very, very miserable.

Someone was at the front door, fumbling with a latchkey. Gertrude hurriedly sprang from her chair, wiped her eyes with her handkerchief and was on her way to the hall when the door opened. The hall was dark; she had turned off the light when she came downstairs; and for a moment she could not see who it was that had entered. She, however, was in the full glow from the electrolier in the library and Mr. Hungerford saw her.

"Ah, Gertrude," he said cheerfully. "Is that you? Don't go. Don't go."

He was at the doorway before she could reach it. He had been dining out with some masculine friends--"old college chums," he had explained when announcing the situation--and was in evening dress.

"Don't go," he repeated. "What's the hurry? Wait a minute and I'll join you."

He removed his overcoat and silk hat and tossed them carelessly upon the hall table. The hat fell to the floor, but he did not heed it. Then he entered the library.

"What!" he exclaimed. "Alone? Burning the midnight oil and all that sort of thing. Where is old--er--where's your father?"

Gertrude replied that her father had retired. She was about to do so, she added. It was untrue, but she was not in the mood for a conversation with anyone, least of all with Cousin Percy.

Cousin Percy, however, appeared decidedly conversational. His face was a trifle flushed and he smiled more than seemed necessary.

"Well," he observed, "this is an unexpected pleasure. Didn't expect to find anyone up at this hour."

Gertrude curtly remarked that it was not late.

"I didn't mean up, I meant in. Did I say 'up'? Most extraordinary. I thought you and Mrs. Dott were playing the political game this evening. Expected to find you out and old--the respected captain, I mean--in the arms of--what's his name?--Morpheus. That's all right, though; that's all right. So much the better. We can talk--you and I."

"I don't feel like talking. You must excuse me."

"What? Don't feel like talking? Cruel! Why not? It isn't late; you said so your-self."

"I know but--really, you must excuse me."

She was moving toward the door, but again he stepped in her way.

"Now, Gertie," he said. Then he broke into a laugh. "Called you Gertie, didn't I?" he said. "Beg pardon. Quite unintentional. It slipped out before I thought. But you don't mind, do you? It's a pretty name. Just a little bit less formal than Gertrude, eh? Don't you think so--Gertie?"

Gertrude hesitated. She was humiliated and angry, but she did not wish a scene. Her parents might hear and her mother must on no account be disturbed.

"Perhaps it is," she answered.

"Then you don't mind?"

"No. Now, Percy, you must excuse me. Goodnight!"

"Wait! Wait! Gertie, I have something to say to you. Been wanting to say it for a long time, but haven't had the opportunity. You have kept out of my way. Ha! ha! you know you have. Perhaps you guessed I wanted to say it. Was that it? Ha! ha! was it now? Confess; was it?"

Gertrude did not answer. She moved toward the door. Mr. Hungerford laugh-ingly blocked the passage.

"No, no!" he cried. "No, no! Mustn't run away. I am going to say it, and you must hear me. Come, don't be cross."

"Mr. Hungerford, will you stand aside? I can not talk with you to-night, or listen. I am going to my room."

The tone in which this was uttered should have been a warning, but Cousin Percy was in no condition to recognize warnings, or to heed them if he had. His smile grew more tender and his tone more intimate.

"Not yet," he smiled; "not just yet. I can't permit it. Gertie, I--"

"If you don't stand aside I shall call my father."

"What? Call the old gentleman? No, you don't mean it. Of course you don't. You wouldn't be so unreasonable. Come, come! we're friends at least. We under-stand each other, don't we?"

"I understand YOU, thoroughly."

"Of course you do," with a triumphant leer. "And you know what I am going to say. Ah ha! I was sure you did. And you've confessed. Gertie, my dearest girl, I--What! Going? Not until you pay toll. I'm keeper of the gate and you must pay before you pass, you know. If you won't listen you must pay. Ha! ha!"

He held out his hands. Gertrude shrank back. She was not afraid of him, but she did fear a scene. She had threatened to call her father, but she could not do that. If she did her mother would be frightened. She moved away, to the other side of the library table.

Cousin Percy interpreted her retreat as a sign of surrender. He followed her, laughing.

"Come!" he insisted. "I knew you didn't mean it. Come, my dear! Just one. I--"

He tripped over the captain's favorite footstool and fell to his knees. With a sudden movement Gertrude jerked the cord of the electrolier on the table. The lights went out. She dodged around the table, through the doorway, into the hall, and up the stairs. Mr. Hungerford, pawing in the darkness at the offending footstool, swore. Then he laughed.

"Good!" he exclaimed. "Very good, but not good enough. You can't escape that way. I shall find you. Where are you hiding? Eh! Ah, there you are!"

He had scrambled to his feet and hurried to the doorway. There were the sounds of footsteps and the rustle of skirts at the other end of the hall.

"There you are!" he cried. "I've caught you. Now you must pay--twice."

He put his arm about a feminine waist and imprinted a kiss upon a feminine cheek. Then his own cheek received a slap which made his head ring, and the hall echoed with a shrill scream.

"Labe!" shrieked Azuba. "Oh, Labe! Help! Come quick!"

Mr. Ginn came up the back stairs three steps at a time.

"What is it? What's the matter, Zuby?" he demanded.

"A man! A man! He--he--"

"Where is he? What's he doin'?"

"He--there he is. Hear him? There!"

Mr. Hungerford, paralyzed with astonishment and dizzy from the slap, had moved, injudiciously. Laban heard him.

"Hey?" he bellowed. "Ah! I've got him. Stand still, dum you! I've got him, Zuby. Who is he? What did he do?"

"I--I don't know who he is," panted the frightened housekeeper. "He--he kissed me."

"KISSED you! YOU? Why--"

"It's a mistake!" cried Cousin Percy, frantically struggling in the grasp of his captor. "I--Stop! Stop! Help! Help!"

The hall became a pandemonium of thumps, struggles, cries for help, and pleas for mercy. Azuba added her shrieks to the tumult. From above Captain Dan shouted and Serena screamed. Then the chandelier blazed. Gertrude had pressed the button at the top of the stairs.

"Let him be!" ordered the young lady, rushing to the rescue. "Don't! don't! Azuba, stop him!"

"Labe! stop! stop!" pleaded the housekeeper. "You--My soul! it's Mr. Hungerford."

It was what there was left of Mr. Hungerford. Mr. Ginn extended the disheveled, whimpering remnant at arm's length and regarded it.

"Humph!" he grunted. "You know him, do you?"

"Know him! Of course I do. But--but I must say--"

Captain Dan came tearing down the stairs, his bathrobe fluttering and a slipper missing. In one hand he held a pair of scissors, the only offensive weapon which he had found available at the moment.

"What in blazes?" he demanded. "Burglars, is it?"

Gertrude answered. "No, Daddy," she said gravely. "It's no one but Cousin Percy. And--and Mr. Ginn. Why, Mr. Ginn, is--is it you?"

Laban nodded. "It's me, all right," he observed grimly. "Who the devil is this? That's what I want to know."

Daniel turned to the captive.

"Why--why, Percy!" he gasped. "What--what's happened to you? Let go of him, Labe Ginn! Percy Hungerford, what--what's all this?"

Mr. Hungerford, suddenly freed from the grasp upon his torn shirt collar, staggered against the wall.

"It's--it's a mistake," he panted. "I--I--this--this blackguard assaulted me. I--I--"

"Assaulted you! I should say he had. Labe Ginn, what did you assault him for?"

Mr. Ginn glared at his victim.

"Blackguard, am I?" he growled. "Humph! Well, if he starts to callin' me names, I'll--"

"Belay! Answer me! What have you been doin' to him? Look at him! What do you mean by assaultin' him that way?"

"What do I mean? When a man comes home from sea and finds another man kissin' his wife, what would he be likely to mean?"

Daniel could not answer. He looked about him in absolute bewilderment. Gertrude choked and turned away.

"Kissin'!" repeated Captain Dan. "Kissin' your wife? Kissin' ZUBA! I--I--am I crazy, or are you, or--or is he?"

Apparently he judged the last surmise to be the most likely. Cousin Percy, frantic with rage and humiliation, tried to protest.

"It's a lie!" he cried. "It's a lie!"

The captain turned to his housekeeper.

"Zuba," he demanded, "what sort of lunatic business is this? Do you know?"

Azuba straightened.

"I don't know much," she announced sharply. "All I know is that I come upstairs in the dark and he grabbed me and--and said somethin' about my payin' him--and then he--he--done the other thing. That's all I know, and it's enough. Don't talk to ME! I never was so surprised and mortified in MY life."

"But--but what's it mean? Can't anybody tell me, for the Lord sakes?"

Gertrude stepped forward. "I think I understand," she said. "Our cousin made a mistake, that's all. I will explain at another time, Daddy. If--if you will all go away, he and I will have an interview. I think I can settle it better than anyone else. Go, please. I'm sure Mother needs you."

The mention of his wife caused her father to forget everything else, even his overwhelming curiosity.

"My soul!" he cried. "She heard this; and--and I left her all alone."

He bolted up the stairs. Gertrude's next remark was addressed to the housekeeper.

"Azuba," she said, "would you and your husband mind leaving us? Perhaps you'd better not go to bed. I--I may need Mr. Ginn later on; perhaps I may. But if you and he were to go down to the kitchen and wait just a few moments I should be so much obliged. Will you?"

Azuba hesitated.

"Leave you?" she repeated. "With--with him?"

"Yes. I have something to say to him. Something important."

She and Azuba exchanged looks. The latter nodded.

"All right," she said decisively; "course we'll go. Come, Labe."

But Laban seemed loath to move.

"I ain't got through with him yet," he observed. "I'd only begun."

"You come with me. Have you forgot all I told you so soon? Come!"

"Hey? No; no, I ain't forgot. Is this part of it?"

"Part of it's part of it; the rest ain't. You come, 'fore you do any more spilin'. Come, now."

Mr. Ginn went. At the head of the back stairs he paused.

"You'll sing out if you need me?" he asked. "You will, won't you? You'll only have to sing once."

He tramped heavily down. Gertrude walked over to the victim of the "mistake" and its consequences.

"I think," she said coldly, "that you had better go."

"Go?" Mr. Hungerford looked at her. "Go?" he repeated.

"Yes. I give you this opportunity. There will not be another. Go to your room, change your clothes, pack your trunk, and go--now, to-night."

"What do you mean? That I am to go--and not come back?"

"Yes."

"But, Gertrude--Gertie--"

"Don't call me that. Don't DARE to speak to me in that tone. Go--now."

"But, Ger--Miss Dott, I--I--don't you see it was all a mistake? I--"

"Stop! I am trying very hard to keep my temper. We have had scenes enough to-night. My mother is ill and she must not be disturbed again. If you do not go to your room and pack and leave at once, I shall call Mr. Ginn and have you put out, just as you are. I am giving you that opportunity. You had better avail yourself of it. I mean what I say."

She looked as if she did. Cousin Percy evidently thought so. His humbleness disappeared.

"So?" he snarled angrily. "So that's it, eh? What do you think I am?"

Gertrude's eyes flashed. She bit her lip. When she spoke it was with deliberate distinctness. Every word was as sharp and cold as an icicle.

"Do you wish to know what I think you are?" she asked. "What I thought at the very beginning you were, and what I have been taking pains to make sure of ever since I came to this house? Very well, I'll tell you."

She told him, slowly, calmly, and with biting exactness. His face was flushed when she began; when she finished it was white.

"That is what you are," she said. "I do not merely think so. I have studied you carefully; I have stooped to associate with you in order to study you; I have studied you through your friends; I KNOW what you are."

His anger and mortification were choking him.

"You--you--" he snarled. "So that is it, is it? You have been using me as a good thing. As a--as a--"

"As you have used my father and mother and their simple-minded goodness and generosity. Yes, I have."

"You have been making a fool of me! And Holway--confound him--"

"Mr. Holway was useful. He helped. And he, too, understands, now."

"By--by gad--I--I won't go. I'll--"

Gertrude walked to the rear of the hall.

"Mr. Ginn!" she called, "will you come, please?"

Laban came. He looked happy and expectant.

"Here I be," he observed eagerly.

"Mr. Ginn," said Gertrude, "this--gentleman--is going to his room for a few minutes. He is preparing to leave us. If he doesn't come down and leave this house in a reasonable time will you kindly assist him? He will, no doubt, send for his trunks to-morrow. But he must go to-night. He must. Do you understand, Mr. Ginn?"

Laban grinned. "I cal'late I do," he said. "Zuba's been tellin' me some. He'll go."

"Thank you. Good-night!"

She ascended the stairs. The first mate looked at his watch.

"Fifteen minutes is enough to pack any trunk," he observed. "I'll give you that much. Now, them, tumble up. Lively!"

At the door of her parents' room Gertrude rapped softly. Captain Dan opened it and showed a pallid, agitated face.

"She's mighty sick, Gertie," he declared. "I wish you'd telephone for the doctor."

CHAPTER XIV

The doctor came, stayed for some time and, after administering a sleeping draught and ordering absolute quiet for his patient, departed, saying that he would come again in the morning. He did so and, before leaving, took Captain Dan and Gertrude into his confidence.

"It is a complete collapse," he said gravely. "Mrs. Dott is worn out, physically and mentally. She must be kept quiet, she must not worry about anything, she must remain in bed, and she must see no one. If she does this, if she rests--really rests--we may fight off nervous prostration. If she does not--anything may happen. With your permission I shall send a nurse."

The permission was given, of course, and the nurse came. She was a quiet, pleasant, capable person, and Daniel and Gertrude liked her. She took charge of the sick room. Azuba--the common sense, adequate, domestic Azuba of old, not the rampant "free woman" of recent days--was in charge of the kitchen. Her husband remained, at Daniel's earnest request, but he spent his time below stairs.

"Sartin sure I won't be in the way, Cap'n, be you?" he asked earnestly. "I can go somewheres else just as well as not, to some boardin' house or somewheres. Zuby Jane won't mind; we can see each other every day."

"Not a mite of it, Labe," replied Daniel earnestly. "There's plenty of room and you can stay here along with your wife just as well as not. I'd like to have you. Maybe--" with a suggestive wink, "maybe you can kind of--well, kind of keep things runnin' smooth--in the galley. You know what I mean."

Laban grinned. "Cal'late you won't have no more trouble that way, Cap'n," he observed. "I guess that's over. Zuby and I understand each other better'n we did. I THOUGHT she was mighty--"

"Mighty what?" Mr. Ginn had broken off his sentence in the middle.

"Oh, nothin'. It's all right, Cap'n Dott. Don't you worry about Zuby and me. We'll boss this end of the craft; you 'tend to the rest of it. Say, that Hungerford swab ain't come back, has he?"

"No. No, he hasn't. He's gone for good, it looks like. Sent for his trunk and gone. That's queer, too. No, he hasn't come back."

Laban seemed disappointed. "Well, all right," he said. "If he should come, just send for me. I'd just as soon talk to him as not--rather, if anything."

The captain shook his head in a puzzled way.

"That business of--of him and Zuba was the strangest thing," he declared. "I can't make head nor tail of it, and Gertie won't talk about it at all. He said 'twas a mistake, and of course it must have been. Either that or he'd gone crazy. No sane man would--"

"What's that?" It was Mr. Ginn's turn to question, and Daniel's to look foolish. "What's that no sane man would do?" demanded Laban sharply.

"Why--why, go away and leave us without sayin' good-by," explained the captain, with surprising presence of mind. "Er--well, so long, Laban. Make yourself at home. I've got to see how Serena is."

He hurried up the back stairs. Mr. Ginn, who seemed a trifle suspicious, called after him, but the call was unheeded.

At the door of his wife's room--his room no longer--Captain Dan rapped softly. The nurse opened the door.

"How is she?" he whispered.

"She is asleep now," whispered the nurse in reply. "You must not come in."

"I wasn't goin' to. But--but--has she been askin' for me?"

"Yes. I told her you were out. If she wakes and asks for you I will call. You may see her then for a minute or two. She is easier when you are with her--or near by."

This was true. The one person Serena wished to see most of all was her husband. She asked for Gertrude, of course, but it was Daniel for whom she asked continually. If he were near her she seemed almost happy and contented. It was when he sat beside the bed that she ceased tossing upon the pillow and lay quiet, looking at him.

"You are a good man, Daniel," she whispered, on one of these occasions. "A dear, good, unselfish man."

"No, no, I ain't any such thing," protested the captain hastily.

"But you are. And--and WHAT should I do without you now?"

"Sh-sh! I'm not much help. Land knows I wish I was more."

"You ARE the help; all the help I have. Gertie--Daniel, you will keep an eye on Gertie, won't you. You won't let her do anything foolish."

"Who? Gertie? She won't do foolish things. She ain't that kind."

"I know, but she has changed so. It worries me. Percy--"

"Now don't you worry about Percy. He isn't here now."

"Not here? Where is he?"

"I don't know. He's gone away--for a spell, anyhow. Maybe that vacation he used to talk about is over. I guess that's it."

Serena was too weak to ask further questions, even concerning so surprising a matter as Cousin Percy's sudden departure. But she did make one further plea.

"Daniel," she begged, "if Annette calls about the Chapter you tell her--"

"I've told her. She understands. She says it's all right."

"Does she? I'm so glad. Oh, Daniel, you'll have to take charge of everything now. I can't, and Gertrude--you must do it, yourself, Daniel. You MUST. Of Azuba and Gertie and everything. I rely on you. You WILL, won't you, Daniel?"

"Sure I will. I'm skipper now, Serena. You ought to see how the hands jump when I give an order."

It was true, too; the hands did "jump" at the captain's orders. He was skipper, for the time being. His wife's illness, Mr. Hungerford's absence, Gertrude's meekness--she was a silent and conscience-stricken young lady--all combined to strengthen Daniel's resolution, and he was, for the first time in years, the actual head of the household. He took active charge of the bills and financial affairs, he commanded Azuba to do this and that, he saw the callers who came and he sent them to the rightabout in a hurry.

His statement concerning Mrs. Black was not the literal truth. Annette had called, that was true; she had called the very next morning after her chief aide was stricken. But she had not declared that everything was "all right"; far from it.

"But can't I see her, Captain Dott?" she begged. "I MUST see her for just a minute."

"Sorry, ma'am, but you can't do it. Doctor's orders. She mustn't be disturbed."

"But I've got to see her. I must talk with her."

"I know, but I'm afraid you can't. You can talk to me, if that will do any good."

"It won't. Of course it won't. Where is Gertrude? Let me talk to her."

Daniel climbed the stairs to his daughter's room. He found her sitting at her desk; she had been writing "regrets" in answer to various invitations. She turned a careworn face in his direction.

"What is it, Daddy?" she asked. "Mother is not worse, is she?"

"No, no; she's better, if anything. But that--er--Annette Black has come and, long as she can't see Serena, she wants to talk to you."

"About her precious politics, I suppose."

"Your supposin' is as nigh right as anything mortal can be, Gertie. That's what she wants."

"I can't see her. I don't want to see her. I don't want to hear the word politics. I--"

"That's enough, that's enough. I'll 'tend to HER. You stay right here."

He descended to the drawing-room, where Annette was fidgeting on the edge of a chair, and announced calmly that Gertrude was not at home.

The caller's agitation got the better of her temper.

"Nonsense!" she snapped. "I don't believe it. How do you know she isn't?"

"Because she said so. Lovely mornin' for a walk, isn't it?"

Mrs. Black rose and stalked to the threshold. But there she turned once more.

"If your wife knew," she cried hysterically, "how I, her best friend, was treated in her house, she--she--"

Daniel stepped forward. "I beg your pardon, Mrs. Black," he said. "Maybe I have been pretty plain spoken. I'm sorry if I've hurt your feelin's. But, you see, we're all upset here. I'm upset, and Gertie's as much so as the rest. She can't talk to you, or anybody else, now. I'm willin' to try, but you say my talkin' won't do any good."

"Of course it won't. Oh, don't you SEE? I'm sorry Serena is not well, but this is IMPORTANT."

"I know, but so's her health, 'cordin' to my thinkin'."

"If I might see her just a moment. It is so provoking. Just at this critical time!

Doesn't my--her election mean ANYTHING to you? Don't you care about the cause?"

The captain shook his head. "All I'm carin' for is my wife, just now," he said. "She's all I can think about. If some of us had thought more about her, maybe--" He stopped, cleared his throat, and added: "I know you'll understand and forgive us, when you think it over. I'll tell her you called. Good-mornin'."

If he supposed this was the end, he was mistaken. Annette was not so easily whipped or discouraged. She called again that afternoon, and again the next day. Each morning for a week she came, and, between times, other adherents of the Black-Dott party called. They all asked concerning the invalid, but their interest plainly centered upon her part in the campaign. Would she be well enough to take part in the election, that was the question. They sent flowers and notes. The flowers reached the lady for whom they were intended; the notes did not. And, after the first week, the calls became fewer. Annette and her followers had, apparently, given up hope of aid and advice from their candidate for vice-president. At any rate they ceased to trouble the captain and his daughter.

"It's all the better, Daddy, dear," said Gertrude. "Mother will have a chance to rest and improve now."

And Serena did improve, slowly at first, then with gratifying rapidity. She began to sit up for a portion of each day and to sleep through the greater part of each night. At the end of the tenth day the doctor announced that the nurse's services were no longer necessary.

"She will be all right now," he said, referring to his patient. "But she must continue to have absolute rest and she must not be worried or permitted to worry. If you and she could go somewhere, Captain Dott, to some quiet place in the country, and stay there for six months, I think it would help her more than anything. Can you do it?"

"I can do it, Doctor," replied Daniel eagerly. "I'd like to do it. I'll go anywhere, if it will help her."

"Good! Then I will advise it and you and Miss Dott must back my advice. Will you?"

"I will, and so'll Gertie, I'm sure. You speak to her, Doctor. We'll do the backin' up."

So the doctor made the suggestion. Serena received it quietly, but, when her husband came to do his share of the "backing up," she shook her head.

"I'd like to, Daniel," she said. "I'd like to, but I can't."

"You can't? Course you can! Now let's think where we'll go. Niagara Falls, hey? You always wanted to go to the Falls."

"No, Daniel."

"No? Well, then, how about Washin'ton? We'll see the President, and the monument, and the Smithsonian Museum, and Congress--we'll see ALL the curiosities and relics. We'll go to--"

"Don't, Daniel. It makes me tired out just to hear about them. I couldn't stand all that."

"Course you couldn't! What a foolhead I am! The doctor said you needed rest and quiet, and Washin'ton is about as quiet as the Ostable Cattle Show. Well, what do you say to the White Mountains?"

"In winter? No, Daniel, if I went anywhere I should like to go to--to--"

"Where, Serena? Just name it and I'll buy the tickets."

"Daniel, I'd rather go to Trumet than anywhere else."

Captain Dan could scarcely believe it.

"WHAT!" he cried. "Trumet? You want to go to Trumet, Serena? YOU?"

"Yes. I've been wanting to go for some time. I never told you; I wouldn't even admit it to myself; but I've thought about it a great deal. I was getting so tired, so sick of all the going about and the dressing up and the talking, talking all the time. I longed to be somewhere where there was nothing going on and where you and I could be together as we used to be. And, oh, Daniel--"

"Yes, Serena? Yes?"

"Oh, Daniel, since I've been really sick, since I've been getting better and could think at all, I've been thinking more and more about our old house at Trumet, and how nice and comfortable we were there, and what pleasant evenings you and I used to have together. It was home, Daniel, really and truly home, and this place never has been, has it?"

"You bet it hasn't! It's been--well, never mind, but it wasn't home. Lordy, but I'm glad to hear you talk this way, Serena! I haven't thought anything else since we first landed, but I never imagined you did."

"I didn't, at first. It has been only lately since I began to feel so tired and my head troubled me so. Daniel, I'm not sure that our coming here wasn't a mistake."

The captain was perfectly sure. He sprang to his feet.

"That's all right, Serena," he cried. "If it was a mistake it's one that can be straightened out in two shakes of slack jib sheet. You stay here and rest easy. I'll be back in a few minutes."

"Where are you going?"

"I'm going to make arrangements for our trip to Trumet. 'Twon't take me long."

"Daniel, stop! Sit down. I didn't say I was going. I said I should like to go."

"That's the same thing. Now, Serena, I know what's frettin' you. You're thinkin' what'll become of this house and all the fine things in it. They'll be all right. We could rent this house in no time, I know it. I ain't sure but what we could sell it if we wanted to. That real estate fellow, the one Barney--B. Phelps, I mean--introduced me to down street one time, met me t'other day and told me if I ever thought of sellin' this place to let him know. Said he had a customer, or thought he had, that knew the house well and always liked it. He believed that feller would buy, if the price was right. Course I didn't pay much attention then; I judged you wouldn't think of sellin', but--"

"Stop! stop, Daniel! You are so excited it makes me nervous again to hear you. I wasn't thinking of the house at all. The way I feel now I had as soon sell it as not. But that isn't it. I can't leave Scarford. I can't!"

Daniel's enthusiasm faded. There was determination in his wife's tone. He sat down again.

"Oh!" he observed wistfully, "you can't? You're sure you can't, Serena? You know what the doctor said. Why can't you go?"

"Because I can't. It is impossible. I couldn't leave the Chapter. Don't you SEE, Daniel? I am a candidate for vice-president. My friends--the truest, most loyal friends a woman ever had--are depending upon me. I couldn't desert them. I told you that before. Would they desert me?"

"I suppose likely they wouldn't," reluctantly.

"You know they wouldn't. No personal considerations, no selfish reasons, NOTHING could make them do it. But I've said this all before, Daniel. You must see why I have to stay. I'd like to go, I'd love to, but I can't. Let's talk of something else."

Captain Dan sighed. "I presume likely you're right, Serena," he admitted. "It would seem like a mean trick, the way you put it. But after the election? You said, when we was talkin' before, that after you was elected maybe you would go with Gertie and me somewhere. And we'll go to Trumet, that's where we'll go."

"All right, Daniel, dear, we'll see. And don't worry about me. I am almost well again and I am going to be completely well. Now won't you ask Gertie to come in and talk with me? I am beginning to think about the election. Gertrude must go. We need her vote and her influence. Has she been helping Annette? I hope she has. Send her to me, Daniel, please."

So the captain, his hopes somewhat dashed, but finding comfort in his wife's new longing to visit the one spot on earth which spelled home to him, left the room to carry Serena's message to their daughter.

He was busy at the desk in the library when, several hours later, Gertrude entered. She was wearing her hat and coat and, coming into the library, stood beside him. He looked up. His expression surprised and alarmed her.

"Why, what's the matter, Daddy?" she asked anxiously. "You look as if something dreadful had happened. What is it?"

Her father put down his pen. A sheet of paper, covered with figures, was on the desk before him; so, also, was the family checkbook which had been, until the illness of Mrs. Dott, in that lady's sole charge.

"Matter?" he repeated. "Matter? Humph! Do I look as if somethin' was the matter? Where have you been?"

"I have been out. Mother was so anxious about the election that I promised her I would see Mrs. Black and some of the others this very day. I have been calling on them."

"Have, hey? Well, what's the prospect? The cause of right and Black, and justice and Dott is goin' to prevail, I presume likely, isn't it?"

"I don't know. I couldn't find out anything. Mrs. Black was not in, at least that is what the maid said; but I am almost sure she was in. I think I saw her peeping between the curtains as I went down the steps."

"That so? Perhaps she was dosin' you with the same medicine I handed her when she called that first day after Serena was taken down."

"I thought of that. But I called on three other leaders of Mother's party--"

"Yours and your mother's, you mean?"

"Yes, of course. I called on three of our leaders. Two of them were in and I talked with them. I could learn nothing from either about the election. They would not discuss it, except to say that everything would be all right. They behaved so oddly and were so embarrassed. It was perfectly obvious that they wanted to get rid of me. I can't understand it."

"There's lots of things we can't understand in this world. Don't fret your mother about it."

"I shan't, of course. But what is troubling you, Daddy? Something, I know."

"Look that way, do I? My looks don't belie me, then. See here, Gertie, I'm stumped. I've been goin' over back bills and the bankbook and the checkbook and--and--well, I'm on my beam ends, that's where I am."

"Why? Don't the books balance?"

"They balance all right. That's what's kicked me over. If they're true--course they can't be, but IF they are--we've spent close to five thousand dollars since we made this town."

"Indeed! Well?"

"WELL! Five thousand dollars! I'm sayin' five THOUSAND; do you understand?"

"I understand. I'm not surprised. Living as we do, and moving in the--in the best society as we have, the expense is large, naturally. You must expect that."

"Expect! Gertie Baker Dott, STOP talkin' that way! Our income, not countin' what the store at Trumet is fetchin' in, ain't over six thousand at the outside. Six thousand a YEAR, that is. And we've got rid of five thousand in a few months! We've got a thousand or so to live the rest of this year on. One thousand--"

"Hush, Daddy! Don't shout and wave your arms. We shall have to use a part of the principal, I presume."

"Part of the prin--Oh, my soul and body! Use part of it this year, and some more next year, and some more the next, and--and--Do you know where we'll be ten year from now? In the poorhouse, that's where."

"Oh, I hope not as bad as that. And, besides, think what a beautiful time we shall have during those ten years. Just as beautiful as we have had so far; better, no doubt, for we have really only begun."

"Ger-tie DOTT!"

"Just think of it, Daddy. We have only begun."

"I--I won't think of it! I'll stop it, that's what I'll do!"

Gertrude smilingly shook her head.

"Oh, no, you won't, Daddy," she said. "You never stop anything."

She turned to go. Captain Dan sat, speechless in his chair, staring at the bills, the figures, the checkbook, and the prospect of the poorhouse. Then he felt her hand upon his shoulder.

"Never mind, Daddy, dear," she said softly. "I wouldn't worry any more, if I were you. I think--I am beginning to hope that YOUR worries are almost over."

She kissed him and hurried out before he could collect his senses sufficiently to ask what she meant. He did ask her at their next meeting, but she only smiled and would not tell him.

The next morning Serena's first remark was concerning the election, which was to take place that evening. All that day she spoke of little else, and when the evening came she insisted upon Gertrude's leaving for the hall immediately after dinner. Laban went with her as escort, Mr. Hungerford's former enviable duty, and one which that gentleman had appeared to enjoy more than did its present occupant, who grumbled at missing his "after supper" smoke. Laban returned early. Gertrude did not.

It was after ten when the young lady appeared. She was very grave when her father met her in the hall.

"How is Mother?" she asked. "Asleep, I hope."

Daniel nodded. "Yes," he said, "she's asleep, for a wonder. She vowed and declared she was goin' to stay awake until you came, but I read out loud to her and she dropped off while I was doin' it."

"Then don't wake her, for the world. Tell her I have returned, that I am tired and have gone to bed, and will give her the news in the morning."

"That won't do. She'll want to know to-night. What is the news? Can't you leave some message? She won't rest if you don't."

Gertrude pondered. "Tell her," she began slowly, "tell her Mrs. Black is elected.

That is all to-night. Perhaps she will take--other things for granted."

But when morning, very early morning, came, Captain Dan summoned his daughter from her room.

"She's wide awake, Gertie," he said, "and she wants to know it all. You'd better come and tell her."

But Gertrude had been thinking. "I think you had better tell her first, Daddy," she said. "I think it may be wiser for you to tell her. Things were said and done at that election which she must not know. They were so mean, so contemptible that she ought never to know. If I am not there she cannot ask about them. I will tell you the result and how it came about and you can tell her. Perhaps that will be sufficient. I hope it may be. Listen, Daddy."

Daniel listened. "My soul and body!" he exclaimed, when the tale was ended. "My Godfreys! and those were the folks she figgered were her friends!"

"Yes."

"And Annette Black--"

"She was the moving spirit in the whole of it, I'm certain."

"My Godfreys! And she--and she--well, I guess maybe Serena'll be willin' to go back to Trumet NOW. She wanted to go before; 'twas only loyalty to that gang that kept her from goin'. She's sick of society, and sick of politics, and sick of Scarford. She said she'd give anything to go back to the old house and be comfortable same as we used to be; she said--"

"Daddy!" Gertrude seized his arm. She was strangely excited. "Did she--did Mother really say that?" she demanded eagerly.

"Sure, she said it! Twice she told me so."

"And she meant it?"

"She acted as if she did. Course we both realized 'twould be hard for you, Gertie, but--"

"Go! Go and tell her about the election. Quick! quick!" She fairly pushed him from her. "Don't wait," she urged, "go."

Daniel was on his way when she called him back.

"I almost forgot, Daddy, dear," she said repentantly. "I was so gl--I mean--well, never mind. What I want to say is that if you think the news will be too great a shock, if you think she is not strong enough to hear it now--"

Her father interrupted. "She's stronger than I've seen her for a fortnight," he declared. "And one thing's sure, she won't rest till she does hear it. I shall tell her, and get it over."

"Then be as gentle as you can, won't you?"

"I'll try. But, Gertie, what did you mean by sayin' you was so--so glad? That was what you was goin' to say, wasn't you? I don't see as there's much to be glad about."

"Don't you? Well, perhaps…. Run along, Daddy, run along."

She closed the door of her room. Daniel, much perplexed, departed on his unpleasant errand.

His wife was eagerly awaiting him.

"Where's Gertie?" she demanded. "Isn't she coming?"

"She'll come by and by, Serena. She isn't quite dressed yet."

"What difference does that make? Why doesn't she come, herself? Didn't you tell her I was dying to hear about the election? She must know I am."

"She does; she knows that, Serena. But she thought--she thought I'd better tell you first, myself."

Serena leaned forward to look at him. His expression alarmed her.

"Why don't you tell, then?" she asked. "Is it--oh, Daniel, it isn't bad news, is it?"

"It ain't very good, Serena."

"You don't mean--why, you said that Annette was elected; you said so last night."

"Yes--yes, she was elected, Serena; but--"

"But--but I wasn't. Is that what you mean, Daniel?"

"Well now, Serena--"

"I wasn't. Yes, it is true, I can see it in your face. I was defeated. Oh--oh, Daniel!"

Captain Dan put his arm about her.

"There! there! Serena," he said chokingly, "don't cry, don't. Don't feel too bad about it. Politics is politics, inside Chapters and out, I guess. I'm as much disappointed as you are, for your sake, but--but don't care too much, will you? Don't make yourself sick again. Don't cry no more than you can help."

Serena raised her head from his shoulder.

"I'm not crying," she said. "Really I'm not, Daniel. It is a relief to me, in a way."

"A RELIEF?"

"Yes. If it had happened a month ago I should have felt it terribly. I was crazy for office then. But lately I have dreaded it so. If I were vice-president I should have so much care, so much responsibility. Now, I shan't. The honor would have been great, I appreciate that. But, for the rest of it, I don't really care."

"Don't CARE! My soul and body!"

"No, I don't. And now," bravely, "tell me all about it. I don't quite see how Annette could win if I did not; but Miss Canby is popular, she has a great many friends. I hope," wistfully, "I hope I got a good vote. Did I, Daniel?"

Daniel's indignation burst forth.

"You didn't get any votes, Serena," he cried angrily.

"What? What? No votes? Why--"

"Not a blessed one. They put up a low-down political trick on you, Serena. They left you out to save themselves. They took advantage of your bein' sick to--to--Here, I'll tell you just what they did."

What they had done was this: Mrs. Lake and Mrs. Black, heads of the opposing factions, each realizing how close the vote was likely to be, had, with their lieutenants--Mrs. Dott excepted--gotten together five days before the election and arranged a compromise, a trade. By this arrangement, Annette was to receive the Lake party's support for president; Miss Canby was to be given the Black support for vice-president; and the united support of both factions was to be behind Mrs. Lake in her struggle for office in the National body. This arrangement was carried through. Serena, not being on hand to protect her own interest, had been sacrificed, her name had not even been brought before the members to be voted upon.

Captain Dan told of this precious scheme, just as it had been told him by his daughter. At first his wife interrupted with exclamations and questions; then she listened in silence.

"That's what they did," cried the captain angrily. "Chucked you into the scrap heap to save themselves. And you sick abed! This was the gang you worked yourself pretty nigh to death for. These were the FRIENDS you thought you had. And Annette Black was the worst of all. 'Twas her idea in the first place. Why, Serena--"

But Serena could hear no more. She threw her arms about her husband's neck and the tears, which she had so bravely repressed at the tidings of her own disappointment, burst forth.

"Oh--oh, Daniel," she sobbed, "take me away from here. I hate this place; I hate Scarford and all the dreadful people in it! Take me to Trumet, Daniel. Take me home! Take me home!"

Half an hour later Captain Dan shouted his daughter's name over the balusters.

"Gertie!" he called; "Gertie! come up here, will you?"

Gertrude came. She entered the room hastily. She had feared to find her mother prostrate, suffering from a new attack of "nerves." She was prepared to obey her father's order to 'phone for the doctor.

But Serena did not, apparently, need a doctor. She was not prostrate, and, although she was nervous, it was rather the nervousness of expectancy, coupled with determination.

"Gertie," said the captain, "I've got some news for you. Your mother and I have made up our minds to go back to Trumet, and we want you to go along with us."

The young lady did not answer at once. She looked first at Serena and then at Daniel. The troubled expression left her face and was succeeded by another, an odd one. When she spoke it was in a tone of great surprise.

"To Trumet?" she repeated. "Go back to Trumet? Not to live there?"

Captain Dan hesitated, but his wife did not.

"Yes," she said decidedly, "to live. For the present, anyhow. At least we shan't live here any longer."

"Not live here? Not live in Scarford, Mother! Why, what do you mean?"

Her father answered. "She means what she says, I presume likely," he observed impatiently. "Think she's talkin' for the fun of it? This ain't April Fool Day."

"But she can't mean it. She can't! Give up the Chapter, and all our friends--"

"Friends! They're a healthy lot of friends, they are!"

"Hush, Daddy; I'm not talking to you. Do you realize what you are saying, Mother? Give up the Chapter, and all your ambitions there? Give up Mrs. Black and Mrs. Lake and Miss Canby--"

"And that twist and squirm, antique Greece disgrace of a Dusante woman--don't forget her. Gertie, you stop now. Your ma knows--"

"Daddy, be still. Be still, I say! Mother, are you willing to give them up? And all our society! You say yourself--I've heard you often--that there is no society in Trumet. Give up our bridge lessons, and our dancing, and our teas, and--"

"For the land sakes! What is this; a catalogue you're givin' us? Stop it! Serena, you tell her to stop."

But Gertrude would not stop. She ignored her father utterly.

"Think what it would mean," she protested. "Think of your social position, Mother, the position we have worked so hard to attain."

Serena shook her head. "I don't care," she said firmly. "Our social position was good enough in Trumet."

"WHAT! Why, Mother! how often I have heard you say--"

"Never mind what I said. I have said a lot of foolish things, and done a lot, too. But I'm through. I'm sick and disgusted with it all. I'm going to be simple and comfortable and happy--yes, happy. Oh, Gertie, DON'T talk to me about society! There isn't a real, sincere person in it, not in the set we have been in. I hate Scarford and I hate society."

"Mother! how can you! And opportunity and advancement--"

"I hate them, too."

Gertrude gasped. "Why, Mother!" she exclaimed. "And it was you who first showed me the way. Who showed me how common and dull and unambitious I had been all my life? Think what leaving here would mean to me. What would Miss Dusante think? I had almost arranged to take dancing lessons of her. Think of Mr. Holway. Is there a young man like him in Trumet? Think of Cousin Percy!"

That was quite enough. Serena rose, her eyes flashing.

"Stop!" she cried. "Stop this minute! Gertrude Dott, your father and I are going back to Trumet and you are going with us."

"Oh, no, I'm not. Why, Cousin Percy--"

"Don't you dare mention his name to me."

"Why not? He is very gentlemanly and very aristocratic. You told me that when I first came, Mother. You were always talking about him and praising him then. And I'm sure he moves in the highest circles; he says he does, himself."

"He is a good-for-nothing loafer. He has sponged upon your father--"

"You have often spoken of him as an honor to the family."

"A good-for-nothing, dissipated, fast--"

"Oh, a little dissipation is expected in society, isn't it?"

"I should think you would be ashamed!"

"Why? I haven't done a thing that you haven't done, Mother. That is, nothing which your friends don't do every day. They are ever so much more advanced than I am. I have only begun. No, indeed, I am not going back to plain, common, every-day old Trumet. I shall stay here and progress. You and your friends have shown me what is expected of a girl in my position and I shall take advantage of my opportunities. Why, Mrs. Black says that, if I play my cards well, I may catch a millionaire, perhaps a foreign nobleman. How would you like to be mother-in-law to a--well, to a count, for instance?"

Mrs. Dott did not answer this question. Instead she turned to her husband.

"Daniel," she cried, "are you going to stand this? Are you that girl's father, or aren't you? Are you going to make her mind, or not?"

Daniel would have spoken, but his daughter got ahead of him.

"Oh, Father doesn't count," she observed lightly. "No one minds what he says. He didn't want to move to Scarford at all. No one minds him."

Serena stamped her foot. "Daniel Dott," she cried, "do you hear that? I call upon you, as the head of this family, to tell that girl what she's got to do, and make her do it."

Captain Dan stepped forward. Gertrude merely laughed. That laugh settled the question.

"Gertie," ordered the captain, his voice, the old quarter-deck voice which had been law aboard the Bluebird, "you march your boots to your room and pack up. We're goin' to Trumet and you're goin' along with us. March! or, by the everlastin', I'll carry you there and lock you in! You speak another word and I'll do it, anyway. Serena, I'll 'tend to her. You're tired out; lie down and rest."

"But, Daniel--"

"Lie down and rest. I'm runnin' this craft. Well," wheeling upon his daughter, "are you goin'? Or shall I carry you?"

Gertrude looked at him and then at her mother. Her lips twitched.

"I'll go, Daddy," she said meekly, and went.

When Captain Dan descended to the lower floor he found Mr. Ginn in the library.

"Hello!" hailed the latter, "you look kind of set-up and sassy, seems to me. YOU ain't had nothin' to drink, have you?"

"Drink? What do you mean by that? Has anybody around here had anything to drink?"

"I don't know. Some of 'em act as if they had. When I came into the kitchen a spell ago I found my wife and Gertie dancin' like a couple of loons."

"Dancin'?"

"Yes, sir, holdin' hands and hoppin' around like sand fleas in a clam bake. I asked 'em what set 'em goin' and they wouldn't tell me. I couldn't think of anything but liquor that would start Zuby Jane dancin'. I don't know's that would--I never tried it on her--but 'twas the only likely guess I could make."

CHAPTER XV

Captain Dan was seated in his old chair, at his old desk, behind the counter of the Metropolitan Store. His pipe, the worn, charred briar that he had left in the drawer of that very desk when he started for the railway station and Scarford, was in his mouth. Over the counter, beyond the showcases and the tables with their piles of oilskins, mittens, sou'westers, and sweaters, through the panes of the big front windows, he could see the road, the main street of Trumet. The road was muddy, and the mud had frozen. Beyond the road, between the shops and houses on the opposite side, he saw the bare brown hills, the pond where the city people found waterlilies in the summer--the pond was now a glare of ice--the sand dunes, the beach, the closed and shuttered hotel and cottages, and, beyond these, the cold gray and white of the wintry sea rolling beneath a gloomy sky. To the average person the view would have been desolation itself. To Captain Dan it was a section of Paradise. It was the picture which had been in his mind for months. And here it was in reality, unchanged, unspoiled, a part of home, his home. And he, at last, was at home again.

They had been in Trumet a week, the captain and Serena and Gertrude. Azuba had been there two days longer, having been sent on ahead of the family to open the house and get it ready. Laban remained behind as caretaker of the Scarford mansion. His term of service in that capacity was not likely to be a long one, for the real estate dealer was in active negotiation with his client, and the dealer's latest report stated that the said client was considering hiring the house, furnished, for a few months and, in the event of his liking it as well as he expected, would then, in all probability, buy.

Laban's remaining as caretaker was his own suggestion.

"Me and the old gal--Zuby Jane, I mean--have talked it over," he explained, "and it seems like the best thing to do. You've got to have somebody here, Cap'n Dott, you've got to pay somebody, and it might as well be me. I'm out of a job just now, anyway. As for me and my wife bein' separated--well, we're different from most married folks that way; it seems the natural thing for us to BE separated. We're used to it, as you might say. I don't know as we'd get along so well together if we wasn't separated. There's nothin' like separation to keep husband and wife happy along with one another. I've been with Zuby for most three weeks steady now; that's the longest stretch we've had in a good many years. We ain't quarreled once, neither."

He seemed to consider the fact remarkable. Captain Dott grinned.

"I suppose that shuttin' her up in the dish closet wasn't what you'd call a quarrel, hey?" he observed.

Mr. Ginn was momentarily embarrassed.

"Oh, that!" he exclaimed. "Humph! I forgot that, for the minute. But that wasn't a quarrel, rightly speakin'. 'Twas just a little difference of opinion on account of my not understandin' her reason for bein' so sot on havin' her own way. Soon's I understood 'twas all right. And you see yourself how peaceable she's been ever since."

So, after consultation with Azuba, the arrangement was perfected. Laban was to receive ten dollars a week, from which sum he was to provide his own meals. He was to sleep in the house, but the meals were to be obtained elsewhere. Mrs. Dott would not consider his cooking in her kitchen.

Serena bore the fatigue of the journey well and the sight of her old home, with the table set for supper, plants in the dining-room windows, and all the little familiar touches which Azuba's thoughtfulness had supplied, served to bring her the contentment and happiness she had been longing for. Each day she gained in health and strength, and the rest and freedom from care, together with the early hours-- they retired at nine-thirty each night--were doing wonders for her. Her husband was delighted at the improvement. He was delighted with everything, the familiar scenes, the smell of the salt marshes, and of the sea, the clear, cold air, the meeting with friends and acquaintances, the freedom from society--he had not even unpacked his dress suit, vowing to Gertrude that it might stay buried till Judgment, he wouldn't resurrect it--all these things delighted his soul. And now, on the Saturday morning at the end of his first week at home, as he sat in his arm chair behind the counter of the Metropolitan Store, looking at the view through the windows and at the store itself, he was a happy man. There was one flaw in his happiness, but that he had forgotten for the moment.

He glanced about him, took a long pull at his pipe, and said aloud: "Well, if I didn't know 'twas the same place, I wouldn't have known it. I never saw such a change in my life."

Nathaniel Bangs, standing by the front window, turned.

"I don't see much difference," he said. "The old town looks about the same to me."

The captain smilingly shook his head.

"'Tain't the town," he observed. "It's this store. Nate, you're a wonder, that's what you are, a wonder."

For, if the view had not changed, if it was the same upon which Daniel Dott had looked for many winters, through the windows of that very store, the store itself had changed materially. Mr. Bangs had wrought the change and it was distinctly a change for the better. The stock, and there was a surprising deal of it, was new and attractively displayed. The contents of the showcases were varied and up-to-date. Neatly lettered placards calling attention to special bargains hung in places where they were most likely to be seen. There was a spruce, swept, and garnished look to the establishment; as Azuba said when she first saw it after her return, it looked as if it had had a shave and a hair cut. In other words, the Metropolitan Store appeared wide awake and prosperous, as if it was making money--which it was.

It was not making a great deal, of course, as yet. This was the dullest season of the year. But the Christmas trade had been good and, thanks to Nathaniel's enterprise and effort, the scallop fishermen, the quahaug rakers, and the members of the life-saving crews were once more buying their outfits at the Metropolitan Store instead of patronizing Mr. J. Cohen and The Emporium. Mr. Bangs was already selecting his summer stock; and his plans for the disposal of that stock were definite and business-like.

"If you don't say no, Cap'n Dott," he had explained, "I'm going to try putting on a horse and wagon this summer. There's no reason why we shouldn't get the cottage trade down at the Neck, and all along shore. Jim Bartlett, Sam's older brother, would like the job driving that wagon. He's smart as a whip, Jim is, and he's willing to work on commission. Let him start out twice a week with a load of hats and oil-skins and belts and children's shovels and pails--all the sort of stuff the boarders and cottage folks buy and that they'd buy more of if it was brought right to their doors--and he'll catch a heap of trade that goes to Bayport or Wellmouth or The Emporium now. What he don't carry he can take orders for and deliver next trip. If you don't say no, Cap'n Dott, I'm going to try it. And I'll bet a month's wages it's a go."

Captain Dan had not said no. On the contrary he expressed enthusiastic approval of his manager's plans and enterprise. Also, he had been thinking of some adequate reward, some means of proving his gratitude real.

"You're a wonder, Nate," repeated Daniel. "I don't know how to get even with you, but I've got an idea. I've talked it over with Serena already and she's for it. I want to ask Gertie's opinion and if she says yes, and she will, I'm almost sartin, I'll tell you what it is."

"All right, Cap'n. Don't you worry yourself trying to 'get even,' as you call it, with me. I've enjoyed being in charge here. I always said there was money in a store in Trumet, if it was run as it should be. One year more and I can show you a few things, I'll bet."

"You've shown 'em already. Land of love! I should say you had."

"Give me time and I'll show you more. We have only begun.... Why, what's the matter? What made you look that way?"

"Oh, nothin', nothin'. Only your sayin' we'd only begun reminded me of--of other things. I don't suppose I'll ever hear 'only begun' without shiverin'. Humph! there's some kind of beginnin's I hope I'll never hear of again. Gertie been in this mornin', has she? She isn't in the house."

"No, I saw her go down street a little while ago. Gone for her morning walk, perhaps. How is Mrs. Dott to-day?"

"Fine. Tip top. I ain't seen her so satisfied with life for two months or more. She's gettin' better every minute."

"That's good. Contented to be back in Trumet, is she?"

"Seems to be. I am; you can bet high on that."

"And--er--Gertie, is she contented, too?"

This question touched directly the one uncertainty, the one uncomfortable doubt in the captain's mind. He looked keenly at the questioner.

"What makes you ask that?" he demanded.

"Oh, nothing much. She seems changed, that's all. She used to be so full of spirits, and so bright and lively. Now she is quiet and doesn't talk much. Looks thinner, too, and as if something was troubling her. Perhaps it is my imagination. When's John Doane coming down? 'Most time for him to be spending a Sunday with you, ain't it? Engaged folks don't usually stay apart more than a week, especially when the one is as near the other as Boston is to Trumet."

Daniel knocked the ashes from his pipe into the wastebasket.

"Oh, oh, John'll be along pretty soon, I shouldn't wonder," he said hastily. "He--he's pretty busy these days, I suppose."

"Nice thing his bein' taken into the firm, after Mr. Griffin died, wasn't it. Well, he's a pretty smart fellow, John is, and he deserves to get ahead. Did he tell you the particulars about it?"

"No. No, not all of 'em. Is that a customer in the other room?"

Mr. Bangs hurried away to attend to the customer. The captain seized the opportunity to make a timely exit. He went into the house, remained a while with his wife, and then returned. Nathaniel had gone on an order-taking trip and Sam Bartlett, the boy, was in charge. Just as Daniel entered the store from the side door Gertrude came in at the front.

"Hello, Daddy," she said. "All alone?"

"Not quite, but I'd just as soon be. Sam, go into the other room; I'll hail you if I need you. Gertie, come here. I want to have a talk with you."

Gertrude came. She took her old position, perching upon the arm of her father's chair, with her own arm about his neck.

"Gertie," began the captain, "what would you think of my makin' Nate Bangs a partner in this concern?"

Gertrude uttered an exclamation of delight.

"Splendid!" she cried. "Just what I wanted you to do. I thought of it, but I said nothing because I wanted you to say it first. It will be just the right thing."

"Ye-es, so it seemed to me. All that's good here in this store is due to Nathaniel. He's made a real, live business out of a remains that was about ready for the undertaker. I ought to give him the whole craft, but--but I hate to."

"You could. You could sell out to him and still have sufficient income to live upon in comfort here in Trumet. You might sell out, retire, and be a gentleman of leisure, one of the town's rich men. You could do that perfectly well."

Daniel grunted in disgust.

"Don't talk that way," he repeated. "I've had enough gentleman of leisure foolishness to last me through. What do you think I am; a second-hand copy of Cousin Percy, without the gilt edges? I might be kissin' Zuba by mistake if I did that."

The story of that eventful evening and the "mistake" had been told him by his daughter since the return home. Gertrude smiled.

"I guess not," she declared. "You are not in the habit of 'dining out'--in Trumet, at any rate. Have you told Mother?"

"Yes, I told her. I don't think she was much surprised. She'd guessed as much before, so I gathered from what she said."

"No doubt; the explanation was obvious enough. Well, Daddy, I did not expect you would be contented to retire and do nothing. That is not your conception of happiness. But, if you do take Mr. Bangs into partnership, let him manage the entire business. You can be in the store as much as you wish, and be interested in it, so long as you don't interfere. And you and Mother can be together and take little trips together once in a while. You mustn't stay in Trumet ALL the time; if you do you will grow discontented again."

"No, no, I shan't. Serena may, perhaps, but I shan't."

"Yes, you will. You both have seen a little of outside life now, and it isn't all bad, though you may think so just at this time. You mustn't settle down and grow narrow like some of the people here in Trumet--Abigail Mayo, for instance."

"Humph! I'd have to swallow a self-windin' talkin' machine before I could get to be like Abigail Mayo. But you may be right, Gertie; perhaps you are. See here, though, how about you, yourself? You've seen a heap more of what you call outside life than your ma and I have. How are YOU goin' to keep contented here in Trumet?"

"Oh, I shall be contented. Don't worry about me."

"But I do worry, and your mother is beginnin' to worry, too. There's somethin' troublin' you; both of us see that plain enough. See here, Gertie, you ain't--you ain't feelin' bad about--about leavin' that Cousin Percy, are you?"

The young lady's cheeks reddened, but with indignation, not embarrassment.

"DADDY!" she protested sharply. "Daddy, how can you! Cousin Percy!"

"Well, you know--"

"I hate him. I've told you so. Or I should, if he was worth hating; as it is I despise him thoroughly."

"That's good! That's one load off my mind. But, you see, Gertie--well, when your mother and I first told you we'd made up our minds to come back here, you--you stood up for him, and said he was aristocratic and--and I don't know what all. That's what you said; and 'twas after the Zuba business, too."

Gertrude regarded him wonderingly. "Said!" she repeated. "I said and did all sorts of things. Daddy--Daddy, DEAR, is it possible you don't understand yet that it was all make-believe?"

"All make-believe? What; your likin' Cousin Percy?"

"Yes, that and Mr. Holway and everything else--the whole of it. Haven't you guessed it yet? It was all a sham; don't you see? When I came back from college and found out exactly how things were going, I realized at once that something must be done. You were miserable and neglected, and Mother was under the influence of Mrs. Black and that empty-headed, ridiculous Chapter and would-be society crowd of hers. I tried at first to reason with her, but that was useless. She was too far gone for reason. So I thought and thought until I had a plan. I believed if I could show her, by my own example, how silly and ridiculous the kind of people she associated with were, if I pretended to be as bad as the worst of them, she would begin by seeing how ridiculous I was, and be frightened into realizing her own position. At any rate, she would be forced into giving it all up to save me. Of course I didn't expect her to be taken ill. When THAT happened I was SO conscience-stricken. I thought I never should forgive myself. But it has turned out so well, that even that is--"

"Gertie! Gertie Dott! stop where you are. Do you mean to tell me that all your--your advancin' and dancin' and bridgin' and tea-in' and Chapterin' was just--"

"Just make-believe, that's all. I hated it as much as you did; as much as Mother does now."

"My SOUL! but--but it can't be! Cousin Percy--"

"Oh, do forget Cousin Percy! I was sure he was exactly what he was and that he was using you and Mother as conveniences for providing him with a home and luxuries which he was too worthless to work for. I was sure of it, morally sure, but

I made up my mind to find out. So I cultivated him, and I cultivated his particular friends, and I did find out. I pretended to like him--"

"Hold on! for mercy sakes, hold on! YOU pretended, but--but HE didn't. If ever a feller was gone on a young woman he was, towards the last of it. Why, he--"

"Hush! hush! Don't speak of it. It makes me disgusted with myself even to think of him. If he was--was as you say, it is all the better. It serves him right. And I think that it was with my--with your money, Daddy, much more than your daughter, he was infatuated. I had the satisfaction of telling him my opinion of him and his conduct before he left."

"Ho! you did, hey? Humph! I wish I might have heard it. But, Gertie," his incredulity not entirely crushed, "it wasn't ALL make-believe; all of it couldn't have been. Even Zuba, she got the advancin' craziness. She joined a--a 'Band,' or somethin'."

"No, she didn't. She pretended to, but she didn't. There wasn't any such 'Band.' She was helping me to cure Mother, that's all. It was all part of the plan. Her husband understands now, although," with a laugh, "he didn't when he first came."

Daniel drew his hand across his forehead.

"Well!" he exclaimed. "WELL! and I--and I--"

"I treated you dreadfully, didn't I? Scolded you, and told you to go away, and--and everything. I COULDN'T tell you the truth, because you cannot keep a secret, but I was sorry, so sorry for you, even when you were most provoking. You WOULD interfere, you know. Two or three times you almost spoiled it all."

"Did I? I shouldn't wonder. And--and to think I never suspicioned a bit of it!"

"I don't see why you didn't. It was so plain. I'm sure Mother suspects--now."

"Probably she does. If I wasn't what I've called myself so much lately, an old fool, I'd have suspected, too. I AM an old fool."

"No, you're not. You are YOU, and that is why I love you--why, everyone who knows you loves you. I wouldn't have you changed one iota. You are the dearest, best father in the world. And you are going to be happy now, aren't you?"

"I--I don't know. I ought to be, I suppose. I guess I shall be--if I ever get over thinkin' what a foolhead I was. So Zuba was part of it all, hey? And John, too? He was in it, I presume likely."

Gertrude's expression changed; so did her tone.

"We won't talk about John, Daddy," she said. "Please don't."

"Why not? I want to talk about him. In a way--yes, sir! in a way I ain't sure that--that I didn't have a hand in spoilin' that, too. Considerin' what you've just told me, I wouldn't wonder if I did."

His daughter had risen to go. Now she turned back.

"What do you mean?" she asked. "What do you mean? Spoiling--what?"

"Why--why, you and John, you know. Whatever happened between you and him happened that night when he come to Scarford. And he wouldn't have come--not then--if I hadn't written for him."

Gertrude was speechless. Her father went on.

"Long's we're confessin'," he said, "we might as well make a clean job of it. I wrote him, all on my own hook. You see, Gertie, 'twas on your account mainly. I was gettin' pretty desperate about you. Instead of straightenin' out your ma's course you were followin' in her wake, runnin' ahead of her, if anything. It looked as if you'd have her hull down and out of the race, if you kept on. I couldn't hold you back, and, bein' desperate, as I say, I wrote John to come and see if he could. And I told him to come quick.... Hey? What did you say?"

The young lady had said nothing; she had been listening, however, and now she seemed to have found an answer to a puzzle.

"So that was why he came?" she said, in a low tone, as if thinking aloud. "That was why. But--but without a word to me."

"Oh, I 'specially wrote him not to tell you he was comin'. I didn't want you to know. I wanted to have a talk with him first and tell him just how matters stood. After you'd gone to Chapter meetin' that night--I always thought 'twas queer, your bein' so determined to go, but I see why now; 'twas part of your plan, wasn't it?"

"Yes, yes, of course. Go on."

"Well, I judge John thought 'twas funny, too--but never mind. After you'd gone, he and I had our talk. I told him everything. He was kind of troubled; I could see that; but he stood up for you through thick and thin. He only laughed when I told him--told him some things, those that worried me most."

Gertrude noticed his hesitation.

"What were those things?" she asked.

"Oh, nothin'. They seem so foolish now; but at that time--"

"Daddy, did you tell him of my--my supposed friendship for Mr. Hungerford?"

Daniel reluctantly nodded. "Yes," he admitted. "I told him some. Maybe I told him more than was absolutely true. Perhaps I exaggerated a little. But he was so stubborn in not believin', that.... Hey? By Godfreys!" as the thought struck him for the first time, "THAT wasn't what ailed John, was it? He wasn't JEALOUS of that consarned Percy?"

Gertrude did not answer.

"It couldn't be," continued Daniel. "He's got more sense than that. Besides, you told him, when you and he were alone together, why you was actin' so, didn't you? Or did he know it beforehand? I presume likely he did. Your mother and I seem to have been the only animals left outside the show tent."

Again there was no answer. When the young lady spoke it was to ask another question.

"Daddy," she said, not looking at him, but folding and unfolding a bit of paper on the counter, "are you SURE you mailed that letter I gave you the morning after--after he went away?"

"What? That letter to John that you gave me to mail? I'm sure as I can be of anything. I put it right in amongst the bills and checks I had ready, and when the postman came I gave 'em all to him with my own hands. Yes, it was mailed all right."

"And no letters--letters for me--came afterwards, which I didn't receive? You didn't put one in your pocket and forget it?"

"No. I'm sure of that. Why, your mother's cleaned out all my pockets a dozen times since. She says I use my clothes for wastebaskets, and she has to empty 'em pretty nigh as often. No, I didn't forget any letter for you, Gertie. But why? What made you think I might have?"

"Oh, nothing; nothing, Daddy." Then, throwing down the bit of paper and moving toward the door, "I must go in and see Mother. I have scarcely seen her all the morning."

"But hold on, Gertie! Don't go. I haven't found out what--Stop! Gertie, look at me! Why don't you look at me?"

She would not look and she would not stop. The door closed behind her. Captain Dan threw himself back in the chair. When Mr. Bangs, returning from his trip after orders, entered the store he found his employer just where he had left him. Now, however, the expression of high, good humor was no longer upon the captain's face.

"Well, Cap'n," hailed Nathaniel cheerfully. "Still on deck, I see. What are you doing; exercising your mind?"

"Humph! What little mind I'VE got has been exercised too blessed much. It needs rest more'n anything, but it don't seem likely to get a great deal. Nate, this world reminds me of a worn-out schooner, it's as full of troubles as that is full of leaks; and you no sooner get one patched up than another breaks out in a new place. Ah hum! ... What you got there? The mail, is it? Anything for me?"

There was one letter bearing the captain's name. Nathaniel handed it to the owner of that name and the latter inspected the envelope and the postmark.

"From Labe Ginn," he observed. "Nobody else in Scarford that I know would spell Daniel with two 'l's and no 'i.' What's troublin' Laban? Somethin' about the house, I presume likely."

He leisurely tore open the envelope. The letter was a lengthy one, scrawled upon a half dozen sheets of cheap note paper. The handwriting was almost as unique as the spelling, which is saying considerable.

"From Laban, is it?" asked Mr. Bangs casually.

"Yup, it's from Labe."

"There was another from him, then. At any rate there was one addressed in the same hen-tracks to Azuba. I met her as I was coming out of the post-office and gave it to her; she was on her way to the grocery store, she said."

Daniel nodded, but made no comment. He was doing his best to decipher Mr. Ginn's hieroglyphics. Occasionally he chuckled.

Laban began by saying that he expected his term as caretaker of the Scarford property to be of short duration. He had dropped in at the real estate office and had there been told that arrangements for the leasing of the mansion, furniture, and all, were practically completed. The new tenant would move in within a fortnight, he was almost sure. Mr. Ginn, personally, would be glad of it, for it was "lonesomer than a meeting-house on a week day."

"I spend the heft of my daytimes out in the Back yard," he wrote. "I've lokated a bordin house handy by, but the Grub thare is tuffer than the mug on a Whaler two year out. I don't offen meet anybody I know, but tother day I met barney Black. He asked about you and your fokes and I told him. He was prety down on his Luck I thort and acted Blue. His wife is hed neck and heles in Chapter goins on. I see her name in the Newspaper about evry day.

"He said give you his Regards and tell you you was a dam lukky Man."

Captain Dan's chuckle developed into a hearty laugh. He sympathized with and understood the feelings of B. Phelps.

"He has sold his summer Plase at Trumet," the letter went on. "Mrs. Black don't want to come thare no more. He wuddent say why but I shuddent wonder if it was becos she ain't hankering to mete your Wife after the way she treted her. He has sold the Plase to some fokes name of Fenholtz. I know thats the rite name becos I made him spel it for me. Do you know them?"

Daniel uttered an exclamation of delight and struck his thigh a resounding slap.

"What's up?" asked Nathaniel. "Got some good news?"

"You bet! Mighty good! Some people I knew and liked in Scarford have bought the Black cottage here in Trumet. I rather guess I am responsible in a way; I preached Cape Cod to 'em pretty steady. The Fenholtzes! Well, well!"

"What I realy wrote you for," continued Mr. Ginn, at the top of page four, "was to tell you that I had a feller come to see me Yesterday. It was that forriner Hapgood who used to work for you. He looked pretty run to seed. He haddent got anny Job since he left you, he sed, and he was flat Broke. I gave him a Square meel or what they call one at the bordin' house and he and me had a long talk. He told me a lot of things but manely all he wanted to talk about was that Swab of a Coussin of yours, that Hungerford. Hapgood was down on him like a Gull on a sand ele. He sed Hungerford was a mene sneak and had treted him bad. He told me a Lot about how Hungerford worked you fokes for sukkers and how he helped. Seems him and Hungerford was old shipmates and chums and had worked your ant Laviny the same way. Hungerford used to pay him, but now that he is flat Broke and can't help no more, he won't give him a cent. Hapgood says if you knew what he knows you'd be intterested. He says Hungerford pade him to get a hold of Tellygrams and letters that he thort you had better not see. He had one Coppy of a tellygram that he says come to him over the Tellyfone 3 days after John Doane left your house. I lent him a cupple of dollars and he gave me the Coppy. It is from John to Gertie, but she never got it becos Hapgood never told her. I send it in this letter."

Captain Dan, who had read the latter part of this long paragraph with increasing excitement, now stopped his reading and began a hurried search for the "Coppy." He found it, on a separate sheet. It was written in pencil in Hapgood's neat, exact handwriting and was, compared to Mr. Ginn's labored scrawl, very easy to read. And this was what the captain read:

"MISS GERTRUDE DOTT,

"No. -- Blank Avenue, "Scarford, Mass.

"Why haven't you written? Did you receive my letters? The firm are sending me on urgent business to San Francisco. I leave to-night. If you write me there I shall know all is well and you have not changed. If not I shall know the other thing. I shall hope for a letter. San Francisco address is--"

Then followed the address and the signature, "John Doane."

The "Coppy" dropped in Daniel's lap. He closed his eyes. Nate Bangs, glancing at him, judged that he was falling asleep, but Mr. Bangs's usually acute judgment was, in this instance, entirely wrong. So far from sleeping, the captain was just beginning to wake up.

"Why haven't you written?" That meant that John had never received the letter which Gertrude wrote, the letter which she had given him--her father--to post. Why had it not been received? It had been posted. He gave it to the carrier with his own hands.

Before the captain's closed eyes that scene in the library passed in review. He was at his desk, Gertrude entered and handed him the letter. He commented upon its address and placed it with the others, the envelopes containing bills and checks, upon the table. Then the postman came and--

No--wait. The postman had not come immediately. Serena had called and he, Daniel, had gone up to her room in answer to the call. But he had come down when the postman rang and.... Wait again! There had been someone in the library when he was called away. He dimly remembered.... What? ... Why, yes! Cousin Percy had come in and--

Daniel leaped to his feet. His chair slid back on its castors and struck the safe behind him. Mr. Bangs looked up.

"Why, what's the matter?" he cried, in alarm. "Is--Where are you going?"

Captain Dan did not answer. He was running, actually running, toward the door. Bareheaded he dashed across the yard. His foot was on the threshold of the back porch of the house, when he stopped short. For a moment he stood still; then he turned and ran back to the store again.

Nathaniel, who had followed him to the side entrance of The Metropolitan, met him there.

"For mercy sakes, Cap'n Dott!" he began. "What IS it?"

Daniel did not answer. He pushed past his perturbed manager and, rushing to the closet in which the telephone instrument hung, closed the door behind him. He jerked the receiver from the hook, placed it at his ear, and shouted into the transmitter.

"Hello! Hello there, Central!" he bellowed. "I want a long distance call. I want to talk to Saunders, Griffin and Company, Pearl Street, Boston.... Hey? ... Yes, I want to talk to Mr. Doane.... NO, not Cone! Doane--Doane--Mr. John Doane.... Hey? ... You'll call me? ... All right, then; be as quick as you can, that's all."

He hung up the receiver and, flinging the door open, dashed out into the store again, and began pacing up and down.

Nathaniel ventured one more question.

"Of course it ain't any of my business, Cap'n Dott," he stammered, "but--"

Daniel waved his hand.

"Sshh! shh!" he commanded. "It's all right. I'll tell you by and by. But now I want to think. To think, by time!"

Ten minutes later the telephone bell rang.

"Hello! Here is your Boston call," announced Central.

"All right! all right! Is this Saunders, Griffin and Company? ... Hey? ... Is Mr. Doane there?... What? I want to know! Is that you, John? ... This is Dott, speakin'.... Yes, Dan Dott.... No, no, of Trumet, not Scarford.... Yes.... YES.... Here! you let me do the talkin'; you listen."

Captain Dan ate scarcely any luncheon that day. He seemed to have lost his appetite. This was a good deal of a loss and his wife commented upon it.

"What does ail you, Daniel?" she asked anxiously. "Why don't you eat?"

"Hey? Oh, I don't know, Serena. Don't feel hungry, somehow."

"Well, it's the first time you haven't been hungry since you came back to Trumet. I was beginning to think Azuba and I couldn't get enough for you TO eat. And now, all at once, you're not hungry. What does ail you?"

"Ail me? Nothin' ails me."

"Don't you feel well?"

"Never felt better in my life. Don't believe I ever felt quite so good."

"You act awfully queer."

"Do I? Don't you worry about me, Serena. My appetite'll be back all right by dinner time. You want to lay in an extra stock for dinner. I'll probably eat you out of house and home then. Better figure on as much as if you was goin' to have company. Ain't that so, Zuba?"

He winked at the housekeeper. His wife noticed the wink.

"What is it?" she demanded. "There's something going on that I don't know about. Are you and Azuba planning some sort of surprise?"

"Surprise! What sort of surprise would Zuba and I plan? She's had one surprise in the last six weeks and that ought to be enough. Laban's droppin' in unexpected was surprise enough to keep you satisfied, wasn't it, Zuba? I never saw anybody more surprised than you was that night in the kitchen. Ho! ho!"

Azuba smiled grimly. "A few more surprises like that," she observed, "and I'll be surprised to death. Don't talk to ME about surprises."

"I wasn't talkin' about 'em, 'twas Serena that started it."

Mrs. Dott was still suspicious. She turned to her daughter.

"Gertie," she asked, "do YOU know what your father is acting so ridiculous about? Is there a secret between you three?"

Gertrude had been very quiet and grave during the meal.

"No," she said. "There is no secret that I know of. Father is happy because we are back here in his beloved Trumet, I suppose."

"Humph! Well, his happiness hasn't interfered with his appetite before. There's something else; I'm sure of it. Why, Gertie! aren't you going to eat, either? You're not through luncheon!"

The young lady had risen from the table.

"You've eaten scarcely anything, Gertie," protested her mother. "I never saw such people. Are YOU so happy that you can't eat. Sit down."

Gertrude did not look happy. She did not sit down. Instead she hastily declared that she was not hungry, and left the room.

Serena stared after her.

"Was she crying, Daniel?" she asked. "She looked as if she was just going to. Ever since she came in from her walk she has been so downcast and sad. She won't talk and she hasn't smiled once. Daniel, has she said anything to you? Do you know what ails her?"

The captain shook his head.

"She and I had a little talk out in the store," he admitted. "I shouldn't wonder if she was thinkin' about--about--"

"About John, do you mean?"

"Maybe so."

"Did she talk with you about HIM? She won't let me mention his name. Daniel, I feel SO bad about that. I'm afraid I was to blame, somehow. If we hadn't gone to Scarford--if ... Daniel, I'm going to her."

She rose. Her husband laid a hand on her arm.

"Sit down, Serena," he urged. "Sit down."

"But, Daniel, let me go. I must go to her. The poor girl! Perhaps I can comfort her, though how, I don't know. John Doane!" with a burst of indignation. "If I ever meet that young man I'll give him my opinion of his--"

"Sshh! shh! Serena! You sit down and finish your luncheon. Don't you worry about Gertie. And you needn't worry about her appetite or mine. I tell you what I'll do: If she and I don't have appetite enough for dinner to-night--or breakfast to-morrow mornin', anyhow--I'll swallow that platter whole. There! A sight like that ought to be worth waitin' for. Cheer up, old lady, and possess your soul in patience. This craft is just gettin' out of the doldrums. There's a fair wind and clear weather comin' for the Dott frigate, or I'm no sailor. You just trust me and wait. Yes, and let Gertie alone."

He positively refused to explain what he meant by this optimistic prophecy, or to permit his wife to go to their daughter. Gertrude went out soon afterward--for another walk, she said--and Serena retired to her room for the afternoon nap which the doctor had prescribed as part of her rest cure. For a time she could not sleep, but lay there wondering and speculating concerning her husband's strange words and his equally strange attitude of confident and excited happiness. What did it mean? There was some secret she was sure; some good news for Gertrude; there must be. She, too, began to share the excitement and feel the confidence. Daniel had asked her to trust him, and she did trust him. He, and not she, had been right in judging Mrs. Black and Cousin Percy, and Scarford, and all the rest. He had been right all through. She had reason to trust him; he was always right. With this comforting conclusion--one indication of the mental revolution which her Scarford experience had brought about--she ceased wondering and dropped to sleep.

Captain Dan and Azuba had a short conference in the kitchen.

"Understand, do you, Zuba?" queried the captain. "A late dinner and plenty of it."

"I understand. Land sakes! I ain't altogether a numskull or a young-one, even if I do have to be shut up in the closet to make me behave."

"Ho! ho! I expect you could have knocked my head off for bein' in the way just at that time."

"Humph!" with a one-sided smile, "I could have knocked my own off for not listenin' afore I come downstairs. If I'd heard Laban's voice I bet you I wouldn't have come. All I needed was a chance to be alone with him and explain what Gertie and I were up to."

"Well, I'm glad you didn't have the chance. I wouldn't have missed that show for somethin'. It beat all my goin' to sea, that did. How you did holler!"

He roared with laughter. Azuba watched him with growing impatience.

"Got through actin' like a Bedlamite?" she inquired tartly, when he stopped for breath. "If you have you can clear out and let me get to my dish-washin'.'"

"I'm through. Oh, by the way, what did Labe say in your letter? I've told you what he wrote me, but I forgot that he wrote you, too."

Mrs. Ginn looked troubled. "I don't know what to do with that man," she declared. "I expect any minute to get word that he's been put in the lock-up. If that house of yours ain't rented or sold pretty quick, so he can get to sea again, he will be. Do you know what he's done to that Hungerford critter?"

"DONE to him! What do you mean? He hasn't seen him, has he?"

"No, he ain't seen him, thank goodness, but Labe is so wrought up over what that Hapgood thief told him, about your precious cousin stealin' your telegrams and so on, that he and Hapgood have gone in cahoots to play a trick on Mr. Percy. Labe says Hapgood told him that Percy was keepin' company now with another woman there in Scarford, a young woman with money, of course--he wouldn't chase any other kind. Well, Hapgood--he's a healthy specimen for my husband to be in with, he is--Hapgood knows a lot about Hungerford and his goin's on in the past, and he's got a lot of the Percy man's old letters from other girls. Don't ask ME how he got 'em; stole 'em, I suppose, same as he stole that telegram from John. Anyhow, Labe and Hapgood have sent those letters to the present young woman's pa."

Daniel whistled. "Whew!" he exclaimed. "That's interestin'."

"Ain't it, now! Laban says the old commodore--meanin' the pa, I suppose--is a holy terror and sets more store by his daughter than he does by his hopes of salvation, enough sight. Good reason, too, I presume likely; he's toler'ble sure of the daughter. Well, anyhow, the letters are gone and Labe says he's willin' to bet that Cousin Percy'll be GOIN'--out of the window and out of Scarford--when papa gets after him. Nice mess, ain't it!"

Captain Dan whistled again. "Well, Zuba," he observed, "we can't help it, as I see. What's done's done and chickens do come home to roost, don't they?"

"Humph! I wish my husband would come home and roost where I can keep my eye on him. He says he's gettin' sick of bein' a land lubber. He'll be aboard some ship and off again afore long, that's some comfort. The only time I know that man is safe is when he's a thousand miles from dry land."

CHAPTER XVI

Serena and Daniel were together in the parlor. It was past dinner time, but Azuba, for some reason or other, had not gotten dinner ready. This was unusual for, if there was one thing upon which the housekeeper prided herself, it was in being "prompt at meal times." She was setting the table now, however, and they could hear her rattling the knives and forks and singing, actually singing.

"Azuba is in good spirits, isn't she," observed Serena. "I haven't heard her sing before for a long time. I suppose, like the rest of us, she has been too troubled to sing."

Captain Dan listened to the singing, shook his head, and remarked whimsically, "There's some comfort to be got out of trouble, then. Say, the 'Sweet By and By' would turn sour if it could hear her sing about it, wouldn't it?"

"Hush, Daniel, don't be irreverent. Why don't you light the lamp, or let me light it? It's getting so dark I can hardly see you."

"Never mind; let's sit in the dark a spell. Gertie comin' down pretty soon, is she?"

"Yes. She's changing her dress, because you asked her to. Why did you ask her? Why should she dress up just for you and me?"

"Oh, just a notion of mine. I like that red dress of hers, anyway; the one with the fringe trimmin's along the upper riggin'."

"That dress isn't red, it's pink."

"I don't care. I thought 'twas about the color of my nose, and if that's pink then I'm losin' my complexion."

"Daniel!" with a laugh, "how you do talk and act to-day! At luncheon you were as queer as could be and now you're worse. I never saw you so fidgety and excited.

What IS going to happen? Something, I know. You wouldn't tell me this noon; will you tell me now?"

"Pretty soon, Serena; pretty soon. Now let's talk about somethin' interestin'; about ourselves, for instance. How do you like bein' back here in Trumet? Ain't gettin' tired of it, are you? The old town doesn't seem stupid; hey?"

"No, indeed! Don't speak that way, Daniel."

"Well, I just mentioned it, that's all. Soon as you do get tired and want to see somethin' new, we'll take that cruise to Washin'ton or the Falls or somewheres. Never mind the price. Way I feel now I'd go to the moon if 'twould please you. Say the word and I'll hire the balloon to-morrow--or Monday, anyway; no business done in Trumet on Sunday."

Serena laughed again. "I shan't say it for a long while," she declared. "I am having such a good time. The house seems so snug and homey. And all our old friends and neighbors have been so kind. They seemed so glad to see us when we came, as if they were real friends, not the make-believe sort."

"Not the Annette kind, you mean. That particular breed of cats is scarce on the Cape--at least I hope it is."

"So do I. I never want to see her again. I am so glad they have sold their cottage here, and that the Fenholtzes have bought it--if they have bought it, as you say you heard. You always liked the Fenholtzes, Daniel. I did, too, or I should if Annette hadn't told me--"

"I know, I know. Some day that woman will tell the truth by accident and the Ladies of Honor crowd'll be mournin' a leadin' light that went out sudden. But never mind her. The folks here HAVE been nice to us, haven't they?"

"Indeed they have! And so thoughtful! Why, Sophronia Smalley even came to ask me if I wouldn't consider taking my old place as president of Trumet Chapter. She is president now, but she declared she would resign in a minute in my favor."

For an instant Captain Dan's exuberant spirits were dashed.

"She did!" he cried. "Well, if that woman ain't.... Humph! Are you thinkin' of lettin' her resign, Serena?"

"No."

"I--I wouldn't stand in your way if you did, you know. I mustn't be selfish. Trumet ain't Scarford, and if you want to--"

"I don't, I don't. I may attend a meeting once in a while, later on, but I never shall hold office again. I have had all the 'advancement' I want."

"Advancin' backwards, some folks would call what you're doin' now, Serena, I cal'late. There! I've said 'cal'late' again. I haven't said it before for a long time. This Cape sand has got into my grammar, I guess. I must be careful."

"You needn't be. Say 'cal'late' if you want to, I am not going to fret you about your grammar any more, Daniel. I've got over that, too. I'd rather have you, just as you are, than any other man in the world, grammar or no grammar."

"Whew! Hold on, old lady! If you talk that way I'll get so puffed up I'll bust into smoke when you touch me, like a dry toadstool. I--Hello! what was that? The train whistle, was it?"

"Yes. Here is the night train in; it is almost mail time, and no dinner yet. What IS the matter with Azuba? I'll speak to her."

She was rising to go to the dining-room, but her husband detained her.

"No, you wait; no, you mustn't," he said, hastily. "Sit right down, Serena. Speakin' of dinners, this talk of ours is like that everlastin' long meal that you and I went to at Barney Black's house just after we landed in Scarford. You remember it took half an hour to get to anything solid in that dinner, don't you? Yes, well, I'm just gettin' to the meat of my talk. And I want Gertie to come in on that course. She is on her way downstairs now; I hear her. Hi! Gertie! come in here, won't you!"

Gertrude entered the room.

"Where are you, Daddy?" she asked.

"Here I am, over here by the window."

"But why haven't you lighted the lamp? Why are you sitting here in the dark?"

Serena answered. "Goodness knows," she replied. "Your father would insist on it. I think he is going crazy; he has acted that way ever since lunch."

The demented one chuckled.

"You see, Gertie," he explained, "'twas on account of my bashfulness. Your mother, she wanted to sit along with me and hold hands, so--. Oh, all right; all right. You can show a glim now, Serena, if you want to. I'll cover up my blushes."

The maligned Mrs. Dott announced that she had a good mind to box his ears. "That's what I should do to a child," she added, "and nobody could act more childish than you have this afternoon."

"Second childhood, Serena. Second childhood and dodderin' old age are cree-pin' over me fast. There!" as the lamp blazed and the parlor was illuminated, "now you can see for yourself. Do I dodder much?"

Even Gertrude was obliged to laugh.

"Daddy!" she cried; "you silly thing! I believe you ARE getting childish."

"Am I? All right, I'm willing to be, at the price. My! Gertie, you look awfully pretty. Don't she look 'specially pretty to you to-night, Serena?"

Serena smiled. "That gown was always becoming," she said.

"I know it was; that's why I wanted her to put it on. And she's fixed her hair the way I like, too. My! my! if some folks I know could see you now, Gertie, they'd.... Ahem! Well, never mind. She looks as if she was expectin' company and had rigged up for it, doesn't she, Serena?"

Gertrude paid little attention to this rather strained attempt at a joke. She mere-ly smiled and turned away. But her mother appeared to suspect a hidden meaning in the words. She leaned forward and gazed at her husband.

"Daniel," she cried, sharply and with increasing excitement; "Daniel Dott, what are you--"

The captain waved her to silence. She would have spoken in spite of it, but his second wave and shake of the head were so emphatic that she hesitated. Before the moment of hesitation was at an end Captain Dan himself began to speak. He spoke in a new tone now and more and more rapidly.

"Serena, don't interrupt me," he ordered. "Gertie, listen. I'm goin' to tell you both a story. Once there was a couple of married folks that had a daughter.... Hush, I tell you! Listen, both of you. I AIN'T crazy. If ever I talked sense in my life I'm talkin' it now.... This couple, as I say, had a daughter. This daughter was engaged to be married. The old folks moved away from the place they had always lived and went somewhere else. There they both commenced to make fools of themselves. The place was all right enough, maybe, but they didn't belong in it. The daughter, she came there and she saw how things were goin' and, says she: 'I'll fix 'em. I'll cure 'em and save 'em, too, by showin' 'em an example, my example. I'll--'"

Gertrude broke in.

"Daddy," she cried, with a warning glance at her mother, "be careful. Don't be silly. What is the use--"

"Hush! Hush and be still! Never mind what she did. All is, she showed 'em and she cured 'em and she saved 'em. But meanwhile her meddlesome old father had got worried, not understandin' what was goin' on, and he put his oar in. He wrote for the young chap she was engaged to to come down and help cure HER. The father meant all right. He--"

Again the young lady interrupted.

"Mother," she said, "this is nonsense, the way father is telling it. I meant to tell you, myself, by and by. I'm sure you have guessed it, anyway, but--"

"There's one part she hasn't guessed," shouted Captain Dan; "or that you haven't guessed either, Gertie, God bless you. I guessed it myself, this very day, and I guessed it because I had a letter from Labe Ginn up at Scarford that put me on the right track. Gertie, that letter you wrote to John WASN'T mailed; the postman DIDN'T get it; John himself never got it."

"Daddy! Daddy, what--"

"Wait! wait! How do I know? you were goin' to say. I know because I know who did get it. Cousin Percy Hungerford--confound his miserable, worthless hulk! HE got it; he stole it from my table, where it laid along with my other letters, when I was out of the room. And--wait! that isn't all. John DID write you, Gertie. He wrote you two or three times and he telegraphed you once. And you didn't get either letters or telegram because that Hapgood butler--Oh, if I had only known this when I chased him out of the back yard! He'd have gone over the fence instead of through the gate--he was helpin' our dear cousin and gettin' paid for it, and HE stole 'em. There! that's the truth and.... My soul! I believe I've scared the girl to death."

He sprang forward. Serena, too, although she was almost as much surprised and agitated as her daughter, hastened to the latter's side.

But Gertrude, although white and shaken, was far from being "scared to death." She was very much alive.

"Are you sure, Daddy?" she cried. "Are you SURE? How do you know?"

"I know because Labe wrote that Hapgood told him. That's how I know about the telegram. And I know that's what happened to your letter because John didn't get it."

"How do you know he didn't get it? Please, Mother, don't worry about me. I am all right. How do you know John didn't get my letter, Father?"

"I know because.... Is that a wagon stoppin' at our gate, Serena?"

"Never mind if it is. Answer Gertie's question. HOW do you know?"

Steps sounded on the front porch. Captain Dan strode to the hall and stood with one hand on the knob of the front door.

"I know," he declared triumphantly, "because I telephoned John this very day and he told me so. And now, by the everlastin', he'll tell you so himself!"

He flung the door wide.

"Come in, John!" he shouted, in a roar which was heard even by deaf old Ebenezer Simpkins, driver of the depot wagon, who was just piloting his ancient steed from the Dott gate. "Come in, John!" roared Captain Dan. "There she is, in there, waitin' for you."

And Mr. Doane came, you may be sure.

Serena and Daniel waited in the dining-room. They were obliged to wait for some time. The captain's triumphant exuberance continued to bubble over. He chuckled and laughed and crowed vaingloriously over his success in keeping the secret ever since noon.

"I was bound I wouldn't tell, Serena," he declared. "I was bound I wouldn't. I told John over the 'phone; I said: 'I won't tell a soul you're comin', John. We'll give 'em one surprise, won't we.' And, ho! ho! he didn't believe I could keep it to myself; he said he didn't. But I did, I did--though I felt all afternoon as if I had a bombshell under my jacket."

Serena laughed; she was as pleased as he. "You certainly exploded it like a bombshell," she declared. "I didn't know at first but that you really had gone crazy. And poor Gertie! you didn't prepare her at all. You blurted it out all at once. The words fairly tumbled over each other. I wonder she didn't faint."

"She isn't the faintin' kind. Serena, we never can be grateful enough to Gertie for what she's done for us. And she sacrificed her own happiness--or thought she did--for you and me and didn't whimper or complain once."

"I know, Daniel, I know. And pretty soon now we must give her up to some-one else. That's the way of the world, though. WE'LL have to be brave then, won't we."

"So we will. But I'd rather give her to John than any other man on earth. The thought that it was all off between them and that she was grievin' over it was about the hardest thing of all."

"So it was. Well, now we can be completely happy, every one of us."

Azuba flounced in from the kitchen. "Ain't they come out of that parlor YET?" she demanded. "I can't keep roast chicken waitin' forever, even for engaged folks."

But the "engaged folks" themselves appeared at that moment. As one of those who, according to Mrs. Dott, were to be completely happy, Mr. Doane looked his part. Gertrude, too, although her eyes were wet, was smiling.

John and the Dotts shook hands. Daniel turned to his daughter.

"Well, Gertie," he asked, "are you ready to forgive me for what happened on account of my sendin' that summons to John--that one up in Scarford, I mean?"

"I think so, Daddy."

"I thought maybe you would be, considerin'," with a wink at Mr. Doane, "the answer you got to my telephone to-day. But, see here, young lady, I want to ask you somethin' and I expect a straight answer. Can I keep a secret, or can't I?"

"You can, Daddy, dear. You kept this one almost seven hours."

"Eight! eight, by Godfreys! 'Twas a strain, but I kept it."

"You managed it all beautifully, Daniel," declared Serena. "I am proud of you."

"We're all proud of you, Captain Dan," said John.

The captain smiled happily.

"Much obliged," he said, "but I ain't the one you ought to be proud of. When it comes to real managin' I ain't knee-high to the ship's cat alongside of Gertie there. She's the one who pulled this family through. No sir-ee! if you've got any time to spare bein' proud of folks, don't be proud of Cap'n Dan, but of Cap'n Dan's daughter. Sit down, all hands. Here comes dinner--at last."

The Codes Of Hammurabi And Moses
W. W. Davies

QTY

The discovery of the Hammurabi Code is one of the greatest achievements of archaeology, and is of paramount interest, not only to the student of the Bible, but also to all those interested in ancient history...

Religion   **ISBN:** *1-59462-338-4*   **Pages:132**
MSRP $12.95

The Theory of Moral Sentiments
Adam Smith

QTY

This work from 1749. contains original theories of conscience amd moral judgment and it is the foundation for systemof morals.

Philosophy   **ISBN:** *1-59462-777-0*   **Pages:536**
MSRP $19.95

Jessica's First Prayer
Hesba Stretton

QTY

In a screened and secluded corner of one of the many railway-bridges which span the streets of London there could be seen a few years ago, from five o'clock every morning until half past eight, a tidily set-out coffee-stall, consisting of a trestle and board, upon which stood two large tin cans, with a small fire of charcoal burning under each so as to keep the coffee boiling during the early hours of the morning when the work-people were thronging into the city on their way to their daily toil...

Pages:84

Childrens   **ISBN:** *1-59462-373-2*   *MSRP $9.95*

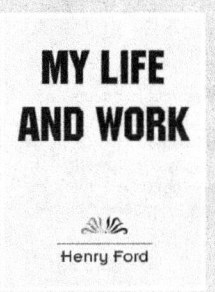

My Life and Work
Henry Ford

QTY

Henry Ford revolutionized the world with his implementation of mass production for the Model T automobile. Gain valuable business insight into his life and work with his own auto-biography... "We have only started on our development of our country we have not as yet, with all our talk of wonderful progress, done more than scratch the surface. The progress has been wonderful enough but..."

Pages:300

Biographies/   **ISBN:** *1-59462-198-5*   *MSRP $21.95*

The Art of Cross-Examination
Francis Wellman

QTY

I presume it is the experience of every author, after his first book is published upon an important subject, to be almost overwhelmed with a wealth of ideas and illustrations which could readily have been included in his book, and which to his own mind, at least, seem to make a second edition inevitable. Such certainly was the case with me; and when the first edition had reached its sixth impression in five months, I rejoiced to learn that it seemed to my publishers that the book had met with a sufficiently favorable reception to justify a second and considerably enlarged edition. ..

Pages:412

Reference   ISBN: *1-59462-647-2*   *MSRP $19.95*

On the Duty of Civil Disobedience
Henry David Thoreau

QTY

Thoreau wrote his famous essay, On the Duty of Civil Disobedience, as a protest against an unjust but popular war and the immoral but popular institution of slave-owning. He did more than write—he declined to pay his taxes, and was hauled off to gaol in consequence. Who can say how much this refusal of his hastened the end of the war and of slavery ?

Law   ISBN: *1-59462-747-9*   **Pages:48**

MSRP $7.45

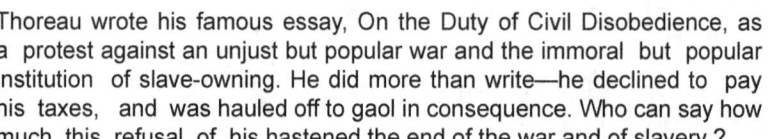

Dream Psychology Psychoanalysis for Beginners
Sigmund Freud

QTY

Sigmund Freud, born Sigismund Schlomo Freud (May 6, 1856 - September 23, 1939), was a Jewish-Austrian neurologist and psychiatrist who co-founded the psychoanalytic school of psychology. Freud is best known for his theories of the unconscious mind, especially involving the mechanism of repression; his redefinition of sexual desire as mobile and directed towards a wide variety of objects; and his therapeutic techniques, especially his understanding of transference in the therapeutic relationship and the presumed value of dreams as sources of insight into unconscious desires.

Pages:196

Psychology   ISBN: *1-59462-905-6*   *MSRP $15.45*

Dream Psychology
Psychoanalysis for Beginners

Sigmund Freud

The Miracle of Right Thought
Orison Swett Marden

QTY

Believe with all of your heart that you will do what you were made to do. When the mind has once formed the habit of holding cheerful, happy, prosperous pictures, it will not be easy to form the opposite habit. It does not matter how improbable or how far away this realization may see, or how dark the prospects may be, if we visualize them as best we can, as vividly as possible, hold tenaciously to them and vigorously struggle to attain them, they will gradually become actualized, realized in the life. But a desire, a longing without endeavor, a yearning abandoned or held indifferently will vanish without realization.

Pages:360

Self Help   ISBN: *1-59462-644-8*   *MSRP $25.45*

QTY

The Rosicrucian Cosmo-Conception Mystic Christianity *by Max Heindel* ISBN: *1-59462-188-8* **$38.95**
The Rosicrucian Cosmo-conception is not dogmatic, neither does it appeal to any other authority than the reason of the student. It is: not controversial, but is: sent forth in the, hope that it may help to clear... New Age/Religion Pages 646

Abandonment To Divine Providence *by Jean-Pierre de Caussade* ISBN: *1-59462-228-0* **$25.95**
"The Rev. Jean Pierre de Caussade was one of the most remarkable spiritual writers of the Society of Jesus in France in the 18th Century. His death took place at Toulouse in 1751. His works have gone through many editions and have been republished... Inspirational/Religion Pages 400

Mental Chemistry *by Charles Haanel* ISBN: *1-59462-192-6* **$23.95**
Mental Chemistry allows the change of material conditions by combining and appropriately utilizing the power of the mind. Much like applied chemistry creates something new and unique out of careful combinations of chemicals the mastery of mental chemistry... New Age Pages 354

The Letters of Robert Browning and Elizabeth Barret Barrett 1845-1846 vol II ISBN: *1-59462-193-4* **$35.95**
by Robert Browning and Elizabeth Barrett Biographies Pages 596

Gleanings In Genesis (volume I) *by Arthur W. Pink* ISBN: *1-59462-130-6* **$27.45**
Appropriately has Genesis been termed "the seed plot of the Bible" for in it we have, in germ form, almost all of the great doctrines which are afterwards fully developed in the books of Scripture which follow... Religion/Inspirational Pages 420

The Master Key *by L. W. de Laurence* ISBN: *1-59462-001-6* **$30.95**
In no branch of human knowledge has there been a more lively increase of the spirit of research during the past few years than in the study of Psychology, Concentration and Mental Discipline. The requests for authentic lessons in Thought Control, Mental Discipline and... New Age/Business Pages 422

The Lesser Key Of Solomon Goetia *by L. W. de Laurence* ISBN: *1-59462-092-X* **$9.95**
This translation of the first book of the "Lernegton" which is now for the first time made accessible to students of Talismanic Magic was done, after careful collation and edition, from numerous Ancient Manuscripts in Hebrew, Latin, and French... New Age/Occult Pages 92

Rubaiyat Of Omar Khayyam *by Edward Fitzgerald* ISBN:*1-59462-332-5* **$13.95**
Edward Fitzgerald, whom the world has already learned, in spite of his own efforts to remain within the shadow of anonymity, to look upon as one of the rarest poets of the century, was born at Bredfield, in Suffolk, on the 31st of March, 1809. He was the third son of John Purcell... Music Pages 172

Ancient Law *by Henry Maine* ISBN: *1-59462-128-4* **$29.95**
The chief object of the following pages is to indicate some of the earliest ideas of mankind, as they are reflected in Ancient Law, and to point out the relation of those ideas to modern thought. Religion/History Pages 452

Far-Away Stories *by William J. Locke* ISBN: *1-59462-129-2* **$19.45**
"Good wine needs no bush, but a collection of mixed vintages does. And this book is just such a collection. Some of the stories I do not want to remain buried for ever in the museum files of dead magazine-numbers an author's not unpardonable vanity..." Fiction Pages 272

Life of David Crockett *by David Crockett* ISBN: *1-59462-250-7* **$27.45**
"Colonel David Crockett was one of the most remarkable men of the times in which he lived. Born in humble life, but gifted with a strong will, an indomitable courage, and unremitting perseverance... Biographies/New Age Pages 424

Lip-Reading *by Edward Nitchie* ISBN: *1-59462-206-X* **$25.95**
Edward B. Nitchie, founder of the New York School for the Hard of Hearing, now the Nitchie School of Lip-Reading, Inc, wrote "LIP-READING Principles and Practice". The development and perfecting of this meritorious work on lip-reading was an undertaking... How-to Pages 400

A Handbook of Suggestive Therapeutics, Applied Hypnotism, Psychic Science ISBN: *1-59462-214-0* **$24.95**
by Henry Munro Health/New Age/Health/Self-help Pages 376

A Doll's House: and Two Other Plays *by Henrik Ibsen* ISBN: *1-59462-112-8* **$19.95**
Henrik Ibsen created this classic when in revolutionary 1848 Rome. Introducing some striking concepts in playwriting for the realist genre, this play has been studied the world over. Fiction/Classics/Plays 308

The Light of Asia *by sir Edwin Arnold* ISBN: *1-59462-204-3* **$13.95**
In this poetic masterpiece, Edwin Arnold describes the life and teachings of Buddha. The man who was to become known as Buddha to the world was born as Prince Gautama of India but he rejected the worldly riches and abandoned the reigns of power when... Religion/History/Biographies Pages 170

The Complete Works of Guy de Maupassant *by Guy de Maupassant* ISBN: *1-59462-157-8* **$16.95**
"For days and days, nights and nights, I had dreamed of that first kiss which was to consecrate our engagement, and I knew not on what spot I should put my lips..." Fiction/Classics Pages 240

The Art of Cross-Examination *by Francis L. Wellman* ISBN: *1-59462-309-0* **$26.95**
Written by a renowned trial lawyer, Wellman imparts his experience and uses case studies to explain how to use psychology to extract desired information through questioning. How-to/Science/Reference Pages 408

Answered or Unanswered? *by Louisa Vaughan* ISBN: *1-59462-248-5* **$10.95**
Miracles of Faith in China Religion Pages 112

The Edinburgh Lectures on Mental Science (1909) *by Thomas* ISBN: *1-59462-008-3* **$11.95**
This book contains the substance of a course of lectures recently given by the writer in the Queen Street Hail, Edinburgh. Its purpose is to indicate the Natural Principles governing the relation between Mental Action and Material Conditions... New Age/Psychology Pages 148

Ayesha *by H. Rider Haggard* ISBN: *1-59462-301-5* **$24.95**
Verily and indeed it is the unexpected that happens! Probably if there was one person upon the earth from whom the Editor of this, and of a certain previous history, did not expect to hear again... Classics Pages 380

Ayala's Angel *by Anthony Trollope* ISBN: *1-59462-352-X* **$29.95**
The two girls were both pretty, but Lucy who was twenty-one who supposed to be simple and comparatively unattractive, whereas Ayala was credited, as her Bombwhat romantic name might show, with poetic charm and a taste for romance. Ayala when her father died was nineteen... Fiction Pages 484

The American Commonwealth *by James Bryce* ISBN: *1-59462-286-8* **$34.45**
An interpretation of American democratic political theory. It examines political mechanics and society from the perspective of Scotsman James Bryce Politics Pages 572

Stories of the Pilgrims *by Margaret P. Pumphrey* ISBN: *1-59462-116-0* **$17.95**
This book explores pilgrims religious oppression in England as well as their escape to Holland and eventual crossing to America on the Mayflower, and their early days in New England... History Pages 268

www.bookjungle.com *email: sales@bookjungle.com fax: 630-214-0564 mail: Book Jungle PO Box 2226 Champaign, IL 61825*

QTY

The Fasting Cure *by Sinclair Upton* ISBN: *1-59462-222-1* **$13.95**
In the Cosmopolitan Magazine for May, 1910, and in the Contemporary Review (London) for April, 1910, I published an article dealing with my experiences in fasting. I have written a great many magazine articles, but never one which attracted so much attention... New Age/Self Help/Health Pages 164

Hebrew Astrology *by Sepharial* ISBN: *1-59462-308-2* **$13.45**
In these days of advanced thinking it is a matter of common observation that we have left many of the old landmarks behind and that we are now pressing forward to greater heights and to a wider horizon than that which represented the mind-content of our progenitors... Astrology Pages 144

Thought Vibration or The Law of Attraction in the Thought World ISBN: *1-59462-127-6* **$12.95**
by William Walker Atkinson Psychology/Religion Pages 144

Optimism *by Helen Keller* ISBN: *1-59462-108-X* **$15.95**
Helen Keller was blind, deaf, and mute since 19 months old, yet famously learned how to overcome these handicaps, communicate with the world, and spread her lectures promoting optimism. An inspiring read for everyone... Biographies/Inspirational Pages 84

Sara Crewe *by Frances Burnett* ISBN: *1-59462-360-0* **$9.45**
In the first place, Miss Minchin lived in London. Her home was a large, dull, tall one, in a large, dull square, where all the houses were alike, and all the sparrows were alike, and where all the door-knockers made the same heavy sound... Childrens/Classic Pages 88

The Autobiography of Benjamin Franklin *by Benjamin Franklin* ISBN: *1-59462-135-7* **$24.95**
The Autobiography of Benjamin Franklin has probably been more extensively read than any other American historical work, and no other book of its kind has had such ups and downs of fortune. Franklin lived for many years in England, where he was agent... Biographies/History Pages 332

Name	
Email	
Telephone	
Address	
City, State ZIP	

☐ **Credit Card**   ☐ **Check / Money Order**

Credit Card Number	
Expiration Date	
Signature	

Please Mail to: Book Jungle
PO Box 2226
Champaign, IL 61825
or Fax to: 630-214-0564

ORDERING INFORMATION
web: *www.bookjungle.com*
email: *sales@bookjungle.com*
fax: *630-214-0564*
mail: *Book Jungle PO Box 2226 Champaign, IL 61825*
or PayPal *to sales@bookjungle.com*

Please contact us for bulk discounts

DIRECT-ORDER TERMS

20% Discount if You Order Two or More Books
Free Domestic Shipping!
Accepted: Master Card, Visa,
Discover, American Express

www.ingramcontent.com/pod-product-compliance
Lightning Source LLC
Chambersburg PA
CBHW080955020726
47505CB00009B/2207